Louise Jensen is a global No. [barcode obscured] gical thrillers. Louise has sold over a million English language books and her novels have been sold for translation to twenty-five territories, as well as being featured on the *USA Today* and *Wall Street Journal* bestsellers lists. Louise was nominated for the Goodreads Debut Author of 2016 Award and *The Guardian*'s Not the Booker 2018. *The Gift* has been optioned for TV and film.

Louise lives with her husband, children, madcap dog and a rather naughty cat in Northamptonshire. She loves to hear from readers and writers and can be found at **www.louisejensen.co.uk**, where she regularly blogs flash fiction and writing tips.

Also by Louise Jensen

The
Family

LOUISE JENSEN

ONE PLACE. MANY STORIES

HQ
An imprint of HarperCollins*Publishers* Ltd
1 London Bridge Street
London SE1 9GF

This edition 2020

1
First published in Great Britain by
HQ, an imprint of HarperCollins*Publishers* Ltd 2019

ISBN 978-0-00-841209-8

MIX
Paper from
responsible sources
FSC™ C007454

This book is produced from independently certified FSC™ paper
to ensure responsible forest management.

For more information visit: www.harpercollins.co.uk/green

This book is set in Sabon

Printed and bound in Great Britain by
CPI Group (UK) Ltd, Croydon, CR0 4YY

For Tim,
This one had to be for you!
With love x

For I know the plans I have for you

JEREMIAH 29:11-14

PROLOGUE

Now
LAURA

It all unfolds with cinematic clarity; the gunshot, the scream. Every detail sharp and clear. Time slows as her eyes plead with me to help her. In my mind I bundle her behind me, shielding her body with mine, but she is too far away and I know I cannot reach her in time.

But still I try.

My legs are weighted with dread as I run towards her; the fist around my heart tightening.

A second shot.

Her knees buckle. She crumples like a paper doll.

The ground falls away beneath my feet and I crawl towards her like the animal I have become. My palms are sticky in the arc of blood that is staining the floor red. Blood is thicker than water they say, but hers is thin and beacon-bright. Adrenaline pulses through me leaving numbness in its wake, as I press against her wrist, desperately seeking a pulse. With my other hand I link my fingers through hers the way we used to, before I brought us to this place that has been our ruin. A lifetime of memories strobe through my mind; cradling her close in the maternity wing; Easter eggs spilling out of the wicker basket looped over her pudgy arm; her first day of school, ribboned pigtails swinging as she ran across the playground.

She can't be gone.

Can she?

Fingers of panic press hard against my skull. The colour leaches from the room. A black and white hue descending upon me. I tighten my fingers around hers, afraid I'm going to faint. Afraid I'm going to let her go.

But then.

A flicker of eyelids. A murmur from her lips.

I lay next to her, gently rolling her towards me, holding her in my arms. I can't, I won't leave her. Family should stick together. Protect each other. Instead, I chose to come here.

This is all my fault.

The drumming in my head grows louder – the sound of footfall. I don't have to look up to feel their anger, solid and immovable.

The acrid smell of gunpowder hangs in the air along with my fear.

Looking up, my eyes meet the shooter's; they are still holding the gun and sensations return, hard and fast. The pain in my stomach is cutting and deep and I am no longer sure if the blood I am covered in has come from her.

Or is coming from me.

Her top is soaked crimson, as is mine.

The pain increases.

Terrified, I tug at her clothes, my clothes. Praying. Let her be okay. Seventeen is no age. Let it be me.

At last I find the wound but before I can apply pressure to stem the flow of blood there are hands on my shoulders. My elbows. Pulling.

Darkness flickers at the edge of my vision but still I fight against it. I fight against them.

My hands are restrained, feet kick out, teeth sinking into flesh, but it's fruitless. I am growing weaker.

Her fingers twitch. Once. Twice.

Nothing.

'Tilly!' My scream rips through me as I am yanked to my feet. 'Tilly!' I scramble for traction, every fibre of my being straining to reach my daughter.

I can't.

I am still wrestling to be free as I am dragged, my feet scraping the ground.

I know they'll never let us leave here now.

Not *alive* anyway.

PART ONE

The Cause

CHAPTER ONE

Before

LAURA

Fears. We all have them. That creeping unease. An aversion to something. For me it's spiders. It stemmed from a nature documentary years before about the black weaver, a matriphagous breed that switches on her babies' cannibalistic instinct by encouraging her spiderlings to devour her. Unable to tear myself away, I had watched through splayed fingers as the mother circled her lair, tapping and vibrating the web, stimulating her young's primal instinct until they attacked her in a frenzied swarm. Hundreds of scuttling legs. Sinking fangs. The sound of the adult being consumed after venom had dissolved her from the inside out had stayed with me. What possessed a mother to sacrifice herself like that? How could her children turn on her? Of course that was long before I was a parent.

The instant I saw Tilly, tiny hands fisted, eyes squinting in the unaccustomed light, I plunged headfirst into a love that was absolute. A fierce desire as her mother to shield her from the world however I could. And she needed shielding. I knew how damaging it could be out there.

I had been damaged.

That morning though I had no idea how I was going to shelter her from the contents of the letter. As I drove towards school, I tightened my grip on the steering wheel as if it might somehow stop the sense of everything spinning out of my control. It didn't.

What was I going to do?

I slotted my rusting Volvo between two shiny 4x4s. Hordes of kids traipsed past the car, spines curved under the weight of the books they carried, dragging their feet towards the black wrought-iron gates. I rubbed my temples, trying to dispel the pounding behind my eyes.

'Do I have to go back to school, Mum?'

I heard the sadness in her voice. I heard it in my own as I said, 'It's been six weeks, Tilly.' As though that was long enough to make everything right.

It wasn't.

She wasn't coping well. Neither was I but, for her, I pretended we'd get through it. We'd be okay. Even if I didn't know how.

'We talked about this,' I said, but not unkindly. 'It was your idea to come back on a Friday. Ease yourself into it. It's one day, Tilly.'

She tucked her unruly dark hair behind her ears as she looked anxiously out of the window. Her face looked smaller, skin ashen, black bags nestled beneath bloodshot eyes. She'd refused the offer of counselling, spending so much of her time shut away in her room that now, being outside was overwhelming.

'You've already so much to catch up on but if you really can't face it I won't make you. You can come and help me in the shop instead. It's time to try to re-join the world.' I spoke slowly, deliberately, although each word was rough, grazing my tongue. Our Family Liaison Officer had said it was best to forge a routine, a semblance of normality, but was it? Sometimes being a parent was torturous. Spinning in circles like a bird with a broken wing. But Tilly was studying for A Levels. It was such an important year. Besides, at school she'd be with Rhianon and, although I knew the cousins were no longer inseparable, I hoped that away from the family drama they could begin to heal.

God knows, we all needed to heal.

'*Fine.*'

It was dizzying how quickly she pinballed between sadness and anger, but I knew it was all part of the hard ball of grief that ricocheted inside her.

She flung open the car door. A lengthy sigh escaping the mouth that no longer smiled.

'Wait,' I called, snatching her lunch from the backseat. 'If it becomes too much you can always ring me.' She snatched the Tupperware from my hands, her expression as hardened as the plastic.

'Try to have a good—' The slam of the car door sliced my sentence in two. 'Day.' A constriction in my throat prevented me calling her back. What could I have said to make things right? She stalked away without a backwards glance, swamped by her black winter coat, which snapped at her ankles as she walked. Weight had fallen off her. Again, I had found her half-eaten breakfast dumped in the bin. On top of the browning banana skin, a smattering of Rice Krispies ground to dust where she had crushed them with her spoon. She never could stand milk.

She stooped as she crossed the road without waiting for the green man, the weight of both her rucksack and the world on her shoulders. I contemplated calling her back but I knew she couldn't hide away forever. If she rang me I could be back there within fifteen minutes, no time at all, but I knew sometimes even sixty seconds could feel like an eternity. The desire to protect her, in the way I hadn't been protected at her age, to whisk her away for a fresh start, was fierce and stabbing, but after that morning's post, it seemed more out of reach than ever.

Tilly merged with the throng of children crunching over the autumn orange leaves that carpeted the pavement. I was reminded of the times Gavan and I would tramp through the forest searching for gleaming conkers, a wellington-booted Tilly nestled between us, her small gloved hands in ours. The smell of moss and earth. It was still so clear to me, the joy of it.

One, two, three, lift! We'd swing her back and forth as she clung on like a baby monkey, her infectious giggles making Gavan and me laugh. Even when she grew too tall, too heavy, she'd raise her knees to her chest to prevent her feet dragging on the floor, as if she couldn't quite accept how big she'd grown. I watched her as she stamped up the drab grey steps, finding it hard to equate the carefree, smiling child of seemingly five minutes ago with this solemn seventeen-year-old. She was a young woman now, lost to me, almost. The days of being able to make everything in her world right again with a mug of hot chocolate and a cuddle were long gone, and I longed to have them back.

The Special Constable with the patchy beard and straggly ponytail, who patrolled the secondary school at 8.45 and 3.15 every day with a ferocity that would put a lioness guarding cubs to shame, half-ran towards me. My rational self knew that he was going to tell me off for parking in the wrong place, but still, my hands were shaking as I released the handbrake. Each time I saw a police uniform it evoked such a physical response, sickness rising like a serpent. I zoomed off the yellow lines before he reached the car, and it wasn't until he disappeared from sight in my rear-view mirror that my breathing began to slow.

I would *always* associate the police with bad news.

With endless, endless questions.

Sometimes it all blended into a swirling, solid mass. The past. The present. Impossible to separate.

The fear has never really left me. Recurrently concealing itself in the layer between skin and flesh, waiting patiently for another trigger. The chance to attack.

I can't remember.

And sometimes, consciously, I couldn't remember. The lie became my truth. The pressure in my head insufferable.

Then, shadowed by night, the bony fingers of the past would drag me back and I would kick and scream before I'd wake. Duvet crumpled on the floor. Pyjamas drenched in sweat. And alone.

Always alone.

The scar on my forehead throbbed a reminder of my helplessness.

Thoughts of the letter filled my mind once more as I drove towards work.

What was I going to do?

CHAPTER TWO

LAURA

The realisation that I was unlocking the door for one of the last times stung like disinfectant being poured onto an open wound.

I drank it all in. The light bouncing off the windows as the day gathered strength. The breeze kissing the 'Laura's Flowers' sign as it creaked its delight. The way the key moulded into my fingers as though it should always be mine. Soon, it would be someone else's key. Someone else's dream.

The door was streaked with dried egg yolk. I told myself it must be from the trick-or-treaters that had roamed the streets the previous night cloaked in black; plastic fangs protruding from bloodstained lips. I really should stop reading too much into things.

But my edginess stayed with me, despite the comforting floral smell that wrapped around me like a hug as I stepped inside.

I couldn't believe it was over.

When I'd opened the shop ten years before I had thought I'd eventually pass the business down to Tilly, or even to my niece Rhianon, who spent as much time at our house as Tilly did at hers. They loved gardening, kneeling side by side, fingernails caked with mud, trowels in hands, digging over the small flower bed that was theirs in the corner of our garden. Nurturing dandelions and buttercups because they were sunshine-yellow bright; pulling anemones and asters which hadn't yet flowered; flashing me gappy smiles as I handed out cherry ice pops. As they transitioned into teenagers, their corner of the garden grew tangled and wild, their interest in flowers lost. For the first time I was grateful they weren't wanting to step into my shoes and walk the endlessly worrisome path of the sole trader; declining business and too many bills.

Crouching, I scooped a clutch of brown envelopes from the doormat and saw 'Final Demand' stamped in red. I dropped them all onto the once-polished counter that was now coated with a thin film of dust. Over the past six weeks I'd been home more than I'd been at the shop; I wanted to be there for Tilly, of course. But it was difficult to know how to be around her when she said she needed space. I'd wandered around the house like a ghost. Touching Gavan's possessions as I'd once have touched his face, wondering who I was if I was no longer someone's wife. I had long since ceased to be anyone's daughter.

I'd had a sick feeling in my stomach for weeks, akin to thrashing around in a boat on a violent sea, but as I stepped inside the shop it was fleetingly as if I'd found the stillness that comes once a storm has passed. The shop gave me space to let my tears flow, unfiltered and raw, without worrying about being strong for Tilly.

Here I could feel.

As I did every morning I checked the diary, though I already knew it was empty. The pain behind my forehead pulsed harder. It wasn't only the fact that I'd been closed more than open recently that had affected business. Ten months ago the scandal had hit and the local papers printed their carefully worded vitriol with their 'allegeds' and their 'possiblys' bringing my family to its knees. It was printed that although Gavan was Welsh, my mother was English; as though that made a difference. Insinuating I didn't belong in Portgellech, the once-bustling fishing town where nowadays fishermen are as scarce a sight as the red kites that once soared across the grey and barren coastline. The community tightened ranks, some even referred to me as 'the English girl' despite me living there all my life. They chose to get their flowers from Tesco, the BP garage, anywhere – it seemed – but from me.

But that wasn't quite fair. Scrape away the thick layer of self-pity I wore like a second skin and my rational self acknowledged that I couldn't compete with the prices of supermarkets or the convenience and speed of online delivery services. Perhaps it was inevitable that it would all fall apart sometime, the whole business with Gavan just sped things up. Still, I was probably overthinking it all again. It was a notoriously quiet time of year. Wedding season was over and there was always a lull until December.

But I won't be here then.

I rummaged through drawers stuffed with ribbon and polka dot cellophane in search of some tablets to ease my headache. Then the bell tinged as the front door opened. I glanced up. My fleeting optimism dissipated when I saw it wasn't a paying customer, but Saffron for the third time that week.

'I'm so sorry.' I popped two paracetamols out of their foil cocoon. 'I haven't sold many.' In truth I hadn't sold any of the Oak Leaf Farm organic veg bags Saffron had been bringing me in to trial – offering me 20 per cent of all sales – but out of guilt I'd again bought two myself. The drawer in my fridge was stacked with limp carrots and browning parsnips.

'That's okay. I guess a florist isn't the first port of call when you want to buy food.' Briefly the corners of her mouth curved into a tense smile.

'It's not the first port of call when you want to buy flowers nowadays.' I grimaced as I swallowed the tablets down dry.

'We'll be okay as long as Amazon doesn't start selling bouquets.'

'They already sell flowers.'

'Then you're buggered.' Her hair, a mass of tight black spirals, sprang as her head shook with a laughter that sounded hollow. She looked as tired as I felt and I knew that despite her jokes she was as worried as I was. It was so tough being a small business owner.

'There's no hope for the independent retailer is there? Not when customers want everything to be available twenty-four-seven,' I said.

'You mean it isn't?' She titled her chin and shielded her eyes, searching for something in the sky. 'Is it a bird? Is it a plane? No, it's a delivery drone.'

I didn't laugh.

'Thanks for the tip you gave me last week, Laura.' She plucked a white rose from the bucket next to the counter and inhaled. 'That new coffee shop around the corner placed a regular order for potatoes. I do love a jacket spud.' She patted her impossibly flat stomach. Give her another ten years and the carbs would settle around her middle, the way they had on mine when I hit thirty.

Saffron chattered on and I tried to maintain my end of the conversation. Normal. I could do normal. But my mind kept returning to the letter. Adrenaline ebbed and flowed. Saffron's sentences fragmented. The words drifted out of my reach.

'Laura?' The way she said my name made me realise she'd asked a question I hadn't answered. Her voice sounded so very far away. I tried to focus but she had taken on an odd tinge. Even then, I put my disorientation down to stress. To grief. It wasn't until a sweet, sickly smell tickled my nostrils that it crossed my mind it was happening again, but it was impossible to think that it could, it had been so long. But I knew I was right when I was hit by a spinning sensation. Arms and legs flailing. I wasn't aware at what stage I fell to the floor, plummeting into blackness, I only found out later that I had. Time became irrelevant. It could have been seconds, minutes, hours later before I became conscious of a distant voice. An odd rasping roared into my ears – my own panicked breath. An angel – a blur of brilliant white light. I thought I was dying.

I thought I was dying again.

But as my hazy vision focused I saw it was Saffron in her white jeans and jumper. Her concerned face loomed towards mine.

'Are you okay?' Her hand was on my shoulder.

I tried to speak but my mouth was full of coppery blood where I'd bitten my tongue.

'I'm calling an ambulance.' The panic in her voice somehow calmed me.

'No.' I sat up. 'Please don't.' Gingerly, I pressed the back of my head where I'd hit it on the floor. I knew from experience that later I'd be sore and covered in bruises, but at the time embarrassment was my overriding emotion as I struggled to my feet. 'It's a seizure. I've had them before.' But not for years, since before my parents disowned me. It was like after they'd thrown me out, my body had fallen into a reverse shock almost – instead of breaking further apart, it had fallen back together. Perhaps Gavan had been the cause of my seizures returning. He had been the cause of so many things. I was thinking of the letter again and it all became too much. I began to cry.

'I'm so sorry.' She looked stricken. 'That looked awful. I didn't know whether to call 999 first or try to help you. It all happened so quickly.'

Although I was fuggy and disorientated and it felt like I'd been out for hours, in reality it had likely lasted less than a minute.

'How are you feeling?' she asked doubtfully, still gripping her phone.

Sick. Exhausted. Afraid.

'Fine,' I said, the bitter taste of the lie and blood on my tongue.

'You don't look it. Are you sure you don't need checking over?'

'No. Honestly, there's nothing the hospital can do for me.' There was a beat and I thought she'd insist on a doctor and all the implications that would bring. 'You could fetch me some water though.' I sat on the stool, elbows on the counter, my head in my hands. Seconds later a glass was placed in front of me and it felt like a dead weight as I lifted it to my dry lips and sipped before wiping the dribble snaking down my chin with my sleeve. 'You can go. I'm going to lock up and head home myself.' I was drained of energy; like I'd been powered by electricity and then unplugged.

Saffron hovered uncertainly. 'I could give you a lift?'

I hesitated. I'd be a danger on the road, but I'd only met Saffron about a dozen times; I didn't want to put her out. 'I'll ring a friend to pick me up.'

It didn't take long to scroll through my contacts. Even if it weren't for recent events, Gavan and I had been one of those couples who spent all our time together, so I didn't have many friends. I hesitated at Anwyn's name. My sister-in-law and I had been so close once, but our fractured family now barely spoke. Still, I called and it rang and rang before her voicemail kicked in. I pictured her watching my name flash up on the screen, choosing not to answer.

I didn't leave a message.

The shop bell pealed. I raised my heavy head. Saffron had cracked open the door; I'd almost forgotten she was still here.

'Are you sure you're okay? I could drive your car and pick mine up later. It's no trouble?'

I was feeling so unwell I couldn't face getting the bus, and I certainly couldn't afford a taxi.

'Yes please,' I said. 'That would be nice.'

But it wasn't nice at all.

Three is a power number, although I didn't know that at the time, I came to learn it later. It took three men to witness three things; a creation, a destruction and a restoration – Noah, Daniel and Job. There were three founders of the Roman Empire. It took three decisions to destroy my life.

Sometimes when something awful happens you sift through memories afterwards, desperate to pinpoint the exact moment things went horribly, horribly wrong.

Saying yes. That was the first mistake I made.

I still had two to go.

CHAPTER THREE

TILLY

They'd changed the classrooms around in the six weeks I'd been off. By the time I'd located my English group I was late.

'Sorry,' I muttered to Mr Cranford.

And rather than snapping at me like he normally would with his stale coffee breath he said, 'That's okay, Tilly. It's good to see you back.' His words were soaked with sympathy and somehow that was harder to bear than his shouting.

All the good seats were taken. Rhianon was sitting at the back with Ashleigh, Katie and Kieron. Katie and Kieron's bodies were angled together, their heads tilted towards each other, and I knew they were no longer purely friends. The thought of his lips on hers made my heart feel like it was breaking all over again. It was only a couple of months ago that he'd told me he loved me as his fingers strayed under my blouse, into my bra.

For God's sake, Tilly. Pull yourself together.

I dumped my rucksack next to an empty desk right at the front. The chair leg scraped loudly across the floor as I pulled it towards me. Mr Cranford waited, whiteboard marker in his hand, until I was settled before he carried on.

'This half term we're going to be studying *Othello*.' There was a collective grumble. 'No need for that. Plays are one of the oldest forms of entertainment.' His pen squeaked as it wrote 'Shakespeare' across the board. 'You can't beat a good tragedy—' He froze. Our eyes met. His were full of apology. I could feel the tears welling in mine. Quickly, he began to speak again. 'Plays were accessible, cheap...'

I zoned out. My mind cast back to the 'theatre' Dad had made me and Rhianon, cutting the front out of a large cardboard box and painting it red. Mum had hung two pieces of yellowing net curtain from a wire. Our audience of Uncle Iwan, Aunt Anwyn, Mum and Dad would queue at the door until Rhianon collected their shiny fifty pence pieces. The stars of the show were the sock monkeys we'd named Dick and Dom – mine turquoise and white striped, Rhianon's red polka dot – and we'd move them from side to side as they spouted waffle we thought was hilarious. There was never a script.

I glanced over my shoulder, certain Rhianon would be sharing the same memory, but I was confronted with the back of her head, long blonde hair hanging silkily over her shoulders. She'd twisted around and was whispering something to Katie and Kieron on the back row. My stomach churned as I assumed it was about me.

It was hard to pinpoint exactly when we'd drifted apart. She hadn't come over recently, but even in the months before that when she'd visited she had spent more time in the kitchen talking to Mum than she did with me. If I snapped at Mum over dinner, when she questioned me endlessly about my day, Rhianon would roll her eyes. Once, she even said, 'Don't speak to your mum that way.' It was rough for her at home, I knew. Her parents were arguing and it was calmer at our house. Mum listened to Rhianon. Mum always found time to listen patiently to everyone. Sometimes I thought Rhianon was jealous of the relationship I had with Mum, when her relationship with Aunty Anwyn was tense and strained, but then teenage girls aren't always close to their own mums are they? Saying that, even I could see Aunt Anwyn had changed. She had become angry I suppose, resentful almost. I guess it must have started with the shit-storm with Dad and Uncle Iwan's construction business. Everything circled back to that. I don't know the ins and outs because my parents only drip-fed me what they thought I needed to know, but Ashleigh's parents bought one of their houses on a new estate. Problem was they had built it on a former landfill site. Ashleigh got sick. Not like a cold and cough sick but proper ill. Leukaemia. That's when it all kicked off. It was months ago, but the memory still smarted; Katie standing on her chair, raising both her voice and her thinly plucked eyebrows.

'Listen up. Ashleigh's in hospital because Tilly's dad built on toxic land. It's *his* fault Ashleigh is sick. She might *literally* die.'

The other kids had started shouting abuse. I raised my palms.

'Honestly, it wasn't toxic land. Basically, there are all these safety checks before a build starts, aren't there, Rhianon?' I turned to my cousin. Our dads were in business together after all.

'I dunno. My dad had no idea about the history of the land. He only deals with finances.' I think I was the only one who could detect the fear in her voice, the shakiness of her words, but that was that. I was singled out. Unfriended. Ignored, ironically, by the majority of the school except Ashleigh who, when she came back after her treatment, wasn't exactly friendly but wasn't unfriendly either. With her illness and the fact she and her parents had crammed into her grandparents' house while checks were being carried out on the new build, she more than anyone had a reason to hate me, but she treated me exactly the way she had before. The occasional hello if we stood next to each other at the lockers, a passing nod if we bumped into each other in town. It was her parents that were furious and wanted someone to blame, I got that. Local papers need something to report on, I got that too. It was harder to understand the actions of the people I thought were my friends, and their parents, the community staging a sit-in at the half-finished building site, circulating petitions. In social studies once we'd examined the psychology of those who participated in protests. A lot of the time those people taking part felt deprived in some way, had felt injustice, inequality, and it didn't even have to be related to the protest they were taking part in. Their shared emotions, sympathy and outrage provided a coming together. A feeling of being part of something that might make a change. Perhaps they were just bloody angry. Or, in the case of our school, scared of Katie. But what was impossible to get my head around was the crack it caused in our family, Aunt Anwyn and Uncle Iwan blaming Mum and Dad for deciding to buy the land, as if they hadn't had any say.

'I'm just the money man,' Uncle Iwan said. 'You source the plots and I do the costings.'

As the business suffered we all suffered. Nobody wanted to buy from or sell to Dad anymore, and his sites remained half-finished. Uncle Iwan got a job with a rival firm. The separation between us widened until it seemed like it was me and Mum and Dad against the world. My opinion of Dad was shaken but it wasn't broken. Not then anyway.

The bell rang for lunch. I realised I hadn't been paying attention to the lesson at all. To look busy, I zipped and unzipped my rucksack until Rhianon reached my desk.

'Hi.' I fell into step beside her. She'd never completely ignored me and I hoped she wouldn't start now.

'Tilly.' Mr Cranford beckoned to me. 'Let me quickly run through what you need to catch up on.'

I made my way over to his desk, hoping Rhianon might wait for me, but instead she slipped out of the door in her new group of four. Katie smirked as she linked her fingers through Kieron's. With the other hand she mimed slicing across her throat with her finger, and I knew exactly where I stood.

Alone.

CHAPTER FOUR

LAURA

Neither Saffron nor I spoke as she drove me home. Exhaustion had carried me beyond the bounds of politeness so when she followed me inside the house and told me she'd put the kettle on, I didn't object. It should have felt odd someone bustling around my kitchen, pulling open the cupboards, popping the lid off the coffee caddy, but in truth it was comforting to have another adult take charge. Filling my space with heady jasmine perfume and normality. I had never coped well alone. I wished I could relinquish control entirely.

The ground seemed fluid rather than firm as I made my way unsteadily into the lounge, still wearing my coat and shoes. I flopped onto the sofa, but despite on some level being aware of the soft sigh of the frame as my weight hit the doughy cushions, I still didn't feel fully present – physically or mentally. I had forgotten how disorientating the period after a seizure is. How debilitating.

'I wasn't sure if you take sugar?' Saffron carried two mugs and a packet of ginger nuts tucked between her elbow and waist. 'And I couldn't find any milk but I take mine black anyway. Do you want a biscuit? I don't know if food helps? I know I'm probably thinking of diabetes but... Are you feeling any better? What happened?'

'A seizure.' I didn't want to call it epilepsy. I'd been free of that label for almost seventeen years. Living without medication for the past ten. My consultant warned me there was a possibility of a relapse. One in twenty-six people will experience a seizure in their lifetime, and with over forty different types they are impossible to predict.

'What brought it on?' The worry on her face made her appear younger than she usually did and sparked my maternal instinct. She shouldn't be the one looking after me.

It was likely that stress had brought it on, but I didn't tell her that. Instead I closed my eyes and counted to ten – your turn to hide – hoping that when I opened them, I would have again found the me of a few weeks ago, who was fit and healthy.

And loved.

Instead, I was confronted with a lonely beam of sunlight pushing through the slats in the blinds, illuminating Gavan's empty chair. The circular stain on the Moroccan orange arm, where he would always rest his after-dinner coffee, despite me sliding a coaster across the side table each evening. The things that had irritated me, I'd now have welcomed; that abandoned tube of toothpaste on the windowsill squeezed from the middle, the toilet seat left up, my razor blunted and clogged with foam and hair. Had I nagged him too much? I tried to think of the last time I told him I appreciated him. Almost every day there had been a new kindness for me to unwrap; the way he'd peel a satsuma for me so the juice didn't sting the sore skin around my fingernails, the giant bar of Galaxy he'd always arrive home with when my period was due, de-icing my windscreen while I was luxuriating under the hot pins of the shower, his patience with Tilly after teenage hormones rendered her snappy and uncommunicative.

And they were just the little things. The big thing, the truth, was that he saved me all those years ago after my parents cast me adrift. He'd be heartbroken to know that I was once again drowning, but this time it was his fault. My eyes were drawn to the letter on the sideboard. I had to save myself, save Tilly. But how? So much was broken, I didn't know where to start.

'Laura?' Saffron's voice was soft. It was a statement, a question, an inviting of confidence, all of this and more. Saffron seeing me at my most vulnerable at the shop had negated the need for social niceties, and all at once I wanted to weep into my coffee. I glanced at her, on the brink of opening up but, for a moment, afraid of what she might think of me.

'What is it?' Her concern gently tugged me over the edge until I plunged headfirst into the unvarnished truth.

'I'm broke. I'm going to lose my house. My business. And I've a daughter to support. Tilly's doing her A Levels and she's already had so much disruption this year.' I didn't elaborate what. Momentarily, I had a fleeting hope that releasing the words from my churning stomach would calm the almost constant nausea I had felt lately. It didn't.

'Oh, Laura. I'm so sorry.' There was a beat. Her eyes flicked to the huge collage in the 'Live, Laugh, Love' frame, hanging above the fireplace. A wall of duck-egg paint and smiling faces. Me and Gavan toasting our fifteen-year anniversary, our heads touching; Tilly and Rhianon starting school, brandishing matching pink lunchboxes and toothy grins; Gavan arched over Tilly's cot, her hair already a shock of black curls, a look of wonder on his face; my wedding dress that clung too tightly to my stomach – seventeen years later, I was still carrying my baby weight. We had wanted to get married before she was born but we couldn't afford it. The photos show us jumbled and out of order, we hop from adults to teenagers, toddlers to babies, and back again. 'It looks like you have a loving family? I'm sure—'

'My husband died six weeks ago.' Chilled, I pulled the coat I was still wearing tighter.

'Christ, Laura, I'm so sorry. And there was me wittering on about fruit and veg boxes.'

There was a pause, her question crackled in the air before she voiced it. 'How did it happen? If you don't mind me asking?'

I plucked out the only answer my mind could make sense of and offered it to her.

'It was an accident.'

'I'm so sorry.' The regret in her voice was genuine. I'd never seen her look so sombre before. It encouraged me to tell her more.

'He fell from some scaffolding at work. The coroner adjourned the inquest pending enquiries, and in the meantime issued an interim death certificate that I sent to our life insurance company. But I've had a letter from them today saying they won't pay out until I've had the death certificate proper.'

'Why? Surely if he's…' her voice dropped. 'If they've proof he died.'

'Apparently they need to establish a cause of death. It's ridiculous. He fell. It was an accident.'

It was. It had to be.

'How long will it be before you get the actual death certificate?'

'I don't know. The coroner said they endeavour to hold all inquests within six months.'

Another court case, and I knew I shouldn't feel so frightened this time – I was an adult now – but somehow I still did.

I swear by almighty God to tell the truth, the whole truth, and nothing but the truth.

But God hadn't protected me then and he still wasn't protecting me.

'I need that money.' My voice cracked. 'I can't pay the rent. We were in arrears anyway and my landlord is threatening eviction. I've reached my overdraft limit. My credit cards are all maxed out. The florist doesn't provide an income anymore. There was an incident a few months ago...' I choked back a sob. 'It's all such a mess. I'd been counting on the insurance money to sort everything out.'

'You must have grounds to appeal? To get an interim payment to see you through at least?'

I rested my head back, staring at Gavan's photo, willing my fight to return. When she was small, Tilly was obsessed with *The Wizard of Oz*. She'd clench her tiny hands into fists and jig from foot to foot like a boxer – 'put 'em up' – the lion found his courage in the end. Where was mine?

'You're right. I must. I only found out this morning. It's so hard, being alone. Everything seems ten times more mountainous than it would otherwise.'

'Perhaps I can help? The man I live with, he used to be a solicitor—'

'That's nice of you but I don't think your boyfriend—'

'He's not a romantic partner. He's...' This time it was she who hesitated, who seemed afraid of being judged. Fiddling with the fraying hem of her jumper. Looking vulnerable away from the wall of jokes that usually shielded her. 'We both live at Gorphwysfa. The farm on Oak Leaf Lane.'

'Of course.' Oak Leaf Organics grew the produce they sold on their farm outside of town. A small community lived there – *bunch of bloody hippies* some of the locals called them – but I didn't know much about them.

'Anyhoo. Alex.' Her features softened as she talked about him. I wondered then if they were more than friends, or if she wanted them to be. 'He might be able to help you with the insurance company. The legal jargon.'

'I can't afford a solicitor.'

'He wouldn't expect you to pay. At the farm it's not just living together, it's... a pulling together I suppose. We share and trade resources. There's always someone on hand with the necessary skill. You're never alone.'

Alone. It was just a word but those five letters triggered such an intense longing, my heart ached.

'But I don't live there.'

'That doesn't matter. You can pay it forward when you can. Help out with growing the veg.'

It was a chance. A possibility. A bright shining star in a dark sky of despair, but although I parted my lips, I couldn't release the *yes* that was stuck to the roof of my mouth. Asking for favours was like stripping back the layers until I was vulnerable and exposed. Open to rejection once more.

'The offer's there anyway. Look. It's almost lunchtime, I'd better go. Let you get some rest.' Saffron stood and smoothed down her top. The words that had poured from me had left my throat and mouth dry. I was more accustomed to the silence that once again filled the room. I pictured Tilly at the cafeteria prising the lid off her Tupperware, and my chest prickled with heat. What had seemed like a good idea at 6.30 this morning, suddenly felt like a horrible mistake. I had a feeling she'd be furious with me after school. Again.

'It's going to be okay,' Saffron said when, lost in thought, I hadn't made a move to see her out.

But I didn't have her certainty. All I had were fears and doubts that threatened to sink me entirely.

'You can't know that unless you can predict the future.' But still, I pleaded with my eyes, wanting her words to be a prophecy. A promise.

Fleetingly, I saw something in her indigo gaze that I didn't understand. I searched her face but couldn't see anything except kindness and understanding.

'Laura, I've been…' She glanced at the floor. 'Low. If it weren't for Alex I honestly don't know where I'd be.' She slipped on her crimson coat and the colour was such a contrast to her stark white outfit it reminded me of another time. Another place. Streaks of blood on virgin white snow.

'I'll jot down my mobile number for you.' She rooted around in her bag. 'If you change your mind, just ask.' And, momentarily, that small, square piece of paper she pushed into my hand was strong enough to keep the tide of hopelessness at bay. Enough to pull me to my feet.

In the hallway I tucked the paper into my handbag while Saffron slipped on shoes that were sturdy and dependable and I told myself I could trust her. She opened the door. A frigid wind gusted through the gap. A shiver trailed its fingers down the back of my neck. I know now it wasn't the icy air that made my hairs stand on end. It was my intuition. That feeling in my gut warned me to stay away from Gorphwysfa.

If only I hadn't ignored it.

CHAPTER FIVE

TILLY

Mr Cranford took forever to load me with homework. By the time I got to the canteen the queue for food was long, not that I had to join it since I had my packed lunch. Mum said we couldn't afford to buy lunch out anymore, like £2.50 would really break the bank.

The spicy pepperoni and melted cheese made my stomach rumble. I was always a fan of pizza day. I slid onto an empty bench, dumping my rucksack at my feet. I scanned the room. Rhianon was at the till paying for her food. Our eyes met. Invisible strands of years of friendship hung between us, frayed and worn. We were so much more than cousins.

I raised my hand. Mouthed, 'Hi.'

Her hand twitched by her side and I willed her to wave at me. Instead, after glancing to see where Katie was, she offered me a weak smile and a barely discernible nod. I'd only spoken to her once since Dad died. After Mum said the post mortem had been carried out and we were free to bury him.

'I can't bear to think of him all cut up,' I had sobbed down the phone. Rhianon had cried too and, for a moment, we were close again.

Now, I patted the seat next to me in a sit-here gesture. She chewed her lip in that way of hers when she couldn't decide what to do.

Katie strode in front of her and then they were all walking in my direction. My stomach tightened and, to make myself look busy, I opened my Tupperware and pulled out a sandwich. Too late I realised my mistake.

'Oh. My. God.' Katie stopped in her tracks. 'Tilly!' She paused for effect, to make sure everyone was looking. 'Has *Mummy* cut your sandwiches into hearts? How sweet!'

My body burned with embarrassment. What *had* Mum been thinking?

'It's like you're seven, not seventeen. No wonder Kieron dumped you.'

Kieron studied his shoes. He used to tell me my eyes were beautiful, but now he couldn't meet them.

Katie began to sing that old song, 'Don't go breaking my heart…' but trailed off when she realised no one was joining in. Rhianon was staring at the floor, an odd expression on her face, and I wondered if she was remembering the same memory as me. The way her mum and mine used to belt out that song whenever they made dinner together, when everyone got along.

'Go and take a running jump, Katie,' I said.

'Like your dad did?'

All the breath left my body in one sharp release. I tried to not picture Dad broken and bleeding on the floor, but the image had snuck into my mind and was scorched there for evermore.

'Katie, don't,' Rhianon said quietly.

'You're sticking up for her?' Katie raised her perfectly drawn eyebrows.

'He *was* my uncle.'

I screwed the sandwich up so tightly in my fist that tuna mayo splattered all over the sleeve of my black top.

'Aww, never mind,' Katie said. 'I'm sure *Mummy* will wash it for you.' She sashayed away while I rubbed at the stain with my fingers, but that only made it worse. I watched as Rhianon and Kieron trailed after her, cramming themselves onto an almost-full table on the other side of the hall.

We had learned about a leper colony in Greece in history once, and as I sat alone, surrounded by empty seats, I realised that I wasn't just a social leper, I was that entire island.

Angrily, I flicked a piece of sweetcorn onto the floor and then felt guilty. Mum tried so hard. I'd been such a bitch to her lately. I wished I could tell her everything. How lonely I was. How afraid. Sometimes I heard her crying in the night. I'd bury my head underneath my pillow. Each day I tried to avoid her. I was frightened that as soon as I started talking to her the truth would just come out. I didn't want to do or say anything that might ruin Mum's memory of Dad; she had enough to deal with. I didn't want her to think badly of me, but I wondered if she *did* know, would she hate him and miss him less? It was impossible to know what the right thing to do was.

As I thought of the way I'd ignored her goodbye and slammed the car door that morning, I began to panic. She was literally all I had left and I wasn't sure what I'd do if she turned her back on me too. I balled my hands as I bit down hard on my lip to stop myself crying. I was shrinking the way Alice did when she drank the potion in Wonderland. The rain hammered down on the corrugated roof and the noise of that, and of the chatter and laughter and the clattering of trays, was unbearable.

'We're off to see the wizard.' I filled my head with Mum's soft voice singing one of our favourite songs.

The pressure released from my lungs, leaving a desire to make up with Mum. I pulled my mobile out of my bag. Straight away it beeped with a message notification from Rhianon.

> Take it from the cute sandwiches you STILL haven't told your mum the truth about your dad?

Dread filled my empty stomach. How much longer would it remain a secret?

Dad's hands cupping my face.

Promise you won't tell, Tilly.

CHAPTER SIX

LAURA

I hugged the pillow tighter, the feathers moulding against the curves of my body. The curves Gavan would kiss on a Saturday morning while I wriggled further under the covers, protesting that it was too bright with the sun glaring through the thin curtains, shining its fiery spotlight on every lump and bump.

'Laura, I've eaten marshmallows off your belly, licked chocolate body paint off your thighs, sucked whipped cream from *everywhere*.' He'd pin my wrists above my head. 'You're beautiful. Don't hide.'

If he were still with me I'd stand in all my naked glory, cellulite and stretch marks on display, and let him love me the way he wanted to. The way I needed him to. I pressed my face against the pillowcase and inhaled, long and slow. Each night I sprayed Boss aftershave on Gavan's side of the bed. The sheets smelled of him, and yet somehow, they didn't. The cologne came from his bottle, the bottle I bought him last Christmas, but it wasn't quite the same. The underlying muskiness of him. His own unique Gavan smell had gone and I just couldn't recreate it.

Music blasted. A thumping bass shaking the wall between Tilly's bedroom and mine, but I didn't shout at her to turn it down. It reminded me that despite the hollow in my chest,

I was not alone. She was up early for a Saturday. Her door crashed open, and seconds later the bathroom door slammed. Seventeen and destined for uni and she still couldn't operate a door handle. Tearing myself away from my too-big-for-one bed I slipped my feet into slippers and shrugged on my dressing gown. It was chilly.

'Morning,' I called from the landing. 'I'm making toast. Do you want some?'

'Not going to cut it into a heart, are you?' she fired through the plasterboard separating us. I hesitated. There was so much I wanted to say but I didn't know where to start, so I jammed my words and my hands into my pockets and traipsed downstairs to put the heating on.

By the time my breakfast was ready the ancient boiler was chugging into life. I ate at the table, the syrupy thick coffee and the sticky tang of marmalade chasing away the last traces of sleep. Once again I read the letter from the insurance company:

Dear Mrs Evans, After careful consideration we regret to inform you that in the absence of...

The words skipped and hopped behind the blur of tears covering my eyes until they rearranged themselves into something different. Something better. A future. I peered into the envelope in case I could find some hope. A second sheet of cheap white paper telling me it was a mistake. Of course they would be paying out. Fulfilling the promises of their slick advertising campaign, featuring impossibly beautiful actors with just the right amount of tension etched into their too-perfect skin.

36

Their smiles chasing away their frowns as Ironstone Insurance reassured, 'We worry, so you don't have to.'

Fucking, fucking liars.

I couldn't wait weeks or even months until the inquest, and what if the coroner didn't think it was an accident?

The truth, the whole truth and nothing but the truth.

I had almost been shattered before. I couldn't be again. I had Tilly to look after.

'Mum?'

I dragged my sleeve across my cheeks, mopping my tears, and attempted a smile. Tilly looked young and uncertain without the thick black lines she normally drew under her eyes, clad in her polar bear pyjamas and penguin slippers.

'I'm fine. I'm popping over to Aunt Anwyn and Uncle Iwan's this morning. Do you want to come?'

Emotions flickered across her face – she had always been so easy to read. Surprise, trepidation, a longing that perhaps everything would be okay. It would go back to the way it was before – sleepovers with Rhianon and family lunches. It worried me that the girls had drifted apart. I could understand Rhianon's loyalty to Anwyn and Iwan, while they unfairly blamed Gavan for the whole sorry mess, but I'd hoped after Gavan died that she'd be there for Tilly. Kieron had dumped her before we'd even had the funeral. I was glad they'd only been together for a few weeks, and I don't think she cared with everything else that was going on, but I was angry with him for letting her down. I knew from experience how uncomfortable death can make adults – avoiding eye contact, avoiding speaking Gavan's name – perhaps it was unfair to expect a seventeen-year-old to be able to offer support. But now that Tilly was back at school

I was sure Rhianon would do the right thing. She was a good girl really.

'It would be nice if you came.' I swept the crumbs that littered the table onto my empty plate. If Tilly was by my side, surely there couldn't be a repeat of last time me and Anwyn were in a room together. The lightning-sharp insults, thundering rage, accusations flung like hail against a windowpane. To my surprise and relief, Tilly said yes.

I had showered, dressed, squeaked the worktops clean with lemon cleaner and clattered too-many-for-one empty wine bottles into the recycling bin, and Tilly still wasn't ready. Upstairs, I tapped on her door and urged her to hurry up before I lost my nerve. It took another half an hour before she stomped down the stairs in a fug of overpowering perfume, wearing a top and trousers that didn't match. She looked like she'd slung on the first things she found on the floor – what had she been doing up there?

My Volvo always smelled of flowers, even when the backseat was empty. I pulled out of our road, opposite the park with the baby swings I used to push Tilly on – higher, higher, higher – as her pudgy hands gripped the metal bar, her head thrown back in laughter. The route to Anwyn's was familiar. I drove on autopilot, oblivious to it all; the traffic lights we must have passed, the rain pattering against the car roof, the swish of the windscreen wipers. I wasn't even conscious of Tilly in the passenger seat as I rehearsed what I'd say over and over, choosing my words carefully, rearranging them into some semblance of order. The last thing I wanted to do was offend them, cause another scene. It wasn't until I parked and yanked the handbrake on that I became aware of the awful heavy metal music Tilly was playing. Some band wanting someone to pour some sugar on them, whatever that meant. Still, as long as she was happy.

It felt odd to be walking up the driveway without holding a bottle of wine for dinner, a homemade trifle for dessert. Without wearing a smile. Rather than heading around the back and walking straight in with an 'it's only us!' I rapped on the front door.

From inside, the muffled sound of shouting. I exchanged a glance with Tilly. We'd arrived at a bad time but I couldn't afford to give up. I knocked again.

It seemed an age before the door opened. Usually well-groomed, I was shocked by Anwyn's appearance. Her hair greasy and unbrushed, the whites of her eyes tinged pink. Around her hung the pungent tang of stale alcohol.

'Laura.' Confused, her gaze flickered between Tilly and I. Before she could react I stepped forward.

'Can we come in? Please.'

'It's not a good time.' The door began to swing towards me and I wedged my foot inside before it fully closed.

I wasn't leaving without a fight.

'Please,' I said, glancing at Tilly. It looked like she was trying not to cry, and Anwyn must have thought the same because she silently turned. I took that as an invitation to step inside, following her down the narrow passageway into the kitchen.

'Tilly, do you want to go and find Rhianon?' It wasn't a question.

In the kitchen Iwan leaned against the worktops, his arms crossed defensively. Two against one. The air was prickly. I closed the door so the girls wouldn't be able to hear. Anwyn wordlessly filled the kettle, lifted milk from the fridge. I used the time it took her to make our drinks to decide where to start, but by the time she slopped the mugs onto the table and we all sat down I still didn't know what to say.

Silently, I slid the letter over to Iwan, studying his face as he read it. He looked terrible. His skin hanging looser around his jowls. His eyes sunken in their blackened sockets. Grief had aged him too.

'Sorry, Laura,' he said after he'd digested it. Anwyn snatched it from his fingers.

She scanned it. 'I can't see what this has to do with us.'

'Anwyn,' Iwan's voice rumbled.

'What? I'm not allowed an opinion on anything now?' She let out a sigh and a cloud of cheap wine fumes.

I addressed Iwan. 'Is there anything you can do?'

'I don't see what I can do. I can't make the inquest happen any quicker.' He ran his fingers through thinning hair.

'Have you been interviewed by the coroner yet? They want to go through the events leading up to that night, as well as find out exactly where everyone was when Gavan fell.'

Anwyn and Iwan exchanged an uncomfortable glance. It was always going to be emotional talking about Gavan's death. I pushed on.

'Iwan, I'm going to lose my *home*.' I wanted to lay down the facts, clear and concise, but my voice splintered under the strain of my uncertain future. 'Isn't there anything else? Business insurance?'

'There isn't a business anymore,' Anwyn chipped in. 'You'll have to get a job like the rest of us, Laura.'

'I've been applying for—' I began but she cut me off.

'Iwan swallowed his pride and began working for someone else after all that hoo-ha with the land. Oh, take that look off your face,' she snapped at me. 'Who cares if it was with a rival firm? He had a family to support. Gavan should have admitted defeat and got a proper job too.'

'Gavan knew he'd done nothing wrong. It didn't matter that the estate was being built on a former landfill site. If it wasn't safe the council wouldn't have sold it to us, or granted planning permission. He didn't give up because he believed in the business. He believed in *you*, Iwan.' I stretched out my fingers towards him but Anwyn placed her hand on his before I could reach him. He snatched it away. 'He never stopped trying.' Tears filled my eyes as I remembered his determination. His optimism that he could turn things around. 'He'd lined up a deal he said would get everything back on track the night he died. He loved what he did. He loved you, Iwan. You were his brother…'

'I think Iwan knows that. Family is important to him.'

'But we're your family. Tilly and I…'

Anwyn snorted. Iwan glared at her. The tension that sat heavy between them when I arrived thickened.

'Laura, I can't help you.' His words were soft but they struck a blow.

'Can't or won't? Please, Iwan. Just be honest with me.'

'Honest!' Anwyn stood so fast her chair toppled backwards and crashed to the ground. 'Don't come here cap in hand and bloody talk to us about being honest, Laura. Don't forget we know the lengths you've gone to in the past to get what you want. The lies you've told. I *know* you.'

I couldn't believe she'd dragged that up and thrown it in

my face. I stood too. My hands flat on the table supporting my weight as I leaned forwards.

'That's a nice way to talk to your family.' My voice was low.

'You're not family.' Her face was inches from mine. Her rancid breath made my stomach roil. 'And neither is that daughter of yours.'

'Let's all calm down,' Iwan said. 'Tilly's family, and Laura is—'

'Laura, you've made your own bed,' Anwyn cut in. 'You're *not* family to us anymore.'

Those were the same words my dad used all those years ago and hearing them felt like ripping off a plaster, raw and painful, the wound gaping wide open once more. Instinctively I slapped her.

'Oh God, Anwyn. I didn't… I…' Shocked, my hand dropped to my side as hers rose to press against her cheek.

'Get out!' she screamed.

But I was already leaving the room, pulling on my coat. Feeling sick, I called for Tilly.

The front door opened. 'Aunt Laura?' Rhianon hesitated halfway across the threshold, sensing the atmosphere. 'Is everything okay?'

Tilly pushed past me, then pushed past Rhianon, and I squeezed my niece on the shoulder as I followed my daughter to the car, knowing I would never set foot in that house again.

Knowing there was only one option left for me, even if the thought of doing it made me feel ill.

But we do what we have to for our children, don't we?

CHAPTER SEVEN

TILLY

I was annoyed I couldn't sleep in. It was Saturday for God's sake. Monday to Friday, Mum had to literally drag me out of bed but that day, with nothing to do and no one to do it with, I was up at eight. I hadn't slept well, thanks to my inability to stop scrolling through Instagram. Sometimes I even put my phone down, only to snatch it up seconds later in case another post had appeared: Rhianon and Ashleigh trying on clothes in New Look; Kieron and Katie sharing a pitcher in the Moon on the Square where they never ask for ID. It was a world where everyone was thinner, happier, more popular than I was. Eating better meals, wearing nicer clothes. I was the stray ginger cat who prowled our garden and sat on the patio, pressing his nose against the glass, purring to be invited in. I could have explained all that to Mum, but I never did. I knew I wasn't the only one having sleepless nights. I could hear the squeak of Mum's bed frame as she tossed and turned. Her footsteps as she padded downstairs for another cup of tea. In the first few days, after Dad died, I wanted to climb into bed with her but it was so weird being in their room without him. His clothes still piled over the elliptical trainer which Mum never used. His brush on top of the chest of drawers. Once I had tugged some of his hair free of the bristles and hidden it in a shoe box at the bottom of my wardrobe, along with a strip of black and white photos of me and Rhianon in one of those old-school photo booths.

I had tried to get back to sleep, but couldn't, so had stomped to the bathroom instead. Mum asked if I wanted toast. I snapped 'not if it's in a heart shape' or something. It was a low blow, but my foul mood was uncontrollable and the words had come out before I could swallow them back down. I had gone downstairs to offer to make her a cup of tea or something. She was sitting at the table crying, and to know I had caused that with my stupid toast remark made me feel like a prize bitch. Mum had tried to do something nice with my sandwiches after all, and I did appreciate it. Some mums don't even bother.

It was a surprise when she asked me to go to Aunt Anwyn's with her. We hadn't seen much of them socially since Ashleigh got sick, and Dad and Uncle Iwan's business stupidly got the blame. I thought it was really unfair because I saw Aunt Anwyn in a coffee shop in town with Cathy Collins, Ashleigh's mum, so they must have still been friends. Mum said things would settle down and everyone would move on. Dad was a scapegoat because Mr Collins needed someone to blame; dads feel like they have to protect their daughters and he must think that he let her down. When I thought of that it made me want to cry. Why didn't my dad want to protect me?

Thinking of the reception we might get, I almost changed my mind about going but Aunt Anwyn and Uncle Iwan were so kind to me at the funeral I thought if we could all come together like a family I might become best friends with Rhianon again, which would make things easier at school. I knew she couldn't completely hate me; if she did she'd never have kept quiet about what I'd told her. Anyway, I owed Mum after the whole heart-shaped toast thing so I agreed to go with her. It was my sorry without saying sorry.

It took ages to decide what to wear. It was the same every morning. Deciding who I wanted to be, painting my skin, covering my body, not wanting anyone to see the real me. Not really sure who the real me was anymore. When we were younger, Rhianon and I were given these books one Christmas. The front page had a paper doll you could pop out, the rest of the pages contained her outfits and accessories. She could be anyone you liked. Biker chick. Catwalk model. Must-go-to-the-ball-and-kiss-a-prince-at-midnight princess. I was that paper doll as I pulled clothes from my wardrobe and stood in front of the mirror trying on new identities; flimsy and fragile. Just like her, I had been so easy to screw up and throw away.

Mum thumped on my door and shouted. I was browsing Instagram as I tried on various combinations of clothes. There was an art to clashing prints and patterns. Finally, I squeezed my feet into my baby blue suede boots and I was, if not satisfied, resigned that this was the best I was going to do. I opened the sample of too-expensive-for-me perfume I'd found in a copy of *Cosmo* that someone had left in the sixth form common room and rubbed it over my wrists, behind my ears, over my neck.

Mum didn't say anything when I came downstairs, let alone bother to tell me I looked nice or that she was pleased I had made such an effort. In fact she didn't speak to me once during the drive. She was either annoyed I had taken so long to get ready, or was still hurt by my toast comment. Who knew?

On the journey I started to think of all the ways my turning up at Rhianon's unannounced was a bad idea. The swarm of bees that constantly filled my head buzzed noisily. Needing a distraction I fiddled with the ancient radio, twisting the dial past the crackle and hiss until I found Planet Rock. Def Leppard vibrated through the terrible speaker in the car door. It wasn't really my sort of music, but I left it on knowing that Mum would hate it, not really understanding why I was compelled to irritate her. But she ignored the music and she ignored me. She clearly thought it wasn't worth the fight, that *I* wasn't worth the fight.

It was when Mum knocked on the front door as if we were strangers that we heard all the shouting coming from inside the house. Aunt Anwyn threw open the door. I was too anxious to speak as we went inside. I couldn't remember ever entering this way, through the cramped hallway with its dark red walls and bookcases, and I had to turn sideward to squeeze past them. Usually we spilled through the light, bright conservatory with the old sofa with a hole in its arm, and the games console Rhianon and I used to play on until we discovered makeup and boys. When we reached the kitchen, Mum ordered me to go and find Rhianon, and virtually slammed the door in my face before I could even say hi to Uncle Iwan. Charming.

Although I'd wanted to see Rhianon, once I was there I had felt too awkward to go upstairs. Instead I sat on the sofa in the lounge. The first thing I noticed was that all the photos of me, Mum and Dad had been removed. There were darker patches on the peacock walls, where the frames used to be. It was quiet at first. But then, from the kitchen, the whisper-shouting started. They didn't think I could hear them, but of course I could. Needing to block out their arguing I pulled the twisted mess of my earbuds from my pocket, and worked the knots free before stuffing them into my ears. My Spotify daily mix played Nina

Nesbitt's '18 Candles'. I would be eighteen next year. An adult. The thought of leaving school calmed me. I started scrolling through Instagram and spotted a new post from Rhianon. A photo of her, Katie and Ashleigh sitting cross-legged on sleeping bags, wearing pyjamas. I think it was taken at Katie's house. 'Great sleepover last night #BFF'

Again that lump in my throat. I'd tell Mum I'd walk home. But when I removed my earbuds I heard Anwyn scream, 'You're not family and neither is that daughter of yours.'

If I wasn't family.

If I wasn't a friend.

Who was I?

I stepped into the hallway and Mum came barging out of the kitchen, just as Rhianon sauntered through the front door with her overnight bag. Her silent yawn shouting she'd had a brilliant sleepover.

I pushed my way past Mum and her, running out towards the car. I never got to tell Aunt Anwyn that even without Dad around to tie her to Mum, I was still her niece. Somehow, even then, I knew I would never be back.

I would never see her again.

CHAPTER EIGHT

LAURA

Tilly thundered upstairs as soon as we got back from Anwyn's. I didn't follow her, knowing I had to make the call straight away before my courage drained away. I sat in the kitchen still wearing my coat. My knee jigging up and down as I conjured up the keypad on my mobile. This wasn't a number that was stored in my contacts, instead it was stored in the dark corners of my mind where cobwebs hung, and memories that were too painful to revisit gathered dust.

Acid rose in my throat as my shaking finger pressed the digits slowly. Through the stretch of time I could see the phone vibrating on the mahogany table with the vase of fake flowers with their too-shiny leaves. I could hear my mother's voice reciting the number every time she answered, in the unlikely event the caller was unaware of who they were trying to reach.

A soft click.

'Hello.' The voice was bright and breezy. Too young to belong to my dad. Too cheerful.

'Hello. I… I'm trying to reach Donald or Linda?'

'You've got the wrong number.'

'Sorry. I… I don't suppose that line is still connected to fourteen Acacia Avenue is it?'

'Yes. But we've been here eight years—'

Numb, I ended the call. Stupid that I'd expected everything in my childhood to have remained the same. Stupid that I'd ever thought my parents would help me, even if they still lived there.

'Laura, you've made your own bed. You're not family to us anymore,' my father had spat after he'd ordered me out of his life. I had hefted a black bag crammed with my possessions over my shoulder, my duvet rolled under my arm, as my scared and confused seventeen-year-old self had stumbled out into the cutting night air. The door slammed behind me but I didn't move. Couldn't co-ordinate my legs and brain to work together. Minutes later I had been flooded with relief as there was the sound of unlocking, my mum framed in the doorway, honeycomb light spilling out into the porch. 'Mum!' Slowly, uncertainly, I had stepped towards her but she had shaken her head, creating an invisible barrier between us, before stretching out her palm.

'Give me your key,' were her last words to me before I handed over my keyring and my identity as a daughter. The door closed once more, leaving me standing alone on the step, my breath coming too fast, white clouds billowing from my mouth like mist, instantaneously disappearing like it had never existed. The kitchen light brightened the garden. I had crouched in the flower bed and peeped through the window as Mum stuck a couple of pork chops under the grill while Dad laid the table for two, and as I turned away I knew – for my parents – it was as if I had never existed.

Still, I couldn't believe how much it hurt to learn they had moved, and I had no idea where they were. If they were alive even. My eyes cast around the tiny kitchen as though somehow

49

I might find them there, coming to rest by the back door. The pencil marks made by Gavan as he balanced a ruler on Tilly's head while she asked, 'How tall am I now, Daddy?' We'd out-grown this house years ago, but I always had an excuse not to move. It was too convenient for Tilly's nursery; for her school. Later, we'd spent the deposit we'd saved to buy our own house on setting up Gavan's business. We'd saved again, but that time our hard-earned cash went on the florist shop. Gavan never complained. Now and then he'd grumble about renting being a waste of money, and that it was ridiculous we didn't own a home when he built them for a living, but he knew that deep down the reason I didn't want to leave was because there, my parents knew where I was. We'd sent them a photo of Tilly asleep in her pram after she was born, with our address scrawled on the back. How could they resist her sweet face? Somehow they did. The void of loss had never fully left me, but gradually over the years I had filled it with a new family: Gavan, Tilly, Iwan, Anwyn, Rhianon; but I always retained the tiniest sliver of hope that one day they might come for me and if that day came I wanted them, I needed them, to be able to find us.

And now *they'd* moved.

When Tilly thumped downstairs hours later, proclaiming that she was starving, I was still sitting at the kitchen table.

Still wearing my coat.

The following day, I was rifling through the fridge, seeing which withering vegetables from the Oak Leaf Organics bag I could salvage for Sunday lunch, when the doorbell chimed.

'Iwan!' My eyes darted left and then right. He was alone. 'Come in.' I stepped back and gestured for him to go into the lounge as I returned to the kitchen to make tea, putting some space between us. I gathered my thoughts as I gathered the milk and the sugar. I needed to repair my shrinking family. Iwan was my last link to Gavan. Their dad had passed from cancer two years ago, and their mum followed six months later. A cardiac arrest, the young doctor had said, but privately we thought that grief had broken her heart in two. There were no other relatives.

My breath caught in my throat as I carried the mugs through. Iwan was filling Gavan's chair, his elbows resting on the arms, fingers steepled together in front of his mouth the way Gavan used to sit when I'd laugh and tell him it looked like he was praying.

'Praying for a kiss,' he'd say and I'd roll my eyes but kiss him anyway.

I'd never noticed before how similar their fingers were, their mannerisms. Iwan cleared his throat. The brothers even had the same husky undertone and I had a crazy impulse to close my eyes. To ask him to whisper 'I love you,' just to hear it one more time.

'Laura, I'm sorry about yesterday, about Anwyn,' he said and the spell was broken.

'I'm sorry too. I should never have slapped her.' Just the thought of it made my palm sting.

'She has a knack of bringing out the worst in people sometimes.' It was a strange thing for him to say about his wife. Again, I wondered what they had been arguing about before we had arrived. The silence stretched. He spoke first. 'I miss him too. It was never... It should never have ended that way. He was my brother and I let him down.'

'He understood.' I told him what he needed to hear. 'That night... He was excited about the business.'

'There was a deal agreed in principle,' he said.

'And now?' Iwan couldn't meet my eye. He didn't speak. 'You've taken the deal to your new firm haven't you?' There was a sour taste in my mouth.

'It's not that, it's… complicated. Look, I'll make some enquiries. See if there's anything I can do. If I can get you some money, Laura, I will. You know what Tilly means to me, what you both mean to me.' He rubbed his fingers over his lips the way Gavan used to whenever he felt uncomfortable. Trying to press the words back inside.

'Thank you.' The pressure on my chest eased.

'Don't thank me yet. Even if I can do anything, it will be a slow process. Months if not longer. There's a situation.' He sipped his tea which was still steaming and I knew it was a delaying tactic.

'Anything I should know about?' I asked.

'Laura.' His eyes met mine. 'Sometimes there are things you're better off never knowing.'

*

'Sorry, there's nothing we can do.'

That was the phase I heard over and over that week. Each day was a battle. After I'd drop Tilly at school there were endless phone calls and visits. The benefits office was sorry but there was a backlog and they couldn't process my claim for weeks. My landlord wouldn't accept housing benefit tenants. There were some flats which would but they were in a rough area and quite far from Tilly's school. The insurance company smothered me with terms and clauses and legalities I couldn't understand. Citizen's Advice couldn't fit me in until the New Year. The landlord of the shop was sorry, but in light of the arrears he'd found a new tenant and he'd be keeping my deposit to cover some of the rent I'd missed.

Sorry. Everyone was sorry.

It was Friday that finally broke me. Although I'd applied for every job going, from cleaning to waitressing, it was the position in the flower department of my local supermarket I had pinned all my hopes upon. I knew it would only be unpacking cellophane-wrapped bouquets from boxes and dumping them in plastic buckets but I was certain I'd get the job.

The white envelope imprinted with the shop's logo dropped onto the doormat. I pounced on it eagerly.

We regret to inform you…

The rejection punched the back of my knees, tore sobs from my throat. I slid to the floor, curling myself as small as possible. The hessian doormat bristled against my cheek as I cried for the things I didn't have; a job, money, a home, but most of all I cried for Gavan, his name rising from the pit of my stomach, spilling out into the cold empty hallway where he would never again kick off muddy boots and trail brick dust over the carpet.

Eventually, I exhausted myself. I shuffled on my knees to the bottom of the stairs and unhooked my handbag from the bannister. It was while I was rooting around for a packet of tissues that my fingers brushed against the piece of paper Saffron had given me.

'If it weren't for Alex I honestly don't know where I'd be.'

Was there such a thing as a truly altruistic person?

I had nothing to lose by asking, but still it was gargantuan to tentatively dial her number, not allowing myself to hope.

'Hello.'

'Saffron, it's Laura. From the florist.'

'I was just thinking about you! The shop's been locked all week. Are you okay?'

'No,' I whispered. The rivers I'd cried had dried my throat. 'No, I'm really not.'

'We can help,' she said.

And those three words were enough for me to drive to Gorphwysfa the following day.

It's easy, with the benefit of hindsight, to realise that taking Tilly was my second mistake. We may have been broke, homeless, longing for support, but nobody had died then.

Nobody had killed.

CHAPTER NINE

LAURA

What sort of people shun society and build their own community? I tried to discuss it with Tilly during our scenic journey to Abberberth but the further out of town we drove, the quieter she became. Tufts of grass sprung in the centre of the unfamiliar road that twisted and turned as it led away from the coast towards Mid Wales. We dipped into a valley, the rolling hills swallowing the car, the tips of their peaks hidden by mist. Free from the buildings that crowded our town, it seemed we were driving into the vast slate-grey sky.

Tilly had her face turned away from me, staring absently out of the window at the bleak and empty fields, her mood as low as the clouds that threatened rain. I wanted to ask her what she was thinking, what she was feeling, but I didn't know how to reach her. I was seventeen when she was born, little more than a child myself. My best friend at the time, Natasha, told me it was really cool I had a daughter. 'You can go shopping together, hang out, you'll be mates.' But I didn't feel like Tilly's friend right then, and with all the ways I was letting her down I didn't feel quite like her mum either. Gavan was always the calmer parent, right from when she arrived red-faced and squalling into the world. He had held her against his bare chest, as he'd read about the importance of skin-to-skin contact, while I was mopped up, stitched up. I fought against climbing down from my cloud of pethidine into reality, where I was responsible for this tiny creature with fisted hands and a furious cry. I wondered how we'd cope, but Gavan was the perfect balance of discipline and fun at each and every stage, coaxing Tilly to finish her vegetables without the onslaught of World War Three. Effortlessly moulding papier-mâché into a castle for her history project, throwing together a fancy dress costume with things he plucked out of the airing cupboard. Although there had been a definite shift in their relationship before he died, a tension which wasn't there before, I put it down to the changes she was going through. Seventeen was impossibly difficult. For me it was an age full of memories I'd locked away.

We'd been driving for forty-five minutes when, almost too late, I noticed the opening between the trees. I swung a hard left, bumping down a rutted track that tapered until hanging twigs scraped against my paintwork. I thought I must have taken a wrong turn. Slowly, I edged forward, looking for a place to turn around. The track widened again. A weatherworn sign speared the ground, a crow perched atop so still at first I thought he was a statue. '*Tresmasers yn Ofalus*' in black peeling letters, and then almost as an afterthought, the English translation, 'Trespassers Beware'. A second sign shouted '*Ffens Trydan*', 'Electric Fence', and a third, newer sign, 'Oak Leaf Organics'. I'd found it. *Gorphwysfa*. Resting place.

An ominous thunder cloud hung suspended over the impossibly tall fences spiked with razor wire. Padlocked chains twisted around the metal gate.

Apprehensively I sat, engine ticking over. In the shadows,

a movement. A figure dressed in black strode out of a small wooden cabin and moved towards us. His head shaven, tattoos wrapped around his neck; a snake, barbed wire, something written in sharp letters that I didn't recognise.

He flung open the gates. Timorously, I cracked open my window. He was younger than I'd initially thought, late 30s I would guess. Shadow fell across his chin that could equally have been bruising or stubble.

'You must be Laura.' He was well spoken. I chided myself for being so judgemental as we shook hands. 'Saffron told me you'd be coming. I'm Reed. Can I just say, we're all very happy that you're here.'

'Umm, thanks.'

'Really. I came here when I was in need and…' He shook his head. 'Anyway, I know you're in a bit of a bind and if anyone can help, Alex can. Carry on straight.' He pointed down the track and his sleeve fell back exposing his forearm, the skin barely visible under his inkings. 'You can't go wrong.'

Still, I didn't move. Wondering how he knew I was in trouble, and wishing he hadn't said anything in front of Tilly. The last thing I wanted was for her to find out just how bad things were. Just what was I driving us into?

'It's okay.' He caught my worried expression. The way my eyes flicked to the rear-view mirror at the signs. 'The fence isn't electrified. Don't be afraid.'

'Mum! What are you waiting for?' Tilly asked.

Flustered, I put the car into gear and released the handbrake. We bunny-hopped forward and I tried not to flinch as the gates creaked shut behind us.

Trapped. I hated feeling trapped.

Out of the cover of the trees it was lighter. In the far distance I spotted smoke spiralling from a chimney, and even without the sun smiling down, the stone farmhouse surrounded by a scattering of outbuildings looked chocolate-box idyllic. I left my sense of foreboding behind with the flattened undergrowth and the worrying amount of security.

That just made it safer, didn't it?

One snowy Sunday afternoon last winter, I had curled up with Gavan on the sofa after too many roast potatoes and herb-crusted pork loaded with apple sauce, and watched a documentary on the Amish.

'It must be lovely to live without technology.' I'd thrown a sideward glance at Tilly. She was tucked up in the armchair, mesmerised by her phone. It was nice to have her in the same room as us, but I doubt she registered we were there, let alone what we were watching. The modern day Pied Piper wouldn't need a magic pipe, he could just wave an iPad. Through my 42-inch flat screen, fingers of tranquillity reached out and caressed me, and as I drove into *Gorphwysfa* that day there was the same sense of being transported back in time. I wouldn't have been surprised to pass a horse and cart. Men in hats and braces. Women in capes and aprons. Children playing with hoops and sticks. Free-range chickens dipping their beaks for seed. Instead Saffron leaned against a Land Rover, waving as she saw us approach. I slotted my car next to a battered old minibus.

'Laura!' The second my feet touched the ground outside the car I was swept into a hug. Momentarily I stiffened. I didn't like being touched, particularly by strangers, but then I relaxed into her embrace. It had been so long since I had been held. Besides, after she'd witnessed me twitching and writhing on the floor last week, the kindness she showed, it seemed churlish to try to maintain a distance between us. 'I'm *so* pleased you're here,' she said. 'I've been so worried. I've a feeling everything's going to be all right now.'

The energy buzzing from her lifted me.

'Saffron, this is Tilly, my daughter.'

Tilly muttered something incomprehensible and I shrugged a *teenagers – what can you do* to Saffron who melted my embarrassment with her hundred-watt smile. 'Tilly, I can't tell you how good it is to meet you! You're genuinely very welcome here. Now, Laura, I'll take you across to Alex.' She gestured away from the farmhouse, towards a woodland. 'Did you want to wait here, Tilly? I'd hate for you to ruin those suede boots. They're fabulous!'

Instead of giving a proper answer, Tilly shook her head. I threw her a *where-are-your-manners* glance.

We all set off, striding across the open field, the first spots of rain blowing into my eyes. My head bowed as I pushed against the blustery wind that snatched my breath. The bitter breeze biting my nose, the tips of my ears.

'Not far now.' Saffron led us into the woods where it was sheltered. I pushed down my hood, breathing in the scent of pine.

Sticks snapped underfoot as we weaved in and out of the autumn-stripped branches and the evergreens. Trees towered above us, blocking the already receding light. Tilly was walking so close to me, our arms brushed.

'I hope you know where you're going,' I said in the tone people use when they're seeking reassurance, but pretending not to.

'You see these?' Saffron pointed to the bright white stones snaking through the gloom. 'They're kind of a path. It does all look the same here, particularly at night.'

A shudder ran through me at the thought of being out there in the pitch-black with the scuttling animals and the rustling bushes.

'We have to be careful.' She gestured with her hand over to the right. 'There's a ravine over there. Don't want anyone falling down it. Hey, what do you call a nun lost in the woods? A Roamin' Catholic. Geddit?'

I groaned.

'Not one of my best! Anyhoo, we're almost there.'

We followed our Hansel and Gretel trail for a few more minutes until we rounded a corner and there it was. A small whitewashed cottage. Smoke curling from the chimney. Storybook perfect. Gingerbread house enticing.

'This was a weaver's cottage,' Saffron said as she pushed open the latched door. 'It's over a hundred years old.'

She kicked off her boots onto the mat in the porch. Tilly and I wobbled as we pulled off our footwear in the confined space. Elbows jabbing into walls. Into each other.

In the lounge, a fire crackled and hissed. The smell of wood smoke was comforting. Dark beams striped the low ceiling. A battered black leather sofa with a cross of duct tape over one cushion was angled by the cracked window. To its side, a coffee table stained with white rings. Two faded mustard armchairs flanked the fireplace.

'Wait here, Tilly,' Saffron said. 'I'll take your mum through and then I'll show you around the farm.'

Tilly's gaze met mine, a *don't-leave-me* expression on her

face, but it was better that I talked to Alex in private. I didn't want her to know how bad things really were.

'You'll have a lovely time, Tilly.' I dragged myself away from her pleading eyes.

'This was a dining room but it's more of an office now,' Saffron said as she pushed open the door to the adjoining room, and there he was.

Alex.

Dark hair curling over the neck of his cream fisherman's jumper. A beard framing lips that spoke my name as if he'd said it a million times before.

'Laura.' His voice a soothing balm on a sting. 'Nice to meet you.' He was only around thirty but he carried the sense of confidence you'd expect from somebody older. He took my hand, his skin rough. His nut-brown eyes, flecked with gold, held mine. I was barely aware of Saffron saying goodbye. Her footsteps receding. The slamming of the front door. Hers and Tilly's voices growing fainter.

'Hello.' It seemed rude to pull my hand away, and if I'm honest, I didn't want to. Instead, I squeezed his fingers, not wanting to feel them slip away from mine. He released me first. Embarrassed, I did what I'd always done in uncomfortable situations; I babbled, cramming the tiny gaps of silence with words, but my voice trailed away when I noticed the shotgun propped against the desk.

In the far depths of my mind a memory slithered to the surface.

There's nowhere to run to.

I couldn't tear my eyes away from it. Panic rising as I remembered the fences, the wire, the locked gate.

'I… I'm not sure I should be here.' I hated weapons of any description. I knew how it felt to be on the wrong end of one. 'I'm going to go.'

'No you're not,' Alex said softly as he reached for the gun.

CHAPTER TEN

TILLY

It had been a shit week at school.

On Monday I'd gone into the sixth form common room. Rhianon was there, alone.

'Hi.' I grabbed a plastic cup and poured water from the cooler.

'Hey.' Her voice was flat. I noticed how pale she was.

'So, the weekend? What was that about?' I tried to act casual as I leant against the wall, uncertain whether I should sit next to her.

'Like, I literally have zero clue. Mum and Dad basically fight *all* the time at the moment.'

'Your mum told mine we're not family anymore.' I shrugged feigning nonchalance.

Before she could answer, Katie burst into the room. 'You'll never guess what Kieron said?!' She noticed me and sat next to Rhianon, cupping her hand against Rhianon's ear and whispering in the way five-year-olds did.

'See you later then,' I said snarkily.

'Yeah. Whatever.' She didn't even look at me as I left.

I hadn't had the chance to speak to her again, spending my free periods in the library. I had only missed six weeks but there was mountains of coursework to catch up on.

And then it was Saturday. I should have been writing up my notes on *Othello* but I was so bored. Mum asked if I wanted to go with her and visit a friend who lived on a farm. I said yes. I'd pictured somewhere pretty with animals I could feed, but we stopped at these massive gates with threatening signs and everything. Honestly, it was as creepy as hell. The man who let us through started talking about how if anyone could help us Alex could, a bit like we were off to see the wizard. I almost expected there to be a road paved with yellow bricks.

We got out of the car. Mum hugged this woman who was stunning. It's so hard to pull off white in the winter but she managed it, with skinny jeans disappearing into black Uggs. She turned to me. I immediately felt six sizes larger than I was, and I wanted to put a paper bag over my head.

'Saffron, this is my daughter, Tilly,' Mum said and I only just managed to push out a shrill 'hi'. I could feel Mum glaring at me and was about to say something really lame about the weather to appease her, but then Saffron commented on my boots. I was so happy I couldn't say anything at all.

It began to rain as we walked across a field. I was glad the wind snatched away the chance of conversation. In the woods it was sheltered. Peaceful. Through the trees there was a cottage. Familiarity soothed my anxious stomach. It looked so similar to the one pictured in the fairy-tale book Mum used to read to me when I was small. I tried to remember the name of the story but I couldn't.

It was bubble bath warm inside the cottage. I sniffed as my nose began to run. Mum pushed a tissue into my hand.

'Wait here, Tilly,' Saffron said. 'I'll take your mum through and then I'll show you around the farm.'

'You'll have a lovely time,' Mum said, in her fake happy voice, as Saffron ushered her through to a different room.

I perched on one of the chairs that was threadbare and faded. The sideboard was chipped on its corner. A dark stain on the carpet near the fireplace. The walls were probably white once, but now had an odd yellow tinge. Somehow all its faults made it look homely, or perfectly imperfect, as someone would say on Instagram.

Saffron returned a minute later.

'Shall we head off, Tilly?'

The buzzing in my mind increased along with my anxiety. Before I could tell her that I didn't mind waiting there for Mum, she flashed me a smile full of white teeth and something I hadn't seen for a long time – friendliness.

Outside, the smell of damp earth hit my nostrils. When I was small I'd love to crunch through autumn-coloured leaves in my wellies, Dad hoisting me onto his shoulders when my legs grew too tired to walk. Now, everything was soggy and limp. The rain sleeting down harder than it had before, the wind gusting it into my face. I knew my makeup would run and my hair would go frizzy. As we hurried through the woods I smoothed my hands over my scalp, wishing my palms could absorb the moisture.

'Your hair is amazing,' Saffron said. My body stiffened as I waited for the punch line. 'No really,' she said when I didn't reply. 'It's really striking.'

'Katie says it looks like pubes.' I inhaled sharply as if I could suck the words back in.

'And Katie is?'

'She's friends with Rhianon. She's my cousin. And best friend. Well, she was. My best friend, I mean. She's still my cousin.'

You're not family anymore.

'Katie sounds… delightful.' Saffron laughed. My jaw tightened until she nudged me with her elbow and I realised she was laughing with me, not at me. And then I was laughing too.

'Your hair's prone to frizz like mine.' She reached out and rubbed the strands that framed my face between her fingers. 'I can give you some tips.'

'Thanks.'

'I was bullied.' She drew her hand away and stuffed it into her coat pocket, leaving me that little bit colder. 'At school. It was a few years ago now and it stopped after I'd moved to a new area but…' She paused and turned to face me and held my gaze. 'It hurt. There are scars we carry, Tilly. Scars that can't be seen but it doesn't make them any less painful.'

I had never really understood what a soul was. Mum used to say mine was old, I was wise beyond my years, but in that moment I was sure Saffron could see into mine. There was this weird kind of connection between us. We were rooted in the woods like the trees, still and silent. There was so much I wanted to say. It had been such a long time since I'd had someone to talk to properly, not just Mum asking me how school was, or if I wanted ketchup with my tea, but to share just how bloody awful everything felt since Dad died.

I parted my lips, wanting to tell Saffron about Dad dying, about what he did before he died, but no words came. Instead I let the rain fall light and cool on my tongue before I swallowed it down with the painful lump that had risen in my throat.

'I'd got to the stage where I didn't know who I was anymore, you know?' Saffron said. I nodded. 'Where I'd spent so long

66

pretending to be someone else I had lost sight of the real me. Putting on an act to impress people who didn't give a toss about me. Joking all the time became a sort of defence mechanism I guess. Pretending I didn't care. Of course now I do care, but I've realised I'm hilarious so the jokes have stayed.' She laughed. I loved that she didn't take herself too seriously.

I stopped worrying about the rain, my hair, as we started to walk again.

'Living here has changed me.' She was serious once more.

'You're lucky,' I said. 'I always wanted to live on a farm.' I had badgered Mum and Dad endlessly when I was small, longing for piglets, lambs, chicks of my own. It wasn't until Rhianon told me where meat came from that I stopped asking.

'It's not a working farm anymore. It's a place for communal living. Do you know what that is?'

Instinctively, I started to nod my head the way I do when I don't know something but don't want to appear stupid. But something told me I didn't need to try to impress Saffron.

'No. What is it?'

'We're a group of like-minded people who have chosen to live together. There're fourteen of us.'

'Why?' I was curious.

'For different reasons. Some because it's just too damn expensive to get on the property ladder. There's a chance of a better quality of life here, splitting the bills, sharing the chores. Daisy is hugely into all that save the planet stuff. Hazel is here because she got divorced. We also get drop-ins. People that temporarily want to step out of their daily grind whether for a weekend or a week.'

'And you? Why are you here?'

'I lost my mum when I was small, and then later I lost my dad. I was confused. I wanted to find out who I was, away from all the pressures of society. Where I fit. What I want to do with my life.'

We were heading towards the farmhouse. Fields and sky merging on the horizon. Without the hum of constant traffic I got at home the world seemed slower. Stiller. Smaller. Or maybe I just felt bigger without the incessant noise and movement.

'It's hard to explain,' Saffron said. 'And I know it sounds a bit arsey to say I'd lost my identity, but that's how I felt.'

'Yeah. I get that,' I said. It was how I had been feeling for months. Mum and Dad had been watching a documentary a while back when she said, 'It must be nice to live without technology.' I thought she was having a dig at me because I was on social media, but when I looked up I saw these women in long dresses and hats on the TV making a quilt. They looked so content and their happiness formed a knot of envy in my chest. I spent so much time taking selfies for Instagram. Running them through a filter to make myself as flawless as possible. Posting them with captions that had to be funnier, snappier than the previous one. It was in that moment I realised I had become a patchwork version of myself. Each photo, each square, had to be brighter, more vibrant, more beautiful than the last. So dazzling people didn't know where to look first, didn't see things too closely. The stitching coming apart. The hem where it's starting to fray. The material dull and fading from constantly being in the light. What everyone saw on the outside never matched how I felt on the inside. I had become a black and white, washed-out version of myself. Tattered and threadbare.

Thunder clapped. Saffron grabbed my hand. 'Run!'

A stitch burned in my side as we tumbled through the door of the farmhouse into the kitchen.

I didn't know what to make of what I saw inside.

CHAPTER ELEVEN

LAURA

There's nowhere to run to.

'You can't leave,' Alex said. 'I know it's incredibly difficult to ask for help but you've taken the first steps coming here. Don't go before we've talked about your situation. Seen if I can help.' He waved the gun. 'I'll put this away. Sorry. I forget it's there.' He must have caught my horrified expression. 'It's Dafydd's, he owns the farm.'

'Is it loaded?' I was repelled and yet strangely fascinated.

'No. Do you want to hold it?'

I couldn't help taking it from him. I'd never held a gun before and it felt cold and heavy in my hands. My finger curved around the trigger. Although it was harmless I couldn't bring myself to squeeze.

'Here.' Abruptly, I handed it back to him.

While he took it out of the room I noticed the clock on the mantelpiece was displaying seven when I knew it was nearly lunchtime.

'I think your clock needs winding,' I said when Alex came back in.

'I purposefully keep it like that,' he said as he sat at the table, gesturing for me to join him. 'We're too governed by time. When

70

we should eat. When we should sleep. We should listen more to our bodies. Our instincts.'

'I can't see my daughter's head teacher being pleased if I rolled up late because I hadn't set the alarm.'

He laughed, although it didn't reach his eyes. I could see a gap in the back of his mouth where he was missing a tooth, but it didn't detract from the obvious. He was incredibly handsome.

'Time is unavoidable in some circumstances, but life is a series of moments and if we clock-watch and plan, we miss the here and now. If you think about it, each moment could be our last and I don't want to spend mine thinking about what I have to do next. It's what I'm doing now that's important.'

I couldn't help trying to picture what Gavan's last moment was like. What his final thought was. Me? Tilly? Did he know he was going to die as he plummeted from the scaffolding?

'Sorry, have I upset you?' Alex lightly touched my arm and I blinked away the film of tears glazing my eyes.

'It wasn't you. It's just…' The choke in my throat was held back by the rest of my words. I pinched the bridge of my nose between my thumb and forefinger. It was several seconds before I could speak again. 'God. I'm glad Saffron took Tilly to look around so she didn't have to see me like this. Everything seems so hopeless.'

'I know how that feels.' This time it was his eyes that filled with tears.

'Are you okay?'

'Yes. Sorry. It's been one of those weeks. What I was clumsily trying to say is that nothing is hopeless, Laura. And you're not alone.'

There's no one to help you. The sour-breathed truth in my ear so many years before had rung true again in recent months.

But perhaps, now, there was someone to help me.

'Saffron told me you have a dispute with your insurance company. I'm so sorry. Let's have a look, shall we? See what we can do?' The way he said 'we' was as warming as the fire. He clicked the end of a ballpoint pen and flicked through his notebook containing rows of figures before he came to rest at a blank page.

'I've been writing a business plan,' he said.

'Look.' I was torn between need and good manners. Politeness won out. 'I know this is an imposition. If you've too much on…'

'Not at all. Sometimes helping someone else is just what you need to take your mind off your own problems.'

'Oak Leaf Organics is a wonderful idea. It just needs time to find its feet,' I said.

'Let's help you find your feet. Tell me all.'

'We've been paying into a joint life insurance policy for years, and never missed a monthly premium. They're supposed to pay out £500,000, but they've said they won't settle on an interim death certificate. The inquest could take months.' Anxiety lifted my voice an octave higher. 'I just don't know what to do. It's all too much.' I dropped my head into my hands. 'We've only just had the funeral and I just want everything to slow down. Stop.'

'The first thing is don't panic.' Alex paused until I lifted my head and nodded. 'It's not unusual to get a no before you get a yes. Some companies will pay out on an interim certificate. Some won't. Who are you with?'

'Ironstone.' I pulled a letter from my bag and thrust it towards him. His eyes scanned the page.

'Evans? Your husband was Gavan from Evans Construction. Saffron didn't mention that.'

'I didn't tell her.' A sinking feeling in my stomach. How stupid to think he wouldn't have heard of us. Toxic waste is probably something they campaign about here. 'Look, I know building on a landfill probably goes against all your principles but…' I fiddled with the wedding ring on my finger. The gold digging into my flesh as I twisted it round and round trying to find the right words.

'We're quick to judge others.' His brow furrowed. 'Too quick.' He placed a hand on my arm and my fingers stilled. 'Here we practise acceptance. I'm sorry for all you've been through.'

He turned his attention back to the letter. The wait for him to speak again was painfully slow.

'Ironstone is one of the newer companies, so it's likely they won't pay out on a suicide. The modern ones rarely do.'

'Gavan didn't jump.' He wouldn't have *chosen* to leave us.

'Of course not. I'm just running through their thought process. They'll be wanting to know what caused the accident. Did he have a blackout from some previously undiagnosed condition? Did he have a heart attack and then fall? Did he have a brain tumour that burst?'

'The post mortem didn't say any of those things. He had a subdural haematoma and midline shift.' Phrases I'd only previously heard on *Casualty* tripped off my tongue. 'It was the fall that killed him.' It was impossible to discuss the love of my life with a detachment I didn't feel. I fished a tissue from my pocket as I asked, 'I don't understand why that's not enough.'

'Gavan was an experienced builder?'

I nodded as I blew my nose.

'Then the inquest will also be asking why he was up on the roof in bad weather? If he'd been drinking? Taking drugs?'

'He had 50 milligrams of alcohol in his blood.' I don't know why; he was supposed to have been at work all day.

'I can't imagine how you feel, losing your husband and… I'm so sorry.' A beat, then, 'Look, I'm not saying it will be easy but it's certainly not impossible to get an interim payment.'

'Do you think…' I trailed off, hoping he would fill in the gaps but he didn't. I started again. 'Do you think you could help me please? I can't afford to pay you right now but Saffron said I could perhaps help out with planting or something.' Even to me, my offer seemed inadequate.

He studied me.

'Here's the thing,' he began, and my spirits sank even lower. 'The policy is in your name, Laura, and I can't speak on your behalf so I can either walk you through the process or you can sign a permission form so Ironstone have to deal with me. I'd need a copy of your policy of course.'

I could have kissed him. 'If you could speak to them directly that would be great. How long do you think it might take to get an answer?'

'I'm not going to lie to you, Laura.' He spoke with such sincerity. 'The inquest might happen sooner than I can get any sort of pay-out.'

I turned away to blow my nose, not wanting him to see my disappointment.

His stomach growled. 'That's my internal body clock letting me know it's lunchtime. Are you hungry? Shall we head over to the main house? Find Tilly?'

'Yes.' We stood. I tried not to show my disappointment that

the insurance wouldn't be resolved quickly enough to cover the arrears on my rent, but he saw it anyway.

'Oh, Laura.' He pulled me into a hug. 'I can promise you I will do my absolute best for you and your daughter.'

His arm encircling my waist. The feel of him. The smell of him. I shivered.

Oddly, even then, something pulled me towards him. The only way I can explain it was that I'd spent weeks dealing with death and all its aftermath. Somewhere, inside my core, I wanted to feel alive.

Alex was magnetic but it wasn't only me he was attracting. I wasn't the one willing to kill for him.

Willing to die for him.

CHAPTER TWELVE

TILLY

I had thought Saffron was wearing white because she was funky enough to carry it off, but in the kitchen were two other women also dressed in white. Honestly it felt a bit weird, it was winter after all, but I tried not to stare.

'This is Tilly,' Saffron said. 'And this is Daisy. She's the youngest here at twenty-three, as she keeps reminding me, because I'm *so* ancient at twenty-seven.'

'Not at twenty-seven,' Daisy said. 'But just wait until you get to twenty-eight! Hi, Tilly.' She gave a little wave. I mumbled 'hello'. She didn't look much older than me with her hair hanging in two long dark plaits either side of her heart-shaped face. She reminded me of Tiger Lily in *Peter Pan*. As an only child I was always envious of the Darling family. Siblings. I used to beg Mum for a brother or sister. She always laughed and said she had her hands full with just me, but her eyes would cloud and I wondered if she meant I was too much.

'*Croeso*, Tilly. Welcome.' The other woman had the biggest smile and rosy red cheeks. Grey hair bobbed to her shoulders but her face only had the odd line. She didn't look properly old and I wondered why she didn't dye her hair.

'And Hazel is—' Saffron began.

'Saffron, don't tell her how old I am!'

'What's it worth?' Saffron held out her hand. 'I was just going to say a fabulous cook.' She blew a kiss.

'You can see how much I love my food.' Hazel patted her rounded stomach and there was something so cuddly about her I wanted to see if my arms would fit around her waist and hug her.

'We all live in this house, along with Dafydd who owns the farm, because we're special.' Saffron fluffed her hair. 'And there are eight others who bunk down in the stables across the way.'

'In a stable?' I couldn't help blurting out.

'It's not a stable in the traditional sense. It's huge and it's been converted into dorms. They've a kitchen and bathroom too. They don't always eat with us, unsociable bunch. Speaking of eating…' She raised her eyebrows.

'I'll start preparing lunch. Do you like soup, Tilly?' Hazel asked.

'Yeah.'

'Vegetable okay?'

'Can I help?' I asked.

'If you want to wash the soil off the veg,' Hazel said.

I must have looked confused because Daisy said, 'We grow our own produce here which reduces our carbon footprint.'

'Mum shops at a greengrocer sometimes.' I didn't know how, but I was sure that must be better than buying everything from a supermarket chain. Supporting local business.

'And where do they get their stock from? It's still a huge amount of fossil fuel to transport food to a local business. On average about one and a half thousand miles is travelled before the food is consumed,' she said, but she wasn't patronising.

'Daisy's our resident environmentalist. *Diolch*. Thank you,' Hazel said as I took the carrots she was holding out towards me. After rinsing them clean, I began to chop. There was something almost therapeutic about the process. Before long, herby soup simmered on the Aga which was nothing like the gas hob we had at home.

'Farmers often put weak lambs in the top oven if their mothers have died,' Saffron told me as I stirred the pot. I must have looked horrified as she quickly added, 'To keep them warm and give them a chance of survival.' She squirted washing-up liquid into running water. Hazel clanked a lid on the soup. I sat at the table listening to the gentle sloshing of water, the rain pattering against the window. The warm, safe feeling weighted my eyelids until they began to droop, only opening properly when Saffron spoke again.

'Here's Alex,' she said, pulling her hands out of the bowl, suds floating to the floor as she dried her hands. Her face brightened. 'Typically he's just in time for lunch.'

Daisy smoothed her hair.

I turned towards the door as it opened. The room disappeared around me. I barely threw a cursory glance over Mum, her hair dripping wet. I didn't register anything but Alex. He was beautiful in a way I never knew boys could be. Once, in biology, we had learned about processing. It takes on average fifty milliseconds for the retina to send visual information to the brain, but those fifty milliseconds were all I needed. The instant I saw Alex, I knew.

I wanted to be in his orbit.

CHAPTER THIRTEEN

ALEX

Alex had known as soon as he laid eyes on her that she was the one, the one who would save him. Save them all. As he kicked off his muddy boots he breathed in the soup and he knew home was more than a building. It was a smell, a feeling. The people you surrounded yourself with.

Her.

The bread timer dinged. He crossed to the sink to wash his hands so he could cut the loaf while it was still warm.

As he scrubbed his fingernails, outside the window a crow swooped – *the* crow swooped – ink-stained wings stretched like a malevolent angel. It perched on the tree stump, claws spiking the rotting wood, head tilted as it appraised him.

Alex tried to look away, but the beady eyes of the bird bored into his. It cawed, the sound sudden and sharp, its head tilted in judgement.

I know, it seemed to say. *I know what you did.*

It was the same crow, Alex knew, that had watched him that day, but this wasn't the same situation. He turned away, facing her instead, and although he could no longer see the bird he could feel it screeching in his head, scratching and pecking behind his eyes, clambering to be free.

She looked at him, already adoring, and the gentleness in her eyes made him want to weep.

He smiled at her but it was forced and tight while, inside, a longing unfurled. More than anything he wanted to drop to his knees, bury his face in her lap and allow her to soothe him. Cool fingers raking his hair, her voice as soft as down. But he had to keep it together.

He couldn't lose control.

Not again.

CHAPTER FOURTEEN

LAURA

'Tilly, this is Alex. He's helping me out with a few bits,' I said.

'Hey there.' He dried his hands on a tea towel and flashed her a smile.

Instead of smiling back she mumbled something inaudible, staring at her shoes as though Alex was something she might scrape off the bottom of her sole. I was embarrassed. She could at least have pretended to be pleased to meet him.

'That smells delicious. Homemade?' I had spotted the peelings heaped by the sink.

'Yes,' said Hazel. 'Let's all sit.'

As we settled around the table the kitchen door swung open and Reed stepped inside.

'I'm not in your seat, am I?' I asked.

'No. I'll take a bowl and eat in my cabin.'

'Join us, please,' Saffron said. 'It's exciting to have Laura here—'

'If he doesn't want to stay, that's fine,' Alex said. 'Sourdough?'

'Thanks.' I plucked a slice of bread from the plate he offered, as Reed carried a tray back out into the rain. It was such a shame, his food would be cold. 'So you all live here then? Tell me how Oak Leaf Organics came to be.'

'I met Dafydd, who owns the farm, about seven years ago,' Alex said. 'I'd just finished my LPC and was on a two-year training contract. He was one of my first clients. There was a dispute over land with the neighbouring farm. I remember how nervous I was.' Crumbs scattered over the table as he tore the crust he was holding into two. 'He was the one who put me at ease. He was grandfatherly. My parents had retired to Spain and I was lonely, if I'm honest. I think Dafydd was too. His daughter, Carys, had settled in Perth, Australia – that's where he is now, visiting her. He told me he'd had to let several of his farmhands go. He wasn't making as much money as he should, supermarkets preferring cheaper imported meat. I started helping out on the odd Saturday or Sunday, and it felt good. Rolling my sleeves up and getting dirty.'

'A bit different to practising law.'

'That was the point. It felt… honest, I suppose. As soon as I joined the firm I'd seen the ugly side of law and seeing it in action, not just reading about previous cases, made working the land more appealing. I had some… stuff to deal with too, and this became my sanctuary. A place to work out my frustrations. Dafydd had arthritis in his hands and talked about selling the farm and I felt…' He looked into the distance, a wistful expression on his face. 'I felt I was losing a piece of my heart.' He laughed. 'A little dramatic perhaps, but there you go.'

'Oh and you're *never* usually dramatic are you, Alex?' Saffron raised her eyebrows.

'I prefer passionate.' His eyes locked onto mine. Goosebumps dusted my arms. 'It was my idea, Oak Leaf Organics. We deliver vegetables the same day we harvest them, to houses within a forty-five mile radius as well as selling at farmer's markets.

Hazel has been mostly responsible for the seasonal recipe cards that accompany each box.'

'Very resourceful.'

'Here's the thing: we don't need much to survive. We live off the land and we've the income from our produce. Saffron arrived and had some brilliant ideas about using some of the land for a retreat. I quit my job. Reed asked if he could stay, and between us we converted the stables and two of the barns into dormitories. There's so much space and it's beautiful here. Last summer we were still getting organised but we hope this year... who knows what this year will bring, but it's been a real team effort trying to get it off the ground. We hold group sessions where we can air any grievances.'

'Therapy,' whispered Saffron conspiratorially to me. 'Alex thinks of himself as a guru. No wonder he grew a beard.'

'Just to annoy you. I know you want me to shave it off.' Alex grinned as he rubbed his hand over his chin.

'I like your face as it is,' blurted out Tilly. It was the first thing she'd said. There was a lull where everyone turned towards her. Her cheeks were blazing. 'Excuse me, I need the loo.' She scraped back her chair and dashed out of the room.

'Sorry.' I contemplated going after her but instead I tried to get the conversation back on track so she wouldn't return to a silent room. 'So... therapy?'

'More of a sharing.' Alex nodded. 'Sometimes it can get a bit emotional, similar people living together, it's good to have an outlet.'

'And you're all living here? Not just visiting on a retreat?' I gestured around the table with my spoon.

'Yes, I'm... visiting,' said Hazel.

'And how long have you been *visiting*?' Saffron's tone was light.

'Umm. Fifteen months give or take. You can't talk.'

'You got me.' Saffron pushed her empty bowl away. 'I was an only child and here it's like having the large family I'd always dreamed of. I can't wrench myself away.'

'I'm divorced,' Hazel chipped in. '*Roeddwn i'n unig.*' She smiled at Tilly as she returned from the toilet. 'I was lonely. I wanted to be among people.'

'Loneliness and social isolation is more widespread than we think, and the increasing cost of living is driving people to take second jobs, live in less desirable areas. Here we provide a short- or long-term fix.'

'I was reading an article in the *Guardian* about housing co-operatives.' I screwed my face, trying to remember the details. 'Groups of people around the country clubbing together to buy property.'

'The housing market is broken and housing should be a right, not a privilege. Communal living is an increasing movement.' Alex nodded. 'This is in a similar vein. Except we haven't had to buy the land.'

'We all chip in financially though,' Saffron added quickly. 'We're not freeloaders. Just all... searching for something and we think we've found it here.'

'And what about you, Daisy?' I asked. She didn't look much older than Tilly.

'I hate what we're doing to the world. To each other,' she said confidently, and at first I thought her very young to have such ideals, but I realised it was *because* she was young, as she added, 'It's my generation and those that will follow that'll suffer for the way the older generations have abused the planet. This lifestyle offers a sustainable future.' I found myself nodding although by the way she gazed at Alex I wondered if the lifestyle was the only attraction. He didn't seem to notice her adoration as he spoke again.

'Half the people that come are drawn to a greener lifestyle, the other half looking for a community. And here we're all about sharing in an opposition to a society based on materialism, moral apathy—'

Saffron cupped her mouth with her hands as she mock shouted, 'Be careful up there on your soapbox.'

'Sorry, Laura. I'm not usually so preachy. I just feel very strongly about things. Fancy a guided tour?'

Nothing waited for me at home except Gavan's empty chair and a pile of unpaid bills.

'I'd love one.' We both stood. Saffron pulled Alex's attention away from me. 'You'll need this.' She stood on tiptoes and wound his scarf around his neck.

'Thanks, Mum!' He hugged her and the easy way he touched her sent a jolt through me. I could almost feel him still touching me. His hand around my waist in his cottage.

The rain had stopped but the ground still squelched as we walked. Everything smelled just-washed-clean. The land seemed to stretch interminably, but if I squinted I could make out the high fences. 'Why so much security?'

'We've one hundred and fifty acres – slightly larger than the average Welsh farm. We put up the fences after our crops were pulled up and left to rot, which was more soul-destroying than if someone had stolen food out of necessity.'

'Who was responsible?'

'I don't know. The change of use has shaken up the locals. The die-hard breed who don't believe it's a proper farm without livestock, Welsh lambs. There were petitions against the retreat. We haven't been made welcome.'

'People can be so judgemental.' I wasn't sure if I was talking about my own experience or his. 'You've done a fabulous job here. What's not to like?' The retreat area was basic but functional. Conifers guarding the perimeter. A wooden sign squeaked as it wafted in the breeze at the entrance. '*Y Lodge.*' The Lodge. Two barn conversions, both coated in stripes of black wooden siding gave a rustic feel.

'There's one for women, a separate one for men, and we'll be adding yurts in the summer for couples. We had planned to build on the retreat side of things. Make use of the ravine. Rock climbing. High wire. That sort of thing.'

'Had? What changed?'

'I don't know. All that pumping adrenaline. It's a bit at odds with the sanctuary of inner peace, isn't it? Besides, it almost always rains here.'

Inside, Alex pulled a cord and overhead the lights flickered and buzzed before sparking to life. Single beds lined the walls like soldiers. The facilities fitted in with the green lifestyle. Solar showers, which Alex admitted weren't effective all year round, but there was also a small conventional shower block, and composting toilets which I thought would smell but didn't.

'It's simple but people don't come here for luxury. They want to get back to nature. Experience how it feels to be alive. Away from technology and distractions. To reconnect.' Alex's mobile began to ring. 'Great advert I am for our ethos.' He smiled wryly.

'I've been waiting for a call from our packaging supplier. I'll be a few minutes. Feel free to wander. I'll find you.' He turned and answered his phone. I headed outside. It was freezing. In the far distance was a small stone structure. There weren't any other buildings visible so I figured that's where we'd be heading next. I set off at a brisk pace, stuffing my hands into my pockets, wishing I'd brought gloves. The air felt thicker as I approached the building. The weather pushing me back, warning me off. Fingers of mist tightened around my throat. The foreboding of unseen danger didn't stop me twisting the handle, ignoring the sense I was somewhere I shouldn't be. The latch, ginger with rust, protested.

I threw a glance over my shoulder. I had a prickling sensation of eyes on me but I was still alone.

The door groaned as I pushed it open. Stepped inside.

It was gloomy; there weren't any windows. The roof was intact bar a couple of missing tiles, which let in a small shaft of light. The smell of mildew was cloying. A scuttling sound. I shivered as I fumbled for my phone. There could be spiders. Rats. I activated the torch on my mobile and cast the light around the room. It was empty, save a glinting underneath the hole in the roof. Metal rings tethered to a post, thick heavy rope coiled on the floor. I drew closer. Trying to hold my torch steady.

A dark splodge.

Blood?

I crouched, straining my eyes.

The stain was dark red, almost black.

Blood.

Abruptly, I was cloaked in darkness as behind me the door slammed shut.

CHAPTER FIFTEEN

TILLY

I like your face.

I like your face!

I was such a fucking idiot.

CHAPTER SIXTEEN

LAURA

There was one horrible, stomach-churning moment when I thought I'd been purposefully locked in that oppressive room. My relief, as I pushed open the door against the wind, and hurried back outside, was immense. From the direction of The Lodge Alex broke into a jog as he spotted me.

'You shouldn't be here,' he said when he came to rest breathless and pale beside me.

'Why?'

'It's dangerous.'

'I like to live dangerously.' I wanted him to see someone different to who I was, when really ordering a tikka masala instead of a korma on a Friday night was my idea of life on the edge.

'Seriously. We haven't had it checked over structurally yet. Don't want the roof collapsing in on you or anything.'

'What was it used for?' I glanced at it again but I had no desire to step back inside.

'It's an old sheep shed.'

'And the metal rings? The rope?'

'That was a lambing post. A throwback from years ago. If the ewe didn't accept her lamb she'd be tied down so her baby could suckle.'

'That's barbaric.'

'Better than letting the lamb die if the farmer didn't have time to bottle feed.'

'And the blood?'

'Sometimes the animal would be tethered if labour was imminent. That's not as awful as it sounds. The weather during lambing season can be biting, and if the ewe gives birth somewhere the farmer doesn't immediately know, under a hedge for instance, there's always a risk of loss. The livestock were contained as far as they could be, but it's inevitable you always get an escapee. Someone who wants to bolt for freedom. Who has to be restrained.' He stared over my shoulder into the distance. There was a beat. I shivered.

'Where to next?' The dismal grey sky was several shades darker than it had been when we set off. Dusk sucking the light from the day. 'Alex?'

'Sorry. I was watching that crow. Let's head back.'

I turned to see the crow but it had gone.

Gorphwysfa loomed into view. I was worried I had left Tilly too long, but as I stepped into the kitchen, which was clouded with steam, she was howling with laughter. The sound was like stumbling across water after an endless thirst. As soon as she spotted me her lips clamped together into that familiar thin line and instead of feeling guilty I had left her, I felt guilty I had returned.

'Having a good time?' I smiled to let her know I was pleased.

She shrugged. 'I've cooked dinner.'

'That's wonderful.' Although we'd eaten a big lunch the fresh air had made me ravenous. I quickly filled her in on the things

I had seen, The Lodge, the derelict sheep shed where ewes were tethered so their lambs could feed, the acres of space that gave the impression the world could be flat and you might step off the edge at any given moment.

'Cool,' she said distractedly as she stirred a simmering pot, pungent with turmeric and pepper.

'It'll be ready in half an hour,' Hazel said. 'Spicy hotpot. Dafydd's favourite. Not that it matters, I expect he's on a beach with a barbecue. Far too busy to send us lot a postcard, isn't he, Alex?'

'I'm sure he'll send one soon. Let's continue your tour, Laura. Leave the chefs to it.' He guided me out of the room, across the hallway. Curled up on a brown velour armchair, studying me with bright green eyes, was a large ginger cat.

'Hello.' I stretched out my hand. He sniffed it tentatively.

'That's Dylan. He's supposed to keep the vermin situation under control but he's infinitely lazy, aren't you, boy? More scared of the mice than they are of you.' He scratched behind Dylan's ear and was rewarded with a low purr. 'So this is the lounge, obviously. And through here's the dining room, but we eat in the kitchen mostly.' Log burners blazed in every room, the air thick with the smell of smoke but it wasn't unpleasant.

We crossed a whitewashed corridor with a flagstone floor, and the difference in temperature was startling. I crossed my arms to keep in my body heat. 'This was the original sitting room, but as it's the largest we use it for the business now.' My eyes scanned the desk, the piles of recipe cards, the boxes heaped in the corner.

'Where's your TV?' I hadn't spotted one in any of the three reception rooms.

'We don't have one. Most forms of media breed negativity and encourage unrealistic expectations.'

'Tilly would hate that – she's addicted to reality shows.'

'Is she happy? Not now, obviously, with her loss, but living vicariously can create feelings of inadequacy.'

I thought about the way she'd changed over the past couple of years. The fake tan she slathered on in the summer, that streaked orange and smelled of biscuits. The perfect arch of her brows. But that was a normal part of growing up, wasn't it?

'There's another loo down there. And that's pretty much it down here.' He headed towards the staircase.

Upstairs, Alex opened the door to the first bedroom and I stepped inside.

'This is Daisy's room.'

Heat lit me from within as I stared uncomfortably at the double bed, remembering Alex's arm encircling my waist at his cottage. The feel of him. The smell of him.

Flustered, I shuffled backwards, treading on his toes.

'Sorry. I...'

But he was already moving on, throwing open the door to the next room.

'This is Dafydd's.'

It was large but dated. Twin beds and a washbasin on a pedestal. Faded wallpaper patterned with roses covered the walls, the edges beginning to peel with age.

'When will he be back from Australia?' I asked.

A gong reverberated.

'Dinner's ready,' Alex said. 'I'll show you the rest later.'

*

There was something comforting about sitting around a table for dinner. Since Gavan died, Tilly and I tended to pick at food on trays in front of a TV programme that we weren't really paying attention to. Conversation buzzed around me. For the most part I was content to sit back and listen.

To my left, Tilly's mouth gaped a yawn as Saffron began clearing the empty plates.

'We really must go.' I pushed back my chair.

'Stay the night,' said Alex.

'I don't know.' I glanced at Tilly. She was almost nodding off.

'The way out isn't very well lit. You're very welcome to both sleep in Dafydd's room.'

I thought of the journey. The rutted track. The brambles scratching at my paintwork. The darkness of the trees.

'Just for tonight,' I said.

After a quick shower I pulled on an oversized T-shirt that Hazel had lent me. 'Barely stretches over my boobs but it'll swamp you,' she said. '*Nos da, cariad.*' She hugged me and I said good-night back, feeling both the warmth of her body and the warmth of being called 'darling' again. I liked her already. Exiting the bathroom, I heard low, angry whispers coming from behind a closed door further down the landing. Hesitantly, I tried to tiptoe across to my room, conscious that the floorboards creaked.

The voices rose in pitch and I recognised the pleading female voice as Saffron's. Not wanting to be caught eavesdropping, I hurried forward, the bottle of shampoo tucked under my arm thudding to the floor. The door flew open and Alex stepped out. He smiled, although it was strained. I was about to ask if Saffron was okay but he spoke first.

'Got everything you need?'

'Yes. Saffron left us a toiletry basket in our room.'

'You have some of what you need then,' he said, pausing. 'I get the feeling you don't have a close family. Nobody to help you out?'

Tears glazed my eyes and I inhaled slowly through my nose in an effort to contain them. It seemed such a failing to admit he was right.

'Look, Laura, with your finances the way they are, if you're stuck, you could come and stay here until you're back on your feet.'

'That's good of you.' My voice quivered. It seemed so long since I had been shown any kindness.

'Dafydd will be gone for a while so you can stay in his room. With Tilly.'

'I'll think about it.' It was so terribly sad that I would have to leave the home Gavan and I had created. The place where Tilly took her first steps. The sunflower-yellow kitchen where we'd stood side by side, her on a blue plastic step swamped by my striped butcher's apron. Her small hand under mine as we'd pressed out gingerbread shapes, later icing on wonky buttons, crooked noses. One eye that was always higher than the other.

'You can bring your memories with you,' he said and that was my undoing. I dissolved into tears. He opened his arms and, confused by my yearning to step into them, I turned away, fumbling for the door handle. Longing to be alone with my grief and my anger and my indecision.

'Laura,' he said, and I hesitated. 'The bottom line is, it's not often a room comes up in the house or the stables. We'd accommodate you of course in the future, in a yurt or dorm if there was space, but the house, that's a rare chance. I need your answer by the morning.'

I nodded.

'Goodnight,' he whispered and the word speared me as I closed the door behind me.

Oddly, it wasn't so much the 'I love yous' or the 'do you fancy a cup of teas' that I missed. It was the 'goodnights'. The knowing that at the end of every good day, of every bad day, there was someone who cared I'd lived through it. That I was going to get some rest. That I'd be rising in the morning to do it all again.

Goodnight.

Just nine letters. An innocuous word falling from Alex's lips. It shouldn't have brought me so much comfort, but somehow it did.

Tilly was already asleep. Motionless under the duvet. I kissed my index finger and lightly touched her forehead.

What was I going to do?

The bed welcomed me with a gentle creak as I climbed between the sheets with my doubts and my questions. My last conscious thought was that I would never settle, but I must have done because at 2 a.m. I was snapped awake by yet another nightmare. My cheeks were wet, my pillow too. But this time instead of Gavan plummeting to his death, it was me I had pictured, spread-eagled in the sheep shed, tethered by a rope to the lambing post, labour pains slicing me in two while a shapeless shadow waited to snatch my baby away because I wasn't capable of looking after her.

I must have dozed again because my mobile vibrating under my pillow roused me. Rhianon. It was barely 7 a.m.

'Just a minute,' I whispered into the handset as I crept out of the room and into the bathroom. 'You okay?'

'Yes. No. Right, so I think Mum and Dad have split up and Uncle Gavan has gone and I never get to see you and everything is horrible.' She strung the words together without drawing breath.

'Your mum and dad have split up?' I sat down on the edge of the bath. The porcelain cold and hard against my thighs. 'Why?'

'I dunno.' She sounded so young and I longed to give her a hug.

'What happened, Rhianon?'

'They've been fighting loads and then a letter came last Monday from the coroner.'

'What did it say?' I asked sharply.

There was silence and I could almost picture her shrugging.

'Rhianon?'

'I was going to get a drink and Mum and Dad were in the kitchen running through what they'd originally told the police. Then they were yelling at each other, saying they needed to get their stories straight about where they were the night Uncle Gavan fell.'

My brain was full of static – an old TV that has lost its signal – and I couldn't tune into one single thought. What might the coroner uncover if he started digging deeper? What could Anwyn and Iwan possibly be hiding? Why had they fabricated a story for the police? Promising Rhianon I'd talk to her again soon, I quickly wrapped up the call and dialled Iwan's number. My head thrumming with the dial tone and all the questions I was going to demand answers to.

CHAPTER SEVENTEEN

ALEX

Breathe out.

Breathe in.

Alex was painfully aware of her in the next room, separated from him by the thick, cold walls. He pressed his palm against the stone. Tried to picture her on the other side. Was she reading? Sleeping? Thinking about him?

His bed was too big. Too empty.

He closed his eyes. Sleep tugged at him but his memories fought against it with a jagged-edged sword.

His sister running to him for comfort. Assurance.

'I'll protect you,' he had promised, and he had tried but it all went wrong.

He could still hear her screams. See her horrified face. The image faded to monochrome before it disappeared under swirling blackness. The crow behind his eyes.

Peck. Peck. Peck.

Keep her safe. Keep her safe. Keep her safe.

CHAPTER EIGHTEEN

TILLY

When I woke the following morning, it all came rushing back to me.

Alex.

Even though during dinner last night I thought he smiled more brightly at me than anyone else in the room, my body still flushed with heat as I remembered the stupid comment I had made about his face. Still, I was humiliated. It reminded me of Mum's favourite film, *Dirty Dancing*, when Baby (and seriously – who's called Baby? And I think *I've* got problems) made a lame comment about carrying a watermelon.

But that wasn't the thing I was most ashamed of yesterday; that had come when I'd been helping Saffron make dinner. The cat weaved in and out of my legs purring for tidbits. I'd felt relaxed. Before I could think it through I'd said, 'Can I ask you a question?'

'Fire away.'

I wasn't sure if I was being rude. 'Umm. Why do you all wear white?'

She put down her potato peeler and turned to me. 'Different colours can affect mood. For instance, yellow can bring wisdom among other things. Green is for balance.

Purple is for spirituality. There's a lot more to it than that but white is an accumulation of all colours. All things. I think in a way it's like stepping out of the darkness. To be honest, Tilly, most of us came here because we were unhappy. Ready for a change. Alex brought in a colour therapist one day who asked us to wear white for the session and it kind of stuck. We don't have to, of course. The drop-ins never do, but I like it. I feel… free. I used to agonise over what I wore every day. How I looked.'

'I think it's cool.' Often I found choosing what to wear every day for school more stressful than my coursework.

'Besides. Everything seems purer, more innocent in white.'

'Imagine if white were the only colour. It would make things so simple.'

'It might make songs a bit boring. "White Suede Shoes".'

'"Perfect White Buildings",' I batted back.

'"Big White Taxi".'

'What about books?' I added. '*Fifty Shades of White*.'

We fell about laughing although it wasn't that funny. I hadn't heard the door open but it must have because Mum was standing there saying, 'You're having a good time' or something, all sarcastic. My face burned with shame. I wanted to tell her that today was the first time I'd laughed since Dad died. It didn't mean I had forgotten him, but honestly, I hadn't thought about him once for the past hour. She was right to think I was a cow. She made some comment about it being great I was helping, but the undertone was that I didn't help at home. Suddenly I was exhausted with everything. After I'd yawned through dinner Mum said we were staying the night so I asked if I could go straight to bed. From downstairs, conversation and laughter drifted and my last waking thought was that they were probably laughing at me.

I was still in bed, wondering if I should get up, when the door opened. I yanked the blanket up to my chin, but it was only Mum swamped by a giant T-shirt.

'Are you okay?' I asked.

'Yes. Sorry, did I wake you? I just slipped out to ring Uncle Iwan but he isn't picking up. Did you sleep well?'

'Yeah.' My stomach growled.

'Let's get dressed and we'll find some food before we head home.'

My appetite disappeared at the thought of leaving. At being back at home surrounded by Dad's things and all my homework.

'I'm not that hungry,' I told her.

'Me neither. Do you fancy a walk?' she asked in a tone that meant it wasn't really a question.

Outside it was freezing. I stuffed my hands into my pockets. I hoped my boots wouldn't get ruined on the damp ground. We stuck to the gravel path, the only sound the crunching of our footsteps. In the distance, Reed came out of one of the barns, dressed in jeans and a thick black jumper. He waved. I waved back, glad it wasn't Alex seeing me in yesterday's clothes, with mad, frizzy hair. I'd found out from Saffron that Alex was twenty-seven, the same age as her. Only ten years older than me! Nine, really, once I'd had my birthday in January.

'Tilly, are you listening to me?' Mum stopped walking. I met her eye.

'Yeah, of course.'

'So what do you think?'

I chewed my lip like I was thinking. Like I had been paying attention.

'Is it okay if we stay here? Do you understand?'

'Yes.' I had nothing better to do that day. I wondered whether we'd stay another night. If I'd miss school tomorrow.

'Thank you. I really am so sorry. As soon as the insurance company pay up we can buy our own house, and start again.'

Her words slammed into me. 'But until then… we're staying here?' She couldn't mean we'd be living here.

'Tilly, I thought you understood?'

'We have to leave our house?' The bees in my head buzzed angrily. I just couldn't process what was happening.

'Yes. I've just explained.'

'But I didn't—'

'It's okay. It's a lot to take in. If you don't want to stay here, we won't.'

'But we have to go somewhere?'

'Yes. But we have options. There are some flats over on the Talbot Estate that welcome housing benefit. We could go there?' I shook my head. She took my hands and rubbed warmth back into them.

'Where else could we go?' My voice was so small and that was the way I felt.

'That's not for you to worry about. I'll figure something out.'

'But our house… My bedroom…' Mum was crying as well, telling me it would be okay. I looked at her pale face. The worry lines on her forehead which hadn't been there a few weeks ago. I knew that I had been the cause of so much stress. If I refused to move I would be the cause of so much more.

'We can stay here,' I said. It was my sorry without saying sorry.

'Are you sure? We—'

'Yes.'

'Good girl.' She hugged me tightly. We walked some more until she said, 'Now. Can you make your way back okay? I need to try Uncle Iwan again.'

'Has something happened?'

'No,' she said but her eyes flickered and I knew she wasn't telling the truth. There was something she was keeping from me. That there were secrets in our family.

Not just Dad's secrets.

And not just mine.

CHAPTER NINETEEN

ALEX

She was here. Unpacking. Staying. Alex felt his heart lift. Fate had brought them together. He had to be careful. Think of the future and all he wanted. He couldn't allow himself to become attached. Inside Alex's chest the crow furiously beat his wings as he remembered what happened the last time he allowed himself to care.

How his sister had held him as he cried, his hands dripping blood.

'It's okay,' she had soothed. 'It's okay. I won't tell.'

But his fury had broiled as he turned to face her and it hadn't been okay.

And nothing had felt right since.

Until now.

Until her.

PART TWO

The Effect

CHAPTER TWENTY

LAURA

The bedroom was still shrouded in darkness as I woke to the creep of footsteps across the landing. It must be time to get up. Across the room I could just make out Tilly. She was curled onto her side clutching the cuddly lion Gavan had bought her when she became obsessed with *The Wizard of Oz*. She called him Cow because she couldn't pronounce cowardly when she was four. My clothes were laid out at the bottom of the bed. I covered my gooseflesh skin with jeans and jumper before tiptoeing across the room, avoiding the floorboard near the chest of drawers that always creaked. Already I was learning.

The first month at the farm had passed in a haze. Leaving the home Gavan and I shared had rocked the earth beneath my feet and I stumbled against the unfamiliar terrain. Without the comfort of Gavan's things it seemed I'd never regain my footing. Dafydd hadn't taken all of his clothes for his trip, and I'd felt guilty packing away the few things that remained so Tilly and I could use the drawers and wardrobe. I folded bobbly jumpers heavy with the pungent odour of mothballs and paired thick woollen socks; cold weather clothes he wouldn't be needing. I worried endlessly about what would happen when he returned in the new year, although there had been much speculation that he might decide to stay in Perth.

'He hasn't even sent us a postcard,' Hazel said, her face dropping. She wore her heart on her sleeve. 'It's like he's forgotten us.'

'He cares about us all,' Alex said. 'The post from Australia takes ages. There'll be something soon, I'm sure.' There was genuine sorrow in his eyes. He must miss him terribly.

Alex had been a great support. He was still fighting with the insurance company, and I still held on to the hope that they would settle before the inquest. A tearful Rhianon had confirmed that Iwan and Anwyn had split up. Neither of them picked up my calls. Rhianon texted me sometimes in the middle of the night and there was such pain in her messages it broke my heart. I wished I were nearer to her. Tilly said she was quiet at school. Not really talking to anyone. I asked her if she wanted to come and stay with us for a few days but she said Anwyn had hit the roof when she'd asked.

My new routine was numbing. Exhaustion had thickened my blood, weighted my bones. It had only been four weeks but getting up at 5.30 a.m. was taking its toll. I moved slower than usual, had less energy, but in a way I welcomed it. Although the physical effects of tiredness were draining, my fears for the future were slothful. Determinedly clinging on but no longer battering me with the same ferocity they once had.

'You look shattered this morning.' Saffron pushed a mug into my hands. I wrapped my fingers around its warmth as I stifled a yawn. 'Sleep well?'

'Fine.' And I had, even if I didn't feel refreshed. No longer was I plagued by nightmares. The long hours ensured I was slipping into sleep before the pillow had sculpted around my head. Still, I couldn't complain. Alex had welcomed Tilly and me, and we were living there rent free. The least I could do was help out. The early starts were essential. Each morning the fruit and vegetables had to be boxed along with recipe cards, and loaded into the minibus to be distributed. I hadn't yet taken a turn at market selling as I was driving Tilly to school for nine each day.

In that environment, I had thought there'd be plenty of time to think, but our days were busy. We were split into threes and assigned our chores, or 'contributions' as they were called. I worked the land, planted, weeded, harvested. It was back-breaking. My hands were chapped and raw from being out in all weathers, but I began to sink almost into a meditative state as I worked. It was restorative to feel the rain caress my skin, the wind murmuring in my ear. A little like recuperating after an illness. Staring into the distance at the horizon binding the sky to the fields was like looking into the future. I'd decided to set up a landscaping business. Not quite working with flowers again but there was something therapeutic about being outside. The connection to the earth. It made me feel closer to Gavan somehow.

'Mum. Can I tell you something?'

'Of course.' Our icy breath fogged the windscreen as Reed opened the gates. I twisted the dial on the heater. The wheels turned slowly over uneven ground as the car trundled out onto the track. I no longer winced at the scratching sound. My paintwork was littered with criss-cross scratches from the undergrowth. Little wonder the drop-ins were brought in by the minibus.

'You can talk to me about anything, Tilly.' I anticipated she'd want to talk about Gavan. I steeled myself to reassure her that whatever she was feeling it was normal and natural and perfectly okay.

'I'm thinking about leaving school.'

The paper bag – we no longer used plastic – containing her lunch fell into the footwell as I automatically squeezed the brake. Thankful we were only travelling at low speed.

'Dropping out? Tilly! No!'

Her head was bowed, hair shielding her face. I stared at her, trying to calm myself, but she wouldn't look at me.

'Why? You've already completed your AS Levels. You've only a few months to go before you're finished for good.'

She shrugged.

'If you can't give me a reason we can't talk about it.'

The engine idled while I lingered. Her unresponsiveness drove me to press the accelerator. She was going to school whether she liked it or not.

'I wish I'd had the chance of sitting A Levels. Getting a degree.' There had honestly never been so much as a millisecond where I had regretted becoming a mum at seventeen, but Tilly throwing away the opportunities she was afforded felt like a slap in the face. Gavan and I had been so proud she'd wanted to go to university. My words continued to tumble. 'What about your plans? You'd have a better chance of getting a marketing job at a higher level with qualifications. Particularly if you still want to work within the beauty industry. It's so competitive.'

Eventually I fell silent too, at a loss to know what to say, what to do. Whether I should give her my blessing to leave. I was desperate to talk it over with someone, but who? A hot ball formed in my throat. Without Gavan there would never be anyone as invested in Tilly as I was. I had to swallow hard before I could eke out a goodbye, but she had already slammed the door behind her. The invisible cord that threaded us together stretched and stretched until I feared it would snap.

After I'd arrived back at the farm I headed straight to Alex's. Over breakfast we'd arranged to talk about expanding our crops. I'd pointed out that being a florist didn't make me an expert.

'You're more capable than you think. Don't underestimate yourself, Laura,' Alex had said, planting a seed I wanted to bloom and grow.

Now, he rattled around in his kitchen fetching drinks while I tried to compose myself, feeling only seconds away from losing it completely as I replayed the school conversation in my mind.

'Fresh smoothie from the house.' Alex brought me out of my thoughts as he handed me a drink. Our fingers brushed as I took the glass from him and an involuntary shiver snaked down my spine.

Unsettled, I took a sip of the green gloop. His was orange and looked far more appetising.

'Everything okay, Laura?'

I shrugged. Not yet ready to talk about Tilly. 'Can I ask you something?'

'Of course.'

'Do you think we should always follow our dreams?'

'It depends on what those dreams are.'

'I want to start a landscaping business.'

'It's good you're thinking about making plans.'

'More than plans. I'm ready to make a start.' Although I didn't want Tilly to drop out of school, there was something admirable in the way she'd made a decision without the endless questions and doubts we grow into as we age. She wanted to plunge headfirst into her future while I was teetering on the edge of mine.

'If that's what you want, but you know there's no rush, Laura. You've been through a lot. There's always something to do here if you want to keep busy.'

'I know, but having something to focus on gives me hope.' And some semblance of control, although I didn't say that.

'There's always hope.'

'Tilly wants to drop out of school.' I sank down onto the sofa.

'How do you feel about that?' Alex asked, and something in his tone caused me to think carefully before I replied. If I scraped away the shock and dismay what was left?

'Disappointed. She's so bright. I don't think I handled it well. We were barely speaking as I dropped her off.'

He sat next to me. 'You want the best for her. That's understandable. I get the sense that your parents didn't support you. They let you down and you don't want to let Tilly down.'

'Who says they let me down?' My defences rose even though he was right.

'I feel it here.' He placed his hand over his stomach. 'The hurt you experienced when you were Tilly's age.'

Without consciously thinking about it, I mirrored his gesture. Feeling the churning heat of a thousand painful memories.

The truth. The whole truth. And nothing but the truth.

'They rejected you.' Alex spoke slowly. Softly. His words

tightened around my throat, the way hands once had. Squeezing, squeezing, squeezing.

'But here's the thing, Laura. You are *not* your mother and you are *not* alone.'

All at once there was a release of pressure and I could breathe.

'Anyone can see Tilly is everything to you,' Alex said.

'I just want her to have the best start, you know? Opportunities. Will you talk to her?'

'I'm not sure that she—'

'Please.'

A beat.

'Okay.'

'Thank you.'

'No need to thank me. I want what's best for you. Listen. I've talked to the insurance company and the coroner about the investigation. Laura—'

Instinctively I knew it was bad news. My mouth dried as I waited for him to finish.

'Are you sure Gavan's death was an accident? Because here's the thing…'

I took a sharp intake of breath and it was almost simultaneous; the sickly sweet smell, the walls crowding in, the ceiling pressing down until I was spinning and falling and welcoming the blackness with open arms.

CHAPTER TWENTY-ONE

TILLY

It was childish, I knew, but sometimes I had to think of the lion from *The Wizard of Oz* and how he realised he was brave in the end, before I could do anything remotely scary. Still, it took forever to summon the courage to tell Mum I wanted to leave school. She went ballistic. Slamming on her brakes. Seriously, I thought we were going to crash.

She asked me why I was dropping out. I wanted to tell her that I was anxious all the time and that I didn't have any real friends at school, but part of me thought that if I told her then she might look at me differently too. Suddenly see what everyone else saw. Anyway, it wasn't just that. Living at the farm, getting to know everyone, particularly Daisy, made me realise there are more important things I could be doing with my time. I couldn't think of how to put it all into words and so I shrugged. Honest to God, you wouldn't think I had wanted to work with words. Mum started rambling about how she didn't get the chance to go to uni. That was awful because I knew she hadn't been able to go to uni because of me. When we got to school she was so angry she didn't even say goodbye.

The first lesson was double English. Mr Cranford tried to catch my eye as I walked into the classroom but I avoided looking at him. I still hadn't caught up properly with the work I'd missed. At night on the farm we talked about the things that mattered. The environment. Our planet. Living in the now. School just didn't seem so important anymore. I sat, spine rigid, ignoring the chatter behind me about the latest episode of some new reality TV show everyone was hooked on. It had been a month since I had last watched TV. I'd missed it at first but in a way it was another pressure lifted. Fewer women to compare myself to. I always came up short.

'Open *Othello* where we left off,' Mr Cranford said. I leaned down to my rucksack to get my book. Rhianon did the same across the other side of the room. The seat next to her was empty. Ashleigh must be ill. I hoped she wasn't back in hospital. The rational part of me knew that the house Dad built hadn't caused her illness, but it didn't stop me feeling somehow responsible.

I texted Rhianon.

Where's Ashleigh?

She glanced over. We hadn't text for ages. At first I thought she wouldn't reply but then her thumbs flew over the keyboard.

She had an eyebrow disaster

I couldn't help snorting. My eyes strayed across the room. Rhianon's shoulders were shaking with laughter too. Poor Ashleigh. I had missed the whole morning on the first day of sixth form because I couldn't get my contouring right, one cheekbone more pronounced than the other. Since living at the farm I'd worn less make-up. Daisy had given me some cruelty-free products, but unless I was going to school I didn't always bother. The way I looked didn't seem so important anymore.

How are things at home?

I messaged back. Mum asked me almost every day how Rhianon was. Mum was still upset Aunt Anwyn and Uncle Iwan wouldn't speak to her.

You're not family anymore.

Aunty Anwyn's words raced around my mind while I willed my darkened screen to light up with an alert. Across the room Rhianon chewed her lip. She was deciding what to reply. Whether to reply.

And then it came,

Shit.

Before I could ask her why my phone lit up again.

Haven't seen Dad. Mum drinking. Drunk rambling about when the trust is gone it's gone.

What do you think he's done?

I couldn't imagine why Aunt Anwyn would have thrown Uncle Iwan out. He was so sweet.

Nothing like your dad...

I looked at Rhianon, unable to tell if she was being spiteful or honest. She was typing again.

Have you told your mum?

This time it was me who hesitated. Deciding what to reply. Whether to reply.

Mr Cranford clapped his hands. I raised my head. 'We're going to be reading aloud.' A groan Mexican waved its way around the room. 'Kieron you'll be Othello, Katie Bianca, Tilly Desdemona...'

I stuffed my phone back into my bag before heading towards the front of the class with my book. I used to love English, but I've had enough drama of my own to last me a lifetime.

'Devil,' Kieron shouted, playing his part. He mimed slapping me. Katie laughed.

The lesson dragged on, long and painful. The bell rang and I gathered my belongings and headed to the library. I had a free period. My phone buzzed, another text from Rhianon.

Lunch by the trees?

We hadn't spent breaks together for months. With Ashleigh off and Katie and Kieron fawning over each other, she probably figured three's a crowd. I hoped she'd help me decide what to do.

Yeah

It was hard to focus as I tried to study. Obsessively checking the time on my phone. Running through conversations we might have. A small, stupid part of me thought that it was over; the bitching, the backstabbing, the hollow feeling of loneliness. Of helplessness.

Just before twelve I headed around to the trees at the back of the school. I hitched my rucksack onto my shoulder. There was a lightness to it. To me. Yes, I'd definitely thought it was over. But then, hands on my shoulder blades.

A hard shove that sent me crashing to the ground.

A sting on my knees.

The warmth of the blood trickling down my shins.

The shadow blocking out the sun.

The laughing.

The kick.

The pain.

I curled into a ball and shielded my head with my arms. In my mind, over and over, Desdemona's line.

'*I have not deserved this.*'

'Tilly!' Rhianon called me as we spilled out of school at the end of the day. She looked shocked as she saw my bruised face. I touched my cheek, conscious of the swelling.

'God. I'm so sorry. I couldn't believe it when I heard.'

'Yeah. Right. Like you didn't set it up?' I jabbed my finger into her chest. Shock flickered across her face.

'What? No? How could you th—'

'No, Rhianon. How could *you*?' She betrayed me. Mr Cranford should have cast her as Iago.

'I didn't know, I swear. Katie literally asked to borrow my phone in Sociology cos hers was flat. She must have read the texts and saw we—'

'So where were you then?'

'Miss Mills wanted to see me after. You know what she's like.'

'So, she basically kept you in all lunch?'

'No, but by the time I got to the trees you'd gone, then I heard what happened. I tried to find you—'

'You didn't look very fucking hard, did you?' I shouted.

Rhianon flinched. 'I couldn't…'

'Call me? Text? Tear yourself away from Katie?'

Rhianon looked away.

'You were with *Katie*! Look at what she did to me.' I touched my cheek.

'I know. I'm sorry.'

'How sorry are you, Rhianon?'

'I'm—'

'Sorry enough not to hang around with her anymore?'

'It's awkward. You know it is. I like Ashleigh, and Kieron.'

'You *used* to like me.' Sadness washed my anger away. I could see she was fighting tears too. 'I miss you, Rhianon. We've always been like sisters.'

'We still are. I know we've grown apart lately. Made different friends but I'd always be there for you, Tills, if you really needed me.'

'I really needed you today,' I said, before I walked away.

I didn't wipe my eyes as I headed out the school gates. For once I didn't want to hide my feelings from Mum. I wanted to tell her how shit my day had been. How shit every day was. Try to get her to understand that I didn't want to leave school on some mad impulse. But Mum wasn't there. Instead, waiting for me was somebody I didn't expect, and I was thrown completely.

Not knowing what to think.

CHAPTER TWENTY-TWO

TILLY

The smile on Alex's face slipped as I climbed into the Land Rover.

'Tilly, what's happened?' He wiped away my tears with his thumbs. Lightly traced my cheek with his index finger.

'I fell.' Despite the look of concern on his face I was reluctant to tell him everything. A fight in the playground really would make me sound like a child, and that's the last thing I wanted him to see me as.

'Are you sure? Because if someone's hurt you…' He ran his fingers through his hair.

God, those fingers.

'I'm sure.' I didn't want to cause any more trouble. 'Where's Mum?'

'She's not feeling well.'

'Sorry you've had to drive all the way here.'

'My pleasure.' He gave me that smile, the one that made me feel I was the only person in the world. That there was nobody else he'd rather be talking to. My cheek didn't seem to throb so much.

He started the engine. We eased into the rush hour traffic. As he raised his hand from the gear stick for a second I thought it floated towards my knee before he placed it back on the steering wheel. I glanced at him but his face was impassive as he studied the road ahead. My mouth twitched into a triumphant smile at the look of disbelief on Katie's face as we drove past her and Kieron at the bus stop. I wondered if she'd thought Alex was my boyfriend. I hoped so.

Alex pushed a cassette into the stereo. I recognised 'Strawberry Fields Forever'.

'Hope this is okay?' Alex asked. 'It's Dafydd's car and the choice is rather limited. Have you ever seen a cassette tape before?'

'Yeah. Uncle Iwan had some in the garage, and some vinyl. Some of them were pretty cool.'

'Were you close to your uncle?' Alex turned the music down.

'Yeah. We spent loads of time together as a family while I was growing up.'

'What was he like?'

I thought for a moment. 'A bit like Dad I guess. But not so annoying.'

'I can't imagine losing your dad at seventeen.' There was so much emotion in Alex's voice I wanted to comfort him.

'I've still got Mum,' I said. 'At least I hope I have. Alex… did she send you today because she's pissed off with me?'

'No. Why would you think that?'

'You know what we talked about the other day?'

'About you leaving school?'

'Yeah.' It had been a throwaway comment I'd made to Alex. He'd asked if I'd had a good day and I'd replied that every day was equally terrible. He asked me why I still went. It had never even occurred to me I had a choice. 'You're in control of your own destiny,' he had said. 'Choose your own path. Don't let anyone influence you. You're a strong woman, Tilly.' And I wasn't sure whether it was him calling me a woman or calling me strong that made me feel different somehow. Empowered. *The Wizard of Oz* lion discovering his courage.

'So, I told Mum I wanted to leave.'

'How did she take it?'

'Not very well. Although I could have put it across better.'

'Perhaps. Learning to communicate is a skill but it's liberating. Bottling things up never did anyone any good.'

'Yeah. Well. I messed up.'

'Don't be hard on yourself, Tilly. It must have been a shock.'

'Maybe,' I said, although I knew that wasn't it. I hadn't explained it properly. There were so many things I wanted to – needed to – tell her but the words had churned round and round in my stomach with my fear and my anger as I wished I could find a way to express myself. I'd ended up not saying anything at all. Mum had said plenty though. 'She kept going on, saying I need a degree to work in marketing but I don't think I do. I dunno. With Dad and everything it's all too much at the moment. I can't focus on studying.'

'Your mum will come around.'

'Thanks so much… Alex.' It still felt odd using his first name but I could hardly call him Mr Draycott like he was a teacher or something.

'You don't have to thank me, Tilly.'

'I did try, but I know she'll guilt-trip me into staying at school and sitting my exams anyway.'

I rested my forehead against the window. The Land Rover chugged up the hill towards Abberberth. Alex turned the music back up. We didn't speak again until we reached *Gorphwysfa*.

Alex wound down his window as Reed opened the gates.

'Everything been okay?'

'Yes, boss.' Reed mock-saluted.

We bumped down the track and pulled up near the farm-house. I was sad our journey had come to an end.

'Thanks for picking me up, Alex.'

I waited for him to say it's okay, but instead he said, 'I had to,' and I felt hurt that he hadn't wanted to. I reached for the door handle.

'Wait. Tilly.' I turned back to face him but he was staring out of the windscreen, fingertips drumming on the steering wheel. He looked so serious.

The hairs on my arms stood on end as I waited for him to continue, second guessing what he might say.

He liked me.

'Look, there's something you should know. It's about your mum.'

'Mum?' I felt heat rise in my cheeks. I'd got it so wrong. 'What about Mum?'

'Here's the thing. She's had a seizure. Another one.'

'What? Wait. Another one?'

'This is really difficult,' he said. 'I shouldn't say anything but—'

'You absolutely should. What's wrong with her?' Even I could hear the edge of panic in my voice.

'You know she has epilepsy?'

I shook my head and then changed it to a nod. 'Yeah, years ago, but she doesn't anymore.'

'She had a seizure today, in the cottage, and one a month or so ago when she was in the shop with Saffron.'

'Christ. Why…' I left my question hanging in the air. Why had it come back? Why hadn't she told me?

'I'm not sure, she hasn't seen a doctor but I've done some research and people can be seizure-free for years, medication-free for years, and then it can return. Possibly it's all the stress she's been under.'

'Did she…' I lowered my eyes, feeling ashamed. 'Did she have one after I told her I was dropping out of school?'

'Yes.'

'I won't. I'll go back, finish my A Levels. I'll—'

'I don't think that's a good idea, Tilly.' Alex took my hand in his. It fit perfectly. 'You're not a child so I'm going to be honest with you. I think the reason she hasn't gone to the doctor and sought treatment is because of you.'

'Me?' Oh God. I was the cause of this?

'A GP would be duty bound to report her to the DVLA.'

'I don't understand…'

'Laura would have her licence revoked until she's been seizure-free for twelve months. She wouldn't be able to drive you to school. With everyone here getting the veg boxes out early there'd be no one to take you. There's no decent public transport to get you there on time. I think it's worry about your education that's stopping her from putting her health first.'

'But Mum needs her licence. Not just for me. She's going to start a landscaping business. She needs to be mobile.'

'The bottom line is, she needs to be alive.' His words hit me like a punch. 'Tilly.' His thumb stroked the back of my wrist. 'Do you realise it's potentially fatal for her to be behind a wheel? What if she has a seizure? It's not just her safety either.

She could easily cause an accident. How would she feel if she killed someone? A child? A baby?'

'Do you think if I leave school and she doesn't have to drive, Mum will see a doctor?'

'Honestly? No. I think she was hoping it was a one-off but now it's happened twice…' He shook his head. 'It's illegal not to report a change in health, let alone incredibly dangerous.'

Images were rubber stamped into my mind. Mum lying in a ditch.

In prison.

In a coffin.

'It's up to us to look after her, Tilly.' Something about the way he said 'us' was comforting.

'Could you please teach me to drive, Alex?' I could ferry Mum around the way she had me.

'I'd teach you all of my bad habits. Besides, it's not that simple. You'd have to pay for the insurance and that would probably cost a couple of grand at your age. Then there's your provisional licence, your tests; theory and practical.'

I didn't have any money. 'What should we do then?'

'You're her daughter. Ultimately it's your decision but if it were someone I loved, I know what I'd do. I'd keep them safe. You can both work here. You won't be stuck with nothing to do.'

He pulled a piece of paper from his pocket. 'This is the number for the DVLA.' He climbed out of the car and then walked around to my side to open my door. My feet felt odd against the ground. The world unexpectedly unsteady. 'I'll keep you both safe.'

Did that mean he loved us? He loved me?

'See you at dinner.' I watched him disappear into the woods.

Alone, I stared at the phone number until the black digits went all fuzzy in front of my eyes.

Could I betray Mum?

Judas.

From my pocket I fished out my mobile and in my hand it felt heavy, like thirty pieces of silver.

CHAPTER TWENTY-THREE

ALEX

He'd been watching them. Unpicking their relationship. Trying to understand the dynamics. Tension crackled between them but underneath pulsed love, strong and steady. A knowing that they'd always be there for each other.

Or would they?

Alex felt a stirring within the blackness that resided inside him, and he didn't know whether it was longing or envy. Once he'd had that trust with his sister. He had thought their bond was unbreakable but in the end it had been cobweb-fragile and easily swept away.

'You'll never look at me the same way anymore,' he had said.

His sister had shaken her head vehemently and promised she would, but he noticed she couldn't quite meet his eyes. Fear had crept into the places familiarity once sat.

He wanted it back, not with his sister of course, that was impossible, but that love. That hope. That faith in something.

In someone.

In her.

He wanted her.

But he needed them both.

CHAPTER TWENTY-FOUR

LAURA

After the seizure I had felt so drained I fell asleep on my bed, waking confused and disorientated. Dusk was closing in outside the window, the moon growing brighter as the afternoon emptied of light. My stomach cartwheeled as I realised I hadn't picked Tilly up from school. I fumbled for my phone which was out of sight in the bedside cabinet drawer, where I now kept it like a shameful secret. Other than Alex and Saffron having mobiles to take veg box orders, and to know what time to leave in the mornings, and Tilly because nothing could prise her from hers, no one else had one. It hadn't been suggested that we shouldn't have phones but I felt awkward that we did. Not following their rules didn't mean I wasn't grateful to be there. There was a text message from Saffron:

Didn't want to disturb you. Tilly home safe and sound.

The red hot panic that gripped me released its hold. The conversation we'd had weeks ago at my house came back to me, 'At the farm it's not just a living together, it's a pulling together. You're never alone.' The words took shape, real and solid. For the first time that faded floral bedroom, smelling of mothballs and lavender furniture polish, felt something akin to home.

From downstairs the chinking of cutlery on china. Laughter. Conversation. The tang of cumin. They'd all be seated around the huge pine table swapping stories about their day like any other family. I wanted to be part of it all.

The kitchen door was cracked open. The lot from the stables, who I hadn't really got to know yet, were crammed around the table. Tilly, her back to me, was sitting between Alex and Saffron. I hovered unseen on the periphery. If I entered the room I knew Tilly's shoulders would stiffen. We needed to talk but it wasn't the time. With a last lingering look at my daughter I headed towards the front door, grabbing my coat from the hook on the way out.

The sky was clear. The night air frigid. Away from the main house I pulled out the Maglite I kept in my pocket for my evening walks. A bright beam of light illuminated the ground before my feet. I got the sense that I was the only person in the world. Sometimes I welcomed the isolation there. Away from pollution, the stars popped in the sky. The air fresh and earthy. But sometimes I found it all horribly oppressive. The silence crushing down on me. I missed the steady thrum of traffic. The aroma of late night chip shops, salt and vinegar mingling with hot oil.

I strode purposefully, my fingers already numb with cold, but my steady footfall, my rhythmic breath, failed to calm the tumult of my mind.

'Are you sure Gavan's death was an accident?' Alex had asked earlier, before consciousness had slipped away from me. Later, after he'd walked me back to the farmhouse, he'd sat on the edge of my bed and told me the coroner hadn't yet set a date for the inquest. 'He says he hasn't finished gathering information. He's been having trouble locating Gavan's brother. Iwan.' I'd only half taken in what he was saying. 'I really hope Iwan doesn't hold things up for you but—'

'I can't believe I've had another seizure.' I'd sunk back onto my pillow.

'Sorry. This isn't the time to talk. I'll leave you to rest. Don't worry,' he said as he left the room, but how could I not?

Shouting drew me out of my thoughts. I looked up. The trees black against a navy sky. Behind them, the main gate. I'd walked further than I'd realised, automatically treading the track I drove down each morning to take Tilly to school.

'You're not coming in.' A voice I recognised. Reed. I wondered if he ever left the gate or if he slept in that small wooden cabin. He never ate at the house.

'I'm not leaving,' yelled a man.

My heart sped, but remembering what Alex had said about the locals trashing the vegetable patches I hurried forward to help him, angry rather than scared. Although I'd only been there a short time I was thankful for the sanctuary the farm had offered me, and protective of everyone who lived here.

'She's our mum!' a girl's voice pleaded.

I hesitated, keeping to the shadows. This didn't sound like a disgruntled local.

'Eilwen!' The man shouted again. 'Mum!'

'She's Hazel now,' Reed said firmly.

'You can't change her name and keep her hidden and expect us to forget she exists. We know she's in there. Mum!'

'She doesn't want to see you.'

'But it's her birthday.' The girl was quieter. I could detect the misery in her words. 'We just wanted to give her a card.'

'You can give it to me,' Reed said.

'Don't give it to him, Saren,' the man said. 'He'll keep it like he's kept Mum and her divorce settlement. Bastards.'

'I haven't kept—'

'The other bloke then. Alex. You're all the same. Mum!'

'You'll pass it on?' The girl sounded broken.

'I promise.' The anger in Reed's voice had softened. 'No one's forcing your mum to stay here. She's happy.'

'But it's Christmas soon.' Her bewilderment, her sense of loss was so raw and familiar I turned away from it, stumbling back towards the house. Towards my own daughter.

Inside, everyone was still gathered in the kitchen. Rather than tucking into Victoria sponge sandwiched with jam and buttercream and dotted with candles, they dipped spoons into soya yoghurt. The sideboard, empty of birthday cards. Saffron made a joke and everyone laughed but rather than depicting the happy family scene it had earlier, the lack of celebration of who Hazel was or where she had come from seemed sinister somehow. Had Alex taken Hazel in to get to her money? Was that what he was doing to me?

Should I tell her I knew she wasn't who she claimed to be or should I conceal her secret along with all the others I carried? Undecided, I slipped away unnoticed and slowly climbed the stairs, weighted with all the things I shouldn't know.

I was in bed when Tilly came into the room. Mug in hand.

'You missed dinner. Can I make you a sandwich?'

'I'm not hungry, but thanks.' I was touched by her unexpected gesture. I hoped this meant she wasn't leaving school, but I couldn't face talking about it. My head too full of the things I'd just seen and heard. 'Is that a bruise on your face?' I peered at her through the half-light.

'Yeah. I walked into an open locker. It doesn't hurt now.' She watched me carefully as I lifted the peace offering to my lips and took a sip. 'Are you okay, Mum?'

'I'm fine. Tired but fine.'

'If you weren't… fine. You could… you know.' She gave me a swift hug and left the room so quickly that if it weren't for the mug in my hand I'd have thought it was a dream.

I drained my tea and curled onto my side, drawing the duvet to my chin. I couldn't stop shivering. Memories of my first meeting with Alex prowled my mind.

There's always someone who wants to bolt for freedom. Who has to be restrained.

The feel of the cold, heavy gun in my hands. The way my finger curved around the trigger.

Up until now I had felt nothing but safe and protected with Alex, but what if my trust was misplaced?

I had half a million pounds coming to me.

Half a million reasons he might not let me leave.

CHAPTER TWENTY-FIVE

TILLY

Mum looked so pale and ill when I took her a mug of tea. My bombshell about school must have made her have a seizure. It was obvious she was sitting there worrying about me. She missed dinner so I offered to make her a sandwich.

It was my sorry without saying sorry, but she didn't want it.

CHAPTER TWENTY-SIX

LAURA

On Saturdays, Gavan used to bring me a bacon sandwich in bed before I had to go and open the shop. When I returned he'd have a coconut bubble bath waiting for me, the room dotted with flickering tea lights. Later, we'd dip poppadoms into mango chutney, sipping a crisp pinot. Despite it being a working day I had always felt relaxed. Now, I was wrenched from sleep by Saffron shaking my shoulder.

'Is it that time already?' I yawned.

'No. It's only just five.'

'What's wrong?' Automatically my eyes found Tilly who was blinking in the artificial light spilling in from the landing.

'Mum?' she asked, small and uncertain.

'What's going on?' I asked Saffron.

'We need an earlier start. Alex has selected a few of us to have a sharing circle at eight. You and Tilly have been chosen.'

Before I could ask what a sharing circle was she added, 'Tilly, you need to pitch in now you've left sixth form.' She slipped out of the door before I could tell her Tilly hadn't left school.

'Tilly. You don't have to—'

'I want to do my bit, Mum.'

I bundled up my clothes and crossed silently to the bathroom.

The tiled floor was freezing against the soles of my feet. Shivering, I twisted on the taps and the ancient pipes gurgled to life. As I waited for the flowing water to heat I caught sight of my reflection in the bathroom mirror. I'd lost so much weight. My cheekbones were sharp under pale skin. My eyes circled with the tell-tale purple rings denoting a lack of sleep.

By eight my hands were numb with cold, arms aching. I had finished loading the minibus with crates of veg brimming with beetroot, celeriac, squash and fennel, all the time watching Hazel carefully as she packed the crates. She stretched, hands massaging the small of her back, a faraway expression on her face. I wondered whether she was thinking of birthdays past. I'd assumed she was happy to be there but what if she wasn't? What if Alex had tricked her into staying? I'd read about brainwashing in the papers. He could have taken her money? Persuaded her to change her name to keep herself hidden. Was she in danger? Was I? Just when I had convinced myself the idea was ridiculous – Alex had been nothing but kind – I'd remember the crack in her daughter's voice. Her distress at not seeing her mum on her birthday. Reed's promise to pass on her card. Had he?

In the cottage, Alex wasn't ready for us, the floorboards settling overhead as he moved around upstairs. The small windows barely let the dull grey light through. Saffron clicked on the honeyed table lamps while Daisy and Tilly claimed seats in front of the crackling fire.

'I'll make some tea,' Hazel said.

'Let me.' I wanted a chance to gather my thoughts.

'*Diolch*, Laura.'

'You're welcome.'

The kitchen was homely. Rustic. Solid wooden worktops with faded patches and criss-cross knife scratches. I sifted through the redirected post addressed to me, piled upon the worktop. Bills I couldn't pay unless the insurance came through. The kettle bubbled. I tipped steaming water into mugs before quickly fishing the teabags out with a spoon before the herbs could properly steep. I opened the lid of the bin. The smell of a banana skin wafted out and just as I was about to drop the teabags inside I saw it, poking out from under some congealing porridge. The envelope torn into two pieces, 'Mum' written in small, curling letters. I fished it out and tried to slot the pieces of card back together but there was a zigzag tear across the centre, a heart that could never be whole again. Inside was written, 'Happy Birthday Mum, Martyn and Saren' and then almost as an afterthought, 'We miss you'. It was none of my business but I was angry, imagining how I would feel if someone tried to keep Tilly away from me? I'd want to kill them.

A noise.

Drifting from the dingy passageway behind me.

A scraping sound.

I stuck my head through to the lounge. Everyone that was supposed to be there was chatting. I could still hear Alex's footfall on the ceiling above me where he was moving around upstairs.

Then who?

Tentatively I crossed the kitchen, stepping into the narrow corridor, not quite sure where it would lead.

I stepped forward once. Twice. My fingers reaching for the handle of the door to my left.

'Hello?' I opened the door. An empty cloakroom.

I was just turning back, convincing myself I must have imagined it, when I heard it again.

Something being knocked over?

I edged further down the passageway, my fingers sliding across the wall until I found the light switch. I clicked it on.

The bulb popped. Darkness fell once more.

The doorway in front of me was shadowed. I stretched my arm forward. Hesitant but not quite sure why. I turned the handle which was loose in my hand and pushed against the door. It was locked.

'What are you doing, Laura?'

'Alex!' I twisted around. 'You scared me! I thought I heard someone.'

'Nobody goes down to the cellar.'

I was intrigued. 'What do you use it for?'

'Nothing. It's damp and mouldy. Not even good for storage. The stone stairs are always slippery. It's a death-trap.'

'But I'm sure…' I rattled the handle once more.

'Come on. We're about to start.' He started to walk away. He was silhouetted in the doorframe of the kitchen when he turned to face me.

'Laura?' There was something in his tone. A command? A warning? I didn't know him well enough to identify it. I trailed after him as he picked up the tray of drinks and took his place in the biggest armchair in the lounge.

The atmosphere was weighted with expectation.

'Let me explain how this works,' he began.

'Let me guess.' Saffron placed her index finger on her chin and furrowed her brow. 'You'll choose three people—'

'We're here to help Laura today.' Alex gave her a look,

something passing between them, thick and private. My nerves increased. Not understanding what he wanted from me. I wanted to grab Tilly and run. Unprepared to share myself. To share her.

'I'm sorry, Alex,' Saffron said.

'Three is a power number, Laura.' He met my eyes. 'It's been significant throughout history and religion, not that we're religious here, but it's a time identifier representing past, present and future.' Uncomfortable, I glanced around the room. Tilly was leaning forwards, mirroring Daisy, staring at him with a rapt expression on her face, although I knew she had no more idea of what he was talking about than I had. 'In numerology numbers one and two are the proverbial mother and father of the universe and three is a product of that union, a child filled with potential and hope.' Inexplicably something twisted in my gut. Although I didn't understand how a number could symbolise anything, there was something about a child filled with potential and hope that resonated with me. That reminded me of the child I once was, innocent and optimistic. My throat began to swell as the profound hurt that I'd been trying to block out for years began to resurface: abandonment and betrayal. I reached for my tea and swallowed it down.

'Here, it's a safe space to share.' He slowly appraised us all, one by one. 'We're family.'

'We're not though, are we?' My gaze flickered from Alex to Hazel. I wanted to add that families didn't lie to each other, they don't keep things hidden, but I knew that they did. I'd been guilty of that myself.

'Not in the conventional sense,' Saffron said. 'We're not a flesh family—'

'Flesh family?' The term made my skin crawl.

'We're better than a flesh family,' Daisy said.

'But you must still see your family, Daisy?' I asked. 'You're so young. Your parents must worry?'

'*Must* they?' I squirmed under her unflinching gaze.

'Here it's about choice, not obligation.' Alex drew the attention back to himself. 'The people we want to spend time with are those who have positively contributed to our quality of life in some way.' As he talked he made eye contact with everyone in turn. 'We build each other up, not knock each other down, like families can. Friends can become more integral to our emotional and physical wellbeing. So no, we're not blood.' His eyes settled on Saffron. 'But we can't imagine being without each other.'

Without consciously choosing to, I nodded. Embarrassed, I looked at Tilly, expecting her to roll her eyes, but she was nodding too.

You're not family. Anwyn had spat her venomous truth. Iwan had let me down. As I looked around the room I knew I'd been shown more compassion and care by those people over the past few weeks than I had from those I thought would always be my support. Still, I was conflicted. Unsure about Alex's motives for inviting us in.

'Unburdening sets you free. Let's share, Laura.' Alex's expectations pinned me to my seat. In my head I heard another question, from another time.

Mrs Evans, where were you this evening?

Feeling hot, I loosened my scarf, those hands around my throat again.

Let's go over your statement one more time.

139

Once again, I didn't have the words. 'Alex, I don't know what to say... I...'

'I'd like you to listen,' he said. 'I'd like you to hear Hazel's story.'

CHAPTER TWENTY-SEVEN

LAURA

'Hazel's story?' I was blindsided. My heart still racing. 'Are you... do you...' I lightly touched Hazel's arm, wanting my fingers to convey what I was having trouble articulating. That she didn't have to speak. But that I was willing to listen.

'I want you to know me, okay?' she asked. I nodded, unsure whether she meant the Hazel sat in front of me, or the woman with an entirely different name. An entirely different identity. The mother. I had been living with her for over a month and she was still a stranger to me.

I supposed I was to her.

'He was a bastard. My ex.' Her voice was softer than usual. I leaned forward so I could properly hear. 'Used to wallop me if I wasn't fast enough making his tea. If I didn't iron the creases in his shirt just right. Once he came in and I was doing his collar wrong and he said... he said I needed to be taught a lesson. He held the iron against my arm. Look.' She pulled up her sleeve. I winced as I saw the pink, puckered scar. 'My children.' Hazel shook her head. 'They were too much like him. It wasn't their fault but...' She shrugged. 'I let them think it was okay to treat me badly.'

'Oh, Hazel.' I forced my shame-filled eyes to meet hers. I'd been so caught up in my own problems, I hadn't once dug deeper into everyone's reasons for being there. Of course, it wasn't a place you would run towards unless you were running away from something. Or someone. 'I'm so sorry.'

And I was. Sorry for what she'd been through. Sorry for not being the friend to her that she had been to me. The home-cooked meals, the laundry. Looking after me when she, more than anyone, deserved to be taken care of. 'What made you finally leave?'

'It was my birthday and I'd made an effort. A couple of months before, he'd split my lip after I'd smiled the wrong way at the man on the checkout at Asda. Leading him on, apparently. Anyway I threatened to leave after that and I meant it. I packed but he persuaded me to stay. Promised he'd change, and it had been so many weeks I started to think he had. I dyed my hair dark brown, put on some red lipstick and wore a new dress, like that could make me into something I wasn't. And that, *cariad aur*,' she turned to Tilly, 'is part of the reason I choose to wear white too. Clothes can be a distraction. Bright colours. Fancy fabric. Plain and simple and nothing to hide behind. Wearing white leaves you nothing to hide behind. It felt like learning to be me. Do you see?'

Tilly nodded.

'Anyway, that day I thought we'd have a little birthday party. He came home early, took one look at me and accused me of having an affair with the neighbour. He... I really believed he was going to kill me.' She paused. I knew she was back in that memory. Terrified. Her body bruised and battered and alone. She was remembering how it felt to be helpless. I knew how she felt. I had felt it once. All of it.

'You don't have to—' I began.

'The kids came home and called an ambulance but when the police interviewed them they said he'd never hit me before. Said he was with them, and someone else must have hurt me.'

'And you never forgave them?' I could understand Hazel felt let down, but I was incredulous to think that she'd never spoken to her children again. We all make mistakes, don't we? Drift from the light towards the dark, hovering in the shades of grey between. I'd forgive Tilly anything, I know. But would she forgive me the same? I glanced over at my daughter. She was gazing at Hazel with a horrified expression on her face, and I didn't know if it was Hazel's actions causing her reaction, or those of her children. I thought of the things I'd kept from Tilly and shuddered. Perhaps we can't all forgive and forget. Some things are best kept secret.

'I made excuses for them, as we do as parents. They were too young to understand, although at seventeen and eighteen they weren't. Not really. They didn't want to choose between us. He never treated them the way he did me – thank God – and he was still their dad. They told me he'd cried and promised he'd never do it again, and they begged me to drop the charges so I did. I came here for a break and once I was here I realised how low I felt. How worthless. Alex said I could stay as long as I wanted.'

'And you haven't seen them since?'

'Every now and then I did, until my birthday last year.'

Hazel's eyes filled with tears. 'You don't have to carry on.' I placed my hand on her arm to comfort her but then I remembered the scar of the iron beneath her sleeve. I pulled away as though I were the one responsible for her pain.

'They turned up here with a card. Reed drove us to a nice village pub and waited in the car while we had our dinner. Saren said she was going to uni and asked me to sign some forms for student finance. I did – well, you would, wouldn't you – but they weren't forms for uni at all. They were forms to give up my share of the house, which had been my mum's before it was mine.'

'So you lost everything?'

'No. Thanks to this one.' She turned and smiled at Alex. 'And his understanding of the law. It all went over my head but he sorted it all out and now I'm divorced with a tidy sum in the bank. I'll never leave here though. It's been my sanctuary. Don't know what I'd have done without this lot. They pieced me back together when I thought I was too broken to repair.'

Hazel was crying hard now. I passed her a tissue and as I looked at Alex I was close to tears myself. I'd doubted him when he'd been protecting her. Did he care about me like that? I wanted him to.

Hazel blew her nose.

'Hazel, do you thi—'

'That's another thing. Hazel isn't my real name.'

I threw a glance at Alex. He was watching me intently.

'I don't get it,' Tilly said.

'I think Hazel wanted to stay hidden…' I began.

'That isn't it at all. When my kids were small I used to read them *The Very Hungry Caterpillar*.'

'I loved that!' Tilly said.

'So you know it's about a dreary caterpillar that can't stop stuffing his face. Every moment is the same for him. I felt like that. My life felt dull. Colourless. But you remember what happened at the end of the story, Tilly, *cariad*?'

'He became a butterfly.'

'Yes, somebody else. Free. Reborn. No one ever called him a caterpillar again. That's what I wanted – to feel free. For nobody to call me Eilwen again.'

'Kind of realising your destiny,' Saffron said.

'But didn't you lose your identity?'

'She created a new one,' Alex said. 'A name change can be a jumpstart to who we want to be. A gift to ourselves.'

'My nana had a hazel tree, growing up, and it was a nod to her as well as to here. All the nature surrounding us. The world is a beautiful place, but I'd forgotten it for a while.'

'But your children…' I thought of the distress in Saren's voice last night.

'Never say never. But it's still too raw. Too painful. I have to put myself first right now. I'll see them when I'm good and ready, but I know one thing. I never want to celebrate a bloody birthday again as long as I live.'

'And you don't have to. We look after you, don't we?' Alex crossed the room and hugged her and unconsciously I wrapped my arms around myself, wanting to be held. Wanting to be held by him, and then immediately loathing myself for it. Gavan was my sun and my moon. I didn't need the stars too.

'It's complex.' This time Alex was looking at me as he spoke and I wondered if everyone felt it, this electricity that crackled between us, and it shamed me to think that they could. That they might think I was willing to let go of Gavan. I wasn't. But still Alex filled my head more than he should.

'We're programmed to think that the relationships with our families are absolute. Our bonds unbreakable. But it's not always the case. Sometimes friends are more loyal, less judgemental. Birthdays are a particularly vulnerable time – all those expectations and often disappointments. The pressure to have one perfect day with people who truthfully you might not even like. I think you've struggled with this, Laura.'

'What, no.' I squirmed under the intensity of his gaze. 'I had a happy childhood.'

'Tell us about it then. This happy childhood.' Despite his words there was only kindness in Alex's voice.

'Well.' I breathed in deeply as I raised my eyes to the ceiling, as though I might find the words I was fumbling for written there.

'Do you have any siblings, Laura?' Saffron prompted.

'No.' I didn't share that I was painfully lonely and once had an imaginary friend.

'Me neither,' Saffron said sadly. 'I always used to badger my mum for a sister, but then she died and it was just me and my dad.'

'I had a sister I loved more than anything, but…' Alex rubbed his lips, reminding me of Gavan, and I wondered if he wished he could send the words that dripped with sorrow back inside his mouth.

Emotions were crushing down on me. I couldn't cope with their feelings. My feelings.

'We can create our own happiness, can't we, Alex? No matter what's happened in the past. Every moment is a chance for a new beginning. Now I have the large family I always wanted.' Saffron gestured around the room. 'This bunch of losers.' She forced a smile.

'It must be… nice. But I was happy growing up. I was.' I didn't know whether I was trying to convince them or myself.

'But you're right.' I tried to smile, but the hot lump in my throat kept the corners of my mouth downturned. 'We do create our own happiness. And marrying Gavan... it was... we were happy.' That much at least was true, but my words were faltering.

'Honestly, there's nothing you would change about your past if you could?'

There's nowhere to run to.

Anger.

Pain.

'I think...' I thought carefully. 'There is perhaps always something we would change if we could.' But even as I said this I didn't want it to be true. I found Tilly's eyes. I didn't want Tilly to ever wish her childhood was anything other than what it was.

'And what was your something? Tell us, Laura.'

My head was heavy with exhaustion. With confusion. I was tired of talking and I'd barely spoken. Part of me, a large part, wanted to share everything about myself. Be accepted. But I wasn't like them, was I? Lost and lonely. I had my daughter there with me.

My flesh family.

I drew my cardigan closer around my body to cover the doubts and fears I was wearing on the outside.

'I don't know what to say,' I lied. 'I can't think of anything specific.'

'I disagree,' Alex said gently. 'I watched the emotions on your face as Hazel talked about having a birthday party. Your parents didn't throw parties for you, did they, Laura?'

My denial was stuck to the roof of my mouth. A hand slipped into mine. Another arm around my shoulder. I wasn't sure if it was the lack of sleep, an accumulation of the emotions of the past few weeks or the stark, simple truth that my parents had never given me a party, although throughout our marriage Gavan had, but then it was me crying. A tissue being pushed into my hand.

'They didn't...' I trailed off. They didn't mean to hurt me. They didn't love me. I just didn't know. 'Gavan arranged parties for me every year, he made me feel special but... my parents...'

'Let go of the struggle, Laura. We need continuous personal growth. Allow yourself to feel the hurt. Feel the pain. Only then can you truly release it.'

When I opened my mouth I wasn't sure whether I was going to defend my parents or condemn them but did they really deserve my loyalty after what they had done to me? My eyes searched for Tilly. She was staring at the floor. Uncomfortable. I hoped Gavan and I had never made her feel anything other than wanted and loved.

'Your dad and I... We've never made you feel like that, have we? Unwanted and unloved. We've never hurt you, have we, Tilly?' It seemed imperative I knew. 'Tilly?' I willed her to answer. 'We've never made you feel like that, have we?'

Her single word answer, jagged and sharp, pierced my already fragile heart.

'Yes.'

The rest of the room faded to nothing as I knelt in front of my daughter and placed her hand in mine.

A hand rested on my shoulder and for one single, solitary second I thought it was Gavan, until reality crashed against me once more. There, with my knees pressed hard against the wooden floorboards, I was sinking, completely out of my depth, the way I had when Tilly was born. But without Gavan I had no anchor.

Tilly swallowed hard and opened her mouth, shutting it quickly again. The back of my neck bristled. I could feel eyes boring into me. I turned to ask for space but everyone other than Daisy had discreetly disappeared into the dining room. A shadow in the kitchen, the tiniest of movements, caught my eye. I turned my head and squinted. It could have been the sway of the trees outside of the window. But I remembered the noises I thought I'd heard coming from the cellar earlier.

I turned my attention back to Tilly, but Daisy was whispering soothing words to her while she held her as she cried. My arms felt cold and empty.

Again, I looked behind me. I still had the eerie sensation of being watched, but there was nobody there.

CHAPTER TWENTY-EIGHT

TILLY

I can't say I was a fan of getting up at 5 a.m. on a Saturday to help. Some of my sixth form would only be rolling home from the pub then. But I knew if I wanted Mum to treat me as an adult I needed to behave like one.

'You don't just get respect,' Dad used to say. 'You have to earn it.' He'd lost mine before he died, and it was awful to think he'd never have the chance to earn it back.

I threw myself into the contributions. In a weird way I enjoyed it. I worked with Daisy and Hazel. They didn't look at me with the sympathy the teachers at school did, or like I was irrelevant, like the other kids did. It was hard though. I could appreciate why Mum had become more and more exhausted since we moved there.

I was starving by the time we got to the cottage. Actually looking forward to muesli and soya milk. Mum was in an odd mood. I couldn't decide if it was the school thing or the fact she'd had a seizure. Probably both. I worried again whether my decision about the DVLA had been the right one. Time would tell, I guessed.

'Have you been to one of these sharing circles?' I whispered to Daisy.

'Yeah, loads.' Jealousy flared because she'd been chosen by Alex before, but it was irrational because I knew this was the first one since we'd been there so it wasn't as if I'd been left out.

'What do you talk about?' I had no idea what I was going to share.

'Couldn't tell you that. We call this *Fight Club* for a reason,' said Saffron tapping the side of her nose.

'Why?' My stomach clenched as my fingers drifted to the bruise on my face.

'Because we don't talk about it afterwards.'

I didn't get what she meant, but before I could ask there was a noise from the stairs. Alex's feet appeared. His body. His beautiful, beautiful face. I sat up a little straighter. So did Daisy and Saffron. I suppose Alex had the same effect on all of us, wanting to be the best versions of ourselves.

Alex talked about flesh families before he asked Hazel to share. I was horrified to hear what she'd been through. I didn't know what I could say, but I moved a bit closer to her. I hope she knew that meant I was on her side. She asked if I'd read *The Very Hungry Caterpillar*. I told her that I had.

'You remember what happened at the end of the story, Tilly, *cariad*?'

'He became a butterfly.'

'Yes, somebody else. Free. Reborn. No one ever called him a caterpillar again. That's what I wanted – to feel free. Do you understand, *cariad*?'

'Yes.' And I did. I pulled the sleeves of my black hoodie over my hands. Embarrassed I was still a caterpillar. Hazel looked different somehow, when she'd finished talking. Almost glowing. Alex said unburdening sets you free. I wished I were that brave but it isn't always easy, is it? Finding the right words. Hazel felt her children had betrayed her by taking their dad's side. Was I taking Dad's side by keeping his secret? Would there be a day when it all spilled out and Mum wouldn't want to see me anymore?

It was Mum's turn next. Alex started asking her questions about her unhappy childhood and I fidgeted, uncomfortable I was hearing things I wasn't sure she wanted me to hear. She never talked about the grandparents I'd never met. She spoke about Dad with such love, how he'd arranged parties for her every year. I wished with all my heart that I could remember only the good and forget the bad.

'There is nothing you would change about your past if you could?' Alex asked her.

'There is perhaps always something we would change if we could.' Mum looked directly at me as she said this. She began to cry.

'I'm sorry,' she said.

'It's okay,' I replied. But it wasn't okay if the something she would change was having me.

In my pocket my phone vibrated and while everyone's attention was on Mum, I eased it out and read the message from Rhianon.

Mum's been on a complete rant about honesty & how lying ruins people's lives. I think I should tell her what your dad did. If it comes out & she knows I knew she'll freak

There was a buzzing in my ears. From a distance I heard Mum say, 'We've never made you feel like that have we? Unwanted and unloved. We've never hurt you have we, Tilly? We've never made you feel like that, have we?'

It was because I was so focused on the text message that I didn't think about what I *should* say. I was honest.

'Yes.'

It all got too much and I cried. Mum kept looking over her shoulder and I felt like saying, 'Why don't you just leave if you want to?' but instead I hiccupped, 'Can we talk? Somewhere private,' to Daisy.

'Of course.' Daisy reached for my hand and pulled me to my feet. 'We can go back to your room if you want?'

I nodded.

I knew I needed to tell someone the truth.

CHAPTER TWENTY-NINE

LAURA

'I'm going out.' I couldn't face another cup of tea. Another conversation pretending that everything was okay when it so obviously wasn't. The intensity of the sharing circle seemed to dissipate for everyone as soon as they got back to the house, but for me, second-guessing what Tilly was saying to Daisy upstairs, my agitation increased. That was the thing about being a parent. You hurt more for them than you ever did yourself.

'Where to?' Saffron asked.

'There's a new marketing firm in town that offers a free twenty-minute consultation. I can't afford to employ them, of course, but I might get some tips on how to grow my landscaping business. How to start it from scratch. The florist was already established when I took it over.'

'If you give me half an hour to finish peeling King Edward's mountain I'll come with you,' Saffron said.

'That's okay.' I needed to remove myself from the house. The urge to burst into our room to try to comfort Tilly was growing. She wasn't alone. I had to learn to give her space.

'Alex doesn't usually like us going out on our own. Sometimes the locals can get a bit mouthy.'

That didn't surprise me after the way I'd been treated. 'Sticks and stones,' I said. Nothing could hurt more than the grief that crashed over me in waves at the most unexpected times, and the guilt of my fleeting moments of attraction to Alex. My confused heart needed some space.

'Can still wound,' she finished off the saying, but it wasn't followed by her laughter. It wasn't like her to be so serious.

'Are you okay?'

'Yes. It's a bit sad to hear you making plans for the future.' Saffron had a wistful look on her face. 'Are you really going to leave us?'

'I think it's best for Tilly,' I said, and perhaps best for me. Rationally I knew the pull I felt towards Alex stemmed from loneliness, I didn't love Gavan any less, and I wasn't ready to move on, but sometimes it seemed too tempting, too easy, to try to lose myself in his arms, however momentarily. But I knew I'd hate myself afterwards.

'How so?'

'She's become so withdrawn. I know she wasn't happy at school but… I don't know. At least she was around people then.'

'What are we, chopped liver?'

'You know what I mean. Being here twenty-four-seven. I'm not sure if it's healthy.'

'It's healing and that's what she needs right now. What you both need.'

'It's been a lifesaver and I'm truly grateful. But long term? I just don't see it, but… You're happy living here, right?'

She swept another mound of peelings into a composting tub. 'I feel safer here than I did outside. It's not perfect…' she trailed off as Alex came into the room.

'What's not perfect?' he asked.

'Not you, obvs,' she batted back and I knew our conversation was over.

It was only when I was waiting for Reed to open the gates that I turned her answer over in my mind and thought it strange. I'd asked if she was happy and she said she felt safe. Were happiness and safety so tightly bound they were impossible to separate? Since I was seventeen I'd always carried a degree of doubt. Suspicion. A niggling fear in the background like a throbbing tooth. But Gavan had made me happy. Tilly. How could we have failed to make her feel the same?

Although I'd been looking forward to getting out, the town – once familiar – seemed louder. Brighter. Clutched tightly in the grips of pre-Christmas mania. A sign on the roof of a department store flashed 'eleven sleeps to go'.

It took me three attempts to park my car. I stood at the ticket machine, slowly picking coins out of my purse like a tourist trying to get to grips with foreign currency. It was so long since I'd had to pay for anything.

It had begun to rain. I zipped up my coat as I headed towards the marketing firm. Illuminated candy canes strung from telegraph post to telegraph post. Everything seemed larger than it had, or perhaps I felt smaller, more accustomed to the rolling hills and limitless sky. Here, buildings crowded in on me. Traffic fumes clogged my throat. Shoes pounded the pavements. Rolls of wrapping paper sticking out of carrier bags banged against my legs. Umbrellas dripped rain down my neck. It was too crowded. The air too polluted. Everywhere I turned I was faced with another person, but instead of the smiles I was used to at the farm, every single person avoided eye contact until I began to doubt my own presence. I glanced at my reflection in a shop mirror to reassure myself I was really there. My movements were slow. Leaden. At the farm I'd almost got used to feeling tired all the time. The early mornings and late nights were now second nature, but among the hustle and bustle of a world I didn't quite fit into anymore, it was worse. Almost without thinking my feet led me to where I didn't want to go.

My shop.

Although it wasn't mine anymore.

The windows were now boarded up. The 'Laura's Flowers' sign missing. Gavan and Iwan had hung it while Anwyn and I stood with a bottle of fizzy wine and plastic glasses. When I tried to venture back inside for my camera, Anwyn placed a hand on my arm and told me to wait. Tilly and Rhianon, pigtailed cute with wide happy smiles, stretched green ribbon across the doorway. I laughed as Anwyn pressed scissors into my hand. Everyone applauded as I announced the shop was open, even though I didn't have any stock, and a big cheer rang out from the queue gathered at the bus stop opposite.

Joy.

Gladiator-powerful but equally fragile. Easily shattered.

As I gazed at my failed dreams, I no longer felt confident that I could start a new business.

Someone pushed past me, knocking me off balance and out of my thoughts. He turned to glare at me. I wrapped my arms around myself wishing I was back at the farm.

'I feel safe here,' Saffron had said and I understood. The world was too big.

Too busy.

Too much.

I hurried across the market and that was where I spotted them.

Ashleigh's parents.

They were arm in arm coming out of Seacrest Solicitors, frail and gaunt. I wasn't sure who was holding who up. Mrs Collins, I could no longer think of her as Cathy, stepped onto the pavement on matchstick legs and even from where I stood I could see the lines on her face were deeper than they had been. As a mother my heart ached for her. Ashleigh was supposed to be in remission, and despite all that had passed between us I hoped she hadn't relapsed. I deliberated whether I should go and speak to them. John caught my eye and his face darkened, spine straightened. Shaking off his wife's arm and ignoring her as she tried to call him back, he marched towards me. Sweat dampened my armpits.

'Standing there as if you haven't a care in the world!'

'Mr Collins, I…' I could feel myself shaking.

'There you are!' Shadows fell as I was flanked by Hazel and Saffron. Their shoulders, solid and dependable, pressing against mine. 'Time to go home.'

'Home?' he sneered. 'In with the freaks are you?'

Saffron ushered me away, but as I glanced back over my shoulder Mrs Collins was staring at me with a strange expression on her face that looked a lot like concern. I think she mouthed 'Be careful' but I couldn't be sure.

'Are you okay?' Saffron asked. 'Alex sent us to find you, he was worried about you.'

'I'm fine, but thanks,' I said as we walked to my car. 'A confrontation is the last thing I needed today.'

'Safety in threes,' Hazel said.

'It's a power number,' Saffron sang. 'I'll drive your car, Hazel can follow with the Land Rover.' She held out her hands and I dropped my keys into them. I climbed into the passenger seat, resting my forehead against the window. We stopped at a junction and through the drizzle streaking the windows I spotted Rhianon waiting to cross the road. I cleaned the fog of breath from the window with my sleeve and pressed my palms against the glass. Rain plastered her hair to her scalp and streamed down her cheeks like tears. Our eyes met. The lights turned to green and then we were gone.

As soon as we arrived back at *Gorphwysfa* I rushed upstairs to call Rhianon, rummaging frantically through my bedside drawer for my mobile. It wasn't there. I checked again, fishing through the sparse contents. I dragged the cabinet away from the wall in case it had somehow fallen behind it. There was nothing but dust. I sat down heavily on the bed. I could remember charging it earlier that morning. Had I perhaps taken it into town and lost it? It could have fallen out of my bag when I pulled out my purse. I couldn't remember taking it, but I couldn't remember not taking it either. My head felt heavy. I was so tired.

There was half an hour before dinner. I didn't feel like joining the others in the kitchen. In the lounge I perused Dafydd's collection of books, running my fingers down the dusty spines, easing a copy of George Orwell's *1984* from the shelf, a novel I'd heard much about but never read. Absorbed in the story, I didn't realise Tilly was in front of me until she spoke.

'Hazel's dishing up.'

I smiled. 'Are you okay? Good chat with Daisy?'

'I feel better now, thanks. Sorry about earlier.' I scanned her face. There was something different about her and initially I thought it was because her features seemed so much more relaxed.

'Mum, can I talk to you?'

'About what you said?' I hesitated. Unsure whether I should bring it up.

'Umm, yeah. I know you love me.' She sat cross-legged on the sofa, facing me. 'It's just... Dad...' I waited while she struggled to find the words.

'It's stupid but sometimes it feels Dad dying meant he didn't love me enough to live.'

'It's not stupid, Tilly.' Irrational, I knew, but I had felt the same. I took her hand in mine. 'He did love you. Very much. As do I.'

Rather than averting her gaze, mumbling a response, she looked directly at me and said, 'I love you too, Mum. I... I don't know what I'd do if anything happened to you.'

'Nothing's going to happen to me.'

'But we never know, do we? People get sick. They die. I bet Hazel never thought when she got married her husband would beat her. Or when she had kids she'd end up not speaking to them. Mum.' Her voice fell. 'I wish I could be more open. I am trying. Alex is right about unburdening, I could see that today, but...' She reached for my hand. 'I couldn't bear it if we didn't talk anymore.'

'Tilly, there's nothing you could do or say that would make me not love you. Not want to speak to you.'

'But Hazel...'

'Hazel's situation is different. She still loves her children, she just has to put herself first right now. Nothing will come between us, Tills. Promise.' But my promise was a cold, hard rock in my stomach, wedged between all the things I could never tell her. 'I love you.'

'I love you too, Mum.' She hugged me and I breathed in the scent of raspberry shampoo. I would build us a new life and it wouldn't be better or worse than what we had lost, but it would be different. And we would be happy.

'Let's go and eat,' I said when I finally let her go.

Dinner was relaxed. The atmosphere lighter as though the sharing circle had brought us all closer. Finally, I was properly part of things. Even when we moved out I would still visit. I was tired but feeling positive. It was only as I climbed the stairs to get ready for bed that it struck me what had been different about Tilly. I vowed to ask her about it when she came up.

I pulled back the duvet and reached for my T-shirt.

I almost didn't see it at first. The envelope. The whiteness of the paper blending with the whiteness of my pillow case. There was no name written on the envelope. I stared at it long and hard before picking it up, a gut feeling telling me the contents would be painful.

Three words.

Just three words shakily scrawled in black marker.

Don't trust anyone.

CHAPTER THIRTY

TILLY

The sharing circle had left me feeling tearful and exhausted. Stupid, considering I wasn't the one who had shared. But, alone in my room with Daisy, I was ready to talk.

'My dad's dead too,' Daisy blurted out as she settled herself cross-legged onto my bed. 'Sorry, have I shocked you? It's blunt isn't it, that word. My mum used to say he was "late" and I always wanted to scream at her, he's not late. He's not coming.'

At first I thought about changing the subject, unsure what the right thing to say to her was, but it was awful when people did that when Mum or I mentioned Dad. Quickly breaking eye contact, looking away, edging away like grief was as easy to catch as a cold. My ensuing embarrassment because I'd believed I'd made them feel uncomfortable. Most of all I knew that sometimes I wanted to talk about Dad. Not the sad stuff either.

'Do you want to tell me about him?' I asked.

Daisy twirled the end of her plait around her finger before releasing it in a springing curl. 'I was thirteen. Mum smoked like a chimney. Me and Dad were always begging her to give up. We were terrified she'd get cancer or emphysema or something. In the end it was Dad who fell ill, and when an X-ray showed a tumour on his lungs it seemed…' Again she played with her hair, twisting it harder around her finger until I could see the tip turn white. 'Unfair, and I know I sound like a cow but if anyone was going to get sick it should have been Mum. Christ.' She wiped her eyes with the back of her sleeve. 'It was ten years ago now. It shouldn't hurt this much still.'

'You don't get over it, you just get on with it,' I said quietly. 'I've read about grief online but I hoped that bit wouldn't be true. Like, I'm not going to forget him but, fuck. Ten years, Daisy, and you're still crying.' It all felt so helpless. I flopped back against the wall. The cold plaster pressing against my spine.

'You kind of get used to it but then something will happen and it all comes flooding back. Last month Reed was whistling "Don't Worry, Be Happy", and it was like being punched in the stomach. Dad always whistled that to me. I couldn't catch my breath. Reed was so apologetic when I told him. But then sometimes I have days where I don't think about Dad at all now, and then I remember I haven't thought about him and I feel like the worst daughter ever.'

'I feel like that. I laughed for the first time the other day and then felt terrible, as though I should never laugh again.'

'He wouldn't want you to be unhappy. Neither would your mum. You can tell how much she loves you.'

'Where's… where's your mum?'

She shrugged. 'I dunno. She remarried when I was sixteen. I left home pretty much straight after my exams. We didn't really get on. After Dad died I endlessly googled cancer and pollution. I resented Mum for smoking, but also for having a mobile phone and Wi-Fi in the house. It's why I love it here.'

'Do you think mobiles can cause cancer?'

'I think everything can cause cancer. It's disgusting how irresponsible people can be. It makes me so angry.'

I couldn't maintain eye contact. I had wanted to tell her everything, but if she found out about Ashleigh's illness she would blame our family for building on a landfill site.

'I'd better go.' She unfolded her body from the bed. 'Alex has asked me to settle the drop-ins.'

She headed to the door. I didn't want to be left alone with my thoughts. I didn't want to have to think about Rhianon's text or how I should answer it.

'Can I come?'

'Alex only asked for me but... I guess.'

I hesitated. Unsure if I was wanted. An image of Alex picking me up at school drifted into my mind. He was smiling *that* smile at me. Mind made up, I followed Daisy out of the room.

All I wanted was one friend. Just one.

It wasn't too much to ask, was it?

Outside the dorms, Alex was already talking to the new drop-ins. Two boys and a girl with black roots poking through straw-white hair. I hated the way she was looking at Alex.

'This is Stuart, Andy and Dannii,' Alex introduced us. 'This is Daisy and Tilly. They'll settle you in.'

'It's fucking freezing here.' Stuart glared at me, and I had to stop myself from snapping, 'I'm not responsible for the weather.'

'We need to share body heat.' Dannii giggled, inching closer to Alex. My hands curled into fists as she licked her red glossy lips. 'Where will you be sleeping?' As she touched his arm my stomach contracted.

'I'm in a cottage in the woods.'

'Ooh, aren't you afraid of wolves? But then you look like you aren't afraid of anything.' She squeezed his bicep. His smile slipped a little and I sensed he was embarrassed. I expected Daisy to roll her eyes but instead the muscle in her cheek was tightening over and over, her expression dark.

'Wolves? This is fucking Wales not Canada.' Stuart shrugged off his rucksack and scratched his patchy beard that didn't look half as good as Alex's. He can't have been much older than me.

'I'll show you where to fetch the wood for the burner,' I said.

'We've got to fetch our own wood?' Andy whined. 'Next you'll be telling us we've got to make our own dinner!'

'We're all about reconnecting with nature here, but don't worry, we'll be providing a hot vegan meal,' Alex said.

'Ooh, vegan. Is that why you're is such great shape?' Again the hair flick. Again my fingernails digging into my palm.

'Let's get this over with,' Stuart said. Reluctant to leave Alex, I led him over to the small shelter where the grasses grew tall. Reed was stacking logs.

'This is Reed,' I said. 'He does lots of the odd jobs and stuff.'

'Hello again. We met at the gate,' Reed said.

Stuart and Andy ignored him. Talking among themselves.

'I thought Dannii said glamping. This is totally basic.'

'Yeah, dude. Don't think we'll be staying. If there isn't anywhere for Dannii to plug her straighteners in, she'll freak.'

'Will she, though? Looks like she's pretty taken with Bear Grylls over there.'

I threw a glance over my shoulder and Dannii was still pressed against Alex, her head thrown back in laughter. Alex was smiling that special smile I thought was mine alone.

My head began to buzz.

'Are you okay, Tilly?' Reed asked quietly. 'Do you need some help with Dumb and Dumber?'

'I'm fine, thanks,' I said automatically. But I wasn't.

Dannii had a hand on Alex's chest now, thrusting out her own.

Anger flared. Alex was the one good thing in my life. I could taste my jealousy in the back of my throat. Dannii's grating laughter pealed once more. The sound kick-started my feet. Suddenly I was running full pelt towards them. Screaming, 'Stop!'

CHAPTER THIRTY-ONE

ALEX

'You look like you aren't afraid of anything,' Dannii said. Her face faded from his consciousness as memories poked and prodded at him. He'd been in turmoil all afternoon since Laura's emotional outpouring.

'Birthdays are a particularly vulnerable time,' he had said, but he hadn't solely been talking about her.

Eight today!

Alex couldn't help feeling excited when he saw the banner draped across the lounge. The clusters of green and orange balloons strung from the bannisters. A fat pass-the-parcel, wrapped in newspaper, rested on one of the wonky camping chairs forming a circle, along with the dining chairs.

He'd never had a party before. Had never been invited to a party before. At his last school he had bowed his head, studied his desk, his shoes, looking anywhere except at the invitations being handed out, knowing his name would never be called. He didn't know why. Mum always said it was their loss, but on Monday morning when the other kids would huddle in the playground talking about how great the bowling party was, the football party, the disco, it always felt like his loss, and he felt it keenly. He tried to be like the other boys, but sport didn't interest him and he was rubbish at PE. He couldn't name any of the players in the England squad, but he could identify almost every tree and species of butterfly.

'You're sensitive. There's nothing wrong with that.' Mum smoothed his hair as he cried.

'You're a freak,' his classmates said.

Finally, after coming home with another black eye, another pair of school trousers ruined where he'd been shoved over and grazed his knee, Mum moved him to a new school.

'We'll invite everyone in your class to your party,' she said. 'It will be a fresh start.'

Mum had talked about the parties she'd had as a child, a wistful look in her eyes, and his enthusiasm grew as together they had googled old-fashioned games. Painstakingly he had painted a donkey. It was Blu-Tacked to the back of the door, waiting for its tail to be pinned on.

At eleven thirty he carefully carried plates balanced full of warm sausage rolls with flaky pastry from the kitchen. On the wallpaper table Dad had set up in the conservatory, there were already mountains of oat and cinnamon cookies, and bowls of bright orange cheese balls. His birthday cake was in a box on top of the fridge. He'd wanted one shaped like a cat, but Mum had bought a *Star Wars* one instead.

He sat on the stairs and watched the clock hanging from the wall. The half hour dragged, each minute painstakingly slow, but Alex felt if he took his eye off the time it might slip away. He was longing for noon. It came and went. The doorbell remained silent. At twelve thirty Mum came and took his hand. 'Don't sit here any longer.'

'I want to.' He shook her off. Perhaps he'd written the

invitations wrong. Put one o'clock instead. He watched the hands tick-tick-tick to one, to two. He couldn't drag himself away.

'It's their loss,' Mum said, as always, but it wasn't their loss at all.

It was his, and his alone.

Later, in the kitchen, Mum rummaged through the junk drawer pulling out tea-towels, a ball of string, packets of seeds.

'Where are the rest?' she muttered, holding three candles she'd found in her hand, the wicks burned from where they'd been used last year.

'Never mind,' she smiled brightly as she'd sunk them into buttercream. 'You only need three candles.'

She lit them and told him to make three wishes.

'Why three?' he asked dully.

'Because it's a powerful number and that's how many wishes genies grant.'

He closed his eyes and puffed the flames to smoke.

At school on Monday nobody mentioned his party and neither did he. At break-time he joined the boys in the playground. They were catching daddy long-legs and plucking off their legs one by one. Alex felt sick but he took a turn. Was that what he had to do to fit in? To maim? To kill?

Just like he told Laura to do, he allowed himself to feel the hurt. To feel the pain.

But he still couldn't release it.

CHAPTER THIRTY-TWO

TILLY

'Stop! Alex!' Both he and Dannii turned towards me. When I saw their shocked expressions I realised how loudly I'd been shouting.

'Umm. Can I speak to you in private?'

Dannii spoke quickly, 'Alex, you haven't finished telling me about—'

'It's important,' I cut in.

'Okay, Tilly.' He stretched out his arm and I stepped into it. His hand rested on the small of my back. I swear to God his fingers felt like fire. As we walked, I imagined how it would feel if he lowered his hand. Hooking his fingers inside the pocket of my jeans the way Kieron used to.

'What's up?' he asked as soon as we were out of sight behind the storage barn.

I didn't know what I was doing until I did it. 'I don't want this anymore.' I pulled my mobile out of my pocket and offered it to him. It felt like I was offering myself to him. There was such a feeling of relief. Now I didn't have to worry about any more texts from Rhianon urging me to tell the truth. I didn't have to reply. I'd no longer fritter away hours on everyone else's Instagram feed while my own remained stagnant.

'Why don't you want your mobile anymore, Tilly?'

That surprised me. I thought he'd be pleased. I was left holding out my phone, feeling like an idiot.

'Because.' I searched for the right words. 'Because I'm sick of how fake social media is. The photos. The filters. There's so much pressure to appear perfect. I know everything on my feed isn't true, and sometimes I post how happy I am even though I feel like shit, I still think everyone else's feed must be... true. They're all having the best time and I... I'm not. Not having the best time.' I was breathless when I'd stuttered it all out.

'I'm proud of you, Tilly. It's a big step.' He was smiling *that* smile again, but that time it was for me and for me alone. 'I know how important all that social media is to you kids.'

'I'm *not* a kid.'

'I guess you're not.' His fingers lingered on mine as he took my phone, never once breaking eye contact. I took a small step forward and then faltered feeling horribly out of my depth as I gazed at him, willing him to see the real me. I noticed it all, the protrusion of his Adam's apple as he swallowed hard, the slight tilt of his head. The way he leaned towards me.

He was going to kiss me.

'Alex! Where are you?' Dannii called. Her brittle voice shattering the moment. 'I need you!'

He straightened up.

'Sorry, Tilly.'

As I watched him walk away, I wondered whether he was apologising for nearly kissing me or for not kissing me. He didn't once glance back. Had I imagined it all? I pressed two fingers against my lips as he rounded the corner. They felt dry and cold.

Running everything through my mind, I strode back to the farmhouse. I didn't think twice about letting myself in through the backdoor without knocking. Relinquishing my phone had made me feel like a member of the family.

'You look thoughtful?' Saffron said.

'Yes. I've given up my mobile.'

'How did that feel?'

'Good. Now I'm not going back to school I want to embrace the lifestyle.'

'One of us.'

'One of you.' For the first time in a long time I fitted in.

'Not quite' she said, and my spirits began to sink until she added, 'Come with me.'

Mum was sitting in the lounge, her legs tucked under her on the sofa, only Dylan keeping her company as he sprawled across the rug in front of the fire, clumps of his ginger fur sticking to the pile. I was nervous when I told Mum dinner was ready, expecting her to criticise my outfit, but she looked pleased to see me. I should have sought her out earlier. She'd found the sharing circle tough too, and I'd left her alone.

'Mum, can I talk to you?'

'About what you said?' she asked.

'Umm, yeah,' I said although it hadn't been about that at all. 'I know you love me.' It was going to be an awkward conversation but I couldn't keep running away from everything I found difficult. I wanted to change. To be more like everyone there. Mum and I should have been on the same team. I sat cross-legged on the sofa and leaned back against the arm, the white of the clothes Saffron had lent me stark against the dark leather. 'It's just… Dad…' I wasn't sure if she'd understand but sometimes I was furious with Dad for dying. To have taken away my chance to ask him why he behaved so badly. If he regretted it. So much was unanswered. So much unresolved. I was the one left fabricating two-sided conversations in my head, always wondering how it would have played out. There were times I had thought I had the harder job, being the one who stayed. He never had to worry about anything again. 'It's stupid but sometimes it feels Dad dying meant he didn't love me enough to live.'

'It's not stupid, Tilly.' She took my hand. We weren't so different, I realised. She must have felt abandoned too. 'He did love you. Very much. As do I.' Mum had often told me she loved me; as I was flying out the door, on the end of a text, before I went to bed. When I was little I used to say it back all the time. I don't know why I stopped, if I was embarrassed or if I just took it for granted that she knew. Imagine if she wasn't there either, and I had never told her how I felt. Another regret I'd carry.

I looked her in the eye and said clearly, 'I love you too, Mum.' The lines on her face became fainter in front of my eyes, and I wondered whether she *had* known it. 'I… I don't know what I'd do if anything happened to you.' The world already seemed too big to cope with. I couldn't bear the thought of trying to navigate it alone.

'Nothing's going to happen to me.'

'But we never know, do we? People get sick. They die.' I wanted to ask whether you could die from a seizure. I'd purposefully not googled it. The internet was always flooded with horror stories, not happy endings. 'I bet Hazel never thought when she got married her husband would beat her. Or when she had kids she'd end up not speaking to them. Mum.' My throat was tight. 'I wish I could be more open. I am trying. Alex is right about unburdening, I could see that today, but…' I had to find a way to let it all out before it drove me completely crazy. She reached for my hand. 'I couldn't stand it if we didn't talk anymore.' That was what it always circled back to. The fear that kept the things I wanted to say inside.

'Tilly, there's nothing you could do or say that would make me not love you. Not want to speak to you.'

'But Hazel—'

'Hazel's situation is different. She still loves her children, she just has to put herself first right now. Nothing will come between us, Tills. Promise. I love you.'

'I love you too, Mum.' We hugged. One of those big, child-hood embraces that I'd always squirmed away from as I got older. I'd forgotten the smell of her. How soft her hair felt against my cheek. I squeezed her harder. I couldn't bear another regret. I just couldn't.

'Let's go and eat,' she said, when I eventually let her go and again, the thing I really wanted to say was left unsaid.

After dinner I sat drinking herbal tea with the others. The taste didn't make me screw my face up anymore, and long for a caramel Frappuccino. Mum was asleep by the time I tiptoed into the bedroom. She hadn't drawn the curtains so I got ready for bed by the light of the moon. The sheets were cold as I slipped between them. I lay there thinking about my future, my new future, tossing up the objections I knew Mum would make and knocking them away with my logic. Alex was going to teach me the business side and involve me in marketing. It made more sense than running up a huge student debt gaining a degree that didn't guarantee me a job. Instead I would gain experience in the field I wanted to work in, and that would look good on my CV when I decided to move on.

If I decided to move on.

My eyes began to feel heavy. Without my phone I had no idea what the time was, but I knew it was late. Night-time at the farm was so black. There had always been the glow of the lamppost outside my window back home, the flash of headlights from passing cars, the light from the landing filtering through the crack under my door. At the farm it was as if I was being covered with a thick blanket. Often the darkness made me feel like the only person in the world. Sometimes I thought I deserved to be, and I had to lie really still and try to calm myself. Other times I liked feeling as if there was only me.

I think it's because it was so dark that it was easy to spot.

The flickering light outside.

At first I thought it must have been a shooting star. Rhianon and I would always make a wish. But then it came.

A faint cough.

If I'd been at home, with double glazing, I probably wouldn't have heard it, but there, with the ancient sash windows that let in a draught, I knew what I had heard.

There was somebody outside.

Instinctively, I swung my legs out of bed and padded over to the window. Peering outside I could see a small shaft of light bobbing up and down. Someone was carrying a torch, keeping to the shadows as they headed towards the woods.

Something was wrong. The back of my neck felt freezing. My heart began to race.

The house was still. Silent. I hadn't heard the front door and I knew whoever was out there wasn't one of us.

I was just about to wake Mum up when I remembered the drop-ins. Dannii. The way she'd looked at Alex. Twirling her hair around her fingers. Asking where he slept. Anger pushed anxiety aside as I imagined her stalking towards Alex's cottage. Climbing into bed beside him.

Honestly, I don't know what got into me but I couldn't resist the urge to go and confront her. Tell her she shouldn't be wandering around at night. I'd had enough of being pushed to the side-lines at school. I wouldn't allow it to happen there too.

Without waking Mum, I inched open the door and padded downstairs. Mum's wellies were on the doormat. I stuffed my feet into them. I dragged her coat from the hook and put it on, grabbing the Maglite out of her pocket.

It was freezing. My nose started running almost as soon as I was outside. The light was dimming. Moving further away. I began to run across the field before I lost sight of it completely.

In the woods, the trees swallowed me up. A shadow. A rustle. I knew that whoever I was following was close.

Edging forward, I shone my torch at the ground, searching for tree stumps that could trip me. I was so intent on watching my feet I didn't see it.

The cold, damp thing that slapped against my face.

Dazed. I stumbled.

The coppery taste of blood in my mouth, in my nostrils.
Raising the torch I spun around. Terror shaking me.
I whimpered, not quite believing what I was seeing.
Hanging from the trees were rabbits.
Skinned rabbits.
It was then I began to scream.

CHAPTER THIRTY-THREE

LAURA

Once I watched a documentary about the bond between mother and baby. A study had proven that a mother could identify their child's cry among other children's. MRI scans showed heightened activity in the caregiving region of the brain when their baby was distressed. The programme explained how a reaction in the mothers of oxytocin and other brain chemicals reinforced the urgency of a child in need, and the average time it took for them to respond was five seconds.

I had jumped out of bed and was halfway across the room before I consciously knew what I was doing.

The scream came again.

Tilly.

Downstairs, my wellies were missing. I jammed my feet into someone else's pair and flung open the door. The night air snatched my breath as I began to run, instinctively knowing which direction my daughter was in.

Five seconds.

It had already been longer.

Oh, how a life could irrevocably alter in five seconds. In four seconds.

Three.

Two.

One.

My mind began to roar as an image sprung at me with sharpened claws.

Tilly, bloodied and bruised.

Please don't hurt me. Please don't hurt me.

I ran.

The scar on my forehead buzzed danger.

My vision tunnelled, the too-big wellies slipping every time my feet slammed against the ground. The image of Tilly begging turned back to me until I was sprinting towards the past, and it was me bloodied and bruised. Me begging, *please don't hurt me*. Hands around my neck morphed into hands around my daughter's neck.

Five seconds.

I was taking too long. My eyes narrowed, my teeth bared as I pounded forward, knowing that I would kill anyone who tried to hurt my baby.

'Tilly!' Momentarily I stopped running and tilted my face to the sky. My scream was primal, filling the infinite space surrounding me. My anguished desire to be with my daughter was palpable. The moon caught Tilly's name with her hands and floated it back down to me in a different form.

'Mum!'

The rush of relief that she was able to answer me seemed to yank the bones from my legs, and I was staggering forwards on rubber, trying to keep upright.

As soon as I entered the woods I saw the torchlight ahead. I could hear Tilly's sobbing. A man's voice. And then nothing.

Five seconds.

I was too late.

My heart was bursting out of my ribs when I found them. Tilly's face pressed against his chest. His arms around her. Her body shaking.

'I heard her screaming,' Reed said. 'Laura, I don't know what sick fuck's done this but it wasn't like this an hour ago when I did the rounds. We need to get her out of here. Now.' He ushered Tilly towards me, while I tried to decipher what 'this' meant. In the moonlight I could see her face was deathly pale. Streaked with blood.

'You're hurt.'

'It's not my blood,' Tilly whispered.

It was then I noticed the rabbits.

My heart stuttered.

Snapping twigs.

Someone was coming.

'Run,' whispered Reed. 'I'm going to find out who did this.'

I grabbed hold of Tilly's hand and ran as though our lives depended on it. I ran as though I could escape the stinging memories of my past.

Please don't hurt me.

As though I could escape my present.

Don't hurt my daughter.

'Mum!'

A wrenching pain in my shoulder as Tilly stumbled, losing her footing. I yanked her upright like a marionette. Tugging her forward. Urging her on. The farmhouse fixed firmly in my sights.

My neck was exposed to the cold air, to the sour breath of the shadow who haunted my dreams and still now, after all this time, lurked at the corners of my mind. My throat vulnerable.

Fingers squeezing. Squeezing.

Run.

The farmhouse door was open – I hadn't closed it properly when I left – and I propelled Tilly forward, releasing her hand so she fell into the kitchen before me. We tumbled to the floor with our fear and confusion. I scrambled to my knees and slammed the door, locking it. Checking the handle once, twice.

'Mum.' Tilly's voice was thin and small.

'It's okay.' I scooped her into my arms, feeling her body tremble against mine as the stitch in my side began to unpick itself.

'The rabbits…' she began to cry.

'It's okay,' I said, although it wasn't.

It wasn't okay at all. She had every right to be terrified.

I was too.

The brandy burned my throat, heated my stomach, but still I didn't feel warm.

'Here.' Alex refilled my glass.

'She was so scared.' I placed my hand on Tilly's leg, partly to reassure myself that she was there. That she was safe. Drained with shock, she'd fallen asleep on the sofa while Alex and Reed cut the carcasses from the trees. I'd draped her with the mint-and-cream crocheted blanket that hung over the armchair, and watched her sleep, the way I had when she was brand new. The rise and fall of her chest. My heart catching in my throat if the pause between breaths stretched too long. The relief as she stirred. I had left the maternity ward clutching my baby and a pink stork helium balloon that floated as high as my hopes that I wouldn't get this wrong. But I also took something else home that day.

Fear.

The new parent terror that something would go wrong had never really left me. We fumbled our way through the stages, Gavan and I, reassuring each other it would get easier. But Tilly grew and the etheric cord stretched as she ventured out into a world filled with things that could hurt her, and I found I never relaxed at all. Not properly.

'Who do you think it was?' I asked again, keeping my voice low.

'Whoever it was has long gone. Reed and I couldn't find anyone.'

'But who could…'

'Shh. Don't think about it,' Alex said.

'I can't stop thinking about it.' The red raw flesh. The blood. 'Perhaps we should leave.'

'That seems a bit extreme?'

'Hanging dead rabbits from trees seems a bit extreme. Even if the locals don't like what you're doing here.'

Alex took a sip of brandy while I slugged mine. 'Here's the thing, Laura.' He swallowed hard. 'I'm not wholly convinced tonight was about us.'

'Who was it about then?' But even as I asked, the expression on his face told me who it was about. 'Me?'

He shrugged. 'I didn't want to tell you because you've had so much on your plate and I'm going to deal with it, but we had a phone call this afternoon from Seacrest Solicitors.'

The name was familiar but it took me a second to place it.

'What did they want?' Worry pulled me to my feet.

'They wanted to confirm this was your postal address. It seems Ashleigh's parents, Mr and Mrs Collins, are building a case against Gavan's estate. They're claiming toxic waste had percolated through the ground water and caused all kinds of diseases.'

'What estate?' Nervous laughter bubbled in my throat, as bitter as the alcohol that swam through my veins. 'But I was nothing to do with the business.'

'Unfortunately on the paperwork you are named as a director.'

'In name only, and solely to enable us to draw dividends without paying masses of tax. What about Iwan?'

'He's liable too, of course. And Anwyn's also a director. I should imagine they've already had letters but the solicitor wasn't sure where you'd moved to. Until today.'

'And what would happen if they were successful?'

'Potentially an unlimited fine and five years in prison for breaching environmental law, but it's highly unlikely they'll win. They're clutching at straws. It seems coincidental though that the day your address is confirmed... well.'

I thought of the look of contempt on Mr Collins's face in town earlier. Could it have been him who hung the rabbits?

I paced over to the window. The glass was a mirror in the darkness. I imagined someone shadowed by the trees staring directly at me. I shivered.

'Reed's going to activate the electric fence. We switch it off to keep costs down. No one will be able to come and go without him knowing. You're safe here. I promise.'

He placed his hand on my shoulder. I leaned back, my spine pressing against his chest. It felt too natural. Too dangerous. Too much of everything I shouldn't feel. His heart beat solid and steady. My wedding ring burned hot against my skin as though it was branding me.

Gavan. I was Gavan's.

'I'll look after you,' Alex murmured.

I stared out at the moon and it stared back at me, but as Alex whispered, 'Trust me,' I stiffened. The words of the note on my bed dried the thank you on my lips. Reluctantly, I stepped away from him.

Don't trust anyone.

CHAPTER THIRTY-FOUR

TILLY

'You're safe here now,' I heard Alex whisper to me. 'I promise.'

White.

I was wearing white, we all were. We were singing and dancing and lighting up the darkness with our brilliance.

I was one of the beautiful people.

Throwing back my head towards the moon I stretched out my arms and began to turn.

Faces blurred and merged into one another; smiling and laughing; everyone loved me.

Dizzy.

I was pirouetting faster.

Stop.

I tried to keep my eyes fixed on Alex.

'I'll look after you,' he said, but he was walking away, his arm around Dannii.

Stop.

Hands touching me, pulling me, spinning me.

Features loomed and disappeared. Daisy, Hazel, Ashleigh. Mum. Saffron. Dad.

Daddy.

He was there again. Real again. Dad's hands cupping my face. *Promise you won't tell, Tilly.*

Stop.

I was slowing. Faces unscrambled their features and it wasn't Mum or Dad or anyone I loved.

Rabbits.

Blood dripping. Flesh hanging from bones. Jaws open. Bared teeth. Snapping. Snapping. Snapping.

I woke. My cheeks wet with tears.

'Trust me,' whispered Alex and I opened my eyes. It took me a second to realise I was on the sofa. In front of the window were Mum and Alex. She was leaning back against him while he murmured soft words that felt hard. I squeezed my eyes shut again as my fingers clutched the crotcheted blanket tighter and tighter.

Feigning sleep still, I rolled onto my side, burying my face into a cushion. Behind me I could hear their whispers but they didn't know I was awake. They didn't know I was crying.

CHAPTER THIRTY-FIVE

LAURA

It was days after the rabbit incident before I could tear myself away from Tilly's side, and during that time I hadn't once suggested she go to school. Each morning at 5.30 a.m., she'd got up without complaint and pitched in with the contributions without being asked. Violet rings circled her eyes. She was pale, as white as the clothes she now chose to wear. Another thing we hadn't yet talked about. After our conversation about Gavan on the afternoon of the sharing circle, I'd been hopeful it had set a tone for a more open relationship, but since her gruesome discovery in the woods she had retreated into herself. I had tried to find out why she was wandering around alone in the dark, but the conversation had been one-sided. Full of shrugs. At least I hadn't had another letter. I hadn't told anyone about it, not sure who sent it. Who to trust.

'Can I talk to you later, Alex?' I asked, as I cleared away his dinner plate. 'In private?'

'Of course. Come over to the cottage.' He slipped his arms into his leather jacket and tugged a beanie low over his head.

Another half hour passed before I'd finished drying the dishes Hazel was washing, and after checking Tilly was okay with me going, I was ready to leave.

'Please keep an eye on her,' I asked Saffron.

'She'll be fine – go!' She half pushed me towards the door when I didn't move. 'We'll have a good time. We're going to try a natural facemask aren't we, Tills? Honey and oats. We'll be like proper sisters!' She slung her arm over Tilly's shoulders, who offered her first smile in days.

'I'm fine, Mum.'

The ground was already frosted, crunching underfoot. The beam from my Maglite, jolting with every step, the yellow light picking out the white stones that led the way to the cottage. Every few steps I aimed the beam upwards, checking the trees for rabbits. Just in case.

Alex was shower fresh as he threw open the door. Hair damp, smelling of soap and shampoo. After taking off my outdoor things, I followed him through to the lounge, closing the porch door behind me to keep out the draught.

'Glass of wine?'

'Please.' I crouched in front of the fire, holding my hands out to warm them. 'Do you have a poker?' I asked as Alex returned from the kitchen. 'The flames are dying down.'

'No. It's one of those things that I never remember to pick up.' He threw another log on. A dullness, a sizzle before the flames roared once more, smoke curling around my nostrils, but I liked the smell.

'What's on your mind?' he asked, bypassing the small talk. He pressed a button on the iPod before slugging red wine into two glasses and handing one to me. Norah Jones sang 'Don't Know Why'. He drank. His lips stained crimson. Settling onto the sofa, I took a sip.

'I still can't find my phone.'

'I wonder if one of the drop-ins stole it? I didn't like the look of those two lads, although I think they were terrified after the rabbit incident, running off home early. I'm glad Dannii decided to extend her stay. She's a sweet girl and it's so quiet this time of year, the money will come in handy.'

'Wherever it is, I need to go into town to get a replacement. It's just that I'm…' I took another sip, larger this time.

'Scared?'

I nodded. Waiting for him to reassure me that my fears were unfounded.

'I think you're right to be cautious, Laura. This business with Mr and Mrs Collins. The suspicion hanging over Gavan's death. You're safer here for now. We've tightened security, switched on the fence. Whoever hung the rabbits won't be back. I promise.'

'But…' I wanted to tell him about the letter. That must have come from somebody there, surely? *Don't trust anyone.* Did that include Alex? 'There's stuff I need to buy for my business. I've only got a few hundred pounds left and the car needs a new exhaust before its MOT. I have to start earning.'

'Speaking of MOTs.' He passed me a brown envelope. 'This came from the DVLA. Your tax must be due, too?'

Shaking my head, I tore open the letter.

Regarding your recent change in health… Please fill in and return the enclosed FEP1 form within fourteen days…

Panic distorted the words in front of my eyes.

'But I don't…' My hands shook as I held out the letter. Alex frowned as he began to read. 'I didn't.' I drained my glass welcoming the way my head began to swim. 'I'm going to lose my licence.'

'And you didn't inform them?'

'No. Hardly anyone knew. You, Saffron, Daisy, Hazel.' I jumped from one name to the next, suspecting them all.

'Tilly?'

'What? She wouldn't…'

'Why wouldn't she?' Alex topped up my glass again. I drank deeply. 'She, more than anyone, would want to keep you safe. She's just lost one parent, it must be terrifying for her to think you could potentially have a seizure while driving. That she could lose you too.'

'But I haven't told her I'm ill.'

'We don't always need words to point out what's in front of us.'

'Yes, but… Oh…' I recalled our conversation:

'I… I don't know what I'd do if anything happened to you.'

'Nothing's going to happen to me.'

'But we never know do we? People get sick. They die.'

'She knows,' I said quietly.

Silence fell, thick and uncomfortable. My skin prickling with the knowledge that again, I'd let my daughter down. And shame. It prickled with shame. Tilly was right to be concerned. I could have killed someone if I'd had a seizure driving. I'd fiercely wanted it to be one-off. I should have reported it myself when it happened again. What was I going to do? Without a car, my business was finished before I'd even started it, but that seemed inconsequential compared to the worry I had put my daughter through. Imagine if she'd witnessed me having a seizure? I should have warned her it was a possibility.

'I should have talked to Tilly myself and explained it all properly,' I said, after Alex had fetched another bottle. 'No wonder she's been tiptoeing around me. Asking if I'm okay. God, what a mess. This could mean twelve months at least without a car. I'll have to live in town so we can use buses when we need to, but that's going to make it impossible to run the business. I'll have to find something else to do.'

'Laura, you don't need to be thinking about that right now.'

'But I do. There's only me to think about this stuff.'

'I hate to point out the obvious but you can't afford to leave yet. It could still be months.'

'Fuck.' I held out my glass for a refill. I was floating on a cloud of alcohol, my words pouring like rain. 'Is this going to be the thing that defines us now? Alex, I'm… I'm so scared that even though Tilly had a happy childhood with two parents who adored her, that this is the thing that will shape her. The thing she'll always remember. That her mum couldn't even provide a real home for her. She'll go through life feeling that I've failed her. That she can't rely on anyone.'

I wasn't sure whether saying the words aloud would make my fears something else. Something less. Or whether giving them weight and shape would allow them to grow. As I finished speaking I exhaled, slow and lengthy. Sometimes it was more exhausting releasing emotions than keeping them in.

'Laura.' Alex paused until my eyes found his. 'Twelve days. Twelve weeks. Twelve months. For as long as you want, this is your home and we'll all do our best to make sure Tilly knows she has everyone's support. She'll be fine. I promise you.'

I placed my hand over his and squeezed gratefully. If it weren't for everyone there Tilly and I really would have been alone.

Flesh family.

Chosen family.

Perhaps the farm was where we belonged, because ultimately isn't that what everyone seeks?

Understanding.

Love.

There was a stirring within me. A longing that I thought had died when Gavan had.

A need.

I should have moved away from Alex when he leaned in and tucked my hair behind my ear.

A tender gesture.

A lie.

The scar on my forehead stung naive.

But I was already lost. Hopelessly, irretrievably lost.

That's the only way I can begin to explain what came next.

CHAPTER THIRTY-SIX

Tilly

It was late at night when I woke. Not yet morning.

Nightmares had filled my sleep again. Rabbits hanging from the trees, swaying in the wind and each time one moved I caught a glimpse of Alex behind it kissing Saffron. Daisy. Dannii who should have gone home by now, but had chosen to stay on without her friends. But never, ever kissing me.

I rolled over.

The moon was bright and white, shining on Mum's empty bed. At least if she was still with Alex, Dannii couldn't be.

And that had to be better, didn't it?

Alex with Danni.

Alex with Mum.

I didn't know which was worse.

CHAPTER THIRTY-SEVEN

LAURA

'If I could wave a magic wand and make everything right for you, believe me I would. All I want is for everyone to be happy.' Alex brushed the hair from my face while I gripped the edge of the sofa, feeling I might float away without a solid weight. I shivered. My body wanting one thing, my head something else entirely, and my heart? It thudded frantically inside my ribcage.

I had felt bone-cold for weeks, in memory of my late husband. Didn't I deserve to feel the warmth of happiness, however fleetingly?

'Laura.' There was something in the way he said my name that reminded me of maple syrup drizzled on warm pancakes. 'Laura.' Almost a whisper. 'Look at me.' The golden flecks in his eyes danced and sang and beckoned me forwards. 'I hate to see you in such emotional pain. I can help you if you let go of the struggle. Stop resisting what you feel. Please.'

Neither of us moved. Neither of us spoke. Gavan and I used to watch wildlife documentaries on the BBC and in that moment I was that quivering antelope full of fear and regret, I was that lion brimming with bravado and hope. In both cases, utterly lost at the mercy of a primal instinct that rubbed its hands together in glee as I pressed myself hard against Alex, my lips on his.

The temperature plummeted as he instantly drew away.

'This isn't what you need,' he said. 'It isn't what you want. You're not ready for a relationship, are you?'

In truth, I had no idea what I wanted but I did want something from him and I thought he felt the same. Still, I quickly said, 'No,' afraid of being judged. I'd only been a widow for a few months and despite what my clumsy advance may have portrayed, I still loved my husband intensely. Embarrassment melded with my loneliness.

'I'm so sorry.' My voice a whisper. My apology not only to him. 'I thought you wanted…' I trailed off, dejected. It had felt raw and natural to kiss him, but his rejection turned it into something dirty and sullied.

'I want to help you heal, Laura. Sleeping together might feel right in this moment, but I think you'd hate yourself tomorrow and feel you have to leave, and I want you and Tilly to stay.'

'I should go.'

'Don't. Please. If you go now it's just going to feel strained and awkward between us and I don't want that, do you?'

'No.' But I was mortified. 'I can't believe I kissed you.'

'No one has to know but if there's tension between us…'

'Tilly can't find out.'

'She won't. Please don't be embarrassed. We're friends. I care about you. You and Tilly.' Alex topped up my wine and I swiftly drained it, waiting for the hard hit of alcohol to numb my humiliation.

'Look, Alex. I don't know what came over me.' I couldn't look him in the eye. 'I don't usually… I mean, I've never—'

'It's okay. Honestly.' But he didn't place a hand on my arm as he usually would when I was upset. There was no comforting squeeze of my shoulder. The thought that I had mistaken his friendly gestures for something else, something more, filled me with shame. I couldn't look up. Couldn't meet his eyes.

'Laura, say something. Please.'

'I don't know what to say.' My cheeks were still blazing. 'I thought…' I picked my glass up again. 'I thought just for a moment I might… I might forget. No, not forget, that's the wrong word. Normal. I suppose I wanted to feel normal, how-ever temporary that feeling might be.'

'You are normal, and very desirable, but—'

'Oh God.' I shook my head. 'You're making it worse.'

'How about we don't mention it again?'

'Please.' Although I knew the memory would slick my skin with a cold, clammy sweat for weeks to come; it wasn't just the rejection making me feel so wretched, it was the fact I'd wanted Alex. I twisted the gold band around on my finger remembering the day Gavan had slipped it on.

Reading me, Alex said, 'Forging a new life for yourself doesn't mean you loved your husband any less. It's not a betrayal to smile again. To laugh again. Even… to love again, one day.'

I shook my head vehemently. 'I'll never fall in love again.' Craving comfort, companionship was one thing, but love? To open my heart up to someone else might mean closing it down to Gavan, and I could never do that.

'Perhaps it's as much about falling in love with yourself as anyone else. Feeling spiritually satisfied.'

I thought about that for a moment, and found myself willing to try to let go of my embarrassment. After all, I was lucky that somebody cared about me. That I had a friend.

'Can I be honest with you?' I tucked my legs under me. The

lingering shards of shame instinctively closing my body as I opened my heart. 'I don't feel strong enough. It's so bloody frightening when I think of a future without Gavan. Wondering what that future will look like. It's terrifying there's only me, and I've no family to fall back on.'

'You have us now.' There was a sincerity to his words that convinced me we could move past the almost-kiss.

'I'm talking about... my flesh family, I suppose. Anwyn, well she's Anwyn... But Iwan? He promised me once that he'd never let me down, but he has. Why did he leave Anwyn, and why did Rhianon say they were arguing about getting their stories straight?'

'About the night Gavan died?'

'Yes.'

'Have you told the coroner?'

'No. I'd already made my statement when I found that out. I was hoping to confront Iwan and ask him to be honest.' I gave a wry laugh. 'Honest. There are far too many skeletons in this family.' Wine loosened my tongue, but not enough to share that I had my own reasons for not wanting the coroner to dig too deeply. 'What do you think I should do?'

'I don't know. It sounds like Rhianon has been through a lot with her parents separating, her dad leaving, her uncle dying, and you and Tilly moving away. Perhaps wait to see what the investigation throws up?'

'You're right.' Rhianon was the reason I was holding back. 'In the meantime I do try to stay positive for Tilly. Make plans to buy our own home, to start a new business, and every time I try I get knocked back down again. The insurance not paying, and now I'm going to lose my driving licence.'

'Perhaps that's the universe stepping in and showing you where you need to be.'

'Here?' I shook my head. 'I don't think so.' Especially not after that night. Despite my confusion I knew that whether they stemmed from loneliness or gratitude, I had developed feelings for Alex. Feelings he clearly didn't reciprocate. And I needed some space between us to unpick them. 'I'm thankful for all you've done. I don't know where I'd be without you, but we don't belong here. Not long term. I want to discover who I am now. To achieve something. To build something. To make Tilly proud of me. I feel I've failed her in so many ways.'

'You can do all of those things here. If you can let go of the past and who you were.'

'How do I do that?' I was desperate to know. Desperate to stop the hurt I felt inside.

'You've the chance for a fresh start. Reinvention. You can be whoever you want to be.'

'What if I don't know who I want to be?' I was no longer a wife. A florist.

'You be brave. Do something out of character. Stepping out of your comfort zone is where the magic happens. Look at Hazel. For years she was downtrodden Eilwen, and then she decided she didn't want to be that person anymore and look at her now. She's happy.'

'Even with a name change you're still the same person inside, aren't you?'

'Or perhaps you become the person you were meant to be. You don't look like a Laura.'

'What do I look like?' My mind sloshed with alcohol. I didn't know what to do. Who to be.

'I don't know.' He tilted his head to one side as he appraised me. 'Aurora?'

'Aurora?' The word dripped with disappointment. Aurora was butterfly soft: fragile wings, easily broken.

'Aurora was the mythical Roman goddess of the dawn.'

Tears stung the back of my throat. Gavan used to call me his goddess. How could I have tried to kiss another man?

'It's emotional to think of shedding your old self, but a new name will be empowering. Laura was given to you by your parents, and they didn't love you, did they? Not really. They cast you aside. You can be anyone you want to be. We never develop if we don't evolve.'

Laura. The name Gavan would whisper in his dreams. I couldn't let it go. I'd be letting go of us.

'I'm happy with Laura.' For the first time in a long while I was certain of something. My name was real and solid, a weight I carried in both hands. A bridge between the past and the present. The now. 'Thank you.' My eyes found his. 'I think I've learned something about myself tonight.'

'That you're settling? Haven't you ever wanted to be someone else? Something else?'

'Haven't you?' I bounced back at him and for a fraction of a second a wave of pain crashed over his face before he rearranged his features into ocean calm once more. But in that millisecond he had been open. Vulnerable.

'Here, I've found the space to be the real me,' he said. 'Will you think about staying, Laura? Longer term?'

'Alex, I just don't know. All I know for certain is that as long as I'm with Tilly, I'll be okay. We'll both be okay if we stick together. Once the money comes through I'll talk to her properly about what she wants, and we'll take it from there.' A thought struck me. 'Alex, promise me you won't try to change Tilly's name while we're here.'

'Isn't it up to…'

'*Promise* me.' My voice was thick with tears. 'Gavan chose Matilda. It's all she has left of him.'

'Don't cry. I promise. It's a beautiful name. Don't cry.'

But still, I did.

The stones glowed white under my torchlight as I hurried through the woods and back to the farmhouse.

Despite the biting cold I could still feel the warmth of his thumbs on my cheek. Alex. The second man I had ever kissed. *The third*, whispered the mocking demon and I pushed it away. I wouldn't think of him. I wouldn't. I couldn't. Alex was the second man. He was. He was. He was.

It was still one too many.

The damp air had chilled me to the bone by the time I tiptoed into the bedroom, quietly closing the door behind me. The room smelled sweetly of honey. I hoped Tilly had had a good time making facemasks with Saffron.

'Are you awake?' I whispered. There was no telltale deep breathing, but she didn't reply. I squinted to make her out but she was curled into a ball, not splayed across the bed, arms spread wide like she'd usually be. I hoped I hadn't disturbed her.

Shivering, I discarded my clothes onto the floor and pulled the T-shirt from underneath my pillow.

An owl screeched and suddenly, inexplicably, there was fear filling the room, my skin crawling with some kind of warning I didn't understand.

I slipped under the duvet and pulled it up to my chin.

It was when I stretched out my legs that I felt it.

Fur.

Dampness.

Immediately the rabbits sprung to mind. My throat swelled with a scream.

My bare feet slapped against the floor as I jumped out of bed. The lamp crashed to its side as I fumbled to switch it on, bulb smashing.

'Mum?'

I whimpered into the dark. Running towards the light switch. A sliver of glass from the broken bulb sliding into my heel. The pain was excruciating. Bright light flooded the room and tentatively I hobbled back over to the bed although I didn't want to know what was there. Not really.

Gingerly I eased back the covers exposing the bloodstained sheet.

Nausea rose as I stared in horror at the thing in my bed.

It wasn't a rabbit at all.

It was a rat.

A headless rat.

CHAPTER THIRTY-EIGHT

TILLY

Sometimes I thought my nostrils still carried traces of the scent of the rabbits. Their flesh. Their blood. But I knew it was impossible for the smell to have lingered. It must have been two weeks, but without the timetable of school I was losing track of time. It was all getting mixed up in my head. The good, the bad. What had happened. What I deserved. I was stupidly tired. Once I had thought school was exhausting. Concentrating in lessons, worrying about exams. The stack of homework. But having left sixth form I was finding my new schedule just as challenging. The hours were harsh. The manual labour gruelling. Alex was going to teach me the business side, but first I needed to experience how everything worked from the ground up. My muscles ached all the time.

'How do you cope?' I'd asked Saffron once.

'You get used to it. It's harder for you because you've started in winter with the lack of daylight. We all feel it more with the dark mornings and evenings. You wait until summer. You'll be leaping out of bed with the larks.'

Her assumption that we'd still be there next year chased away my tiredness, putting a smile on my face that lasted the whole day.

I was working with Mum and Daisy. We were in the dining room sorting through the packaging collected from customers. We aimed to reuse everything ten times if we could. I placed another icepack on the pile for the freezer, and checked the wool we wrapped around them to keep them cool was okay to use again.

Dylan batted my shin with his head.

'Hello, you.' I leaned forward and scratched him behind his ear. He half-closed his eyes and purred. 'He's so sweet.'

'You wouldn't say that if he'd left a rat in your bed,' Daisy laughed. Mum didn't.

'I still don't thi—'

'Mum! Every time you say that you're literally accusing someone here of beheading a rodent!' I wished she'd stop. Talk about unforgiving. The atmosphere wasn't always great with her around lately. There was tension between her and Alex, but I didn't think she should blame him for Dylan's natural instincts. It wasn't fair.

'It's better he hunts,' Daisy said again. 'Cats have a larger carbon footprint than you'd think. The meat production for their food—'

'Don't you listen.' I covered Dylan's ears. 'They love you really.'

'Yes well, when we leave, please don't ask me for a cat,' Mum said.

Dylan sprang from my lap and ran out of the room like he understood. Like he knew better than to grow emotionally attached to me the way I had to him. The way I had to them all.

Temporary. This is only temporary.

One day we would leave and I'd never see Alex again.

Every afternoon we had a break from the contributions. 'Reflection time', Alex called it. Daisy had tried to teach me to meditate, but I just didn't get it.

'I can't stop having thoughts.'

'You don't have to,' she said. 'It's about becoming an observer. Seeing the thoughts rather than being them.'

But I was too restless to sit still. Edgy. Automatically thrusting my hand in my pocket to pull out my phone to scroll through social media, forgetting I didn't have it anymore.

'It doesn't matter if meditation's not for you,' Saffron said. 'Use the time to think about what you can learn from the past to improve the present.' But I was too worried about the future.

'When we leave.'

'When we leave.'

'When we leave.'

My boots drummed out the rhythm of Mum's words as I stalked across the field into the grey, angry sky, wishing the expanse of nothingness could swallow me up. The woods were to my left, the branches bending in the wind towards me, leaves rustling in my ear.

Temporary, this is only temporary.

I dragged my sleeve across my cheeks, wiping away frustrated tears.

A shout sliced through the buzzing in my head. I jumped, wondering what I'd done wrong. There was no one to be seen.

An angry voice.

Alex?

Hesitantly, I edged towards the sound. Behind the shield of

the first row of trees I saw that I was right. I was surprised. Alex was always calm. He was shouting at Saffron, who shrank away from him. It looked like she was scared but why would she be scared of Alex? He would never hurt anyone. But there was a furious, unfamiliar expression on the face I'd committed to memory. My heart pounded as I wondered whether I should do something, but before I could react Reed jogged over to them, shouting at Alex to back off. Saffron began to cry. Reed put his arm around her and led her away.

Alex spun around and began to walk in my direction. Panic glued my feet to the ground.

'Tilly?'

'Hi. Umm. I was just… it's reflection time and I… Is Saffron okay? Were you arguing?'

'Just talking. She's… It's complicated, but she's all right. But what about you? You look like you've been crying.' There was such concern in his eyes, the angry Alex of a few minutes ago skipped from my mind and I let him go.

'Tilly? You can talk to me.'

'I'm fine.' I burst into tears.

He didn't speak but he took my hand.

Temporary, this is only temporary.

The thought that this might be the only time his fingers entwined with mine made me cry even harder.

He led me through the trees until we were outside his cottage. Inside.

On the sofa. Thighs touching.

'God, sorry.' I pulled my sleeve over my hand and scrubbed at my cheeks. 'I must look an ugly, horrible mess.'

'You're beautiful, Tilly.'

That set me off again because I know I'm not and worse than that, I'm ugly on the inside. At the farm I was safe. My secrets tangled with the barbed wire on the gate. The high fences keeping Mum's love for me contained. We couldn't go back to the outside. It would all unravel. Alex pulled a white handkerchief from his pocket. I pressed it against my nose, breathing in his smell as I tried to calm myself. Alex fetched a glass of water. I took a sip.

'Mum's talking about leaving,' I said quietly.

A flicker of alarm crossed his face. He was going to miss me too. 'And you're crying because you're happy about that, or sad?'

'I don't want to go.'

'So don't.'

It sounded so simple but I couldn't leave Mum.

'I have to.'

'Why?'

You're not my family anymore, Aunt Anwyn had screamed. 'Mum's only got me.'

'But that doesn't make you responsible for her. We're responsible for our own happiness. Our own choices.'

'It's not that easy.'

'It can be. You've left school, so you know you're capable of making an informed decision. You're a woman now, but your mum can't see it. Like calling you Tilly. It's a lovely name for a little girl but—'

'You don't like my name?'

'I'm not saying that. This isn't about your name, exactly. It's just that I don't think you're a child.'

I thought about Hazel's hungry caterpillar story. How a name is a gift you can give yourself. But I was named after my

206

grandmother. It had always felt like a gift from her. 'It's short for Matilda, you know? Do you think I should change it?'

Alex hesitated. 'No. I don't think you should change it. Matilda is perfect.'

'No one has called me Matilda for years.'

'I will,' he said softly. 'Matilda.' The three syllables rose and dipped and had never sounded so sweet.

Dad had chosen my name. There was a photo of us in the maternity ward after I was born. I was small and wrinkled, my head too large, but Dad gazed at me like I was the most precious thing in the world. He'd adored me once. The hot lump rose in my throat again. I closed my eyes, trying to hold in my unshed tears, but they escaped nevertheless, leaking down my cheeks. Alex mopped them with his fingertips.

Dad's hands cupping my face. Promise you won't tell, Tilly.

'Matilda. Please look at me.' Wanting to block out the images, the feelings, I opened my eyes. Before I could think it through I awkwardly angled my body towards his, not knowing where to rest my hands, and then it happened.

I kissed him.

He drew away.

'This isn't what you need.'

'It's what I want.'

'Tilly, I—'

'Don't call me Tilly. I am *not* a child.' Our eyes met until all I could hear was his breathing, my breathing. My whispered words, 'Please, Alex.'

'Matilda.'

'Don't.' My voice thin. 'Please don't talk.' My eyes flickered to his mouth, back to his eyes.

That mouth.

'Alex...' I took his hand. 'I need...'

I slowly shook my head, not sure what I needed. He leaned forward.

His kisses were gentle. Different to kissing clean-shaven Kieron, but I liked the feel of his beard against my chin.

I relaxed into his arms until I was lying beneath him, his body blocking out the light. But he was my sun.

His hands tangled in my hair. His lips on my neck.

My chest rising and falling. A longing. A wanting. A need. I was lost in him but it was the kind of lost that felt like being found.

'Please.' I nearly cried with frustration.

'Please what?' he whispered in my ear.

'Please touch me.'

His trailed his index finger up and down my arm.

'Please.'

He ran his thumb between the waistband of my top and my jeans.

'Please.'

'You're too young.'

'I'm not. I'm an adult and I know what I'm doing. You're only ten years older than me. Nine soon.'

'It's wrong.'

'It's right.'

'Matilda,' he moaned. 'Are you sure?'

'Yes. Touch me.'

His hand slipped between the sofa and my back. I almost blurted out that wasn't where I wanted him to touch me, but there was a tightening of my bra strap, a release. His hand

208

cupped my breast, thumb running over my nipple. I gasped as I fumbled with the button on his jeans.

He reached for my wrist and stopped me. 'Matilda. Do you really want me?'

I almost cried out my yes.

'I want you. I want you to be my first.'

He hesitated. Straightened his arms until he was looking directly into my soul.

It felt like forever until his lips butterflied mine again. His hands roaming over my body.

It was as though all the versions of myself I'd tried on in the past were all leading to this.

To him.

He unzipped my jeans. I raised my hips so he could slide them down my thighs. I avoided looking at him as he undressed but out the corner of my eye I could see him rolling on a condom. When he was back on top of me I pressed my face against his neck, breathing in his smell. Spice and wood. Breathing out my nerves. He hooked my right leg around his back and pushed gently.

'Is this okay?'

I bit my lip, trapping inside my desire to tell him yes. No. To speed up. To slow down. It hurt.

I nodded.

My body tensed but then he was rolling my nipple between his fingers, kissing my neck. Until I was moving with him, crying out his name, digging my nails into his skin until he cried out too.

Eventually he kissed the top of my head, before rolling off me. My body felt cold without the cover of his. I shifted onto my side, trying to read his expression as he studied my face. 'Matilda.' Again, he tucked my hair behind my ear. 'You are so incredibly beautiful.'

The sun was beaming through the window. It poured through me, lighting me from the inside out, and I knew that I was glowing. That time when he told me I was beautiful, I believed him.

'My mum will have a fit.' I hated that she sprung to mind.

'I know she would, and that's why it must stay between us. I would hate to come between you and your mum.'

'But she'll find out if we're… Are we…' I tugged my T-shirt down, covering as much as my body as I could.

'Matilda, I don't regret what just happened. Neither should you, but… I don't think… *everyone* would be happy for us.'

'Is that it then?' I was despairing that my first time – our first time – might have been the last.

'It doesn't have to be, but I don't think we should tell anyone yet. Can you keep a secret?'

Promise you won't tell, Tilly.

If that was what it took, I could keep a secret.

Another one.

'I won't tell anyone, if that's what you want. I'll wait.' I touched his face. 'Alex, I'll do anything for you.'

I'm not sure what I thought 'anything' might cover. Not the unimaginable, the unthinkable, the things that lurk in nightmares.

But a promise was a promise.

CHAPTER THIRTY-NINE

ALEX

Once, Alex had been on a school trip to a castle, and the museum-calm of the exhibition hall had been such a contrast to the rowdiness of the classroom, the playground where he was tormented on a daily basis. He felt a peace he had never experienced before as he wandered among the brutal display of swords and cannons and battleaxes. Back on the coach at the end of the day, Alex had twisted around in his seat, his nose pressed against the window. The brakes hissed before they lurched forward, taking Alex away from the place that had felt like a world of its own. He wished there was a safe place where all the good people could live, and shut all the bad ones out. Somewhere that felt as tranquil as the museum.

Later that night his door was pushed open, a rectangle of light from the landing pooling over his carpet as his sister slipped into his room. He pulled back the covers. She climbed into bed beside him.

'I've had another nightmare.'

He wrapped his arms around her and quietly sang until she stopped shaking with fear. Alex thought back to the suits of armour he had seen that day. His arms felt as protective as steel.

They still felt the same way, but he needed to remember

who he wanted to protect and why. He needed to remember the endgame.

Mother-daughter.

Daughter-mother.

Impossible to separate, or were they?

He needed structure. Order. A plan. He couldn't descend into dizzying chaos. Not again.

Whenever he did, people got hurt.

And it wasn't just hearts that got broken.

CHAPTER FORTY

LAURA

Slowly I turned my head as the bedroom door cracked open. It was Saffron, a tray balanced in her hand. My stomach roiled at the stench of scrambled eggs.

'How are you feeling?'

I levered myself to sitting.

'Rough.' I'd had another seizure. My third. I knew I needed to see a doctor, but some days even getting dressed took colossal effort. 'Is that…?'

'Brunch. You slept through dinner yesterday.'

My eyes sought out Tilly's bed. I hadn't seen her since the beginning of reflection time yesterday. At least I thought it was yesterday.

'She's fine. She slept in with me last night. We thought it better not to disturb you.' She set the tray down and passed me a glass of orange juice. 'Freshly squeezed.'

'Thanks. What time is it?' My mouth stretched into a yawn. I knew from the thin winter daylight pressing against the windowpane, the sun high in the sky, that I'd missed boxing-up.

'Now you know we're not governed by clocks.'

'I don't even know what day of the week we're on anymore.'

My head was constantly brimming with nothing. 'We must be close to Christmas.'

'Laura.' Saffron looked at me with sympathy. 'That's been and gone.'

I froze, the glass halfway to my lips. 'It can't have done. We haven't been here that long, surely?'

'Eight weeks.'

'But…' I wanted to say we didn't have a Christmas tree, we didn't have Santa. It wasn't just myself I was disappointed for. 'Tilly loves Christmas.'

'I'm so sorry, Laura. We don't mark it here. Alex doesn't like… I didn't realise you were religious.'

'I'm not. But…' I forced orange juice down my hot, swollen throat and tried to pull myself together.

'We're all about not conforming, breaking the mould. Alex wants us to create our own traditions here. Anyhoo, tonight we're having a celebration.'

'Of what?' I asked dully.

'Of ourselves.'

'I'm not sure if I'm up to it.'

'Everyone will be there. The guys from the stables, Reed, Dannii. It'll be fun.'

'Can you ask Tilly to come and see me?'

'Of course.' She closed the door behind her, and that was when I allowed myself to cry. As much as I had been dreading the first Christmas without Gavan – without Anwyn and Iwan; we took it in turns to host each year – I would have made an effort for Tilly.

As painful as it was, I mentally travelled to the year before. Five years before. Ten years before. I had dug holes in my mind and buried the memories from that time, which were now bittersweet, but nevertheless I clawed at them, fumbling to unearth them.

Tilly and Rhianon, bulging stockings embroidered with their names propped up against their cots as the adults drank mulled wine downstairs. Tilly and Rhianon vigorously sprinkling icing sugar over warm-from-the-oven mince pies until it looked like it had been snowing indoors. Gavan pacing the garden, boots dipped in flour, leaving Santa-sized footprints. Iwan standing on the landing, shaking bells, until the girls declared they could hear Rudolph and rushed over to the window to pull back the curtains. Quality Street. Hangovers. Too many games of Monopoly. It was over. All of it.

Later, the sound of china rattling roused me. While I was reliving the past I must have slipped back into sleep. Daisy balanced a dinner tray in her hands.

'Are you okay, Laura?'

'Fine.' But I wasn't. My eyes were sore and gritty. My pillow soaked with misery.

'Tilly's getting ready with me. See you outside soon?' She didn't wait for an answer.

As I picked at dry and tasteless quinoa, it occurred to me.

I'd been by myself all afternoon.

Tilly hadn't come.

My daughter was slipping away from me.

I flexed my fingers.

I could almost feel her letting go of my hand.

My fingers shook as I threaded a belt through the loops of my jeans. They used to dig into my waist, but now felt loose on my hips. I pulled my navy fisherman's jumper over my head. The floor seemed to rock but thoughts of Tilly forced me to trudge downstairs. The house was quiet, the kitchen empty. I pulled on my boots, buttoned my coat and stepped outside. Far across the field the sky was hazy with the orange shimmer of fire. Incessant drumming pounded like a heartbeat. My footfall adopted the same urgent rhythm as I stumbled across the field. A sense of foreboding that came from nowhere building inside me.

A premonition?

A mother's instinct?

I slowed, breathless. The atmosphere was electric, manic almost. Towering, roaring flames. Reed slapping the African drums. The beating sound filling the air. Filling my head. Dancing figures dressed in bright white dipped and twirled. Singing. Laughing. I loitered on the periphery, feeling conspicuous in my blue jeans and jumper. A cup was pushed into my hand but I didn't register who gave it to me, my eyes seeking out Tilly.

And there she was: recognisable, and yet unfamiliar.

Her face was shining, eyes wide and bright as she tilted her face towards Alex. There was an almost ethereal quality about her that made my heart ache. Hesitantly, I approached them, feeling I was intruding somehow. I think I knew deep down that there was something between them.

Something that would destroy her.

They didn't notice me, although I was close enough to stretch out my hand and touch her. Touch him. Painfully close and yet a continent away.

I was tiny. Invisible. Insignificant. Horribly out of place with my dark, dark clothes and my dark, dark heart which was breaking all over again.

She was gazing at him the way I had when I had tried to kiss him. The way most people there did.

'Matilda,' Alex murmured. She parted her mouth but rather than correct him, to tell him she hated being called anything other than Tilly, she smiled. 'Matilda,' he said again. And that was when I knew for certain. Everything became white noise. His mouth moved with words I could not hear over the furious pounding of my pulse in my ears. One thought. Just one thought consumed me.

He had touched her.

Any lingering feelings I had for him were swept away by that knowing.

He had touched my little girl.

She was only seventeen.

The age the world is most dangerous.

Leave her alone, I wanted to scream, but my throat was constricted, the words contained.

She belongs to me.

But as I watched her gaze at him with such utter adoration, I knew she didn't belong to me, not anymore.

I'd be damned if I'd let him have her.

'Listen everyone.' Alex clapped his hands together and instantly the dancing stopped. The chatter. The only thing remaining was the beat of Reed's drum which had slowed – thump-thump-thump – combined with the anger kicking inside my ribcage until I couldn't tell what was me anymore, what was the music. I drained my drink to push my rage back down. It was bitter and potent. My head began to swim.

Rapt faces glowed orangey-red in the light of the fire which threw shadows over the fields. On the edge of the woods, the branches of the trees scratched against each other in the wind. My jaw clenched so hard I drew blood from my tongue. Inside that forest was his lair. The place he had laid hands on her.

'Matilda,' I bristled as he called her that, 'is going to hand out paper, envelopes and a pen. I want everyone to write two things. What they are, and how that makes them feel.'

'What do you mean?' asked Hazel.

He cleared his throat, low and loud. 'For example, I am a warrior and I feel powerful.'

The compostable cup crumpled in my fist as I fought to gather control. Tilly snaked through the throng. This wasn't the time or the place for a confrontation. She moved effortlessly, basking under the warmth of responsibility Alex had bestowed upon her. I struggled to find the before-Tilly, with her thick black makeup and mismatched clothes in this poised young woman, with her white flowing dress and her face bare and beautiful.

'Here you go, Mum.' I took the pen from her fingers and pictured the way they used to be, small and chubby, moulding animals from brightly coloured Play-Doh. The purple giraffe indistinguishable from the green elephant.

I closed my eyes against the painful image.

'Are you okay?' she asked with concern. It wasn't like her to be so tuned in to my emotions, it was like she'd grown up overnight.

'Tilly…' My voice a whisper as I gazed at her face.

'It's Matilda now,' she said quietly, without breaking eye contact. 'Are you okay, Dannii?' Her attention was dragged away from me as Dannii jostled her shoulder as she rushed past.

'Yeah. I just wanna ask Alex how he sees me.' She giggled. Thrust out her chest.

'No,' Tilly snapped. 'This is about how you see yourself, not anybody else.'

'I dunno. I guess living here, being a resident, being free from all that shit outside.'

'You're going to stay?' Even in the fiery hue, Tilly's face visibly paled. 'Forever?'

'Dunno about forever. Not much lasts that long, does it? I'm gonna ask Alex.'

At the mention of his name Tilly rushed back to his side as though she was magnetised. And it wasn't so much a moving away from me. It was a pulling away.

'Once you've written who you are and how that makes you feel, put it in your envelope and seal it,' he commanded.

Everyone was scribbling, angling their paper towards the fire so they could properly see.

Who was I?

How did it make me feel?

No one else seemed to falter, words flowed freely. And then it came to me. There was only one thing I could write. Without a hard surface to lean on, my sentence was almost illegible, but it was all there in those eight words. Everything I was. Everything I felt.

'Here's the thing.' Alex spoke again and a hush fell over the crowd. 'We are so quick to define ourselves. To put ourselves in a box. But at the end of the day you are *not* who you think you are.' He scanned the crowd and I hated myself for nodding. 'You are so much more. You don't always know how you feel and that's okay. We're going to break out of the box.'

'Fuck the system,' shouted Reed, still that thud-thud-thud of the drum.

A roaring cheer.

'Fuck the system.'

My nerves jangled.

'We're going to head down to the ravine and throw our paper in the abyss. On this journey of self-awareness we're going to shed who we think we are and become who we're meant to be.' He held a long stick aloft like a hunter brandishing a trophy and lit the end.

Another cheer.

Before long everyone was holding a blazing stick, including me. I didn't want to be there, but I found myself transfixed. Unable to leave. Unwilling to leave Tilly. Fleetingly, I wondered about trudging through the woods with fire, but Alex led our odd procession around the side of the woods as we walked two by two. Animals into the ark. The chosen ones.

An elbow in my side. A blonde head bobbing in front.

Dannii squeezing in between Tilly and Alex. Giggling and tossing her hair. I watched Tilly's thunderous face and I knew it was worse than I thought. She hadn't just slept with Alex.

She loved him.

The edge of the ravine loomed sudden and dangerous. Automatically I sought out Tilly, checking she was safe. I'd never been there before, and as I stared down into the blackness a strange urge to step off the edge snuck up on me. I shuffled backwards.

'Now,' said Alex. 'I want you to close your eyes and think about who you want to become, and once that's clear in your mind, let go of your letters and your limitations.'

Again a cheer.

I closed my eyes. The envelope tight in my hands. The wind

trying to tug it from my grasp. But I didn't want to let go of who I was.

Whooping filled my ears as people began to release their envelopes but then something else.

A scream that immediately made my blood run to ice.

Tilly.

My eyes snapped open, scanning the crowd.

I couldn't see her.

Alex's anguished cry: 'No. God, no. She's fallen over the edge.'

The world lost its grip on me. My knees slammed into the floor; an animalistic keening spewing from inside my gut.

Tilly!

CHAPTER FORTY-ONE

ALEX

Wings and claws whirlwinded inside of him as his panic spun and grew.

So young.

So beautiful.

So dead.

It was happening.

It was all happening over again.

CHAPTER FORTY-TWO

LAURA

Oh, Tilly.

Oh, my baby.

My heart broke for you.

CHAPTER FORTY-THREE

TILLY

When I was four, Mum and Dad spent weeks telling me how I was going to start big school. I didn't want to go. They kept assuring me I'd love it. That it'd be this huge adventure. Rhianon was so excited. Aunty Anwyn had hung her uniform on the front of her wardrobe, and she tried it on every day. Whenever I thought about it there was a sick feeling in my stomach which when I was older I recognised as a sense of foreboding. But then I formed a plan and it all seemed a little easier to bear. On that first Monday, when my parents came to wake me, I refused to open my eyes. I figured if I couldn't see, they wouldn't make me go. Dad lifted me out of bed and carried me downstairs. He spooned Weetabix into my mouth, the way he had when I was a baby. Eventually, when Mum had washed and dressed me, and I was still pretending I couldn't open my eyes, Dad began to tickle me.

'Let me see those indigo eyes, Tilly.'

I peeked at him through lowered lashes.

'That's better. You know I'm coming to take you to school, and I'll be waiting for you afterwards. I *promise* you everything will be okay.'

Reassured, I let him put on my new shoes that felt stiff and uncomfortable, and zip up my coat. We walked, hand in hand. I was snuggly-warm, wrapped in my anorak and his promises. And when he kissed me goodbye and told me again that I'd be okay, I knew that I would be. And I was. After all the excitement, Rhianon was the one who clung to Aunt Anwyn at the gates. The one who wouldn't go inside.

At seventeen I was old enough to know better, but again I kept my eyes tightly closed as people entered and left the room. Talking in low whispers about the police. I had the same sense of foreboding, but there was no one holding my hand, telling me it would be okay, because it wouldn't.

I didn't have a plan.

Dannii was dead. I just couldn't get my head around it. It had only been a few hours ago she was flicking her hair, flirting with Alex, giggling like she was the happiest person in the world. Now she was gone. I couldn't begin to process what had happened. There had been such horror on her face as she tumbled backwards and realised she was falling. What was she thinking as she fell? What had Dad thought? In my mind, their images strobed bright and piercing. Dad-Dannii-Dad-Dannii. Flashing faster and faster until they become one person plunging into blackness.

From the landing, Saffron murmured to someone. 'Thankfully it was quick. She didn't suffer.' But she must have done. I saw how scared she was, and even though it was probably all over in seconds, for her it probably lasted a lifetime.

'Tilly.' Mum's voice soft in my ear. I fought my panic and kept my breathing measured. 'Are you awake?' She brushed my hair back from my forehead. It took every ounce of self-control not to move or speak. Eventually she crept away. My skin felt cold and empty where her touch had been.

Tired. I was so tired but sleep wouldn't come. The memories I had been trying so hard to repress fired at me, no longer vague and shapeless but as sharp and pointed as the fire sticks we'd carried last night. I tried to stuff them back inside the box in my head, but the lid kept springing off. I faced the window, staring out into the starless sky until the darkness flickered and folded in on itself, rushing towards me, carrying me to places I did not want to go.

Falling, falling, falling. At first I thought it was me but I was the one watching; feeling the disbelief, the denial, the terror. Horrified screams ringing in my ears.

The sickening thud.

The silence.

The nightmare poked and prodded until I woke, my chest heaving, my sheets damp with sweat. My skin red hot with shame. Why hadn't I done more? Why were my reflexes too sluggish? Too slow. I had been frozen to the spot as arms stretched out towards me. If only I'd grasped the hands that brushed against mine.

It wasn't my fault.

My breath was coming in short, hiccupy gasps.

It was an accident.

Shaking, I reached for the water on my bedside table.

Was it an accident? asked a voice in my head. *Was it really?*

Yes. Yes. Yes.

But as my fingers closed around the coolness of the glass I noticed how my palms were tingling and it felt like a memory.

Pushing.

The glass slipped from my grasp. I furled and unfurled my fingers but the heat, the pins and needles, the memory remained.

Did I push?

Falling, falling, floating. Rising up towards the ceiling. Looking down at myself coiled into a ball, on the bed.

Sleep.

Nightmares lurking in the shadows, hugging the walls, ready to spring.

It was an accident.

A moan escaped my lips as I shook my head. Down on the bed, completely detached from myself, I observed the other me do the same. I didn't know if I was awake or asleep. If any of this was real. If I was real.

I didn't know if I wanted to be.

Because if I pushed, what did that make me? *Who* did that make me?

Tilly-Matilda-Tilly-Matilda.

I peeled open my eyes, forcing sleep and the nightmares away, but I knew they were still there, crouching in the corners where the ceiling meets the walls. The monsters poised to leap and I wasn't one of them, I wasn't.

Matilda-Tilly-Matilda-Tilly.

'Shhh.' Alex. Hands soothing my hair. The squeak of bedsprings. His body against mine. 'I've got you, Matilda. You're safe. Shhh. You're mine.'

Footsteps.

'Tilly,' Mum said. 'The police are downstairs. They need to speak to you.'

I turned my face into my pillow and wept.

CHAPTER FORTY-FOUR

LAURA

Time was long and slow. I sat silently at the kitchen table with two police officers, waiting for Tilly to come downstairs, my mind reliving the previous night. My skin still clammy with the tidal wave of fear that had washed over me in those first few seconds when I believed it was Tilly who had fallen over the edge. The onslaught of relief when I discovered it wasn't. Bile rising hot and acidic in my throat at the realisation it was Dannii. Still somebody's daughter. Somebody's friend. The police would be knocking on a different door this time. *We regret to inform you.* The uniforms, the crackle of walkie-talkies brought it all back. Every single torturous second. Although I can't remember exactly what was said on the night Gavan died, I can remember how it felt. Every word a swift, hard kick to the stomach.

At last there were footsteps on the stairs.

'This is Tilly,' I said as she entered the room, shadowed by Alex.

'Matilda,' he corrected me, as he pulled out a chair for her, sitting her down as though she was so fragile she might break. Over her white T-shirt and jeans she wore Alex's hoody, unzipped, the cuffs hanging loose over her hands.

'Hello,' the police officer said, her eyes flickering between Alex and I as she tried to unpick the dynamics. 'Matilda, is it?'

Tilly nodded.

'I'm her mum,' I said with more bite than intended.

'I'm PC Stanway and this is PC Hughes. We're taking initial statements relating to Danielle's death. And you are?' she addressed Alex.

'Alexander Draycott. I'm the manager of The Lodge and Oak Leaf Organics.' There was an edge to his voice. He was uncomfortable.

'You own the land?'

'No, that's Dafydd Thomas.'

'We'll need to speak to him too.'

'He's in Australia with his daughter, Carys.'

'We'll take his contact number.'

'I don't have one for him. He doesn't have a mobile.'

'So you haven't spoken to him? He doesn't know about the death on his land?'

'No.' Alex ran his hand through his hair. The underarms of his shirt were damp with sweat.

'And he didn't leave an emergency contact? Carys's landline?'

'No.'

'An address?'

'Perth.' Alex splayed his hands. 'Sorry it all sounds so vague. We never thought anything like this would happen.'

'And when is Mr Thomas due back?'

'I… I'm not sure. A few weeks yet, I think. Sorry.'

'We'll try to trace him. Now, Matilda, we're going to ask you a few questions if that's okay? It's nothing to worry about.

We're speaking to everyone present, trying to build up a picture of what happened to Danielle. How old are you?'

'Seventeen.'

'You can have an adult with you.'

'I'll stay with her.' Alex placed a hand on her shoulder.

'I think that—' I began.

'Matilda, who do you want?'

Tilly raised her hand to her shoulder and linked her fingers through Alex's. Her eyes filled with sorrow as they met mine.

'Can they both stay? I need them both.'

'Of course. Can you tell me what happened last night? There was a celebration?'

'Umm, yes?' Alex's fingers squeezed her shoulder reassuringly. She cleared her throat. 'Yes, there was.'

Tilly's account of the evening was slow, faltering. Hesitations peppered with glances to Alex. PC Hughes chewed the end of his pen while we waited for a response.

'And at the ravine,' PC Stanway probed. 'I believe you were standing next to Danielle?'

'I… It was dark. I don't know.'

'You were standing between Dannii and I, Matilda,' Alex said softly. 'Remember?'

'No. I… Someone brushed against me. I don't know.'

'That's okay. It must have been horribly confusing. Tell me what you do remember,' PC Stanway asked.

'The beat of the drum. The fire. The shadows. I think…' Tilly closed her eyes. 'I heard some stones fall over the edge and Dannii's blonde hair caught my eyes. I tried… I think I knew she was falling but I don't know how… My hand… I tried to grab her to pull her back… Someone screamed. I think her. Or me.

I don't *know*. I can't remember.' She began to cry, the mirror of me all those years ago, scared and confused. *I can't remember.*

'Tilly. If there's anything else you can remember you should…' I began. I knew the questions wouldn't stop until the police were satisfied.

'No, that's enough, Matilda.' Alex crouched down next to her and took her hands. 'You've done really well. You can go upstairs and rest now.' He looked up. 'Unless you have any objections?'

I opened my mouth to answer but then realised he was addressing PC Hughes, not me.

'No, that's fine.' He snapped his notebook shut. 'Thank you, Matilda. You've been really helpful.'

Alex helped Tilly to her feet and she crumpled into him. I stepped forward to take her other arm.

'Laura,' said PC Stanway. 'If we could talk to you next, please.'

The room tightened around me as Alex and Tilly left. Neither of them looked back.

Gavan was at the forefront my mind as I gave my scant account of the previous evening. Afterwards I was craving fresh air. While the police began talking to Saffron, I yanked on my coat. Dannii's death had stirred up so many feelings. More than ever I was desperate for the inquest. Desperate for closure. My restless feet tramped over fields. The hem of my jeans wet with dew.

It wasn't until I heard a sound I couldn't identify that I looked up and realised that I had returned to the ravine. Blue and white police tape flapped in the wind. Sickened, I darted into the woods to loop back towards the house, and I hadn't gone very far before I saw them trapped inside a holly bush.

231

Three envelopes.

The wind can't have been blowing in the right direction the previous night to carry them across the ravine. My fury built again at Alex's recklessness, and I ignored the thorns that snagged at my clothes, snatched my hair, as I yanked the letters free.

It felt intrusive but I couldn't help opening them.

I am independent and I feel strong; read the first one. Fleetingly I wondered if it was written by Tilly and her new-found bravado last night. The writing didn't quite look like hers, it was shaky, but there had been nothing to lean on. I opened the second letter. *I am a resident and I feel free.* Instantly I knew this was Dannii's letter. She was right about nothing lasting forever. I began to cry for her, for her family, and then I was crying for Gavan, for Tilly and myself, and everything got turned inside out and upside down. I just couldn't pull myself together until I tore open the third letter. *I am a mother and I feel love.* That one I knew. I had written it and the words drew strength to my limbs, dried my tears as I began to hurry back to the farmhouse.

I was on the periphery of the woods when I spotted another letter, caught within a Y-shaped branch. I almost didn't stop to retrieve it. I almost didn't read it.

Sometimes I wish I hadn't.

It was virtually illegible. I held it closer to my eyes to read it better.

I am a murderer and I feel sorry.

CHAPTER FORTY-FIVE

ALEX

The truth will set you free.

CHAPTER FORTY-SIX

TILLY

Exhausted after the questioning, I'd fallen into a restless sleep. The first thing I did when I woke and remembered what had happened was to burst into noisy tears.

'Matilda. Please don't cry. Please.' Alex's hands stroked my back. Before I'd have given anything to have been touched by him, but I didn't want to be Matilda anymore. The barrage of police questions had terrified me. I wasn't sure if they thought I was lying. If I had something to do with Dannii falling. I could barely remember. It was all so muddled. I had tried so hard to answer everything calmly, but I couldn't tell them what they needed to know. It didn't reassure me that they were going to be talking to everyone. I was sure they'd be back for me. I didn't feel ready to be a grown-up. I wanted to be Tilly again. Tilly who had two parents who loved her and could make everything better.

'I want my mum.' My voice was muffled. Cotton pillowcase against my mouth.

'What did you say, sweetheart?'

Dad used to call me sweetheart. Hearing it from someone else's lips just made my cry harder.

I wanted him.

Dad's hands cupping my face. Promise you won't tell, Tilly.
No!

I wanted Mum.

Anwyn, Iwan, Rhianon.

I wanted them all.

'I want my mum,' I said again, turning my face to the side.
'I want to go home.'

'You are home—'

'No! My real home. I want my mum. I want my dad. I want
everything to be okay again.'

'But your dad—'

'He's dead. I know. But that doesn't stop me wanting him.
When I was small he was… he was… How could he…'

The bed shook with the force of my sobs but I just couldn't
stem the flow of tears. I didn't even know what I was crying for.
Who I was crying for. All of them, I suppose. All of it.

'Daddy. Daddy.' I was getting myself more and more worked
up.

'Shhh.' Alex tried to calm me. I slapped his hand away.

'I *want* my parents.' I just wanted to feel normal again. To
be bitching about homework. About the boring documentaries
Mum used to watch. My chest burned with painful hiccups. My
head so hot I thought it might burst. Dad was gone. Gone, *gone*.
So was Dannii and, ridiculous I know, all of a sudden it seemed
too final. Stupidly, I had been half-expecting Dad to appear
again one day and say, 'That was a bit shit being dead. I didn't
like it much so I thought I'd come back. Did you miss me?'

Panic attacked from all sides. I sat up, wrapping my arms
around my knees, holding them close to me along with my
misery and my memory of my father.

The room was filled with a weird moaning sound. I began rocking back and forth.

'Matilda!' Alex said sharply. The noise stopped and I realised it had been coming from me. He took my hands and gripped them tightly. 'I know it was a terrible shock seeing Dannii fall but please, calm down.' There was an edge of anxiety to his words that I recognised. My words were often smothered with it.

'No! Where's my mum? My dad?' Short breathless gasps, the room beginning to spin.

'I'm here.'

I shook my head. He wasn't the one I wanted. The one I needed.

'Matilda.' His hands released mine and cupped my cheeks. 'Look at me.'

'I don't want—'

'*Look*. At me.'

Reluctantly, my eyes met his. 'I can fetch your mum but you can't have your dad, you just can't.'

'Because he's dead.' Basically I'd spent months avoiding the 'D' word, and now I couldn't stop saying it.

'Because you don't know who he is.'

I stopped rocking. Stopped breathing.

'Matilda, I'm so sorry, but here's the thing, Gavan, he isn't... He wasn't your father.'

The words fell from Alex's familiar mouth and whatever his intention, they felt mean and spiteful, and it was like I was back at school, lost and alone. The edges of the room darkened and I pinched the skin of the back of my hand, hard, to make sure it wasn't some awful dream.

'Why... why would you say that?' I couldn't grasp why he was trying to hurt me. Why everyone seemed to turn against me.

236

'So… so you'll stop calling for him. Sweetheart, it's tearing me apart—'

'You're wrong.' He had to be mistaken. Again I dug my nails into the back of my hand, squeezing hard, welcoming the physical pain. Something I could understand.

'Gavan wasn't your biological father, Tilly. I'm so sorry.'

'Who told you that? They were lying.'

'Look maybe I shouldn't have…' Alex looked stricken. 'It *is* true though.'

'It isn't!' I screamed, hating him. Hating myself for trusting him.

The bees in my head became a frenzied swarm. I could see Alex's lips moving but I couldn't hear what he was saying above the buzzing noise. It couldn't be true, could it?

Promise you won't tell, Tilly? Dad's hands cupping my face as I tried to equate the Dad I knew with his actions, but what if he knew I wasn't his real daughter? It changed everything.

You're not my family, Anwyn had said. I'd thought it was because she had fallen out with Mum, but what if she *had* meant I wasn't her family either, because I didn't share their genes?

Niece. Daughter. Cousin. I wasn't any of the things I thought I was.

Who was I?

Tilly-Matilda-Tilly-Matilda.

I threw my head back and howled, 'No!'

Alex drew me to him. This time I clung to him like he was the only thing I had left in the world, and in that moment, it felt like he was.

The door pushed open. Mum. She hesitated when she saw Alex, biting her lip the way she sometimes bit back her nagging.

237

I didn't care. There was only one thing I could say to her. It came out in a torrent of bitterness that almost knocked her off her feet.

Sticks and stones may break bones, but sometimes one chosen word can wound.

And it did.

CHAPTER FORTY-SEVEN

Alex

Lies. Lies. Lies.

Alex had only wanted to create a safe environment. A haven. To help.

He never intended to hurt her. To hurt any of them.

If he'd known it would all have gone so wrong, would he have done things differently?

He liked to think he would.

CHAPTER FORTY-EIGHT

LAURA

'LIAR!'

The word thundered towards me bowling-ball fast and just as hard. I staggered backwards, one hand steadying myself on the door frame for support.

'Tilly, I—'

'Liar.' Her tone was quieter and somehow that was worse. I began to shake, trying to figure out what she was referring to. Lies. There had been so many.

'I haven't lied to you.' It had become so ingrained to tell Tilly what I thought she should know that I was incapable of telling the truth. 'I've never—'

'You've *never*?'

'Tills—'

'Don't. Call. Me. That.'

'Sorry. I… You used to like it when Dad called you that.'

'Gavan? THAT MAN WAS NOT MY FATHER.' She hurled Cow the lion towards me, where he splayed on the floor, legs at odd angles, as though he too was broken, and it felt like a rejection of Gavan.

My knees snapped. My heart too. My whole body shattering. There were so many things I should have said, could have said, to ease the pain she must have felt, but instead I blurted out, 'How did you find out? Did Anwyn tell you? When did you speak?'

One night when Tilly was small, Gavan, Anwyn, Iwan and I had sat around the table, drinking too much wine.

'When are you going to tell her the truth?' Anwyn slurred. 'It might be easier while she's young.'

Uneasy, I looked towards Gavan. 'We're not,' he affirmed. 'If I'm happy raising her as my daughter, that should be good enough for you, Anwyn.'

'Yes, it wouldn't do Tilly any good to know the truth,' Iwan chipped in. 'As far as she's concerned I'm her uncle, you're her aunt. Don't take that away from her.'

'But who—' Anwyn began.

'It's none of our business,' Iwan said.

'Mark my words, it'll come out in the end,' Anwyn said. 'Secrets always do.'

She was right.

'So it *is* true?' Tilly looked so small. 'And everyone knew except me? Rhianon?'

'Just Iwan and Anwyn. Tilly, I'm so sorry.' Tentatively I stepped forward.

'Get out.' Her words stopped me in my tracks. 'GET. OUT.'

'You need to give her some space, Laura,' Alex said.

'No.' I should have told her. The risk of her discovering Gavan was not her biological father was always there, smouldering away, before Anwyn poured the petrol of truth upon it, but I had no one to blame but myself. If I couldn't extinguish the flames, she'd be lost to me forever. 'You're upset. That's understandable.'

'Just pack your things and go, Mum.' Her shoulders slumped. 'I don't want you here anymore.'

'I'm not leaving without you.' All those weeks ago I had thought I came to *Gorphwysfa* with nothing. I was wrong.

I still had her, then.

'Nobody has to go,' Alex said.

'We should both go, Tilly. Spend some proper time together, just the two of us,' I pleaded.

'I'm staying.'

'You can't, it's dangerous.' My words fell out in a garbled rush. 'The rabbits, Dannii dying. There's a killer here. I found a note. I was going to give it to the police. Look.' I fumbled in my back pocket. It was empty. 'There was one, I swear. We have to leave. Someone has *died* here.'

'People die out there.' Her voice was weary.

'I'm not leaving you. Alex, please give us some space. I need to talk to my daughter.'

'I want him to stay. I want you to go.' She raised her bloodshot eyes. 'Please.' The word was painful. I couldn't bear it.

My body turned away, but my heart? My heart very much remained with her.

Still remains with her.

'You have to give her space, *cariad*.' Hazel pushed a mug into my hand. 'Drink.'

I sipped, expecting pungent herbs, but it was tea. Proper tea, loaded with sugar.

'Secret supplies,' she said.

The second sip made my head spin. I hadn't had anything sweet since I'd arrived.

'I want to leave,' I said again, but I knew I wouldn't. Not without Tilly. 'We should never have come here. Alex thinks we should stay but—'

'You'd do well to listen to him. Alex is a good man.' Hazel spoke sharply. 'A kind man. I know he'd do anything for us, just as we'd do anything for him.'

'I can't just sit here drinking tea. I have to talk to her.' Ten minutes, surely she'd give me that? I stood. Hazel's fingers snaked around my wrist.

'Laura, if you push her hard now, you'll push her away, for good. That's what I did with my kids. Tried time and time again to make them see their dad was bad, until they felt forced to take sides. If I'd given them some space to process it all, they'd have seen it clear as day. How much I loved them. Give her some time. She's had a horrible shock, seeing Dannii fall.'

I didn't sit down again. I didn't walk away either.

'Let her rest up tonight. I promise you we'll look after her and tomorrow you can try again. Everything seems better after a good's night's sleep, my nana used to say.'

'OK,' I relented. 'I'll wait.' But only until the morning. Tomorrow we were leaving whether she liked it or not.

The Lodge was gloomy and unwelcoming. Bleak against the backdrop of naked trees, shadowed against a lacy mist. Not so much a haven but a thing from nightmares. The ghost of Dannii danced around the converted barn, head thrown back in laughter. The front door was stiff and heavy, scraping against the wooden floor as I pushed it open. Inside, my hand fumbled for the light cord. There was a flicker as I pulled it. Darkness. Blood pulsed in my ears as I yanked it again. This time the flicker bloomed into harsh white light. I stepped inside, my breath clouding in front of me. Pulling my sleeves over the heel of my hands for warmth, I headed straight through to the sleeping quarters and scanned the room. There was only one bed made up, sheets crumpled, pillow dimpled where her head had rested. It was ridiculous, but I began to straighten the covers, smoothing down the bedding even though Dannii's sleep was now eternal and she didn't need a bed. On the bedside cabinet sat a pot of peppermint lip balm and a hairbrush tangled with long blonde hairs. I lightly touched the brush with my fingers, vowing to make sure her mum got it back, those scant remains of her daughter.

The log basket was empty.

One night.

Just one night there. Tomorrow I'd gather Tilly, along with our possessions and our faded dreams for the future, and I'd make it right. All of it.

Every muscle in my body ached. Rather than chopping wood for the fire I gathered all the blankets I could find and slipped into the bed next to Dannii's. Even though she wasn't physically there, strangely I didn't want her to feel alone. My stomach ached with hunger. I'd skipped lunch but I wasn't going back to the house for food. I'd let Tilly have the space she craved and tomorrow, when she was ready to talk, ready to listen at least, I'd go to her with an apology and a plan.

Mentally I prepared a list of things I needed to do; chase the coroner for Gavan's hearing date – I was still horribly worried about what they might uncover at the inquest; badger the insurance for an interim pay-out. Speak to Ashleigh's parents face to face. Parent to parent. Ask them – no, beg them – to drop their legal proceedings. Suddenly I was incredulous that I'd left everything to Alex. Of course nothing had been resolved yet. He wouldn't have felt the same urgency I did.

A fresh start.

A home of our own.

Perhaps I'd start a new business, making Tilly a partner, on the condition she sat her A Levels.

I was cold, hungry and alone, drifting into sleep. Trying to fool myself that it would all be okay tomorrow, when I knew it wouldn't be. An apology wouldn't make everything right. At the very least Tilly would want an explanation. She'd want to know who her real father was.

But how could I tell her that?

Although I was exhausted I didn't sleep for long, cold and hunger tugging me awake. The others must have eaten already. Dusk was pressing hard against the windows. Nobody had brought me any dinner. I climbed out of bed, draping a blanket over my shoulders, and began to stalk up and down the dorm in a bid to warm up. My energy depleted fast. I sank into a chair and gazed out of the window at the rising moon, imagining Tilly at the farmhouse seeing the same moon, missing me as I was missing her.

So many emotions scrambled for prominance inside me. Guilt that I hadn't told her the truth, pitted against anger that someone had. But overriding them all was utter despair that my relationship with my daughter was in tatters. How could I even begin to stitch the frayed edges of us back together, when she wouldn't give me the chance to explain?

Outside, a movement caught my eye. Alex slipping between the trees. He must have been going back to the cottage.

Tilly would listen to him. He could persuade her to hear me out.

But would he?

Light spilled from the cottage as Alex opened the front door. 'Laura.' From the way he said my name, I knew he'd been expecting me.

'Can we talk? About Tilly?' I tried not to sound hostile.

He opened the door wider. I twisted off my Maglite and dropped it into my pocket and stepped inside, kicking my boots onto the mat, hanging my coat on the hook in the porch.

'I'm glad you came,' he said, as I settled myself on the sofa. 'I was worried about you.'

He touched my hand and I tried not to recoil. Tried not to think of those fingers on my daughter. He wasn't my enemy. I needed him on my side.

'Drink?' He set a bottle of brandy and two glasses on the table.

'I'd better not on an empty stomach.'

'Didn't you eat the dinner I sent over?' He frowned.

'I didn't get any food. But it's okay, I want—'

'It's not okay. You didn't eat lunch either, did you?'

I shook my head.

'We need to look after you. I don't know what the mix-up was. I'll nip back to the farmhouse and fetch your plate. It must still be in the kitchen.'

My stomach growled at the thought of a meal, louder than the 'no' I was about to say.

While Alex was gone I washed my hands in the tiny cloak-room. Splashed my face with water, ignoring my haunted eyes staring back at me from the mirror. Afterwards, I detoured past the cellar door, remembering the noises I had heard. Pressed my ear against the wood.

All was silent.

In the lounge, the wood burner crackled and hissed.

I ate quickly, conscious of Alex watching me. Thanking him as he cleared away my empty plate and pressed a tumbler of brandy into my hand.

'How's Tilly?' The alcohol slipped down my throat, burning away my resentment at having to ask someone else how my daughter was. The guilt that it was my fault I couldn't ask her myself.

'She was sleeping when I left.'

'How did she find out?' I asked, but I didn't wait for an answer, feeling the need to share. Besides, it must have been Anwyn, and I couldn't blame her for the mess I was in. It was me who had fought to keep the truth hidden. 'Gavan wanted to tell her when she was sixteen, you know.' My mind travelled back. Gavan taking my hand between his. His rough thumb rubbing mine. *'One day, she'll find out, and if it hasn't come from us she'll think we're ashamed of her. That we don't love her. She needs to know how loved she is. It's time.'*

'But you didn't want to?' Alex asked.

'I didn't want her to know who her real father was. I thought it would... confuse her.'

'You have to tell her.'

'I can't.'

'Laura, you have to.'

'It's complicated. It will make things worse.'

'How much worse can they be?'

'Can you talk to her, please? Ask her to hear me out. She'll listen to you.'

'Hear you out, so you can tell her more lies?'

'Not lies exactly… but perhaps not the whole truth.'

'Tell me.'

'Tell you what?'

'All of it. Unburdening sets you free, Laura. I want you to be free. You and Tilly. I promised you when you came here I'd do the best for you both. Nothing has changed.'

'But you're…'

'Your friend.'

God knows I needed one. I drained my brandy. My eyes watered. He topped up my glass.

'Okay. I'll tell you.' It wasn't only to prepare for what I'd need to say to Tilly. Filter out the bad from the terrible. Practise the shape and taste of the words I never thought I'd say. I just couldn't bear it any longer. My shoulders were heavy from the weight of the fiction I'd created throughout Tilly's childhood.

Alex took my hand. 'Good girl. Let go of the struggle, Laura. Let it all out.'

And I did.

CHAPTER FORTY-NINE

TILLY

Alex brushed his lips against my forehead and whispered he'd see me tomorrow. I pretended to be asleep. I was good at pretending. But not as good as Mum. I pressed my face into my pillow and screamed with frustration.

My whole life had been a lie.

I cried until my chest burned. When I ran out of tears I was left with a sick, empty feeling. I threw back the duvet and crossed the room to Mum's bed. The T-shirt she wore to sleep in was still bundled underneath her pillow. I raised it to my face and inhaled. The scent of my childhood, of biscuits and flowers, was gone.

I gazed out of the window at the moon. Whenever Dad worked away and I missed him, Mum would say, 'Look at the moon, Tilly. It's a link to Dad. The same moon he'll be looking at.'

The furious bees buzzed louder in my mind as I thought about him.

Dad.

But that wasn't Gavan, was it? Who was my real dad? Did he know I even existed? Had he ever made any effort to see me?

More than anything, I wished I'd never found out the truth.

My feelings see-sawed once more as I realised that some secrets were best kept buried, so they didn't hurt anyone.

I hadn't believed that at the sharing circle. That day, I had so wanted to tell Mum everything. *Unburdening sets you free,* Alex had said, and I had so wanted to be free. I'd listened to Hazel's story. I wanted to become that butterfly, shedding the lie of my caterpillar shell. *Let go of the struggle.* And that's what life had felt like the past few months. A struggle.

But after the circle, I was unable to start the awkward conversation with Mum. It occurred to me it might be easier to pour everything into a letter, but the words wouldn't flow and the page remained blank until, frustrated, I had scrawled, *Don't trust anyone.*

I was about to crumple it up and throw it away when I thought it could open up a conversation if I left it on her pillow, reasoning she'd show it to me and we'd start talking about trust. I'd be able to tell her she shouldn't trust me. She shouldn't have trusted Dad. But she never mentioned it, and over the following three weeks since I'd left it I'd begun to doubt myself. Perhaps I never wrote it at all, I just intended to. We were all so tired there. It's easy for the mind to play tricks. A blurry line between the real and the imagined.

Outside, a shadowy figure caught my eye. I followed them with my eyes, into the woods.

Don't trust anyone. The tables had turned. All along I shouldn't have trusted Mum.

Is karma a thing? If you do something bad, hurt someone else, does it really all come back on you? If it does then I should be careful.

And so should she.

CHAPTER FIFTY

LAURA

Disapproval rolled off my parents in waves the instant I told them that Jonathan Campbell had invited me to the Christmas sixth-form disco. From my dad's reproachful gaze, as he silently studied me over the rims of his tortoiseshell glasses, you'd have thought I'd just announced I was intending to auction off my virginity online. I squirmed, wondering whether that was how it felt for those standing before him in the dock, awaiting their fate. My words fell out in a gibbering rush, cutting off any objections he might have, but his expression didn't soften. The excitement in my voice descended into nerves as I garbled the no-alcohol policy, reassured him there would be teachers chaperoning, promised the rest of the school would be strictly off limits – there'd be no sneaking off to empty classrooms. My best friend Natasha would be there with her boyfriend, Rich. Safety in numbers. Eventually, my voice rose to a pitch only dogs could hear. I clamped my jaw shut, anxiously waiting. The silence expanded and expanded like a balloon, until Dad, both judge and jury at home, popped it with one word.

'No.'

'But—'

'Butts are for goats, Laura. You know that.' He turned his attention back to his laptop and I was dismissed.

'Mum!' I trailed her into the kitchen where she yanked a paring knife from the block and began taking out her anger against the vegetables. 'Mum?' I couldn't ascertain whether she was furious with me or Dad. I was certain the carrot in her hand hadn't offended her. 'I'm seventeen! Everyone's dating but me. I want to date.' I wanted to have sex, and Jonathan was definitely the one, but I wasn't going to share that with her.

'And you can,' she said. 'Just not him.'

'Why?' Jonathan was smart and funny, with eyes the colour of hazelnuts.

'Dad sentenced Jonathan's older brother. He's doing seven years, along with his cousin. His mum had a go at me in Asda because of it. They're a bad lot, those Campbells. Jonathan has probably only asked you to get back at Dad somehow.'

But I knew that wasn't it. The way Jonathan looked at me, you couldn't fake that. He wanted me. And I wanted him.

'If you go out with him you'll live to regret it,' Mum warned. I had tutted under my breath.

The Friday of the disco was one of those freezing winter days, where the light was sucked from the sky by tea time. Natasha came home with me after school, the dress she was going to wear neatly folded at the bottom of her rucksack. We sat cross-legged on my bed, crunching bacon Frazzles and rehearsing our parts in the play of deceit we would perform once my parents arrived home.

'Rich has dumped me, Mr Stirling.' She practiced swooning, pressing the back of her hand against her forehead.

'Boys,' I chipped in. 'I'm glad I'm not dating.'

'I'm so happy I've got you to go to the disco with, Laura.' She choked back a pretend sob before collapsing into a fit of giggles, but I didn't join in. It sounded as fake as it felt. My father had reduced grown men to tears in a courtroom. I didn't think he'd be fooled for a second.

As it was, he worked late, and it was Mum we had to convince. And I thought we had until, just as we tumbled out of the front door in a cloud of peach body spray and sparkly silver eyeshadow, she said in a voice so low only I could hear, 'You know how we feel about liars, Laura. If this goes wrong, you've only got yourself to blame.' She was calm and controlled but I was full of anticipation and hormones and I didn't stop to listen.

In the few short hours since we'd left, the school had been transformed into a winter wonderland. The huge plastic rubber plants that usually flanked reception had been dragged into the sports hall. Fairy lights wrapped around their leaves. They wink-wink-winked at me – *I'll keep your secret*. Black fabric swathed the wooden wall bars. The smell of rubber trainers and sweaty feet was temporarily masked by too much aftershave. A plywood bar was erected on piles of bricks, shielding the piano that banged out hymns on a Monday morning, causing us to collectively stare at our shoes and mumble-mime. Inside a huge glass bowl, slices of oranges and apples bobbed in a sea of crimson cranberry. Lee Miller hadn't yet arrived with his contraband Smirnoff, so the juice was as innocent as I was.

At first it was awkward. Jonathan whispering to his best mate Darren. Natasha and I sucking our drinks through straws, between flicking our hair and throwing our heads back in a riot of laughter, even though neither of us had said anything remotely funny. Tapping our feet to 'Papa Don't Preach'. Nobody wanting to be the first to dance.

Rich appeared, whisking Natasha off to a darkened corner. Darren slapped Jonathan on the back and wished him luck and then we were alone. Except for 120 other teenagers, four teachers and five parent helpers.

'Shall we sit?' Jonathan asked, and we squeezed onto a bench near the toilets. The incessant opening and closing of the door, the urine-tanged chemical smell, faded to nothing as he began to speak. His words barely registered as I fought the urge to trail my fingers across the curve of his chin, to dip my tongue into the hollows above his collarbones, to skim my lips against his. Seventeen and, ridiculously, I had never been kissed, and oh how I longed for it to happen there, among the swirling mosaic of the glitterball, the music pulsing like a heartbeat. I can recall with clarity most of the details about that night; the crumple of the plastic cup in my nervous grip, greasy pastry flakes from cheese straws spilling onto my skirt. I can't remember what it was we talked about, but the jitter in my stomach, the flush of my cheeks, convinced me it was love. Of course he wasn't dating me for revenge. You couldn't fake a connection like ours.

Later, we had shimmered around the dance floor. I think we both thought we were high on life, on love, on promise, not knowing then about the vodka we'd unknowingly consumed. 'Don't Leave Me This Way,' Jonathan had sung, flailing his arms in the air and I had silently promised I'd never leave him. He'd pulled me into his arms as we'd swayed to 'Lady in Red', and I'd thought how perfect it was that I had chosen to wear my ruby top. Meant to be.

At the end of the night, I couldn't find Natasha. Jonathan

offered to walk me home and I remember thinking what a gentleman he was. How Dad would like him, if he'd only give him a chance. Darren had leered, 'Don't do anything I wouldn't,' and licked his lips as we left, his eyes fixed on my cleavage, and I had shivered. Jonathan mistook my repulsion for coldness, and had wrapped his coat protectively around my shoulders, and that one, pure moment of unadulterated joy was the last one I experienced. Since that night, there has always been a wariness bubbling under every emotion I have ever felt. My happiness forever tainted with the knowledge that the world isn't always good and bad. Evil comes in all shades of grey and sometimes it looks like you.

Sometimes it looks like me.

As we walked, snow began to fall, thick and heavy, like something from a romantic movie, swirling halos around our heads. Jonathan's coat slipped from my shoulders and after he had hitched it up he slung his arm around me. Our footsteps slowed as we reached the park opposite my house, my pulse light and rapid, my shallow breath an unspoken invitation.

'Laura. Can I see you again? Tomorrow?'

'Yes,' I said without hesitation. 'In the park at twelve?'

He nodded, linking his fingers through mine. 'I'll see you to your door.'

'Best not. Dad would have a fit if he saw you.'

He stepped forward. My senses were on high alert. I could smell the lemon shampoo he used. The trace of washing powder on his shirt. Clean. He smelled clean. I was both nervous and excited, my chin tilted, lips parted, waiting for what came next, but Jonathan pecked his hot mouth against my icy cheek. 'Goodbye, Laura.' As I watched him leave, I pressed my fingertips against the skin his lips had brushed, wishing I could trap his kiss, wondering if it counted as my first. Oddly I knew that one day I would look back on that point and remember what it was like to feel truly happy.

Under the orange light of the lamppost I checked my watch. I only had two minutes until my curfew. Although I shouldn't have done, although I'd been told a thousand times not to cut across the park on my own, after dark, I was invincible, euphoric, the impenetrable bubble of the first throes of love protecting me. Keeping me safe.

Except it didn't.

I'm not sure when but creeping unease nudged aside my happiness. I grew aware that I was being watched. I froze, my legs betraying the gut instinct that screamed at me to run, but alcohol had dulled my senses. Before I could force myself to move he came from nowhere. Before I could release the scream that tore through my throat, I was lying on my back, my skull thundering with pain, one hand clamped over my mouth, one around my neck, squeezing, squeezing, squeezing. Alcohol hazy, my reflexes were slow, my thoughts muddied. I tried to bring up my knees. He slapped my cheek, hard.

'Stop struggling. There's nowhere to run to. There's no one to help you,' the middle-age voice growled. My body bucked and twisted. I wanted to get away, with every fibre of my being. My head slammed against a stone as I scrambled for freedom, my vision exploding scarlet before shrinking to fearful grey. My body limp.

These are the memories I carry from that night, the heavy weight of a body on mine, suffocating the possibility I had felt five minutes earlier. The smell of cigarettes and alcohol. Sweat.

Dirt. He smelled dirty, the way I felt. The taste of blood in my mouth where my teeth had clamped around my tongue. The feel of it trickling down my cheek from the wound on my forehead. Bristles prickling my skin. Metal blade glinting in the moonlight. 'Don't. Make. A. Sound.' The pain, sudden and sharp between my legs. I thought I was dying. The stars blurring together through my tears. Thrusting. Grunting. Crushing. The rush of air as he pulled his hand away from my mouth. The revulsion as his lips pressed onto mine. 'Count to a thousand before you move.' His lumbering figure retreated, mass of thick black hair bobbing as he ran, before he was swallowed by the darkness. I sobbed as I straightened my clothes. Rubbed and rubbed at my lips as though I could make that kiss disappear. As though it didn't have to be my first. As I rolled onto my knees, crimson blood streaked below me, onto the stark white snow.

It was a secret I clutched against me the next day as I huddled under my duvet, feigning illness, trying not to picture Jonathan waiting at the park I would never enter again. It was a secret I carried like the baby that grew in my belly.

'I warned you,' roared my father. 'What would happen if you went out with Jonathan Campbell.' I still never told. He thought me a slut. If I told him I was a victim of rape I knew the disgust in his eyes would still remain, if he believed me at all. Damned if I do, damned if I don't. Those fairy lights at the disco winking-winking-winking, *keep your secret close*. And I did.

My parents threw me out. 'Let the Campbells bloody take care of you.'

I stayed with Natasha, got a job on the tills at Tesco. That was where I met Gavan, when he came in to buy ham rolls, with his grubby builder boots and his beanie hat. His big ideas for the future and his brilliant, brilliant smile. He was a few years older, a million times kinder, and I unexpectedly fell in love. It hadn't mattered to him that Tilly wasn't his, he loved her with all of his heart.

What makes a father? It has to be more than the biology. How could those few seemingly interminable minutes of being held down – forced – override years of getting up for night feeds, the blowing out of candles, the teaching to ride a bike? They can't. They don't. Gavan was her father. He was.

Except she knows he wasn't, and how she guessed didn't seem so important anymore. Gavan was right. The truth will always out.

It was six months later, shortly before Tilly was born, that I saw his face staring out at me from a newspaper, and all at once I could smell his smell. Feel his hands around my throat. *There's nowhere to run to. No one to help you.* He'd raped again in a neighbouring town, and this time she was only thirteen. I ran to the bathroom. My shame and my guilt splattering the toilet bowl until I was empty. Hollow.

It was Gavan who'd held my hand as I falteringly made my statement to the police. Gavan whose eyes comforted me in court, as I stammered out what I could remember, but there were things I couldn't, and not because it was so long ago but because my mind had blocked them out. Had he worn a wristwatch? A wedding ring? Could I identify his tattoo? All of those things I didn't know, but I knew his smell. His touch. The feel of him watching me as I gave my evidence was identical to the feel of him watching me that night. The thirteen-year-old girl remained hidden as her testimony was presented via video. Thirteen. It almost broke me at seventeen. The jury learned he lived thirty miles from where he'd committed his atrocious crimes. That he had a daughter of just ten. Disgust churned when this was revealed. Was he thinking of her when he ripped away my virginity? I'd never know, but my relief when he was convicted was fierce.

I thought that was the end of it. I thought Tilly never need know. If she ever googled me, the article was so far down the list of results, I felt secure she would never stumble across it. I had waived my right to anonymity, as my relief that the judge wasn't my dad was overridden by a strong sense that I wanted my parents to know what had happened to me. I'd thought they might get in touch when it featured in the paper but they didn't.

'If you go out with him you'll live to regret it,' Mum had said, but I didn't believe her, and even now I can't say for sure if I do regret it. The memories from that night often spring at me with sharpened teeth and pointed claws. They nip and scratch and taunt me with their rancid breath, asking that if I knew what was to come, would I have stayed at home? Their goading leaves my skin cold and clammy, my breath tight and ragged, because despite the horror and the pain and the humiliation, if I had stayed at home Tilly wouldn't exist. I say to those whispering demons, yes. Yes, I would still have gone, and they flick their tails and laugh and laugh but I can't change my answer. I won't. For my daughter, I'd go through it all again in a heartbeat. And honestly, naively, I thought that night was the most frightened I could ever feel. The most I'd ever have to endure. I was a fool. The worst was yet to come. Because the prospect of life without Tilly, that white-hot searing pain of loss, nothing *had* ever, *will* ever, come close.

Although I didn't know it at the time, that was my third

mistake. Not leaving there and then, insisting Tilly came with me whether she liked it or not, but draining one more glass of brandy.

It wouldn't hurt, would it?

Oh God. I was *such* a fool.

CHAPTER FIFTY-ONE

ALEX

Threes.

Alex knew all about Laura.

And Tilly.

He knew everything.

He knew Dannii was dead.

Threes. Threes. It always came in threes.

CHAPTER FIFTY-TWO

LAURA

Speaking the truth had left an acetic taste in my mouth, and I swallowed the last of my brandy to wash it away.

'Oh God, Laura. I...' Alex ran his hand over his beard. 'I had no idea, that must have been so horrific. Did—'

'Please don't ask me anything.' It had been exhausting reliving it all and I was scared. Not just of the things I had revealed, but the way that revealing them made me feel inexplicably bound to Alex. But I was painfully aware I couldn't be. He was not mine to want.

'You've done well, Laura. It's draining, sharing.' His face was serious and there was something else there. Sympathy? Understanding? A desire to make me feel better? All of it? None of it? I couldn't tell.

'I think I should go back to the dorm now.' Half of me hoped he'd try to talk me out of it.

He didn't.

In the porch I stuffed my feet into my boots, zipped up my coat and turned away from him and all the feelings I should not have felt.

*

The air was biting, stinging my cheeks, my nose. I strode forward purposefully, feeling in my bulging pocket for my Maglite. Alex closed the door of the cottage and the soft creamy light that was spilling out was once again contained within its four stone walls.

My fingers brushed against tissues and a half-eaten tube of Polo mints.

No torch.

I slowed. My hand slipping into my left pocket. It was empty. I stopped. Casting my mind back, recalling arriving at the cottage, jamming the torch into my pocket. How certain was I? My mind was fugged with brandy, the trees swaying around me. Did it drop into my pocket, or had it fallen unnoticed onto the soft leaves as I stepped inside?

A fist of panic squeezed inside me.

As I turned, the cottage fell into darkness, except a pinprick of light coming from the bedroom upstairs.

I pictured Alex sitting on his bed, tugging his T-shirt over his head.

He was not mine to want.

Shame held the cold at bay while I contemplated what to do. The moon was bright, even under the shadow of trees. The white chalk stones glowing like the solar lights that once framed my flower beds. The memory of Gavan, pulling weeds, raking the earth, was enough to make me turn away from Alex. Carefully, I picked my way through the woods, uncertain and afraid. I told myself that the stone trail would keep me safe, lead me away from the ravine and instead towards the clearing where I could turn left instead of right and head back to The Lodge. I told myself that I'd be okay as long as I took it slowly.

I told myself lies.

I wasn't safe at all. Even though I never once tore my gaze away from the stones; not when an owl screeched his hunger, or when a bat flapped fast and low. Cloud drifted across the moon and momentarily the darkness was absolute. I waited, catching my breath. I'd been walking for what felt like hours but in reality couldn't have been more than five or ten minutes. I began to shiver uncontrollably. It wasn't because I had stopped moving that I was trembling.

It was because I was scared.

The gloom heightened my other senses. My hearing razor-sharp.

A scuffling.

A fox, I told myself. Nothing but a fox.

But still I moved away from the sound of scrunching leaves, of snapping twigs.

Forgetting that my path was no longer lit.

Alcohol clouding my judgement.

Almost plucking a direction out of thin air.

One step.

Two steps.

Quicker.

Feet pounding onto the hard earth.

Three steps.

Four, and then my feet were flailing, my arms windmilling. A scream wrenched from the pit of my belly as I plummeted into blackness. I couldn't tell you now whether it would have been less terrifying to see where I was heading, or more so. My body slammed into rock, blood filling my mouth.

My last conscious thought was that the stones should have led away from the ravine, not towards it.

Somebody had moved them.

CHAPTER FIFTY-THREE

ALEX

Alex wished he could release the pressure that built inside his head. The crow stretched out its wings, filling his mind, and there was no space for thought. No room for hope. It pecked and pecked at the inside of his eyes. He dug his fingers hard into his scalp, wishing his nails could pierce the hard bone of his skull. The crow could slip through the hole and soar into the sky, its words growing fainter and fainter with every beat of its wings.

But the bird remained inside him. Outside him. Everywhere he looked he saw it.

Heard it.

Don't hurt her. Hurt her. Don't hurt her. Hurt her.

Don't hurt her.

But it was too late.

CHAPTER FIFTY-FOUR

LAURA

Hands on me.

Gavan.

Stroking my face, my hair. Holding me close.

Hands on me.

Alex.

Around my waist.

Brushing my fingers.

Hands on me.

Weight against my shoulder blades.

Pushing.

Falling.

Hurt. Everything hurt.

Hand around my throat. Pressure. Squeezing.

Hands everywhere. Real or imagined?

It was so very hard to tell.

Cold. So cold.

I pulled sleep towards me and we danced twirling faster and faster until I was floating, soaring, spinning in the darkness.

Until I was nothing at all.

CHAPTER FIFTY-FIVE

TILLY

Saffron and Hazel talked in low whispers like I wasn't only sitting five feet away staring blankly into space.

'She's not in the dorm and her coat and boots are missing. I can't find her anywhere, Hazel.'

'I told her to give Tilly some space. She's probably gone away for a few days. Tilly, *bach*?' Her voice louder. 'Have you seen your mum?'

I shook my head.

Don't trust anyone.

I wouldn't think about her, I wouldn't.

Don't trust anyone.

Even when Daisy found Mum's broken torch while she was jogging in the woods.

Don't trust anyone.

CHAPTER FIFTY-SIX

ALEX

Alex stared at the broken clock. The hands stiff and unmoving, but still he could hear time marching on.

Tick-tock, tick-tock, tick-tock.

And it wasn't just marching on.

It was running out.

CHAPTER FIFTY-SEVEN

LAURA

It was dark.

So dark.

The smell of the damp earth I was lying upon, cloying.

Where was I? Somewhere enclosed. Cold. A coffin?

Panic formed a ball in my stomach that grew and grew, rising into my throat, cutting off my ability to draw in a breath.

My lungs burned for air as I frantically stretched out my hands to feel the space around me.

Not a coffin.

I pushed myself to sitting, chest heaving, the ball expanding, blocking my airway

Breathe.

I shook my head hard, trying to kick-start my lungs. The ferocity of my headache as I moved forced me back to lying. It took minutes for the pulsing pain to subside and the sickness in my stomach to settle.

I moved again. Rope bit into my wrists, my ankles. My fingers groped in the dark until they connected to hard metal rings that held me prisoner.

The lambing post.

I was in the sheep shed where Alex never let anyone come.

'*It's too dangerous.*'

Dizziness overcame me. I curled my bruised and battered body back into the floor.

When I came to again there was a chink of light through the gap in the roof. It was the most beautiful sight I'd ever seen. I dragged myself to kneeling. Waited for the world to stop swimming before I weakly tugged at my binds.

How had I got there?

I cast my mind back. Leaving Alex's cottage, following the stones, stepping into nothing. Teeth clattering inside my jaw as I slammed onto a ledge, and it was this and only this that had saved my life. Had someone intended on killing me? Alex? He was a long time fetching my dinner plate from the farmhouse. He'd had time to move the stones.

Pain sliced inside my skull once more. I gingerly prodded my head, wincing at the solid bump. My fingers came away sticky. I was bleeding. Drifting. Drifting.

Awake once more, my nails tore as I clumsily tried to unknot the rope and when that didn't work I tried to force it over my wrist until my skin was torn and bleeding.

My headache sharpening.

Drifting. Drifting.

Dark again.

Mouth dry.

'Help.' My voice hoarse, knowing the walls were too solid, too thick for my words to penetrate. Knowing that even if they did, nobody ever came down this end of the farm. But still I screamed, 'Help!' over and over until my voice became a croak.

An exhausted sleep carried me away.

Scuttling? Rats? I curled my body into itself but it wasn't the scratch of claws but the patter of hundreds of legs. A frenzied swarm of spiderlings rushing to devour me. Sinking fangs. Venom flooding through my veins.

Weaker and weaker I grew.

Spider legs scurrying across my face. Lips pursed together, screaming on the inside. The arachnids scrambling inside my ears, my nose. I puffed out air through my nostrils but I couldn't dislodge them as they scrambled towards my brain. I grew dizzy with the lack of air until I was forced to open my mouth. They climbed inside, the spiders, slipping under my tongue, down my throat, laying eggs in my gut that would grow until they hatched, splitting my skin, consuming my flesh, until all that was left of me was bone.

I woke to the acrid stench of urine, my jeans damp around the crotch. It was then I began to cry, but my sobs were dry and heaving. I had no tears.

Above me, through my hole to the world, grey watery light was visible. It was hard to gauge as I'd drifted in and out of consciousness, but I thought I'd been a prisoner for two days. The pain in my head was now a dull ache, my mouth sawdust-dry, stomach spasming with hunger. I knew I could survive roughly three weeks without food but it was imperative I drank or I'd be dead by the end of the week. Sitting up slowly, nausea shook me hard. I swallowed back the bile that rose in my throat. I couldn't afford to become any more dehydrated than I already was. My lack of tears was worrying. At least it wasn't hot. If I were sweating I'd rapidly be losing fluid.

I squinted until indecipherable shapes blurred and shifted.

A scratching.

Two bright eyes.

I scrambled away from the rat, the binds pulling hard against my wrists, slicing into soft flesh. For the longest time we stared at each other, him and I. I had a vision of biting his head off, drinking his blood, teeth ripping into his flesh. The fist around my stomach tightened and I vomited, tasting the brandy I'd drunk with Alex as it flooded through my mouth. Eventually I was spent. Weak. Shaking. My eyes scanned for the rat but he had scuttled towards the wall, his tail disappearing with a flick, leaving me with a semblance of hope. If he found a way in, surely there must be a way out?

Think, Laura.

My fingers pulled at the metal rings but they were heavy. Immovable. Again I tried the knots. Scrunched my fingers together and tried again and again to force the ropes over my wrists until blood dripped from raw and open wounds. A flash. Being here with Alex. Asking about the bloodstains in this very spot. A ewe in labour, he had said, but what if it wasn't? What if somebody else had been tied here before? Did they escape? How?

Think, Laura.

Gingerly I stood, the room tilting and swaying. I stretched out my arms and moved as far as the rope would allow. I could touch one wall, it was cold and slimy and for a second I imagined licking the moisture from it.

Exhausted I sat back down, my eyelids drooping heavy, but then something brushed my cheek. I pressed my fingertips against my skin, feeling the wetness as I raised my face towards the missing roof tile.

Rain.

A few spots at first, and then heavier and heavier.

I opened my mouth and stuck out my tongue. I had honestly never tasted anything so wonderful. So pure.

It was a sign.

I was going to be okay. I had to be.

Thunder rumbled and lightning cracked. Hypothermia became my main concern as the downpour continued. I was freezing and soaked to the skin. Each time I edged away, seeking out a dry spot, the raging wind blew the rain in a different direction. The rope that tethered me wasn't long enough to enable me to find shelter. The ground beneath me was damp. I miserably tugged at the metal rings on the ground once more, and there was a slight movement. A give. I clawed at the earth with my fingers, mud crusting under my nails. Could I dislodge the rings? Make my escape. The rain blew into my face as I knelt, digging furiously, thoughts of freedom blossoming into strength. Once I'd dislodged the wet earth it was harder. My fingers ached. I moved away, letting the rain fall onto the dry earth, my eyes searching for something, for anything to use as a spade. There was nothing.

I patted my pockets in the irrational hope I might find a trowel.

They were empty. I willed the downpour to continue softening the ground. Pins and needles attacked my legs and I stood, stamping my feet. My heel slamming into the ground. My clumpy heel! Quickly, I tugged off a boot and drove the corner of the solid, chunky heel into the ground. I dug until my vision was speckled and my arms felt like lead. I dug until I struck something hard and immovable. Concrete. The rings were concreted in. Disappointment and fatigue trudged through my veins.

I curled into a ball and slept.

There was still some light as I woke. I think it must have been the same day but I couldn't be certain. My tongue was thick and heavy in my mouth. Throat parched. Eyes staring at me.

'Hello, rat.' I was too weary to move. It shuffled forward. Two steps. Stopped and stared. Two more. Whiskers brushing against my forehead, its nose twitching with curiosity, sharp yellow teeth and pointed pink claws. Disinterested, it scurried back over to the wall and slipped away.

Where did it go?

I picked up my boot and crawled after him. The ground there wasn't as firm as everywhere else. It crumbled beneath my fingers. There had to be a way out. Even though I couldn't release myself from the rope, if I could make a hole to the outside there was a chance, however slim, that somebody might hear me scream. It was a long shot, but better than nothing. The desire to leave, to live, flamed hot and bright. I dug my heel into the earth and dug.

It wasn't far down when I hit something hard. I plunged my hand into the earth to feel what it was.

It was hard not to vomit as my fingers ran over the familiar shape. I pulled my hand back sharply.

Fear drummed my heart.

I told myself I must be mistaken.

It must be something else. Anything else. But I knew that it wasn't.

As much as I didn't want to, I worked at the hole again until I uncovered it properly.

A human hand.

CHAPTER FIFTY-EIGHT

ALEX

*D*on't be dead, don't be dead, don't be dead.

Alex had stared in horror at the motionless body. He imagined he saw maggots crawling from the open wound, the mouth, the nostrils.

What had he done?

He touched his cheeks, they were wet, but it wasn't until he removed his fingers he saw they weren't coated in tears, but blood.

Wake up, wake up, wake up.

But it was too late.

Afterwards he could still smell death. Hear his sister's screams.

A crow appraised him from a nearby tree stump and Alex picked up a stone and hurled it as hard as he could towards the bird. It flapped its wings and screeched out its anger but instead of retreating it edged towards him.

'Go away!' In that moment he blamed it for everything that had come before. And everything that would come after.

The bird fixed him with a mocking stare.

Alex threw his head back and let out an anguished cry.

His mind a jumble of chaotic thoughts, flapping for attention.

The bird flew into his brain and pecked to be free. But Alex couldn't release the bird any more than he could release his guilt.

He'd never be free again.

He wept for his sister.

He wept for himself.

The crow laughed and laughed and laughed. Alex pressed his hands against his ears and dropped his head to his knees.

But he still heard it.

CHAPTER FIFTY-NINE

TILLY

The mirror-me looked different. My eyes smaller without kohl lining the rims. Lashes shorter without mascara.

I was a caterpillar.

Mum had been gone for three days.

Dad, Iwan, Anwyn, Rhianon. All of the people who had slotted into my life vanished, along with the biological father I had never met. My fake life tumbling down like Jenga.

But I still had Alex. He was right; a chosen family could be more integral to our emotional and physical wellbeing. And… what else? I paused, my hairbrush suspended in my hand. I kept losing my train of thought. Something about positively contributing to our quality of life. He'd also said… what was it? The buzzing in my mind grew louder, making it harder and harder to focus. I was so tired.

Again, I dug the bristles into my scalp. My frizzy hair a mass of static. Pubes, Katie had likened it to, but pretty hair, Saffron said. Just like hers.

Here… Here I was loved.

Alex said out of the rubble and destruction flesh families leave, chosen families build something stronger in its place.

Something honest.

Matilda. I stared into my own eyes. *Matilda.*

I still had Alex.

Let go of the struggle.

A release.

I still had Alex.

Suddenly I understood it all. The journey of self-awareness. The importance of self-development.

The buzzing quietened. I waited for it to start again but there was nothing but stillness.

Peace.

Matilda.

Never breaking eye contact with my reflection, I dragged the brush through my hair over and over.

I'd let go of the struggle.

Broken out of my cocoon.

I was a butterfly at last.

And it was beautiful.

CHAPTER SIXTY

ALEX

Matilda was soft in his arms. Malleable.

He dropped a kiss on the top of her head.

A tap on the bedroom door. Daisy pushed her way inside before Alex could move.

'Laura wouldn't be very happy if she could see you all cosy.' Her eyes flashed fury.

'She's gone away for a few days. To give Matilda some space,' he said.

'Well, watch yourselves. She could be back any minute. Hazel says to tell you dinner's ready.' The door slammed behind her.

'Let's go and eat, Matilda,' he said. She nodded.

It was a shame about Laura, but with her gone there was nothing, there was no one, standing in his way.

CHAPTER SIXTY-ONE

LAURA

There was a body buried beneath the earth that I was lying on. I couldn't begin to process it. My teeth clattered together as I violently shivered. My head, already fuzzy, tried to make sense of it all. Who was buried there? I'd dropped the hand in shock and to my shame scooped the earth back over it as if it were nothing more than rubbish. If I couldn't see it, it wasn't really there. But I knew the image would be forever scorched onto my mind. Thoughts circled like angry sharks, hungry for answers. The body can't have been there too long because flesh still wrapped around bone.

Dafydd.

Did he bury somebody and run away to Australia? It was, after all, his land.

What if… a million spiderlings scurried over my skin. What if it was Dafydd buried there while everyone waited for a postcard that never came. Alex was uncomfortable with the police.

'Mr Thomas doesn't know about the death on his land?' they had asked.

Alex had been visibly agitated; the underarms of his shirt were damp with sweat. He'd been unable to provide a contact phone number or an address for Dafydd. Unable to provide a return date.

My mind began to hop. Had Dafydd wanted Alex to leave? Had Alex imprisoned him while he tried to think his way out of a bad situation. I thought of the noises I had heard coming from the cellar that was always kept locked.

'*Dangerous,*' Alex had said.

Unable to think of a solution and unwilling to leave, Alex could have killed Dafydd. Buried him here.

This last thought was torturous as I pictured the way Tilly had gazed at him that night, during the celebrations, and in my mind the hand I'd uncovered morphed into Alex's hand, touching me. Touching Tilly. A lover's hand.

A killer's hand.

I screamed out my frustration as I yanked at my binds again and again until the welts on my wrists had deepened to grooves.

I screamed as the image of the hand strobed between what I'd seen and Tilly's hand. Tilly's fingers. Blunt nails with chipped blue varnish, speckled with tiny white stars.

I screamed until my voice disappeared, hiding somewhere with the dark thoughts my mind could no longer cope with. My body shut down. Fear and exhaustion collaborating, dragging me into sleep. When I woke, it was dark. It could have been any time between 4 p.m. and 8 a.m. My calf muscles cramped. I stretched out my leg and my foot connected with something. There was a light thud. Warily, I groped around, my eyes adjusting to the gloom.

A bottle of water.

It was heavy. Full.

Was somebody there?

Instinctively I held my breath, craning my neck forward, listening for sounds of movement.

Nothing.

I twisted off the cap and hesitated. Somebody had hurt me at best, tried to kill me at worst. If they had left the bottle it could contain some sort of poison. Acid. My thirst was raging. I couldn't help myself gulping greedily, drops spilling from my lips, dripping down my chin.

My stomach began to cramp but I didn't stop drinking until I'd drained the bottle and it was only then, when I began to lower my arm, I noticed the ropes around my wrists were missing.

I was free.

Or was I?

Something didn't feel right.

It was impossible to know how many hours, days, I had dreamed of getting out of that room but now I had the chance I was hesitant. No, more than hesitant. I was scared.

Was it a trap?

A nightmare?

Had I really seen a body?

I looked at the place where I thought I'd uncovered one, and the earth was flat. There was nothing to be seen. Was I mad? I crawled over to the spot and furiously dragged the looser earth into a pile and there it was again, the hand.

Whimpering, I stood, backing away until my spine pressed against the door. I turned, pressing my ear against the wood. Listening.

My fingers gripped the door handle. I had no desire to move or to stay. This was neither fight nor flight, just cold, hard dread.

Was someone out there?

Slowly, slowly I opened the door. My breath shallow and light. I took one step forward, still clinging onto the handle like it was a raft and I was drowning and it felt as though I was. Darkness and fear and trepidation sucking me underneath the surface.

A second step.

My fingers releasing their grip.

And then I was exposed in the milky moonlight. I steeled myself, inhaling deeply before I could run on legs that felt too weak to support me. I stumbled as I hurtled towards the open field, towards my past.

Hands gripping me. Fingers squeezing my throat. There's nowhere to run to.

I threw a glance over my shoulder. A shadow. A movement.

The scar on my forehead burned.

I whimpered.

The indeterminate shape blurred before sharpening into focus.

It was a bird, nothing more.

The crow perched on a bale of straw, his eyes burning holes in me. A coldness trickled down my neck as I remembered the same crow atop the 'Beware' sign the day Tilly and I first got there.

It felt like an omen. I didn't stop to question what was possible and what wasn't. What was real and what wasn't.

I ran.

CHAPTER SIXTY-TWO

LAURA

Weak.

I stumbled through empty fields that were waiting patiently for spring. I'd almost expected to encounter a search party. They must be worried. Except 'they' wouldn't be. One of them, if not more, had rearranged the stones, perhaps hoping I'd fall to my death. Why would somebody do that? A sob rose in my throat but I wouldn't release it. Now was not the time to fall apart. All the same the thought that if I hadn't survived, then Tilly might have believed I'd purposefully jumped into the ravine, perhaps out of grief for Gavan, out of shame that she'd discovered her mother was a liar, sent a searing pain through my heart. She must be frantic, wondering where I was. She needed me. I had a ferocious desire to see her. Eventually I'd explain everything but first I had to get her out of there. Get us both out of there.

Cold.

My hands and feet were numb by the time the farmhouse loomed ahead. Its thick grey walls, the smattering of outbuildings standing sentry looked chilling. How did I ever think it looked warm and inviting? The adrenaline surging through my veins, urging my feet to run faster and faster drained away. I was dizzy. Sick. Afraid. The lump on my head throbbing, my stomach spasming.

Hungry.

I slowed, circled around the side of the house away from the stables, pressing myself into the shadows so I couldn't be seen.

Now, I was the hunter.

Light glared from the kitchen. Through the cracked-open window the heady smell of garlic. It must be time for supper.

Tilly would still be in our room. Her room. After the shock of Dannii's fall and my disappearance, she'd have retreated into herself just like she did after Gavan's death, craving solitude. Silence. Eyes rimmed red. Face puffy from crying. Mentally I traced a route. In through the front door barely anyone used, up the stairs avoiding the third that creaked, across the landing stepping over the loose floorboard. It was there I needed to be careful, I'd be standing directly above the kitchen. In my mind I crept into the room, my index finger over my lips, warning Tilly to keep quiet. The joy on her face. I'd come back. As if I'd ever leave her. There'd be no need to waste time packing. Clothes, possessions, they were all so disposable, so easily replaceable. It was people we needed to hold tight to and never let go.

I eased myself onto my hands and knees. Began to crawl past the window. Slowed. Stopped. Every instinct in my body screamed at me to move but I couldn't help myself. The desire to peek inside, to identify who had hurt me, imprisoned me, set me free, was too strong to resist.

I began to raise my head.

One centimetre.

Two.

An inch.

My eyes level with the taps on the sink, beyond them the table.

A brush against my cheek.

My head jerked upwards. Soft flakes of snow were sprinkling the ground white.

I turned my attention back to the sight in front of me. A family dinner. My mum grilling pork chops all those years ago, Dad laying the table for two.

Hazel, waving a butter-loaded knife as she talked animatedly, a piece of sourdough in her other hand. Daisy, nodding, eyes shining bright. Saffron smiling, handing out laden bowls. Alex sitting at the head of the table, elbows resting on his placemat, chin cradled between his hands.

But it was the other end of the table that drew my attention. The pain was so sudden and sharp. So physical. My hands instantly fluttered to my chest.

Tilly.

In the chair directly opposite Alex that usually remained empty.

Tilly.

She wasn't in her room crying. She was smiling.

Smiling.

As though she didn't miss me at all.

As though I'd never existed.

The wind blustered freezing snow into my face as I stumbled away from the farmhouse.

Flesh family.

The term still made my skin crawl but that's what they all looked like gathered around the table. A family.

286

When Tilly started school it left a hollow in my chest.

'Let's have another baby?' I suggested to Gavan one evening, as he picked dry plaster from his calloused fingers. He didn't answer, his expression thoughtful as he rinsed his hands under the sink. Dried them carefully with a towel.

My lips twitched with the beginning of a smile as he turned to face me. I waited for his yes. To be swept into his arms.

'I don't think we should,' he said. My head tilted to the side, waiting for the punchline. It didn't come.

'Are you serious?'

'Laura.' His toffee eyes darkening. 'In different circumstances I'd jump at the chance of having more children but it doesn't feel right.'

'Different circumstances?' My mind hopped, trying to make sense of what he was telling me. 'Don't you love me? Tilly?' My knees turned to rubber as I sank onto a chair.

'Of course I love you, you daft thing.' He crouched down and took my hands. 'And I love Tilly. She's my little girl and one day… one day we're going to have to tell her that I'm not her real father, and when that time comes, I want her to be certain that she's absolutely the centre of my world. I don't want her looking at a brother or sister thinking I must love them more. I don't…' His voice so sincere. 'I don't want her to feel *less*. Do you understand?'

I nodded. Swallowed the hard lump in my throat as I hugged him tightly. And then I packed away my hopes and dreams and covered my longing for another child with a thick blanket of love for the child I already had. Sometimes, just sometimes, when Rhianon came to stay, her fair head dipped next to Tilly's dark one as they set out their dolls for a tea party, I pretended she was mine too. That they were sisters.

My flesh family.

My chosen family.

Neither wanted me anymore.

Wearily, I trudged to the gate, reluctant to leave Tilly but I needed to fetch help. My fuddled mind couldn't quite make sense of all the crimes that had been committed. Attempted murder? False imprisonment? I bandied around phrases I'd only ever heard on TV. Murder. The body under the soil. I began to move faster, traces of bile coating my throat.

I pictured Tilly in the kitchen eating dinner. She was safe for now, but for how long?

The gates were visible before I realised I didn't have a plan. A soft light billowed from the window of Reed's wooden cabin. I deliberated what would happen if I rapped on his door and asked him to open the gates for me. It wouldn't take much to bring tears. Tell him I had a sick relative I needed to get to urgently. But then surely he must have known I was missing? Perhaps Alex even sent him out searching for me.

Don't trust anyone.

Reed might let me go, but then he might not.

I hurried away, hugging the cover of trees, down the dip and up the steep, slippery incline. The snow beginning to freeze. There the fence was lower. I thought I could scale it. If I made it as far as the main road I could flag down a car. I didn't think I had the energy to walk to the nearest village but then a mother's strength could never be underestimated, could it?

My eyes scanned the top of the fence. There was no barbed wire.

I nodded.

I can do this.

But then I remembered that ever since the rabbits were found hanging in the woods, the fence had been electrified. If I touched it I could die.

What now?

CHAPTER SIXTY-THREE

TILLY

I'd skipped dessert and been excused from clearing up, slipping back into my room while everyone else was still gathered around the table. I pulled my old clothes from my drawers. I was so accustomed to wearing white I'd almost forgotten how dark my old wardrobe was. I must have looked such a state when I'd arrived there. Angry, black T-shirts, jeans shredded at the knees. I stuffed them into the same suitcase I'd unpacked them from all those weeks ago, or was it months? It didn't matter.

I was leaving.

My eyes lingered on Mum's bed. Her sleep T-shirt still neatly folded on her pillow. I'd been sleeping in a white shirt Saffron had given me. I folded that and packed it too. The top drawer was stuffed full of toiletries. As Tilly, I hadn't realised how harmful these products were to the environment. The aerosols. The chemicals. But as Matilda, I did.

It shamed me to think I'd once wanted to market the items that were destroying the earth. I'd learned such a lot from Daisy. I'd take that with me.

My makeup bag felt weighted in my hand. I couldn't believe I once wanted to work in the beauty industry. It was all so superficial. How much time had I wasted each morning painting on a new persona when I could have just been me?

Matilda.

'You are enough, exactly as you are.' Alex nuzzled my neck and slipped the makeup bag back inside the drawer before sliding it shut. 'The cause of all unhappiness is resistance to something. What are you resisting, Matilda?'

'Nothing anymore.'

The buzzing had gone. My mind as clear and empty as the sky. I was calm.

Loved.

'Ready to move into my cottage?' He held out his hand and I willingly took it.

We were one.

CHAPTER SIXTY-FOUR

LAURA

The cottage was in darkness – a gingerbread house, I had thought when I first set eyes on it. I should have remembered the gingerbread house contained a witch. Even though I knew everyone was still gathered around the table, would linger over dessert and clearing up, my heart still pumped furiously in my chest. There was no landline there but I'd slip in, find the mobile Alex rarely carried with him out of office hours, and call the police. I would hide until they came.

A plan of sorts. I couldn't think of anything better.

It was unsurprising the front door to the cottage was locked. For all his talk of family and trust, Alex was guarded, secretive even. I shivered as I thought of the body I'd unearthed. What else did he have to hide? Danger hung in the air. Snow blanketed the ground, throwing an eerie brightness through the shadows of the trees. Once I'd loved the winter, sledging, packing snowballs, building snowmen, but it had never been the same since that night I'd been held down, numb with cold. With shock. With fear. My blood streaking the white crimson.

The terror from the past merged with the terror I felt as I raced around the perimeter of the cottage. Rattling windows, trying to heft up the old-fashioned sashes from the outside.

I couldn't.

The back door held firm as I shook the handle. I knew I had little choice but to break in if I wanted to get inside, but where? Somewhere it wouldn't be too visible if Reed passed by on one of his security checks.

From the front I fetched one of the white stones that should have guided me to safety, but didn't. I circled the cottage once more, ruling out the lounge window, the kitchen. Tucked against the house, almost obscured by a layer of snow, I noticed a flutter. The wings of a crow perched on the window-well to the cellar. It soared into the inky blackness. I dropped to my knees and peered through the smeared glass into nothing, feeling an icy anticipation. I was certain that must have been where Alex kept Dafydd before he buried him.

I raised the stone in my hand and smashed it against the window. Shards of glass still clung to the frame. I pulled my sleeve over my hand and knocked them loose.

Hesitantly, on my hands and knees, I shuffled backwards towards the window until my feet were through the hole. The ground was wet as I dropped onto my stomach, dampness filling my nostrils, fingers freezing in the snow as I tried to bury them into the earth to give myself some grip, but the ground was too hard. I plummeted into nothing.

A searing pain in my knee.

A fragment of glass tearing at my cheek.

And then the smell hit me like a fist.

Covering my nostrils and mouth with my forearm I placed my other hand on the wall, gagging at the slimy surface. Wincing as I put weight on my knee, I inched around the outside of the room until I located the light switch. I steeled myself. Did I really want to see what this room contained? Part of me wanted to climb back out of the window but where would I go? How else would I fetch help?

Three things happened at once.

A scraping sound.

Two eyes shining in the dark.

My hand slapping the switch, heart stuttering as bright light from a bare bulb flooded the cellar.

A squirrel. It was just a squirrel. I let out a short, loud laugh of relief as it scurried away. There must be a drey here. Could that have accounted for the noises I'd heard?

The room was strewn with furniture and boxes, an old-fashioned bureau and a couple of chairs with broken legs. Littered with animal droppings. Thick green mould clinging to the walls like ivy. Beads of moisture dripped from the ceiling onto the floor. The fungus clogged my throat.

The steps were treacherous, twice I nearly slipped. Alex was right about it being a death-trap. It was only when I reached the top I remembered the door was locked. Frantically I rattled the handle, claustrophobia gripping my lungs tightly.

'Let me out,' I screamed. Not caring who might hear. I needed to be out of the cellar. Into the light and the space and the air that didn't feel rancid in my lungs. There was a give, a weight dropping into my hands. The handle. Without waiting to see whether someone had released it from the other side. Without urging myself to be quiet. Be careful. Prepare myself in case there was someone waiting, ready to pounce, I hurled myself forward and tumbled into the passageway.

CHAPTER SIXTY-FIVE

LAURA

The smell of mildew clung to me as I rushed away from the cellar. The passageway was silent. Adrenaline propelled me into the kitchen. The moonlight shimmered silver through the large windows and that, combined with the brightness of the snow meant there was no need to switch on the light. I knew I didn't have time to waste but still I hunched over the sink, gulping water from cupped hands. When my thirst was sated I grabbed a banana from the fruit bowl and peeled it quickly, eating almost without chewing. I was ravenous. Stuffing grapes into my mouth as I stalked around the kitchen, checking the worktops and pulling open drawers. The mobile was not here although its charger was plugged in next to the kettle. I clung onto the kernel of hope that it would be in the dining room office. The phone was mainly used for business, 'and emergencies', Alex had said, 'although I can't envisage us having one of those here.' It would be the second time recently it had been used to call the police, the first being Dannii of course. The table lamps in the lounge cast a buttery glow, ready to welcome Alex home. Hurriedly, I checked on the coffee table, stuck my hand down the side of the sofa cushions just in case. Something crinkled beneath my fingers and I pulled it out. A condom wrapper. I curled my fists at the thought of that man's murdering hands on my daughter. Alex's desk was meticulously tidy. Pen and notebook. Indents of doodles from a discarded page which I knew would have come from Saffron. A plant with shiny, polished leaves, but no phone. Panic was rising as I rifled through the drawers.

Where was it?

I took a deep breath and tried to calm myself. They'd likely still be eating dessert, if not washing up. I still had time.

Think.

If I couldn't find it, I didn't have a Plan B.

Most people would keep their mobile by their bed. Alex wasn't most people. Nevertheless I thundered up the stairs, two at a time, flinging open the door. Stomach rolling as I saw the bed. Had Tilly laid there?

There was nothing on, or in, the bedside tables.

The spare room housed dark, mahogany furniture. In the corner, out of place, a filing cabinet. The drawer screeched in protest as I yanked it open, rummaged through the suspension files all neatly labelled. Invoices. Orders. Recipe cards. The next drawer down. Utilities. The Retreat. And there it was at the back. The last folder. The white tab containing a neatly printed label.

LAURA.

CHAPTER SIXTY-SIX

TILLY

Not everyone was thrilled with the news I was moving into the cottage with Alex. Saffron smiled tightly, the kind that doesn't quite reach the eyes. Daisy didn't even bother to try to hide the sneer on her face.

'She needs looking after properly,' Alex had said. 'With Laura leaving, well… You can't always rely on flesh families can you? We know that.'

I looked pleadingly at Hazel, she'd almost become a second mum. One person. Just one person happy for us would be enough. She threw a glance at Daisy and Saffron before averting her eyes and moving pointedly across the kitchen to stand shoulder to shoulder with them.

Threes.

Alex was right.

I didn't see it before.

Saffron, Daisy and Hazel.

Rhianon, Katie and Kieron.

Always threes.

Outside, the world was lighter and brighter than it usually was after dinner.

'Snow!'

Winter was absolutely my favourite time of year. The excitement of looking out of the window to see the drab winter garden draped in white.

'Have you looked outside?' Rhianon would squeal.

'Horrible stuff, snow.' Mum shuddered, lowering the blind. 'Still, I suppose you both want to go out and play.'

She'd help Rhianon and I pull on too-tight wellies over thick, chunky socks, navigate our hands into the gloves which tried to trick us every single time, thumb always sliding into the wrong finger-hole.

'Have fun.' She'd kiss us both before Dad took us to Beaker's Hill where we'd race down the slope on blue plastic sleds. Running up the incline again and again, the bobbles on our hats wobbling. Our legs grew tired and Dad would heft me onto his shoulders, Rhianon on his hip. We'd trudge slowly, slowly back to the top where we'd decide we wanted a snowball fight instead. Freezing fingers despite their woollen cocoons, numb noses and hot chocolate with a swirl of whipped cream and marshmallows on the way home. The best times. I never understood why Mum wouldn't come with us. We called her boring but she never changed her mind.

Crunching across the field with Alex towards the woods I was warmed by my memories. That sense of early childhood security. As if nothing bad could ever happen when it snowed.

In the darkness a bird screeched.

CHAPTER SIXTY-SEVEN

LAURA

My pulse was skyrocketing at the sight of my name. I pulled out the folder. It was heavier than I expected, but as I opened it I saw why. There wasn't only paperwork inside. There was something else.

My phone.

The phone the drop-ins had supposedly stolen.

A hot rush of fear swept from my feet to my scalp as I realised that whatever Alex's plan for me was, it was not a whim. It was cold and calculated and he'd likely been putting it into place since I'd got there. That thought was even more frightening.

I had to stop him.

I grasped at my phone, dislodging letters that spilled in front of me. I gave them a cursory glance. My stomach clenching as my eyes picked out my name. I couldn't deal with them right now. I needed to call for help.

My hands were shaking as I pressed the power button, fully expecting the battery to be flat, but the screen lit black and white where it had switched into power-saving mode. I noticed the date. The 24th of December. We hadn't missed Christmas. Another lie. If you stacked them all up they'd be as high as the barbed wire fence that isolated us from the outside world.

Alex's talk of creating our own traditions was just another way of making us dependent on each other.

On him.

Despite the injury to my head and lack of food I found I was thinking more clearly than I had been in weeks. All along he'd been controlling us.

What would happen if we disobeyed him?

Bile stung my throat again as I recalled discovering the body in the sheep shed.

I fumbled to unlock the keypad. There were several missed calls and texts from Rhianon.

I miss you & Tilly

Can you call me Aunt Laura – I need someone to talk to

Will I see you over Christmas?

The last one broke my heart. She must have thought that I'd forgotten her. That I didn't care.

There was also a text from Cathy Collins, Ashleigh's mum. It was so long I almost didn't read it, she wasn't my priority right then and I was certain it was informing me she was taking legal action against me, but one word caught my eye.

Sorry.

Hastily, I began to read.

Laura, I know we haven't always seen eye to eye but I wanted to let you know we're moving away for a fresh start. We'd just signed the contracts for our new house when we saw you. I wanted to speak but it was difficult with John there. He's still so angry, because he feels he failed Ashleigh. It wasn't your fault, or Gavan's, that Ashleigh became sick but we were frightened & that was our way of trying to make sense of it all. It was unfair. I am so very sorry about the way you've been treated. It's none of my business but I wanted to tell you to be careful at Gorphwysfa. There's something odd with the man there. Dangerous even. I'm going to be honest with you & tell you Anwyn had an affair with him. Iwan found out & he's left her. Anyway he treated her terribly. He's a bad lot. Please be careful. Wishing you all the best for the future. Cathy.

There were so many implications it was difficult to know where to start. 'Mr and Mrs Collins are building a case against Gavan's estate,' Alex had said. 'You're named as a director.'

I hadn't questioned him, assuming that when Hazel, Saffron and I had seen them coming out of the solicitors', they'd been instructing their claim against me. In truth they'd been there for conveyancing.

The floor rocked and the walls closed inward as I read the message again, trying to untangle it all in my mind.

Alex had slept with Anwyn. Iwan had left her because he found out. That explains why they'd been fighting when Tilly and I arrived. Why the atmosphere was so taut.

I chewed my thumbnail as I ran through the facts. What did I know?

Rhianon had overheard them rowing about the night Gavan died, needing to 'get their stories straight'. It was likely Anwyn had been with Alex that night. No matter what Iwan thought of his wife, he would never want Rhianon to know that her mum was responsible for tearing the family apart. That Anwyn had betrayed her daughter as much as she had betrayed her husband.

She had betrayed me.

It all slotted together like a jigsaw forming a dark and terrible picture. The way Alex knew personal things about me. Things he 'sensed'. Did he feign interest while Anwyn talked about her family? Did he ask probing questions until he got the information he wanted? It was sickening, the thought of them discussing the private things I'd thought only a handful of people knew.

My parents disowning me. Did she tell him I had a fear of losing people?

Poor Laura.

Stupid Laura.

'You're not alone,' he'd said on that very first day, playing on my biggest fear. Taking my weakness and chipping away at it.

'Your parents didn't throw you birthday parties did they, Laura?' All that stuff he could supposedly 'feel', and I fell for it.

I fell for it all.

My upset burned to rage as I realised Anwyn had shared with him the story of my rape. Of Tilly's conception. He knew that Gavan wasn't her biological father, and he told her, to try to drive a wedge between us.

'You're not my family.' Anwyn had lashed out at me and I couldn't dispute that. There was no blood between us, or shared genes between her and Tilly. But loyalty. I had expected loyalty. Not the bitter anger I'd been greeted with when Iwan had uncovered her affair.

Had Alex deliberately targeted Anwyn? And if so, why?

To get to me.

But that didn't altogether make sense either.

What was he up to?

I rifled through the papers spread on the carpet in front of me.

There was a recent letter from the council.

> After thorough investigation we are happy to confirm all
> the necessary checks had been completed on the former
> landfill site before it was sold, and it was also checked again
> before planning permission had been granted. The reports
> are attached for your perusal.

Although I knew the land wasn't toxic, and we were not to blame for Ashleigh's illness, reading it in black and white still brought a burst of relief. It wouldn't stop Mr and Mrs Collins taking further action if they had wanted to, but it made it almost impossible for them to build a solid case.

I dropped the letter onto the carpet and scooped up a bunch of paperwork held together with a paperclip. Now that I had begun searching I just couldn't stop. This was correspondence from the coroner.

> Despite being unable to contact Iwan Evans we have enough
> information to call a hearing for 25th November…

My stomach tightened. I'd missed the hearing.

I grappled through the letters until I found the coroner's conclusion. Accidental death. Again, under the anger and the confusion, relief.

Next, was a copy of Gavan's actual death certificate to

replace the interim one I had been issued with. My vision started to mist with tears as I traced his name with my fingertips vowing to keep his memory alive. Never let him be reduced to a bunch of letters on a piece of paper. To convince Tilly that he couldn't have loved her any more if he had been her biological father.

Tilly.

The thought of her spurred me to grasp my phone. I needed to call the police but before I could a familiar letterhead caught my eye.

Ironstone Insurance.

They'd pay out now that accidental death had been established.

It was all going to be okay.

The first few letters I scanned were long-winded wordy replies to questions Alex had posed. But it was the fifth one that caused my heart to jump.

It wasn't possible.

I read it again.

We are pleased to confirm… Action on behalf of Mrs Evans…
We've transferred the sum of £500,000 to Alexander Draycott
as per the client's signed release. We trust that…

Trust.

The same moment kept coming at me, leaving me panicky sick. Alex on the very first day: 'The policy is in your name, Laura, and I can't speak on your behalf so I can either walk you through the process or you can sign a permission form so Ironstone have to deal with me.' How readily I'd agreed. How grateful I was. I always was *such* a fool.

My eyes sought out the date of the letter.

22nd December.

The money had appeared in Alex's bank account the day I was forced off the edge of the ravine.

If I wasn't sure before that he had tried to kill me, I was then.

Fucking, fucking bastard.

Now, he had my money and my daughter.

He wasn't keeping either.

CHAPTER SIXTY-EIGHT

ALEX

As they stepped under the cover of trees it fell silent, the bird in his head. No longer squawking and pecking and fighting to be free.

He'd known it the instant he'd laid eyes on Matilda in the kitchen all those weeks ago, that she'd be the one to save him. To save them all.

He searched his pocket for his keys. He was almost home.

He smiled at Matilda.

They were almost home.

CHAPTER SIXTY-NINE

LAURA

Despite Anwyn's recent behaviour I felt a sense of solidarity with her – we had both been fooled by the same man. But we had something he hadn't accounted for: eighteen years of friendship, and that couldn't be wiped out with a few angry words spoken out of fear. Together we would have enough evidence to send him away for a very long time.

My fingers flew over the keyboard punching out a text to her.

> I know everything!!! It isn't just you he deceived but me & Tilly too. We're in trouble up at Gorphwysfa. I'm calling the police & when they come I'm coming to yours. We can sort everything out X

Alex had ruined so much I wouldn't let him be the ruin of this. Quickly I dialled 999.

It rang once.

Twice.

Nothing.

The screen was black, the battery dead.

Fuck.

I shook the handset violently in the unlikely event that it might release a smidgen of energy. It didn't.

Think.

I held my hands in prayer position, rapidly drumming my fingertips together.

The charger next to the kettle.

I pounded out of the room, the heavy door swinging shut behind me as I sped down the stairs. I dived on the cable, fumbling to fit it into the port of my phone.

It wouldn't.

The lead was incompatible with my handset.

A noise.

I froze, cable in one hand, phone in the other, as I heard the front door open. My legs trembling so much I could barely stay upright as it slammed shut. Panic shook me hard as footsteps entered the lounge, slow and leaden.

Slowly, slowly I put down the lead. Looked around for somewhere to hide.

The sound of Alex clearing his throat, low and loud. The same as he had at the celebration, before he gave his example for our letters.

'I am a warrior and I feel powerful.'

Just as I was retreating, something else.

Tilly's voice.

I would not leave without my daughter.

Silently I slid the boning knife from the wooden block next to the toaster.

Now, I was the warrior and Alex would discover just how powerful I was.

I would not run away.

CHAPTER SEVENTY

TILLY

Alex unlocked the front door and hesitated, glancing at me.

For one stupid moment I thought he was about to sweep me into his arms and carry me over the threshold like they did in movies, but I think that's perhaps when you get married? We're just... The truth was I had no idea what we were. When Alex asked me to move into the cottage he didn't say... No, wait. I couldn't remember if he did ask me or tell me. I couldn't remember answering at all.

'Matilda?' He gestured with his hand. I realised he was waiting for me to go in first. A proper gentleman. Dad would approve. He always walked nearest the kerb in case a car leaped onto the path towards Mum, and other random stuff like... oh yeah, things such as opening the car door for her and helping her out like she couldn't manage it without his hand. All those little gestures made it worse somehow, when I discovered who he really was. What he really was. Our family had been held together with lies. Fake. It was all so fake. With Alex it was real.

Honest.

The lounge was cosy. Alex had left the lamps on. I yawned. I hoped Alex would carry my case upstairs and put it in his room, because although I thought we were a couple, there was a small part of me that wasn't sure. Had he invited me as a friend? Did he expect me to sleep in the spare room? Again, I tried to recall his exact words but it was hard to focus. For the brief snatches my mind became clearer, it filled with thoughts of Mum. Dannii. Of Dad. I didn't want that. Feeling like my head was stuffed with straw was a good thing. The scarecrow in *The Wizard of Oz* wanted a brain – I wanted an empty space. Peacefulness. Nothingness.

Instead of climbing the stairs, Alex put my case by the side of the sofa. 'Shall we have a nightcap?' He strode towards the kitchen before I answered.

'Make yourself comfortable, Matilda. Put on some music if you like.'

The iPod was one of those huge ones that wouldn't fit into a pocket and didn't have Wi-Fi. I scrolled through the artists, giving up when I got to 'C', as I didn't recognise any of the names. I was too exhausted to think. I selected Clannad and 'The Theme from Harry's Game' filled the room.

'Matilda?'

My eyes snapped open. I'd dozed off.

'Sorry I was so long, I made some kale crisps while the wine was breathing.'

'Right.' I didn't know what to say to that. Didn't want to question why the wine needed to breathe, but I liked that about being there. I didn't have to question anything. Who I was. What I wanted to do for the rest of my life. I could just… be. I thought that's what Saffron said. There we could just *be*.

'I'm going to light the fire. There's a draught coming in from somewhere.'

I sipped my wine.

'I'm glad you're here, Matilda. I think I'll take you off contributions for a while.'

'Okay.'

'You can work here, with me, focusing on marketing. It's what you wanted to do isn't it?'

'Yes.' I tried to recall the excitement I used to feel when I thought about creating campaigns, the artwork, the slogans, the passion I had, but I couldn't conjure any of it. A magician with nothing to pull from an empty hat.

'I've had a couple of ideas for the direction of the business. Let's discuss them and see what you think. I value your opinion, Matilda.'

We talked, the fire crackling, the music soothing. The Clannad album finished and was replaced by Enya. Mum liked her. I gulped my wine until the feeling of sadness went away.

Alex refilled our glasses. His fingers linked through mine. Our eyes met. I knew he was going to kiss me. I remember thinking that it was the perfect moment. It was *my* perfect moment. Even then I somehow knew it would turn into a memory I would hold close, and that whatever happened no one could ever take it away.

No one would ever ruin it.

But that was before Saffron burst in, bringing a flurry of snow and cold air.

'Alex. Alex, I…' She scrubbed at the tears that were spilling down her cheeks.

He crossed the room and wrapped his arms around her. The warm spot on my thigh where his leg had pressed against mine, colder.

'You love me don't you, Alex?' Her arms looped around his neck, her face pressed against his chest. 'Tell me you haven't stopped loving *me*.'

He disentangled her arms and I found myself nodding. Encouraging him to tell her it was me he loved. But he didn't even look at me as he cupped her face between his hands. He didn't look at me as he planted a kiss on her forehead.

And he didn't look at me as he looked deep into her eyes and said, 'Saffron, I'll never stop loving you.'

CHAPTER SEVENTY-ONE

ALEX

Lonely. That's how Alex felt the first few years of his life. His parents played with him whenever he asked, but as he grew he craved the company of another child. Mum had cradled him on her lap and patiently explained that when he was born they'd had to take away the part of her that could grow another baby. Alex felt he'd ruined something for them all. He began to blame himself, questioning whether they blamed him too. On his eighth birthday, as Mum sank those three candles into his buttercream-iced cake, telling him to make three wishes, he knew just what he wanted, even though one of them was impossible.

He wanted a sister.

He wanted someone other than his parents to play with him.

He wanted to feel loved.

Alex didn't think much more of it until he came home from school one day. A skinny girl with wild black hair perched on the sofa, picking at her nails.

'Alex,' said his mum. 'This is Saffron. Your new sister.'

His head spun. How could he now have a sister? But his parents explained about fostering. How Saffron's mum was dead and her father was on bail and couldn't look after her.

'Hello.' He stepped towards her, hesitant. Unsure. He'd long stopped trying to make friends. After the one time he'd hurt an insect, he'd gagged as the other boys laughed and called him a pussy, but he didn't care. He was disgusted with himself and decided if that was what he had to do to make friends, he was better off alone.

She lowered her hands, looked up. Instead of amusement or disdain or any of the things he saw in the eyes of the kids at school, he saw fear. Something twisted inside his gut. A desire to protect her.

'I'll show you around if you like?' He held out his hand and she slipped hers inside of his and he knew, his three wishes had come true.

Alex was the same age as Saffron but it was him who she turned to when she had yet another nightmare, slipping into his bed. Into his arms. He'd quietly sing to her and promise her it would be okay. Her dad would be home soon. But those words impaled him like the spear he'd seen at the museum, the thought of her leaving, painful.

Months passed and life before Saffron became a blurred memory. Not quite real. They tumbled through the front door after school one day, dumping satchels at the bottom of the stairs, heading into the kitchen for hot chocolate and cookies. Sat around the table were his parents and the woman from social services with the wobbly chins who sometimes came to check that Saffron was happy.

'Come and sit down, Saffron.' His mum patted the chair beside her. Dad stood and ruffled his hair before closing the kitchen door. Alex was left in the hallway, alone with an overwhelming fear that Saffron was going to be taken away from them. Although he didn't believe in God, he began to pray.

Please keep her here. I'll be so good if she can stay. Please.

His eyes were closed, lips moved silently

From inside the kitchen Saffron screamed. The same tortured scream from her nightmares, and he knew whatever was being said was bad.

Very bad indeed.

The door flew open and she pushed past him and thundered up the stairs. Alex made himself as small as possible as the social worker waddled to the front door.

'Saffron's going to be staying,' Mum said to Alex, but instead of relief he felt confusion. Saffron was distraught. Had she wanted to leave? But more than confused, he felt responsible somehow, as if his deal with God was the definitive factor in her still being there.

Hesitantly, he entered her room. The curtains were drawn. Her body a mound under the duvet.

'Saffron?'

He was met with silence.

'Saffron.' He peeled back the duvet. She glared at him with eyes that glistened through the gloom.

'Dad's gone to prison. You told me he'd be coming home.' Alex felt wretched, although he hadn't purposefully misled her. He'd only been trying to make her feel better, but the things he said had been a lie.

'I'm so sorry. I'll make it up to you.'

He had made a promise to her and to God. He'd be a good person. He'd never lie again.

The years rolled past. They both left school with plans to go to uni, but Saffron's dad was released and she chose to live with him. Alex visited the dingy bedsit where mould clung to the ceiling and walls and condensation streamed down the windows, and he watched as she faded before his eyes. Alex completed his law degree and as soon as he got his first job he asked Saffron to come and live with him. She wouldn't, but pleaded with him to send her money for food. He set up a direct debit, pleased there was something he could do to help. The next time he saw her she was even thinner. Eyes glassy. The light inside her extinguished. Needle marks pinpricked her arms. Alex begged her to come and live with him but she wouldn't leave her father.

By that time Alex had met Dafydd, and was helping out on the farm. Dafydd allowed Alex to spend more and more time there, and he worked out his frustrations. Losing himself in the endless sky and fields that stretched as far as the eye could see.

He remembered the day he received the phone call. It was the perfect summer day. Shimmering sun and fluffy white clouds. The sort of day where everything in the world seemed right. Darkness twisted around the receiver, snaking down his throat and gripping his heart.

'This is Newtown Hospital. We've admitted your sister, Saffron. You're down as her next of kin. She's had an overdose. I think you should come.'

He rushed to her side.

'Saffron.' He took her hand, her fingers as thin as twigs and he didn't let go of her until her eyes flickered open.

'Dad's in prison again,' she whispered. 'He's never going to change, is he?'

'Don't cry. I'm here.' He wiped away her tears. 'I'll look after you.'

When Saffron was discharged Alex drove her to rehab.

'I feel so helpless,' he told Dafydd as he drove his spade furiously into the earth.

'Bring her here,' Dafydd said. 'Fresh air. Open space. It'll do her good. I'm planning on selling the farm, Alex. My hands aren't up to it but she's welcome to stay until then.'

Alex felt the potential loss of the farm keenly. Ideas flitted through his mind as he dug, until one stuck.

'What if…' Alex placed a pot of tea on the pine table at the end of the day. 'I moved here and with the money I've saved, financed an organic fruit and veg company. You wouldn't have to do anything. There's so much land here. So many possibilities.'

Dafydd balanced a tea strainer over his cup and as he poured the tea, proposals poured from Alex. A green lifestyle. A community.

'I've nothing to lose,' Dafydd said.

But Alex had everything to lose. He handed in his notice immediately and worked hard on his plans. By the time he picked up Saffron from the facility twelve weeks later, he couldn't wait to tell her about his future haven away from the outside world and all its temptations.

'Can I bring a friend I've met here?' she asked.

'Of course.'

And they built on what he'd started until it became the thing he'd always dreamed off. A sanctuary.

Saffron began to smile again and he knew he was fulfilling his childhood promise.

He was a good person.

He was looking after her.

And he knew he'd do whatever it took to keep her safe.

CHAPTER SEVENTY-TWO

TILLY

'I love you, Saffron,' Alex said again.

I told myself that it didn't mean anything. That Alex loved everyone but all the same, the buzzing in my head returned, barely audible, white noise in the background.

'Even if I've done something terrible?'

'Tell me what you've done.'

As they held each other with their eyes, something silent and intimate passed between them. Saffron's expression slid from sorrow to fear to horror.

'You know, don't you, Alex? How?'

'Tell me.'

'I've never been able to keep anything from you, have I? Please don't hate me.'

'Tell me.'

'You don't need me to say it. You know… I can't.' Her eyes flickered to me. 'Tilly…'

'It's Matilda. Unburdening sets you free, Saffron. You know that.' He wiped away her tears with his thumb. Jealousy jabbed sharply into my side. 'Let it all out.'

'I can't…'

Again, Alex cradled her face with his hands so she couldn't look away.

'Release the struggle, Saffron. There's so much love in the room. I promise you. It's okay.'

But I wasn't feeling love. I was only feeling hate.

'I…' She inhaled deeply. Her chest juddering as she exhaled. 'I moved the stones that lead from your cottage back to the farmhouse, the night Laura was here.'

'Why?' My thoughts gathered and scattered like petals on the flowers I used to help Mum arrange, as I tried to second-guess why Saffron would have done something like that.

'And…' she continued, ignoring my question. 'I came into the porch and stole her torch from her coat pocket, so that she wouldn't see the stones had been moved, and… and she'd be so focused on following them in the moonlight she'd lose her sense of direction and fall into the ravine.'

'What?' My eyes darted between Saffron and Alex, thinking I must have heard wrong. My exhausted mind playing tricks on me. Saffron can't have just said she'd tried to kill Mum and yet, I thought she had. I pinched the skin on the back of my hand, hard. I was awake, but I just couldn't make sense of it. 'Mum didn't though, did she… follow the stones… fall?' Even as I asked, I knew the answer. It was so out of character for her to disappear. My angry words ordering her to leave after I found out the truth about Dad wouldn't have driven her away.

And then it came.

As swift and as hard as the kicks Katie aimed at me on my last day of school. Mum had fallen to her death, just like Dad.

Dannii.

'Mum is… Is Mum…' I just couldn't say it. I couldn't

comprehend how Saffron and Alex were standing still and silent while my heart was rattling against my ribcage, shattering into pieces. 'Mum fell into the ravine?' I was uncertain once more. Sure I must have misunderstood. I tried to break it down into bite-sized chunks. *You can't eat an elephant all at once,* Mum used to say. She couldn't be dead.

'Saffron! What's happened to Mum?' All I could think of was getting answers, I couldn't begin to process her involvement. '*Please* tell me.'

'She's okay, Tilly.' Saffron still didn't look at me.

'It's Matilda,' Alex said.

'She did fall, but she was lucky.'

'Lucky?' There are many words I'd use to describe Mum: brave, beautiful, selfless; words I wished I'd realised while she was there. Lucky wasn't one of them. But she'd never once complained. And now…

'She knocked herself out when she landed on a ledge but she's okay. I swear,' Saffron said.

'Is she in hospital? I need to see her. Alex, you *have* to take me.' I was crying. Feeling horrible that after everything Mum had been through she could have died thinking I didn't love her. Thinking I'd never forgive her.

'She's not in hospital,' he replied. Something inside me shrank as I realised: if he knew where she was, he must be a part of it. He was supposed to be my safety, my Kansas, instead I was spinning and floundering and hurtling towards Oz where nothing made any sense.

'Please.' Everything in my body had shifted in panic, my organs squeezing together. 'Somebody tell me what's going on.'

'Tell Matilda where Laura has been these past few days,' Alex gently prompted.

'Alex, please. Can we talk alone?' Saffron begged.

'Each moment is the chance for a new beginning. You don't have to be the person you were even five minutes ago.'

'SHUT UP!' I screamed, the blinkers slipping from my eyes. Living in the moment didn't negate the past. Something awful had happened to Mum and somebody had to be accountable, but first I needed to find her.

'Saffron! Is she still at the ravine?'

'No,' she turned to me. 'I moved her.' In the dim light from the lamp her skin looked like a waxy mask, covering all the things she'd wanted to keep hidden. I thought we'd grown close, but there she was, revealing herself as the Wicked Witch. But instead of attacking with wolves and crows and bees, she'd defeated Mum with kind words and empty promises.

Lies.

'Moved her where?' When I was small and had sneaked biscuits from the barrel, or chocolate from the cupboard, Mum would patiently coax the truth out of me piece by piece, but I didn't have her patience. All I had was fury and fear and a fierce desire to shake the truth out of Saffron. 'FUCKING TELL ME!'

'To the sheep shed. I tied her to the lambing post but now she's gone.'

'Gone *where*?'

'Honestly, I don't know.'

My hands drifted to my scalp, fingernails digging into bone. The bees in my mind were back with a vengeance, loud and relentless. Should I go out and look for Mum? Demand my mobile back and call the police? Would Alex even let me have my phone? Whatever this was, he was clearly involved. It struck me that I could run to the main house and tell Hazel, but then I remembered it was her who told me Mum had gone away for a few days because she needed space.

They were all in it together.

I wasn't just frightened for Mum, I was frightened for me too. I took a deep breath and tried to calm my voice. 'Why did you tie Mum up, Saffron?' I asked like I wasn't angry or scared or any of the things I was feeling. Like it was a perfectly reasonable thing to have done.

'Because it all went wrong.' Saffron tried to wriggle free of Alex's grip but he wouldn't let her go. 'I thought Laura would like it here. We're all a family and she was so alone. I thought she'd invest the insurance money in us, but she kept talking about leaving. I thought… If she wasn't around you'd inherit everything, Tilly, and if you were with Alex…'

He had used me. Used her. I could feel myself cracking. All along I'd wished for courage when it was a brain I had needed. I didn't know what to do. How to get away from them both. How to find Mum. They wouldn't just let me leave. It all seemed so hopeless.

'Matilda,' Alex said.

Saffron had tried to kill Mum. I was going to die there. I dropped to a crouch. Yanking at my hair. The buzzing in my mind deafening.

'I love you,' Alex said, but that didn't excuse what he'd done. 'Matilda, look at me.'

Slowly I raised my face expecting to see the monster he had become, but he was Alex. Just Alex. I began to cry. 'I want my mum.'

'I had nothing to do with this,' he said. I met his eyes, the eyes that had scanned my body and told me I was beautiful, and I so badly wanted to believe him but how could I?

'Please let me go.' I wiped my cheeks with my sleeve.

'Matilda, no one's forcing you to be here.' He looked hurt. 'When you both came here I wanted to help your mum. I wanted to help you. I love you, please believe me. I didn't know about the stones. I didn't know about any of it.'

'But you did.'

'He didn't,' said Saffron. 'He wasn't involved.'

'I found Laura earlier,' Alex said. 'I'd thought it was out of character for her to leave you here. She's gutsy, not the sort to give up on anything. Especially not on you, Matilda.'

Shame pulsed through me. He'd believed in her love for me when I hadn't.

'How did you find her?' Saffron asked.

'I saw you heading over to the sheep shed this afternoon with a bottle of water and coming out empty-handed. I was shocked when I found her, but I understood why she was there. You were trying to save us – the farm, our community – but it wasn't the right way, Saff, and you know that.' He turned to me. 'She was sleeping but looked okay. She stirred when I untied her.'

'You deliberately let her go?' The disbelief on Saffron's face told me that I *could* trust Alex.

'You couldn't keep her there forever, and if you'd wanted to… dispose of her, you wouldn't have taken her water. It was the right thing to do, Saff.' Alex's voice was soft.

'But she'll call the police and—'

'She might, but I think she's had enough of them, with eve-rything she's been through. She'll need to see Matilda at some stage, but I'm hoping she'll want to put all this behind her and start again. There's half a million pounds in her bank account, now that I transferred—'

'The insurance paid out?' Saffron narrowed her eyes. 'That should have been ours! You bastard.' She sprung at him, nails raking down his face.

'Stop!' I grabbed her hair. Pulled her off him. She pushed me hard and I fell on the floor, scrambling back to my feet. I sprung at her again. Alex stepped between us, arms outstretched, keeping us apart. She stood facing him, hands on hips, chest heaving.

'You gave away our money.'

'Saffron, it was never our money, and I would never have agreed to taking it. You know that. I didn't take any money from Hazel when she offered it. It wouldn't be right.'

'You and your fucking ideals. Your rose-coloured glasses. Yes, it's a shit thing to do but the world is shit. It's dog-eat-dog out there. It was the answer to *everything*. This…' She swept her hand around the room. '*This* community you're trying to create, it isn't real.' She began to cry again. Hard to soft and back again. 'You fucking idiot! We're going to lose the farm. Lose everything, while you stand there sheltered by your veil of honesty. Don't you *care*? Why couldn't you have fallen in love with Laura instead of *her*.' She flashed me a look of pure hate. 'She'd have wanted to stay then.'

'Don't fucking look at me like that.' All those times I should have stood up for myself at school, all the outrage I could never feel for myself, came tumbling out now. For Mum. 'We have to find Mum. Now. She's out there alone.'

'She's right,' Saffron snapped. 'Laura's still on site somewhere. Reed would have known if she'd left. Alex, please… it's not too late, is it? The money?'

'It's not ours. It never was.'

'And what do we have?' Saffron was crying again.

'We—' Alex opened his arms. 'We have each other. We'll get by. We always do.'

'Not this time.' Saffron wiped her nose with the back of her hand. 'We have to find Laura and bring her back.'

'And then what?' I asked quietly, fearing the answer.

'And then we have to…' Saffron began.

'Let her go,' Alex said.

'We can't,' Saffron said, and there was something in her voice that turned me to ice. 'Laura's been digging in the sheep shed. She… she's uncovered the body.'

CHAPTER SEVENTY-THREE

ALEX

It had all started a few weeks ago. Alex had strolled into the kitchen at the main house, unaware that that was the moment his life would begin to spiral out of control.

Leaning against the Aga, hands wrapped around a mug, was a blonde woman.

'Alex, this is Carys,' Dafydd said delightedly.

'Carys? Your daughter?' Alex's smile stretched as wide as Dafydd's. He knew how much the farmer missed her. 'It's so good to meet you.' He offered his hand before wrapping her in a hug instead. Any family of Dafydd's were family to him too. She was stiff in his arms. Pressing against his chest, pushing him away.

'Sorry.' Alex shook his head laughing. 'I'm just so pleased you're here. I didn't know you were—'

'I thought I'd surprise Dad.' Her Australian accent was prominent, but underneath was still the faint Welsh lilt. She didn't return his smile. 'I haven't heard from him for ages and I was worried. But I was the one who was surprised, finding a house full of strangers.'

'She's met Daisy and Hazel—' Dafydd began.

'Yes, once I got past the electric fences and barbed wire gate.

Both women wearing all white.' She raised her eyebrows. 'Dad says that's a thing here?'

'Yes. Well…' Alex was uncomfortable. Aware it looked odd to an outsider.

'And you're the leader, I understand.'

'Not exactly a leader, but Oak Leaf Organics was my idea…'

'Ah yes. The fruit and veg. If it wasn't for that I'd almost think you've turned Dad's farm into some sort of… *cult*.'

'Ah, there's no sacrificing goats at midnight, I'm afraid.' Dafydd's eyes twinkled. He seemed unaware of the change in atmosphere.

'Glad to hear it,' Carys said. 'Or I'd think Alex here had taken advantage of a vulnerable old man.'

'Less of the old!' Dafydd placed his mug on the table. 'I can't wait to show you around, Carys. Show you the changes.'

'Of which there are many, I bet.' Again, she flashed Alex a look.

'Yes. There are. Alex implemented most of them. Along with Saffron. She's his sister. Oops.' He covered his mouth. 'We don't tell people that. Alex wants everyone here to feel like one big family. No favourites. It's not the past that matters is it, Alex, but the now?'

Alex averted his eyes so he couldn't see the disdain on Carys's face. Dafydd continued.

'Reed. You met him on the gates. He's been here since the beginning. He arrived with Saffron. They met in rehab.'

'Rehab! Dad. Let's go for a walk. Talk properly. Just *family*.'

And that one word contained enough bitterness and doubt for Alex to know.

It was all going to fall apart.

Carys only stayed for a few days but that was long enough to ruin everything.

After she'd gone, Alex stood at the ravine jotting down notes on his clipboard.

'Alex,' Dafydd said. 'We need to talk.'

'Yes. I'm thinking rock climbing, high wire, that sort of thing to start with and then we can…'

'I don't think that's possible,' Dafydd said in a low voice.

'I know there's a lot to sort out with insurance and everything, but I really believe—'

'It's not the insurance.' Dafydd couldn't look Alex in the eye. 'Look, you've been like a grandson to me and I love what we've achieved here, but I'm not getting any younger and…' The farmer's voice was regretful. 'I'm going to Australia.'

'That's great.' Alex smiled. 'The heat will do your arthritis the world of good, and Carys wasn't here for long enough. When you come back—'

'That's the thing.' Dafydd raised his face. Alex could see he was battling tears. 'I won't be coming back. I'm selling the farm.'

'But…' Panic clutched at Alex. 'What about the retreat? Where will we go?' It wasn't just him and Saffron, there was a whole community now. 'Hazel, I can't send her back to her husband and kids. Daisy doesn't speak to her mum. You *can't* sell.'

Alex had to stop him.

CHAPTER SEVENTY-FOUR

TILLY

Alex seemed to fold into himself, shrinking before my eyes, while Saffron pleaded with him to run away with her.

'What body?' I was shaking.

He shook his head, eyes wide.

'Alex, *please*.' I had to know. 'What have you done?'

And when he told me, something deep inside my core shattered.

CHAPTER SEVENTY-FIVE

ALEX

'Please don't sell the farm. It's our home,' Alex begged.

'I know,' Dafydd said. 'I really am sorry but Carys has asked me to go and live with her in Australia and… she's *family*. I'm getting old. I want to retire.'

'I'll buy the farm,' Alex cut in. He wasn't sure how he'd raise the money but he would try. 'I'll draw a business plan and—'

'It's too late, son.' Hearing that cut Alex to the quick. 'Carys has already found a buyer. A deal's been agreed.'

Back at the cottage Alex sank into a chair and buried his head in his hands, after he'd recounted the conversation to Saffron. It was over. He'd let everyone down.

'I'm so sorry,' he muttered. 'I don't know what we'll do.'

'Don't tell the others,' Saffron said. 'They'll only worry. We'll make a success of Oak Leaf Organics,' she said. 'I'll go door to door further afield, with all the local businesses. Persuade them to stock us. We can raise the money, I know we can.'

Alex didn't have the heart to tell her it was too little, too late.

The atmosphere was strained and awkward.

Days later, Dafydd dragged a suitcase down the stairs. Placed a hand on Alex's shoulder.

'I really am sorry. You know how fond I am of you. I think

it's best that I go and stay with Carys until the sale goes through. It could take weeks. You've time to find somewhere else to go. You're a bright lad. You can recreate all of this somewhere else.'

'Please don't tell everyone you're selling. Let me be the one to break it to them, when I've made a plan.'

'I'll tell them I'm just visiting Carys,' Dafydd said. 'Keep it vague.'

'Thank you,' Alex said. 'I'll drive you to the airport.'

'I was going to give you the Land Rover anyway.' Dafydd pressed the keys into Alex's hands.

Alex sat in the car thinking as the engine idled while Dafydd said his goodbyes. By the time he climbed into the passenger seat the tip of his nose was red, his cheeks stained with tears, and Alex knew he loved them all in his own way.

They were his chosen family.

But Dafydd wanted to be with his flesh family.

It was impossible to compete.

Dusk closed around them as the Land Rover hugged the narrow roads. The Beatles song 'Hey Jude' floated out of the tape deck. The traffic grew in volume as the mountains shrank in the rear-view mirror.

The airport was bright and busy.

'I'll come…'

'Best not.' Dafydd's voice was gravel as he squeezed Alex in a tight hug. 'When I've a firm date for the sale I'll be in touch.' It was hearing this that made Alex realise that their relationship had irrevocably altered. There was no promise of postcards, photos. A friendly sharing of news.

Alex watched the farmer carry his battered old case into the terminal without once looking back. A tear slid down his cheek as he said a silent goodbye to the man who had been like a grandfather to him.

He missed him already.

For weeks there was no word. Alex kept Oak Leaf Organics viable. Saffron doubled her efforts selling to shops, while he drew up a business plan, meeting with estate agents, banks. Trying to find them an alternative site, finance.

He couldn't.

But the lack of news caused him to wonder whether Dafydd had had a change of heart. Wondering if they'd be able to stay.

But that was before his mobile rang.

'Boss,' Reed said. 'There's a man at the gate says he's here about the sale.'

Alex felt the heavy weight of defeat round his shoulders.

'Bring him to the cottage.' Alex tossed his phone onto the table and turned to Saffron. 'I think this is it,' he said sadly.

Alex paced the room and Saffron chewed her nails as they waited for Reed to show the man into the lounge.

'I'm Alex—'

Before he could finish introducing himself the man flew at him.

The first punch made his teeth rattle in his head. The second knocked him off his feet.

'You bastard,' the man shouted. 'I should fucking kill you.'

'Stop!' Saffron screamed as the man lunged forward again.

Alex spat out blood and a tooth onto the carpet. Reed grabbed the man's arms and began dragging him towards the door.

'Let him go, Reed.' Alex deplored violence. He pulled himself onto the sofa, making it clear he wasn't going to fight back. 'What the hell do you think you're doing? *You're* buying our home. I'm the one who should be angry with *you*,' Alex said.

'I don't understand…' Saffron was crying. 'Who are you?'

'My name's Iwan Evans, from Evans Construction. Carys agreed to sell the land to my brother Gavan before he died.' His voice was hard and angry but his eyes were full of sadness.

Saffron took a sharp intake of breath and despite his bruised jaw, Alex also felt pity for the man standing before him. He'd suffered. 'I'm sorry for the loss of your brother.'

'I don't want *your* pity,' Iwan said.

'What *do* you want?' Saffron asked.

'I decided I wasn't going to pursue the sale. I wasn't interested in the land, and I'd heard the people living here didn't have anywhere to go. I felt they had enough to deal with, coping with a scumbag like you, and it seemed harsh to make a whole community homeless, but then…'

'Scumbag? I don't think—'

'Oh I don't *think*. I *know*.'

'Don't make me out to be the bad guy. I know there's a lot of money at stake and—' Alex began.

'The money wasn't for me. There's a delay in Gavan's life insurance policy paying out to his wife. She's about to lose her florist shop and her home.'

'And family comes first.' Alex wiped his mouth with a tissue. It came away crimson. 'I admire your loyalty but—'

'I don't *want* or *need* your fucking understanding.' Iwan's face was growing red once more. 'You can't talk about loyalty, you—'

'Don't judge me. You don't know—'

'I *know* you've been fucking my wife and I *know* she was

333

with you the night Gavan died. It all came out after I'd driven to her friend's to pick her up and she wasn't there and her cover was blown.'

'I don't—'

'And,' Iwan was shouting again, 'although I thought after Gavan died I didn't want the sale, now I've met you it will be my greatest pleasure to buy this farm and kick you out.'

'Your wife?' Alex gave a swift shake of his head. His vision lurched and settled. 'I have no idea what you're talking about.'

'Anwyn. I *know* you've been having an affair with her. I found condoms in her handbag. I had a vasectomy after we had our daughter, Rhianon. She's seventeen! It's not just my life you're ruining, you home-wrecking—'

'I don't know anyone called Anwyn.' Alex's head hurt and he couldn't grasp what was happening.

'Liar! She said the guy from *Gorphwysfa*. That's—'

'Me,' Reed said quietly. 'Me. Not Alex. I'm sorry.'

'You?' Iwan's jaw hung open as his eyes drank in Reed's tattoos, his bald head. 'But… how?'

Reed sighed. 'We met by chance. I stopped to help her change a flat tyre and we… what can I say? We clicked.'

'You bastard!' Iwan clenched his jaw, his fists. He drew his arm back once, twice, throwing his weight behind his punch, again and again. Bone on bone. The crunch of cartilage.

'Stop!' Saffron cried. 'Leave him alone! Leave us *all* alone!'

There was so much noise. Screaming and shouting. It was so chaotic he felt dizzy. Alex had lost control. Helpless, he saw Saffron lift the poker from the hearth. Swing it high above her head. Bring it down on Iwan's skull. He crumpled to the floor,

Saffron falling to her knees beside him, a horrified expression on her face.

What had Alex done? He had just sat there and allowed it to happen.

They all watched transfixed as Iwan's blood stained the carpet.

Time stretched and bent around the silent clock with the hands that never moved.

'Is he...' Saffron asked eventually.

Alex kneeled down and pressed his fingers against Iwan's throat. His fingers warm with the blood that streamed from the wound in Iwan's head. He shook his head and began to cry. 'It's okay,' Saffron said, wrapping her arms around him as his hands dripped blood. 'It's okay if we don't tell. I won't tell...'

'We need to call the police,' Reed said. 'I'll tell them it was my fault, I'll...'

'No!' Saffron reached and grabbed his shirt between her hands. 'Please, Reed. Don't say anything. I've seen what it's like in prison. I've seen what it did to my father. I'd never cope. You owe me. You had nowhere to go after rehab and if I hadn't helped you. Given you a home.' She began to sob. 'Alex?' He turned to face her. The torment in her voice made his fury at what she'd done melt away.

'It'll be okay,' Alex said robotically. 'It'll be okay.' But he didn't know how.

Later, Reed had driven into town and dumped the poker in a skip, while Alex and Saffron scrubbed at the blood on the carpet which wouldn't come out. Under the cover of darkness, while the stars remained hidden beneath a blanket of clouds,

Alex and Reed clumsily half-carried, half-dragged Iwan's dead weight over to the sheep shed where no one ever ventured. Saffron passed him the spade.

'I don't think I can—' Alex began.

'Alex. You promised. You promised to look after me.'

'If I do this you'll never look at me the same way again. I'll never look at you the same way again.' He knew the trust he'd had in her was gone, but the love. The love was still there. 'There's no going back from this, Saffron. And if Dafydd doesn't sell the land to Iwan, there'll be somebody else. It's crazy to think we can keep this hidden.'

'I can fix it,' Saffron said, but she couldn't quite meet his eyes. 'I can fix it so we can buy the land. Stay here. Trust me.'

'How? How can you possibly fix this?'

'You wouldn't… I can't… I've had an idea. I need to check something first but let me try. Please.'

There was desperation in her tone, and although Alex knew there was no way she could fix the unfixable, he didn't know what else he could do to protect her, except dig.

As Alex stumbled out of the sheep shed he was streaked with mud and tears and another man's blood. He was an altogether different person to the one who had gone inside. A crow appraised him from a nearby tree stump, judging him. Alex picked up a stone and hurled it as hard as he could towards the bird. It flapped its wings and screeched out its anger, but instead of retreating it edged towards him.

'Go away!' In that moment he blamed it for everything that had come before. And everything that would come after.

The bird fixed him with a mocking stare.

Alex threw his head back and let out an anguished cry.

His mind a jumble of chaotic thoughts, flapping for attention. The bird flew into his brain and pecked to be free. But Alex couldn't release the bird, any more than he could ever release his guilt.

He'd never be free again.

He wept for his sister.

He wept for himself.

The crow laughed and laughed and laughed. Alex pressed his hands against his ears and dropped his head to his knees.

But he still heard it.

Even now.

He still hears it.

CHAPTER SEVENTY-SIX

TILLY

My body was trembling.

Saffron had killed Uncle Iwan.

Reed had had an affair with Aunty Anwyn.

'Laura will call the police and they'll come and arrest us all. We have to leave, Alex. NOW!' Saffron took his hand and tried to drag him towards the door.

'No!' He shook his hand free.

I put my hands over my ears. The buzzing. My thoughts. I wanted… I needed everything to slow down. To stop.

Uncle Iwan was *dead*.

Mum was missing.

The police were going to take Alex away from me.

My Jenga life was toppling once more, when I'd finally thought I was rebuilding it.

I was going to be left alone if I didn't stop this. Stop *her*.

It was easy slipping out of the room unnoticed.

It was easy lifting the gun propped against the wall in the dining room.

It was easy curling my finger around the trigger.

It was what came next that was the hard part.

PART THREE

The Aftermath

CHAPTER SEVENTY-SEVEN

LAURA

Everything seems to happen simultaneously. From my hiding place in the kitchen where I'd listened in disbelief to the confession, I hear Alex shout, 'Put down the gun, Matilda,' and instantly I'm pelting through the kitchen, catching my hip on the sharp corner of the worktop. Reed's voice snarls, 'Look who I've found wandering around outside the gates.' Roughly dragging Rhianon by the arm.

'Aunt Laura.' She tries to reach me. 'I got the text you sent to Mum that Tilly was in trouble. I got a taxi. I want to prove to her...'

Noise. There is so much noise.

Tilly swings around with the gun. Her shoulder jerking backwards as her finger squeezes the trigger.

There's a split second of disbelief, perfect, perfect silence before time kicks in again and it all unfolds with cinematic clarity; the gunshot, the scream. Every detail sharp and clear. Time slows as Rhianon's eyes plead with me to help her. In my mind I bundle her behind me, shielding her body with mine, but she is too far away and I know I cannot reach her in time.

But still I try.

My legs are weighted with dread as I run towards her; the fist around my heart tightening.

'Tilly, stop!' The words are painful as they tear from my throat.

A second shot.

Rhianon's knees buckle. She crumples like a paper doll.

The ground falls away beneath my feet and I crawl towards her like the animal I have become. My palms are sticky in the arc of blood that is staining the floor red. Blood is thicker than water they say, but hers is thin and beacon-bright. Adrenaline pulses through me leaving numbness in its wake, as I press against her wrist, desperately seeking a pulse. With my other hand I link my fingers through hers the way we used to, before I brought us to this place that has been our ruin. A lifetime of memories strobe through my mind; cradling her close in the maternity wing as an exhausted Anwyn was stitched; Easter eggs spilling out of the wicker basket looped over her pudgy arm as she toddled after Tilly in the garden; her first day of school, ribboned pigtails swinging as she ran across the playground hand in hand with Tilly. Cousins. Best Friends. How had it come to this?

She can't be gone.

Can she?

Fingers of panic press hard against my skull. The colour leaches from the room. A black and white hue descending upon me. I tighten my fingers around hers, afraid I'm going to faint. Afraid I'm going to let her go.

But then.

A flicker of eyelids. A murmur from her lips.

'Rhianon.' I try to whisper life back into her. Needing her to know she is not alone. 'Rhianon.'

I lay next to her, gently rolling her towards me, holding her in

342

my arms. I can't, I won't leave her. Family should stick together. Protect each other. We should never have come here, Tilly and I. I should never have texted Anwyn that we needed help.

This is all my fault.

The drumming in my head grows louder – the sound of footfall. I don't have to look up to feel their anger, solid and immovable. Saffron and Reed tower above me.

The acrid smell of gunpowder hangs in the air along with my fear.

Looking up, my eyes meet Tilly's. Her face is a mask of utter despair. Her mouth opening and closing but no words forthcoming. Reed snatches the gun from her hands and I berate myself for not taking it.

Sensations return, hard and fast. The pain in my stomach is cutting and deep and I am no longer sure if the blood I am covered in has come from Rhianon.

Or is coming from me.

Her top is soaked crimson, as is mine.

The pain increases.

Terrified, I tug at her clothes, my clothes. Praying. Let her be okay. Seventeen is no age. Let it be me.

At last I find the wound but before I can apply pressure to stem the flow of blood there are hands on my shoulders. My elbows. Pulling.

Darkness flickers at the edge of my vision but still I fight against it. I fight against them.

My hands are restrained, feet kick out, teeth sinking into flesh, but it's fruitless. I am growing weaker.

Rhianon's fingers twitch. Once. Twice.

Nothing.

'Rhianon! Tilly!' My scream rips through me as I am yanked to my feet. 'Tilly! Rhianon! They're just kids. Leave them alone!' I scramble for traction, every fibre of my being straining to reach my daughter. My niece.

I can't.

'Alex!' I plead for help but he is banging his fists against the side of his head as if he is trying to release something, a low moan of despair falling from his lips. 'Alex!' I call again but it's fruitless.

I am still wrestling to be free as I am dragged, my feet scraping the ground, but I'm losing the fight against Reed as Saffron pushes a compliant Tilly after me.

I know they'll never let us leave here now.

Not alive anyway.

CHAPTER SEVENTY-EIGHT

TILLY

It builds and builds. The fear. The noise. The confusion.

The thought of Alex being taken away crashes into me. A mist descending. Everything seems further away, out of focus. The buzzing in my ears deafening.

It all happens so fast. The door swings open. I don't even take the time to register who is standing in front of me. I have to keep Alex safe. With me.

Noise. So much noise.

I don't consciously squeeze the trigger but it happens anyway. Twice.

The gunshot cracks. My *Wizard of Oz* courage drains away as I fragment into tiny, tiny pieces.

Now, the buzzing in my mind is louder than ever before. Filling me. Consuming me until I am the sound and the sound is me.

Out of the fading light I hear a voice. 'Come back to me, Tilly.' But I don't want to come back.

Ever.

I don't deserve to.

CHAPTER SEVENTY-NINE

LAURA

'Come back to me, Tilly.'

Slumped on the damp floor of the cellar I cradle my daughter in my lap. Reed is banging nails into wood, boarding up the small window I climbed in through probably only a couple of hours ago. It already feels like another lifetime. He has already screwed the door handle back on, while Saffron stood over us with the gun.

The last chink of moonlight is sucked away. I swallow hard, tasting my terror at the back of my throat. As terrified as I am for Tilly, I'm frantic with worry about Rhianon. The gratitude I feel that she came to help is pitched against fury that she could be so reckless. But my rage is misplaced, I know. The one consolation is that I think she must have fainted. She wasn't the one who was shot. I know that because although at the time adrenaline had numbed my body, now the spasms of pain in my side are brutal.

I press the heel of my hand against the wound, trying to stem the flow of blood. I imagine Rhianon out there alone, waking from her faint, scared and confused when she'd only come to help.

Alex was right. Blood isn't always thicker than water. The

bond between chosen families can run deeper than flesh families. When I agreed to marry Gavan, when he dropped to one knee, and uncertainly offered a ring, I was saying yes to Anwyn. To Iwan. To Rhianon.

Gavan may not be Tilly's natural father, she may not share the same genes as Rhianon, but although they've been through a rough patch, when it counted Rhianon came through. That's family in my book.

Alex.

I'd thought he was manipulating us. Assumed he was the one who had tried to lead me to my death. Locked me up. I'd got it so very, very wrong. He'd been trying to protect me from Saffron. He was the one who set me free. He didn't want my money at all.

He wanted my daughter.

'Come back to me, Tilly.'

He loves her.

I love her.

She's somewhere else and I need to reach her. 'Tilly, do you remember how obsessed you used to be with *The Wizard of Oz*? We watched it over and over.' Sticky popcorn. Sticky kisses. The memory has a warm amber glow. 'You used to pretend to be the lion. You'd curl your tiny hands into fists and bounce from foot to foot like a boxer. "Put 'em up. Put 'em up," you'd say. Do you remember, Tills?' I can't see her expression in the dark. She is limp lying across my lap, giving no indication she even hears me. I tighten my arm around her, wanting to hold her together, stop what little of her there is left from unravelling. 'You need to find your courage now, my baby. You need to be strong. Come back to me, Tilly.' I pause.

Listen.

Nothing.

I place my hand on her ribcage, the way I used to when she was a baby, when I'd jolt awake in the middle of the night, convinced something was wrong, rushing to her cot, feeling the rise and fall of chest. Reassured.

'Do you remember when Dad stuffed the hay we'd bought for Peppa, the hamster, under the cuffs of his sleeves like the scarecrow and sang "If I only had a brain".'

Nothing.

'And I'd march around the room like a robot, made of tin.' But oh I have a heart, I can feel mine breaking. 'Tilly, come back to me.' The deluge of memories are losing their colour, the happiness of that day tainted now. 'Please remember.' I begin to sing 'Over the Rainbow' wishing we were soaring high in a clear blue sky with those ruby shoes and promises of home. I shift my weight. Pain pulses through me in red-hot waves. I press my hand harder against my wound. The bottom half of my top is saturated with blood now. 'Tilly.' The word is a plea. I feel myself beginning to slip away too.

Skies are blue.

My mind muzzy, the smell of mildew fading, replaced by the smell of roses.

Roses on my wedding day.

'Gavan.' He is light and bright and all things good. 'You're here.'

He smiles. 'I'm always here.'

My shoulders relax, my hand growing limp. The blood gushing through my fingers no longer warm but cold.

It's so very, very cold.

'Gavan.' He begins to fade. 'Take me with you.' Panic bubbles.

'She needs you.' His eyes on mine. 'Our daughter needs you.'

Then the floorboards above us shift.

The sound of the key scraping the lock.

Someone is coming.

CHAPTER EIGHTY

LAURA

I'd watched a documentary about it once, hysterical strength. Feats stretching the boundaries of what should be humanly possible in times of crisis.

By the time the door groans open, a wedge of light creeping into the room, I have manoeuvred Tilly off my lap and am staggering up the stairs, feet slipping, hand gripping the rail to prevent myself from falling backwards. Panic and pain pitted against a monstrous desire to get us out of here.

To live.

Saffron is framed in the doorway. She shoves a weeping Rhianon towards me. It's such a relief to see she's awake. This time I do bundle her behind me. Shielding her with my body. I hear her clatter down the stairs towards Tilly.

'What's going to happen now... to us? I need an ambulance. For God's sake I've been *shot,* Saffron.'

'I don't know...' Fear raises her voice as she backs away. I can't let her leave now. We'll never get out.

Calm. I need her to be calm. Keep her talking.

'I don't understand.' I am fumbling for words, playing for time. My mind sifting what I *can* do from what I *should* do. What I am capable of is something else entirely.

'Understand what?'

'Any of it.' My voice catches. I realise that under my delaying tactic is a need to know whether any of this was genuine, this place I thought of as home. These people I'd come to regard as friends. Family. 'Was it always about the money?'

'No. Meeting you was coincidental. I'd visited all the shops in the area asking them to stock Oak Leaf Organics. I knew the farm was being sold and I thought if I ventured further afield I might be able to generate more income for us.'

If only I hadn't been there the day she passed by.

'When I saw you have a seizure I felt sorry for you. Part of me genuinely wanted to help but the other part... The other part knew we were going to have to move out of the farm and I did wonder, after you told me about your problems with your life insurance, whether there was a way we could use your money to start again. Then the following week we met Iwan, of course.' She pauses. 'When he mentioned his sister-in-law and her flower shop, it was obvious it was meant to be. I'd already met you! I'd already offered you help!'

'You had no idea I was married to the man who tried to buy the land when we first met?'

'No. Dafydd never shared details of the sale with us. It wasn't until Iwan turned up here... God... Iwan.' Tears slide down her cheeks. 'That really was an accident. I promise you.'

I glance at Rhianon but she is huddled next to Tilly. I can just about make out a vacant expression on her face.

'I googled you after Iwan had... gone, and it confirmed who you were. I found out... everything. And then I *knew*. I absolutely *knew* it wasn't a coincidence at all. Fate had led me into your shop. It was destiny, Laura, believe me. We were *always* meant to meet.'

'I don't believe in destiny.' How could Gavan's death, my rape, any of it be part of some grand plan?

'But you *must*. The six degrees of separation is real. We are all intrinsically linked. When you came here, Laura, I was so happy. I thought it was the answer to everything, not just our problems but yours. I genuinely thought you could find a home here, the way Reed and I did. That you'd willingly use your insurance money to save us. Then we wouldn't have to worry about moving, or about the new owners discovering Iwan's body. And Tilly... Getting to know Tilly was a joy.'

I hate her saying my daughter's name. 'And Alex approved of using us like that?' I'd heard him deny being a part of it, but I wasn't convinced.

'Alex didn't know anything. He would never have agreed. He's a good person. Hazel and Daisy don't know anything either. Really. I am sorry. I never meant for anyone to get hurt.' She reaches for my hand but I pull away. 'It all sounds so desperate but I was desperate. I told Alex I'd fix everything. Reed knew bits and pieces about your family from his relationship with Anwyn, and he shared it with us. Alex wasn't trying to be manipulative, mentioning things about your childhood. He wanted to help you heal.'

Does she expect me to be *grateful*? 'And Anwyn?' I can't help but wonder about my sister-in-law. 'Reed's cast her aside, I take it? Who's going to help her heal?' She must have loved Reed. She'd never have risked everything for a fling. Never have shared so much of herself. Of all of us.

'She wanted him to move in with her once Iwan had moved

out, but this is the only real home he's ever known. She didn't take it well when he ended it. She keeps texting him saying Iwan has walked out on her, and begging him to try again. I suppose she'll find out now Iwan's... never coming back.' She steps backwards. The sound of Reed fixing the window has stopped. 'I have to go.'

'Wait!' I am running out of time but there is something I genuinely need to know. 'Alex knew Gavan wasn't Tilly's biological father. But...' I lower my voice so the girls can't hear. 'Did Anwyn tell Reed I was raped?'

The word that made me feel dirty and ashamed for years has lost its power. Nothing is as important as the desire to survive this. But part of me needs to know whether Anwyn had knowingly betrayed me, as she had her husband. We had been so close once.

'No.' Saffron keeps her voice as low as mine. 'I... I'm sorry you were raped, Laura, but out of that came Tilly. So much suffering, but she's the result. She's such a gift. She almost makes it all worth it. You should tell her. She could find out via the internet if she ever searched. The truth will always out.' She glances towards Tilly and her expression softens. 'Anwyn told Reed that you and Gavan got together after you fell pregnant. That's all. How at first he treated you like you were made of glass. Always worrying in case you had a seizure.'

'I hadn't had a seizure for years before... before I met you.' I don't think she had anything to do with that, but the uncomfortable expression on her face tells me she did. 'What did you do to me?' I whisper.

'Laura, I'm sorry. After you had a seizure in the shop I researched epilepsy and learned that extreme stress can cause a one-off episode. I also discovered that old-school antihistamines can sometimes trigger seizures in epileptics. I've been putting them in your drinks here. They rarely worked, but...'

'Why?' I ask. But I know why. So I'd lose my car and my independence, leaving me weak and vulnerable. Easy to manipulate. I think of the constant exhaustion I've felt. How I put it all down to grief. Manual labour. I haven't been able to think clearly since I arrived.

'It was for you and Tilly as much as us. So you'd settle here and see how different life can be out of the rat race. How *good*.' She makes it all sound so rational, my knees shake harder. She really is capable of anything.

My stomach is a burning mass of pain. My hand dripping with blood. I am dizzy but determined to keep her talking until... I don't know what, but something. There has to be *something* I can do.

'And I bet you took no pleasure reporting me to the DVLA.' My knees buckle and I lean against the wall. Stars exploding behind my eyes.

'That was Tilly. Alex told her how worried he was about you. He always wants to do the right thing. The honest thing. It was the same when I mentioned to him that Seacrest Solicitors had rung. I pretended they had told me Mr and Mrs Collins were taking legal action against you. They hadn't rung, of course, but I knew after seeing them coming out of the solicitors, you'd believe it.'

'And the rabbits?'

'Reed. That was awful. I love animals.'

'Let us go. Please, Saffron. I know you're not bad. Not really.' My voice is growing weaker, along with my body.

'Laura... I don't know what we'll do, but I can promise you I'll never hurt Tilly, and not only because she'll inherit half a million pounds if you're not around. You...' She swallows hard. 'It might be too late for you.'

'And Rhianon?' My heart is breaking.

She shrugs. 'It's not my fault.' Her voice is tinged with hysteria. 'If you could have *just* stopped banging on about starting a business, buying a house, been... been a little *grateful,* we could all have stayed together, been a proper family.'

'You're no family of mine. We're...' I gesture weakly towards Tilly and Rhianon. 'We're a family. Are you *really* going to be responsible for tearing us apart?'

A sob escapes her throat.

She glances at Tilly.

For the split second her eyes are away from me I wonder whether that's my chance to push past her, but I hesitate too long. Her attention returns to me. She leans forward, puts her mouth against my ear, her breath hot. She whispers. I have no choice but to listen and when I do my fear hardens into a rage that is absolute.

Everything shrinks. There is nothing in the world except her and I.

Coincidence.

The knife I'd taken from the kitchen flashes to mind. Automatically, my hand snakes around to my back pocket where my hand grips the handle.

Fate.

The drumming of my heart kicking against my ribs, hers pounding in her chest. The sound rising frantically until I cannot tell what is coming from her and what is coming from me.

Destiny.

I plunge the blade as hard as I can into her yielding flesh.

The drumming stops.

Blackness comes to claim me. I let it drag me under.

PART FOUR

Eighteen Months Later

CHAPTER EIGHTY-ONE

TILLY

It's been eighteen months since I saw Mum and in that time I've grown up. A journey of self-awareness. Alex would be proud. I shake my head to try to dislodge his voice which is both pleasant and painful to hear. I've helped build a school in India, laying foundations and trying to bury the sense that everyone I loved has betrayed me. I've taught English to too-thin children with visible ribs and beaming smiles. Tried not to envy them with their bustling homes containing parents, grandparents, aunts, uncles and cousins. Despite having nothing, they knew who they were and where they had come from. They knew that they were loved.

I've roamed the world tasting exotic fruits, fragrant spices, but nothing can mask the taste of bitterness in my mouth. The hustle and bustle of refugee centres can't drown out the buzzing in my head. All my life I'd believed Gavan was my dad. But all the time Mum knew my real father was festering in prison. I've tried to picture him but I can't. He's vague and distant. Not quite real to me. A cartoon character baddie. A cloaked queen offering a poisoned apple. Rumpelstiltskin wanting the firstborn child. I wasn't wanted. It still hurts.

I've flown thousands of miles. Hitchhiked. Walked until

my feet blistered and bled, but I've carried my thoughts along with my rucksack and I still feel dirty. Ashamed. How could my mother love me? I was the result of an act of violence and control. How could anyone want me? But Alex had. I no longer think of him as coated in gold. He isn't capable of shifting planets, moving moons after all; like the Wizard of Oz he turned out to be just a man – human and fallible – but he tried to save me nevertheless. He had loved me. I quickly turn my mind to something else. There's no room inside my head for him today. Happy thoughts only.

In Africa I volunteered at an orphanage and just last week an American couple came in and lifted a baby from a cot, his nappy gaping under skinny ribs. They gazed at him with such love. Such devotion.

'We're going to be your new mummy and daddy,' the lady whispered. 'Where you've come from. What you've been through. It only makes us love you more. Want you more.' She cradled him to her chest with such tenderness. 'We have chosen you.' Something that had shattered inside me began to fuse back together and I couldn't help it, I began to cry. My mum could have had a termination after she was raped. She could have given me away, but she chose not to. Casting my mind back I couldn't think of one single instance where she made me feel unwanted. Unloved. I walked back to the dorm I was sharing and stuffed my belongings back into my rucksack. I had realised that no matter how far I travelled I was never, ever going to escape myself. Mum had been an easy target for my anger, when really it was me I was angry with. It dawned on me that I could have lost her too.

It was time to put things right.

Restack my Jenga life one block at a time.

I wrote three emails.

One to Mum, one to Aunt Anwyn, and one to Rhianon.

Aunt Anwyn never replied. I don't think I'll ever see her again. Rhianon and I are texting, just general stuff. Nothing too profound but our connection is still there and it's strengthening by the day. And Mum…

Today I am full of nerves and trepidation and yet there is a sense of underlying excitement. I check the map once more. Mum's new cottage should be at the end of the lane. I stop for a moment. Gather my thoughts. A queasiness in my stomach and a bunch of chrysanthemums in my hand. My sorry without saying sorry. I don't know what exactly I'm apologising for. For falling in love with Alex? For pushing her away? For lying? For Dad? For something else? Something worse.

A few days before Dad died – I'm not sure if I should even call him Dad anymore, but Gavan is too weird and Dad is still how I think of him – I had been to the cinema on my own like Billy-no-mates. It was freezing when I came out. I texted him and asked if he could pick me up but he said sorry but no. He was at the Walker Street site working late. I had literally just read the text when I walked past that posh new Italian that Mum wanted to eat at, but Dad said they couldn't afford, when I saw him. Sitting opposite this trampy-looking blonde. Although the restaurant was dim, flickering candles on every table, I could see he looked so happy.

As I stood watching them I didn't notice the cold anymore, just a hot, angry feeling deep in my belly. The jalapeños I'd eaten with my nachos bursting into flames. They couldn't take their eyes off one another. I swear, they wouldn't even have noticed if a bomb had dropped or something. Dad held out her coat and she put it on. When she turned around and hugged him I ran away.

I sat on a bench in the bus station and rang Rhianon. Although we'd begun to drift apart, I had no one else to talk to and okay, I guess there was a part of me that thought a bit of drama might bring us together again. That she might feel sorry for me.

'My dad's having an affair.' Burst out of my mouth as soon as she answered the phone.

'You have to tell your mum,' she said and, panicked, I cut the call. I couldn't let Mum know. I couldn't be responsible for her feeling like me, betrayed and confused. I was alone with the posters covered in graffiti and the chewing gum stuck to the floor and an empty, empty heart.

When I got home, Dad was there.

'How was *work*?' I hoped the tone of my voice would tell him that I knew where he had been. He would laugh and offer me a reasonable explanation. Reassure me that he wouldn't leave like Katie's dad had. That he and Mum wouldn't get divorced but instead he answered, 'Fine.'

I waited for Mum to ask him why he smelled of garlic. Why he said he didn't want any dinner. But she didn't, and by failing to tell the truth my dad had turned me into a liar.

I jumped every time Mum's phone buzzed, terrified Rhianon would tell Aunt Anwyn and she would tell Mum. I'd be from a home as broken as I felt. The days rolled into each other and I could hardly bear to look at Dad. I couldn't talk to him, snapping whenever he tried to make conversation. Mum asked me what was wrong and I almost told her, wanting her to make everything okay again the way she had when I was small. Dad made an extra effort with me. Just when I began to think that maybe I was mistaken, he announced he was going out with Iwan for a drink one evening. But the way he carefully ironed a shirt, splashed aftershave onto his cheeks, told another story.

He was lying.

I slipped out of the house after him, following him as he strode down the road. At first I thought he was going to The Cricketer's Arms where he drank with Iwan, until he turned left at the end of Green Street, instead of right.

'Dad!' I called.

He turned. Under the orangey glow of the streetlights I could see him pale.

'You've passed the pub?'

'I'm not... I wasn't...' I'd never heard him lost for words before. 'Look.' He cupped my face in his hands. 'Promise you won't tell, Tilly? I'm not meeting Iwan in the Cricketer's. I'm organising a surprise for Mum.'

'Yeah, right.'

'Have I ever let you down?'

And then I was the one uncertain. Lost for words. I shook my head. He planted a kiss on his fingertips, pressed them against my cheek.

'Good girl. Go home.'

I turned and walked away but I'd only reached the corner when I threw a glance over my shoulder. He was patting his hair and that small gesture combined with the aftershave made me turn around and follow him again.

I saw her standing outside a hotel, checking her watch. Her face lit up when she saw him and they hugged. She kissed him on the cheek and they disappeared inside. There were no windows I could see through, and there was no way I could risk going inside. I sat on a low wall at the end of the road and imagined the worst. Rain began to fall. A light shower turned into a heavy downpour. I was soaked. Freezing. It was another hour before Dad came out alone. I had visions of her waiting for him in bed. Perhaps he was heading out for condoms. My stomach rolled at the thought. Again, I followed him as close as I dared. At one stage I thought he must be able to hear my pounding heart, but the wind howled and the rain beat down. It was almost impossible to see where I was going. It was several minutes before I realised Dad had disappeared. I looked around in confusion before I realised we were in Walker Street, next to his site.

A crashing sound.

I jumped.

Once I realised it was the wind turning over a wheelie bin I suddenly felt furious. Why should I be the one skulking in the shadows when I had done nothing wrong? He was the one who was going to tear our family apart.

Today, I'm not sure what my intentions were as I tried the front door, and found he'd left it unlocked. I followed him inside, carefully clicking the door shut behind me so it didn't bang. His footsteps were pounding up the concrete steps. I followed.

One flight.

Two flights.

Three flights.

Four.

The door to the flat roof terrace was open. Dad knelt, fighting the wind for a piece of tarpaulin. Yanking it down only to have it whipped out of his fingers again. Rain plastered into my face, my mouth, my eyes. I stood there and let it wash over me.

'Dad,' I said, but my voice was small and carried out into the night. 'Dad!' I shouted and this time he heard me. He jumped to his feet and spun around. He was standing so close to the edge.

Too close.

CHAPTER EIGHTY-TWO

LAURA

It's been eighteen months since my daughter felt ready to see me and in that time I've tried to forge a new life, using the insurance money that almost cost me mine. I skirt on the edge of sleep most nights, waking with my breath rasping, feeling the handle of the knife as I thrust it into Saffron, the resistance before the give, the slight pop before it slid into her abdomen and pierced her liver. I'd expected to go to prison for manslaughter at the very least, told myself it was worth it as I was stretchered to an ambulance. At the hospital, I was told I was lucky that despite the pain I experienced I'd only been grazed by stray pellets rather than taking a direct hit. By the time the nurse had cleaned away the blood and dressed my wounds the sun had begun to rise.

'Happy Christmas,' the nurse said. 'We'll find you some turkey a bit later.'

Later, I made a statement, firmly relaying the words Saffron had whispered to me before I stabbed her, 'I pushed your husband from that roof to stop the sale and now I'm going to kill you.'

I was lying.

That wasn't what she said at all, but I was prepared to do

whatever it took to keep that woman away from my daughter, to keep my daughter away from the truth. That black weaver spider, the one in the documentary that had repulsed me, and I aren't that different after all. As parents we'd go to the ends of the earth to protect our young, wouldn't we? In light of everything else the police uncovered, Saffron's death was deemed self-defence. I was free.

Physically free.

Mentally, I'm not sure when I'll recover.

If I ever will.

It's been lonely. I've moved away. It's the fresh start I've always craved, but I've been reluctant to make friends. To trust. I haven't spoken to Anwyn but Rhianon emails me from time to time. She's at university now. I wish Tilly would settle.

Looking out of the window for the hundredth time, I see her. Black hair springing as she ambles down the lane. I want to run to her but I'm rooted to the spot. The sky is the brightest shade of blue, hedgerows polished green, but it all pales into insignificance. I can't tear my eyes away from her. She ducks, disappearing from view, and momentarily I'm confused until she bobs into sight once more, holding a primrose under her nose, inhaling deeply. She always did love flowers as much as me. A memory comes. Tilly must have been around two and it was my birthday. She rushed into my bedroom clutching a bunch of orange and white chrysanthemums in her pudgy hands, tied with one of the red polka dot ribbons I bowed around her pigtails.

'Flowers!' I exclaimed as she clambered onto the bed, petals falling like confetti.

'They're chr, chr.' Her face screwed up in concentration. 'They're Mum's,' she said triumphantly.

'They are Mum's flowers.' Gavan balanced a tea tray containing triangles of toast and thick-cut marmalade.

'Mummy, 'mell them.' She thrust the bouquet towards me and I breathed in the sweet, floral smell, and love. I breathed in love. Gavan joined us on the bed, helping Tilly spread butter, spoon sugar into my tea. I had such a feeling of peace. Something I thought I'd never have again since I'd lain bruised and bleeding in the park that night, full of shame and revulsion for the man who raped me. Full of revulsion for myself. And in that instant when Tilly handed me a plate, marmalade coating her fingers – 'like Paddington eats' – the disgust I had seen in the eyes of my parents, that had lodged itself into the bottom of my stomach, disappeared. It had all been worth it. For Tilly. For Gavan. I think that was partly why I was always so happy pottering around the florist shop. We've all experienced that perfect moment haven't we? That was mine, and the scent of flowers always brought it back to me.

My stomach is doing the dip of the dragonflies that hover over the pond, swooping low, jolting upwards. I wonder if she's nervous. My eyes cast around the cottage. The cushions are plumped, wooden floors gleaming. From the kitchen wafts the smell of freshly made bread. I'm an estate agent's cliché. I tell myself to relax, I'm not trying to sell the place, but I so want it to feel like home for her. In her tiny room in the eaves, Cow the lion rests on her pillow. I've decorated in the same shades of lemon and lilac that covered the walls in our last house, even though I know it's ridiculous. Home isn't a colour, or a smell, or anything tangible, is it? It's a series of emotions.

Above the fireplace I have hung the canvas of Gavan, Tilly and I. We're lying in the garden. Tilly's dark hair spread over the grass, our two fair heads either side of hers. We all share matching, toothy smiles, flecks of happiness sparkling in our eyes. It takes more than blood to weave a family, doesn't it? It takes threads of kindness and understanding; love and patience. But is she ready to see him? My fingers twitch with indecision, a small part of me wanting to take the canvas down and hide it behind the sofa with the rest of the secrets and lies. I can feel them, brewing, bubbling, ready to come to the surface.

But it's okay.

I've gone to unimaginable lengths to keep it all contained.

I'll make sure Tilly never finds out.

CHAPTER EIGHTY-THREE

TILLY

For eighteen months I've been tired. So tired, but sleep won't come. The memories I've been trying so hard to repress fire at me like bullets. I've tried to stuff them back inside that box in my head, but again the lid keeps springing off. I've lain on my side, staring out into the starless sky until the darkness flickers and folds in on itself, rushing towards me, carrying me to places I do not want to go.

Falling, falling, falling. At first I thought it was me but I was the one watching; feeling the disbelief, the denial, the terror.

Horrified screams ringing in my ears. The sickening thud. The silence. My skin red hot with shame, my stomach icy cold. Why I hadn't done more. Why were my reflexes too sluggish? Too slow. I had been rooted to the spot as arms stretched out towards me. If only I'd taken the hands that reached for me and pulled, although logic told me I'd have gone over too.

It wasn't my fault.

It was an accident.

'Dad!' I had called as he teetered too close to the edge.

I remember darting forwards full of hate and rage and sorrow and fear.

I remember raising my hands as he stretched his towards me.

I remembered nothing else until Mum found me crying in my bedroom.

But I don't want to remember, even if the memory might prove to me once and for all I wasn't to blame.

But even as I tried to convince myself it was an accident I recall the letter I had written at the celebration.

I am a murderer and I feel sorry.

My subconscious remembers.

It knows.

But I do not know whether it was my fault because I was there. If I hadn't called his name. Made him jump. He'd never have lost his balance, would he?

Or was it something else?

My palms tingle as they often do.

Did I push?

I can't have pushed him, can I? He was my father and I loved him. But Dannii?

I don't believe I have evil in me. The truth is I just can't remember and it scares me that in my dreams there is always someone falling.

Dad.

Dannii.

Faceless figures. Their screams echoing through my mind. I wake up drenched in sweat and I doubt myself.

Did I push?

His hands cupping my face. '*I'm arranging a surprise for Mum.*'

Mum was asleep in hospital and I was curled up next to her bed, when the nurse brought over an elderly man and a younger woman.

'Hello.' The man cleared his throat. 'I'm Dafydd. I can't apologise enough for what you've both been through on my property. This is my daughter, Carys.'

I recognised her straight away. The woman Dad had met for dinner. The one I thought he was having an affair with. It was Dad who agreed the sale with Carys that would net our family a lot of money.

I'm arranging a surprise for Mum.

And he was.

Now, my thoughts drift away as I realise I am here. Mum's cottage is chocolate-box pretty. It reminds me of Alex's cottage in the woods. The gingerbread house. But I can't think of him. I won't.

I push open the garden gate but my feet don't want to carry me inside.

CHAPTER EIGHTY-FOUR

LAURA

The rusted garden gate squeals as Tilly opens it. I throw a last, lingering glance at the picture.

Gavan she had called him at *Gorphwysfa*, his name coated with poison. Even now I can't think of that place without feeling cold. I've heard it's still unsold. Falling to ruin. Dafydd is now settled in Australia with Carys. He avoided charges, insistent he had always kept the shotgun locked away in a cabinet. Leaving it loaded and accessible was another thing blamed on Saffron. And the dead can't defend themselves, can they?

But enough of the past. Today is about the present. The future.

Should I take down the picture of Gavan?

My nerves are zinging. Why is she taking so long?

I fling open the door.

She lingers at the bottom of the path. The sight of her causes happiness to burst from me. A meteor shower of joy.

I spread open my arms. She walks towards me falteringly. First steps. First words.

'Mum.' She can't meet my eye, instead she thrusts a bunch of chrysanthemums into my hands.

'Tilly!'

'Matilda,' she says quietly as she steps inside. She drinks everything in. I hold my breath as her eyes rest on the picture.

Her body begins to shake before she crumples into tears. I hold her gently because she is precious and fragile and I'm scared that she will break.

My eyes close as I bury my nose in her hair, inhaling as much as I can. Johnson's baby shampoo had long since been replaced by the apple shampoo I always favoured, but now there's something unidentifiable to me, but it's still there; the unmistakable smell of my daughter. The essence of Tilly. Her fingers dig into my shoulder blades as she clings on. I am the floating branch in her torrent of pain. I won't let her drown. I am buoyant enough for the both of us, although I too am crying now.

'It's okay,' I murmur. 'I love you.' Over and over. 'It's okay.'

I am reassuring her.

Reassuring myself.

Eventually her grip releases. She wipes her face with her sleeve, glancing at the photo again.

'Dad,' she says. The three letters dripping with her pain.

I cast my mind back to the last time I heard her call him that. The night he died.

Times had been hard since Gavan had been blamed for causing Ashleigh's cancer by building on a landfill site. Money short. Friends and neighbours avoiding us. When he texted that evening and said the surprise deal he'd been working on was going ahead, he told me to put the champagne on ice. He needed to stop off and secure the tarpaulin covering the roof at the Walker Street site, before the predicted high winds hit, and then he'd be home. Years ago, after Gavan landed his first deal, I'd gone to the site he was working on with a bottle of cheap fizzy wine, and two glasses. After the builders had left for the day he'd spread his coat on the concrete floors and we had toasted our change of fortune. I thought it would be nice to do the same; good news had been a long time coming. I grabbed the bottle of champagne that was gathering dust at the back of the cupboard and called up the stairs to Tilly that I'd see her later. She'd been shut in her bedroom all night. I had hardly seen her those past few days and when she ventured downstairs she was sullen. Snapping one word answers to Gavan, and sometimes he couldn't help biting back. Now he had this deal, much of his stress would be alleviated and the atmosphere at home would lift, I was sure. I had visions of us going out for a celebratory family dinner on Saturday evening. Chinking glasses. Making plans.

It wasn't until I stepped out of the front door I realised how bad the weather was. The wind blustered rain into my face, shoved me back when I tried to walk forwards. By the time I reached the end of our road I was considering turning back, but Walker Street was only ten minutes away and I was already soaked through. I bowed my head, shrouded in a hood, ignored the freezing raindrops dripping down my collar and pushed forward.

I was on the opposite side of the road to the site, metres away from the huge building covered in scaffolding when my shoelace became undone. I crouched down to tie it under a streetlamp. Something reflected in the puddle drew my eye upwards. A shadow. A scream. A falling figure.

My husband.

I toppled forward onto my hands and knees. My bowels

loosening, stomach churning with the need to vomit. I had forgotten how to breathe.

A figure came rushing out of the door.

'Dad!'

My mind registered it was Tilly. I sucked in a lungful of air but before I could call out her name, she ran away.

The shell of my husband lay on the ground, broken and bleeding. I knew there was no way he could have survived. I rocked myself to my feet and approached him. His wide, unseeing eyes stared back at me. Instead of falling apart I experienced a moment of absolute stillness.

Absolute silence.

It was as though I had also ceased to exist but seconds later my heart kicked in again, strong, determined and metronome-steady. I had to make a choice. Tilly was alive. Tilly needed me. What might she do after witnessing something so traumatic? With one last, lingering look at Gavan, my maternal instinct drove me after my daughter as I fumbled for my phone to call for help, but I couldn't speak and run and, rightly or wrongly, Tilly was my priority. She was fast. Faster than me. And by the time I had rounded the corner she had disappeared. I knew she was heading for home. My feet splashed through puddles she'd have splashed through moments before. I don't remember thinking anything, feeling anything, as I flung open the front door and pounded up the stairs. I didn't have a plan. Outside Tilly's room I hesitated, rested my forehead against the wall. Her muffled sobbing tore at my heart. I shucked off my wet coat and threw it over the bannisters. Without knocking, I opened the door, crossing the room to sit on the bed beside her, cocooning her in my arms, wishing we could stay that way forever. I needed to call the police but my body had been emptied and filled with concrete. It was impossible for me to move. It seems like ages we sat there. She didn't speak and I couldn't. Eventually the doorbell broke us apart. I patted her hand. I opened the door to the two officers I had been expecting, but still it felt like a complete shock and when they broke the news my grief was real and raw. A primal scream ripping through me. I was led to the sofa and when I looked up Tilly was framed in the doorway. She told the police we had both been home all evening. How could I betray her? Call her a liar? They'd have taken her away for questioning, and she hadn't done anything wrong, had she? My head was swimming with the right and the wrong and all the shades of grey between.

'Mrs Evans?' I was prompted.

'Yes.' My voice cracked. 'We've both been here all evening.' Nobody noticed my jeans were damp, and if I had been asked why, that might have been my downfall. My thinking was slow. Muddled. All I knew was Gavan had gone and I couldn't lose Tilly too. Subject her to endless questions. She wasn't strong enough for that. The police interviews I'd been a party to at her age had been relentless and, while not ruthless, they'd made me question if it *had* been my fault. If I *had* been to blame just because I had been in the wrong place at the wrong time. I wouldn't put Tilly through the same experience.

But two lies don't make the truth, do they? In the following days, weeks, we were both heartbroken. Neither of us thinking clearly. And it seemed better for her to pretend she hadn't watched her father fall to his death, if that's what she wanted to do. If that's what she needed to do to get through the darkest days. Now I wonder if it had just been better for me. Time marched on and her anguish, her guilt, seemed to amplify, and I longed to talk to her so she didn't have to carry the burden alone, but I didn't know when or how to bring it up. She seemed happier pretending, and sometimes if you tell the same story often enough it becomes your version of reality. Who was I to wrench that away from her? I'd been so anxious about the inquest. Worrying whether the coroner would somehow discover that Gavan hadn't been alone on the roof, and think Tilly's lies meant she had something to do with his death. But all I could do was stick to my story – Tilly's story – and hope for the best.

I wrap her in my arms again and rest my chin on the top of her head.

She's here.

She's home.

It's all over.

I'll never tell her that I know.

It is not the only lie I've told.

Not the only secret I keep.

CHAPTER EIGHTY-FIVE

ALEX

Alex swallows the tablets on his tongue and opens his mouth so the nurse can check it's empty. It doesn't matter what medication they give him, he can still see it, the crow. Even though he'd screamed and screamed until they'd covered up the window in his room with cardboard and tape, he knew it was still there.

Watching.

Waiting.

Nights are always the worst.

The darkness around him

The darkness within him.

As he tries to sleep he imagines he hears it. He can't cover his head with his pillow, the nurse took it away. Instead he draws his knees to his chest, trying to make himself as small as possible, and clamps his hands over his ears but it's still there. The rush of beating wings coming at him.

Coming for him.

'Please,' he whispers. 'Please leave me alone. I'm not a bad person.' The crow caws and caws as he hears this, and Alex begins to rock, his skull slamming against the wall with each backward movement until his tongue clamps between his teeth and he tastes blood. Then the bird quietens, his hunger fed by

Alex's suffering. But he never stays silent for long. The bird will never let him go. Let him forget. It will never forgive him and this Alex knows because he will never forgive himself.

How had it come to this? All he ever wanted was to create a good place for good people.

He'd always done his best for the residents of the farm. For Laura. He'd taken her phone and hidden it because he hadn't wanted her to somehow find out that the date of the inquest was set, and mention it to Saffron. Even then, part of him must have known that if the coroner's conclusion was in Laura's favour, and the insurance company paid out, she was in danger. Saffron was a threat.

One little lie.

It was for her own good.

He was protecting her from his sister.

He was protecting his sister from herself.

It has changed him, Saffron's death.

Sometimes he cries so hard it feels his skeleton is breaking apart. Sometimes he lies rigid on his thin mattress, his veins molten with anger. Missing Saffron is a physical ache throbbing beneath his skin. He'd cradled her in his arms as her life ebbed away.

'I told Laura,' she rasped. 'She told me I'd never be family.' She tried to twist her mouth into a smile but it was more a grimace. 'She was wrong.'

'What did you tell her, Saff?' Alex soothed her hair away from her head.

'That it was my dad. My dad who raped her. I found out when I googled Laura and worked out the dates. Tilly is my half-sister.' Her chest rattled. 'We'll always be blood.' One last breath and then she was gone.

Alex hadn't wanted to believe it, but he knew it must be true. How could Saffron have kept that from him? He had trusted her. He questioned whether he really knew her at all, but that didn't make him feel her loss any less.

He never told the police; he didn't want Matilda to find out that way that her mother had killed her half-sister. He'd be the one to break that news. Matilda has a right to know she wasn't an only child, doesn't she? Honesty. You can't have a relationship without honesty, can you?

Endless questions plague him and sometimes Alex can't move his head because of the sharpness of beak and claws inside of him. Sometimes he bangs his skull against the floor, hoping it will split in two and the crow will fly free.

Where will it all end? They won't keep him here forever. Already they are talking about letting him out, needing the space.

He has nowhere to go. His safe haven gone. His darling Matilda gone.

Sometimes he envies Reed being in prison. Out of a sense of loyalty, Reed said he'd acted alone, helping Saffron bury Iwan. Alex might have escaped jail but he was a different kind of prisoner, trapped by his own ferocious thoughts.

The slap of shoe leather on vinyl floor. A throat clearing. The kindly orderly who sometimes brings Alex treats. Who listens to him in a way the therapists don't. Never questioning. Never judging. Understanding what he'd lost. Who he'd lost. Promising to help, if he could. A rustle. Something appearing under his door.

A letter.

He reads the first two words printed in thick black ink.

Two words that make his pulse race. His blood heat.

She's back.

Underneath, a scrawled address.

Alex draws the paper to his nose, imagining he can smell her. Closes his eyes as he remembers what it was to taste her.

Matilda.

He knew she'd return. Soft and gentle and beautiful.

He was her first.

He'll be her last.

Suddenly, through the chemically induced fug, Alex knows he's ready to rejoin the world once more. In his mind's eye, her face lights up as he calls her name. She runs into his arms and begs him not to leave her again. He promises he won't and as his lips graze her cheek he whispers in her ear, 'You are my family.'

He fantasises about buying a piece of land. Building a community. Reed will need a place to stay when he's released. Although Alex has refused visitors, Hazel and Daisy have written and told him they are waiting. Their tone is darker, anger crouching between their scrawled lines, and Alex knows they have been damaged too. He will help them heal. A safe haven, but this time it will all be his, by whatever means necessary. Saffron was right. It's dog-eat-dog out there.

The more he daydreams, the more his ideas take shape. Matilda, her hair hanging loose, a baby on her hip. They could do anything. Be anyone.

She's a wealthy young woman.

Or she would be if Laura was dead.

He fantasises about that too. And this is how he knows he is broken. Where once his head was full of communities and happiness. Laughter and love. His mind now travels from dark thought to dark thought.

Don't hurt her. Hurt her. Don't hurt her. Hurt her.

They *could* kill her.

How angry will Matilda be when she finds out the truth about Saffron? Finds out that Laura had lied to her, again.

Alex knows it's not over.

It's only just beginning.

Matilda would do anything for him.

Wouldn't she?

Acknowledgements

I can't believe I'm writing the acknowledgements for my fifth psychological thriller! Writing a book can be a solitary process, but publishing one is such a collaboration. I've many people to thank. Firstly, huge gratitude to Lisa Milton for welcoming me to my new home at HQ, and the whole team at HQ – I'm excited to be in your capable hands. My fabulous editor Manpreet Grewal for her understanding and expertise in bringing this story to life. Thank you to Lily, Janet, George, Cara and and the production team for all you have done. The team at The Blair Partnership, in particular my agent, Rory Scarfe, for his patient guidance.

Sally Abbott and Helen Armitage for answering my endless questions regarding inquests, and Lisa Hardy for her police procedural expertise – any mistakes are purely my own.

All the writers who I spend far too much time interacting with online – it's fabulous to know I'm not alone. Emma Mitchell – bloody love you. The Cotes Ladies – you're such a supportive group and I love our get togethers. Lucille Grant, a much loved and valued friend. Darren O'Sullivan, for so many coffees and cakes! Hilary, Sarah, Natalie and Sue – I may not see you as much as I'd like, but I treasure your friendship dearly. My family, particularly my mum, Pete, Glyn, Bekkii, and my sister, Karen.

My husband Tim who can now throw a meal together at short notice while I write 'just one more page', and without whom I'd likely almost never eat.

Callum, Kai and Finley – I'll never stop striving to make you a fraction as proud of me as I am of you.

And Ian Hawley. For you, I try to be the best version of myself every single day. Still. Always.

The following letter
contains spoilers

Dear Readers,

Thanks so much for taking the time to read my fifth psychological thriller, *The Family*. I do hope you enjoyed it.

The book would probably never have come to fruition if it weren't for yet another incident of terrorism on the news. My youngest son asked why people committed such acts, if they were just born 'bad'. I told my son that although it might seem that way, I believe it wasn't always the case and explained to him the concept of brainwashing. Infinitely interested in psychology, he had a million questions that I couldn't answer and so I started researching. I found it both saddening and fascinating to learn that in the right circumstances, over time, almost anybody could be indoctrinated into behaving in a way that was out of character.

I began to wonder what would happen if you placed two extremely vulnerable women in an environment that was out of the ordinary. Would they feel the same? React the same? What would happen if there was a charismatic leader they were both attracted to? What if the women were mother and daughter?

Tilly and Laura came to me immediately and their grief felt real and raw. Alex was more complex. Charming and idealistic.

It took several rewrites for me to realise that he really was sensitive and vulnerable, as open-hearted as he appeared. Full of love, he longed to make the world a better place.

By the end of the book, of course, Alex has come around to Saffron's way of thinking and Tilly is completely under his spell. How far will she go for him? Far enough to betray her own mother? To kill? I've left it up to you to decide.

Human instinct is to make snap judgements based on snippets of information we are presented with. A segment of the news. The opening of a book. Sometimes the one we think is the manipulator could be the one being manipulated. I do hope the twists took you by surprise. In fiction, like life, things are rarely how they first appear.

Do join me next year when my next psychological thriller, *The Stolen Sisters* will be released, and in the meantime, you can keep up to date with my news and events via www.louisejensen. co.uk.

Love, Louise x

P.S. If you're interested in exploring brainwashing further I highly recommend reading *Terror, Love and Brainwashing: Attachment in Cults and Totalitarian Systems* by Alexandra Stein.

Book Club Questions

1) During the opening of the book we learn that someone has been shot. Who did you think this was?

2) Laura had kept a huge secret from Tilly. Did you feel any empathy towards her or do you think she should have been honest with her daughter?

3) *'We're programmed to think that the relationships with our families are absolute. Our bonds unbreakable. But it's not always the case. Sometimes friends are more loyal, less judgemental.'* Do you think the bonds between family are greater than friends? Is blood thicker than water?

4) Tilly is keeping a secret from Laura because she thinks the truth would hurt her mum. Is keeping secrets ever justified, or is honesty the best policy?

5) *'We all make mistakes don't we? Drift from the light towards the dark, hovering in the shades of grey between.'* Are any of the characters in the book completely good or completely bad?

6) Tilly made a gruesome discovery in the woods. Who did you think was responsible for that?

7) *'Promise you won't tell, Tilly.'* Could you understand Gavan's reasons for wanting Tilly to keep his secret? Did you think it was unfair?

8) What did you assume about Alex throughout the book? How did this change by the end?

9) What do you think the future holds for Laura and Tilly?

10) What is your opinion on brainwashing? Do you think, in the right circumstances, over time, anyone can be manipulated into behaving out of character?

Turn the page for an extract
from Louise Jensen's next novel,

The Stolen Sisters ...

CHAPTER ONE

Carly
Then

When Carly looked back at that day the memory was in shades of grey as though the trauma had sucked the blue from the sky, the green from the freshly mown grass after it had received its last cut of the year. She had sat on the back door step, the coolness of the concrete permeating through her school skirt. The late afternoon sun warming her bare arms. Carly remembers now the blackness of a beetle scurrying down the path, disappearing into the freshly dug borders. The stark white of the twins' socks, bunched below their knees.

Inconsequential details that later the police would jot in their notebooks as though Carly was somehow being a great help but she knew she wasn't, and worse than that, she knew it was entirely her fault.

It had all been so frustratingly normal. Leah and Marie shrieking mock disgust as Bruno, their boxer, bounded up to them, drool spilling from his jowls. But their screams then still carried an undercurrent of happiness, not like later when their cries were full of fear and there was nowhere to run to.

The things that have stayed with Carly are these.

The way her fingers gripped the cumbersome Nokia in her hand as though she was clutching a secret. Her annoyance as she angled her screen to avoid the glare, never dreaming that soon she would be craving daylight.

Fresh air.

Space.

The pounding in her head increasing as the girls bounced a tennis ball between them across the patio. The way she snapped at the twins as though it was their fault Dean Malden hadn't text her. Of all the things that she could, that she should, feel guilty about, she had never forgiven herself that the last words she spoke to her sisters before they were all irrevocably damaged was in anger rather than kindness.

Although in truth, she had never forgiven herself for any of it.

'Shut up!' She had roared out her frustration that the first boy she loved had shattered her thirteen-year-old heart. Ridiculous now to think she once thought the absence of a text was the end of the world. There were far worse things. Far worse people than the floppy-haired blond boy who'd let her down.

Her younger sisters turned to her, identical green eyes wide. Marie's sight trained on Carly's face as she chucked the ball for Bruno. Carly's irritation grew as she watched it fly over the fence.

'For God's sake.' She stood, brushing the dust from the back of her sensible pleated skirt. 'It's time to come in.'

'But that's not fair,' Marie looked stricken as her gaze flickered towards the fence.

'Life isn't fair.' Carly said feeling a bubbling resentment that at nine years old the twins had it easy.

'Can you fetch our ball please, Carly?' Marie pleaded. The twins weren't allowed out of the garden alone.

'Fetch it yourself. And shut the gate *properly*.' She turned and pushed open the door, stepping into the vast kitchen that never smelled of cakes or bread. It never smelled of anything except freshly roasted coffee. Carly clattered her phone onto the marble island and yanked open the fridge. The shelves that were once stocked with stilton and steak, groaning under the weight of fresh fruit and vegetables were woefully bare. There was nothing except a shrivelled cucumber and some out of date hummus. It was all right for her mum and stepdad out for the evening at yet another corporate function. They spent more time on the business than they did with their children nowadays, although Mum had assured her it wouldn't be for much longer. She'd soon be able to be at home more but in the meantime it was left to Carly to sort out tea again. It wasn't as if she got paid any more for watching her sisters. She sighed as she crossed to the shelf above the Aga and lifted the lid from the teapot. Inside was a £10 note. Chips for tea. She wondered whether the money would stretch to three sausages or if they should split a battered cod.

Minutes later the twins tumbled into the kitchen.

'Yuck.' Leah dropped the tennis ball coated with slobber into the wicker basket where Bruno kept his toys.

'Wash your hands,' Carly snapped as she checked her phone again.

Nothing.

What had she done wrong? She thought Dean liked her.

Marie perched on a stool at the breakfast bar, swinging her legs, the toe of her shoes thudding against the kick board. How was Carly supposed to hear her text alert over that? Marie had her chin in her hands, her mouth downturned. Carly could see the way her lip trembled with already being in trouble but she couldn't help roaring again.

'Shut. Up.'

Marie slid off the stool. 'I… I left my fleece in the garden.'

Carly jerked her head towards the back door before she clicked on the radio. The sound of Steps flooded the room. Marie paused and momentarily their sisterly bond tugged at them all. '5, 6, 7, 8' was one of their favourite songs. Usually they'd fall into line and dance in synchronicity.

'Let's do this!' Leah flicked her red hair over her shoulders and placed her hands on her hips.

'It's childish,' Carly snapped although inside of her shoes, her toes were tapping.

'It doesn't work unless we *all* do it.' Marie's voice cracked. 'We have to be together.'

Carly pulled the scrunchie she'd been wearing like a bracelet from her wrist and smoothed her long fair hair back into a ponytail. Leah smiled. Waited. Carly reached for her phone and tried to ignore the pang of meanness that flitted through her as the smile slipped from Leah's face. Marie's small shoulders rounded as she headed back out into the garden.

Minutes later she raced back in, socked feet skidding across the tiles, tears streaming down her freckled cheeks. 'Bruno's got out. The gate was open.'

'For God's sake.' Carly could feel the anger in her chest form a cold, hard ball. It was one of the last times she ever allowed herself to truly feel. 'Who shut the gate?'

Marie bit her lower lip.

'I did,' said Leah.

'You're supposed to bang it until it latches, you idiot. You know it's broken. Three times. You bang it three times.'

The girls pelted into the garden, calling the dog's name.

Marie hesitated at the gate. 'Perhaps we should wait—' Under her freckles, her skin was pale. She'd been off school yesterday with a stomach ache and although she'd gone back today, she didn't look well. Carly knew she should ask if she was feeling okay, instead she shoved her roughly into the street. 'It's your fault, Marie. You search that way.' She pointed down the avenue lined with beech trees.

Marie grabbed Leah's hand.

'No,' Carly snapped. 'Leah can come with me.' The twins could be silly where they were together and she had enough to worry about without them getting into trouble.

'But I want...' Marie began.

'I don't *care* what you want. Move.' Carly grabbed Leah's arm and led her in the opposite direction, towards the cut through at the side of their house which led to the park.

It all happened so quickly that afterwards Carly couldn't remember what order it all came in. The balaclava-clad face looming towards hers. The forearm around her neck, the gloved hand clamped over her mouth. The sight of Leah struggling against arms that restrained her. The scraping sound of her shoe as she was dragged towards the van at the other end of the alley. The sight of Marie, almost a blur, flying towards the second man also clad in black, who held her twin, pummelling him with her small fists.

'Stop! You can't do this! Don't take her. I don't want you to take her!'

The soft flesh compacting against hard bone as Carly bit down hard on the fingers that had covered her mouth.

'Run!' she screamed at Marie as the man who held Leah grabbled to find something of Marie's he could hold onto, clutching at her collar, her ginger pigtails, as she dodged his grasp.

'Run!'

CHAPTER TWO

Leah
Now

It's impossible to ignore the urge to run back into the room and check; dread crawls around the pit of my stomach until I push open the door and step inside. The kitchen is exactly as I left it, not surprising as I am the only one home but nevertheless I twist the dial on the oven three times to make sure that it's off, even though I haven't yet cooked anything today.

Safe.

I have to keep us all safe.

My compulsions are worsening again. If I was being kind to myself I'd think it's not surprising considering what I've been through, what I've yet to face over this coming week.

I'm rarely kind to myself.

But still, I remember what happened the last time everything got out of hand. The build of pressure. The loss of control. Despite the scrutiny I'll be under over the next few days I have to hold it together this time, if not for me, then for George and Archie.

The silver-framed faces of the three of us at Drayton Manor Park beam down at me from the dresser. Archie has inherited bits of both of us. My fiery red hair but instead of being poker-straight like mine it's curly like George's dark mop would be if he didn't keep it so short, and it always smells of the apple shampoo I wash it with each night. Momentarily I allow myself to relax until an incoming text lights up my phone.

I need you.

I tell myself I can just say no but anxiety rises as quickly as Archie's tears do when he's overtired. I force my eyes to travel around the room and name three things to ground myself.

Archie's cuddly labrador curled up in its wicker basket, a fake bone between its paws. He's forever begging for a puppy.

George's sheepskin gloves on top of the microwave; he always forgets where he's left them.

A canvas print of three girls holding hands on a golden beach. I don't know who they are but when I saw it hanging in the window of a local gallery I stood there for the longest time unsure whether it made me feel happy or sad. For three years it's hung on my wall and I still feel a flurry of emotions when I catch sight of it. I still can't unpick what they are.

A second message buzzes.

It's important.

I can just say no.

But I won't.

I can't delay it anymore. Peeling off my disposable gloves I snap on a fresh pair and gather my keys and my mobile. On the doormat is a business card from a reporter with 'call me' scrawled across it.

I won't.

Although I'm late, I'm in no hurry to get there; part of me knows what she'll want to talk about and I don't think I can face it.

I'm careful as I drive, headlights slicing through the gloom. The dark skies give a sense of early evening rather than mid morning. We're barely into autumn and it already feels like winter. I'm mindful of the traffic. Peering into cars wondering who's inside and where they're going.

If they're happy.

I'm almost halfway there when I notice the fuel gauge is almost empty. Inwardly, I curse. George was supposed to fill my car up last night, he knows I find it difficult. I can't bear the smell of fumes. I was sure he'd gone to do it while I gave Archie his bath and read him a story but I must have been mistaken. He probably got caught up in another long work call. The hours he's putting in at the moment are ridiculous but I'm lucky he's working so hard towards our future, even if we don't always want the same thing.

It's tempting to go home but I'd still have to refuel before picking Archie up from nursery so I indicate left and pull into the forecourt of the BP garage. The instant I step out of the car the smell of petrol invades my nostrils and I have to swallow down bile.

My hand is shaking by the time I replace the pump and go and pay.

The sole cashier is busy with another customer and as I wait I impulsively pick up a KitKat for Archie and a Twix for George. I don't snack, preferring proper meals. My debit card is already in my hand ready to tap it on the reader but I've gone over the contactless limit and so I stuff the card inside the machine. Out of my peripheral vision I notice a white van pull up alongside my car. Flustered I enter my pin number incorrectly twice before I remember what it is. A man with spiked black hair steps out of the van and I scan him from his boots to his scalp. He's young. Younger than me, and he looks happy but still, that doesn't mean he's not dangerous, does it? We all wear a mask sometimes, don't we? I'm guilty of it myself. The calm mother, the carefree wife. That's unfair. I'm being hard on myself again. I've had periods of months, years even when I've almost, if not forgotten what I've been through, come to terms with it. Learned to live with it I suppose like the patches of eczema that used to scab my skin when I was stressed, but that was before my rituals became all consuming. Oddly as my mental health plummeted, my physical health problems disappeared almost overnight.

'You can take your card.' The sharp tone of the cashier's voice tells me this is not the first time he's asked me. I mumble a thank you to him, an apology to the van driver standing behind me, whose eyes I do not meet, and I hurry outside.

I'm just passing the van when I hear a thud coming from inside. I hesitate, ears straining. There's nothing to be heard except the steady thrum of traffic coming from the main road but still I cup my hands and peer through the driver's window.

'Oi!'

I turn at the noise, sweat prickling under my arms as the driver jogs over to me. 'What do you think you're doing?' His manner as spiky as his hair.

'Do you have anyone else in the van?' I ask.

'What's it gotta do wiv you?'

I keep my gaze steady, waiting him out.

'No. Just me.' He jabs his key into the lock but before he can climb inside, we both hear it. The shuffling coming from inside his vehicle.

'I'm DC Ross,' I lie. 'Do you mind opening your back door, sir?' I stride to the back of the van with a confidence I don't feel.

'I've told you there's no—'

'Then you won't mind showing me, will you?'

Tutting he unlocks the back doors. My heart races as he yanks them open and I make sure I'm not standing too close. There's a delighted yelp and a Staffie launches himself at his owner.

It's just a dog.

I back away, feeling his glare on me. Fumbling to start my car, gears crunching as I pull back out onto the road, breathing heavily. I'm edging forward at the T-junction, waiting to turn left when I catch a flash of the profile of the driver who slides past me in a black car, indicating right.

It's him.

The man who nearly broke me.

I'm frozen to my seat, neck rigid, willing my eyes to take a second look.

I catch him again as his car turns into the traffic. I'm not as certain as I was a few seconds ago that it is him. The jawline is wrong. A horn blasts behind me and in my rush to move forward I stall my car. I'm trembling as I twist the key to fire the engine to life once more.

It *can't* have been him.

It's impossible.

As I pull forward, I imagine him in his cell. The thick iron bars that contain him.

It's the anniversary that's made me so skittish, I know. Twenty years. It's been almost twenty years.

I'm no calmer by the time I pull up outside Marie's flat, even when I notice Carly's car is already there.

Soon we'll all be in one room.

Three sisters.

Nothing good happens when we're all together.

I can just say no.

Above me the grey clouds break apart and rain lashes against my windscreen.

It feels like an omen. A sense of impending doom.

ONE PLACE. MANY STORIES

Bold, innovative and
empowering publishing.

FOLLOW US ON:

@HQStories